UK Praise

"*The Return* should be required holiday reading for anyone going to Spain." —*Daily Mail*

"Hislop carefully choreographs her way from a long-distance fascination with Spain to a novel about domestic experiences in the Civil War. . . . Though she writes to entertain, her depth of research is frequently harrowing." —*The Spectator*

"Hislop wraps another British-innocent-abroad envelope around a meaty—and moving—slice of modern history." —*Independent*

"An accessible, compelling page-turner. It tugs the heartstrings but also gives you a crash course in a large part of twentieth-century history." —*Sunday Express*

"The descriptions of war-ravaged Spain, of hand-to-hand fighting, bombardment of civilians, brutal atrocities by both sides, and Europe's cold reception of refugees are very powerful." —*Guardian*

"What sets Hislop apart is her ability to put a human face on the shocking civil conflict. . . . Stirring stuff." —*Time Out London*

Angus Muir

VICTORIA HISLOP read English at St Hilda's College, Oxford, and writes travel features for the *Sunday Telegraph*, the *Mail on Sunday*, and *Woman & Home*. Her first novel, *The Island*, was an international bestseller, has sold one million copies, and has been translated into more than twenty languages. She lives in Kent, England, with her husband and their two children.

# THE RETURN

Also by Victoria Hislop

THE ISLAND

# THE RETURN

## VICTORIA HISLOP

**HARPER**

NEW YORK • LONDON • TORONTO • SYDNEY

For Emily and William, with love

# HARPER

First published in Great Britain in 2008 by Headline Book Publishing, a division of Hodder Headline.

HarperCollins books may be purchased for educational, business, or sales promotional use. For information please write: Special Markets Department, HarperCollins Publishers, 10 East 53rd Street, New York, NY 10022.

FIRST U.S. EDITION

Library of Congress Cataloging-in-Publication Data is available upon request.

ISBN 978-0-06-171541-9

09 10 11 12 13  OV/RRD  10 9 8 7 6 5 4 3 2

# ACKNOWLEDGMENTS

With thanks to: Ian Hislop, David Miller, Flora Rees, Natalia Benjamin, Steve Bowles, Emma Cantons, Professor Juan Antonio Díaz, Rachel Dymond, Tracey Hay, Helvecia Hidalgo, Gerald Howson, Michael Jacobs, Herminio Martinez, Eleanor Mortimer, Victor Ovies, Jan Page, Stewart, Josefina Stubbs, and Yolanda Urios.

Spain, 1931

*I*n the shuttered nocturnal gloom of an apartment, the discreet click of a closing door penetrated the silence. To the crime of being late, the girl had added the sin of trying to conceal her surreptitious homecoming.

"Mercedes! Where in the name of God have you been?" came a harsh whisper.

A young man emerged from the shadows into the hallway and the girl, who was no more than sixteen, stood facing him, her head bowed, hands concealed behind her back.

"Why are you so late? Why are you doing this to us?"

He hesitated, suspended in the uncertain space between total despair and uncompromising love for this girl.

"And what are you hiding? As if I couldn't guess."

She held out her hands. Balanced on her flattened palms was a pair of scuffed black shoes, the leather as soft as human skin, their soles worn to transparency.

He took her wrists gently and held them in his hands. "Please, for the very last time I am asking you . . ." he implored.

"I'm sorry, Antonio," she said quietly, her eyes now meeting his. "I can't stop. I can't help myself."

"It's not safe, querida mia, it's not safe."

PART 1

# CHAPTER 1

*Granada, 2001*

J ust moments before, the two women had taken their seats, the last of the audience to be admitted before the surly *gitano* slid the bolts decisively across the door.

Voluminous skirts trailing behind them, five raven-headed girls made their entrance. Tight to their bodies swirled dresses of flaming reds and oranges, acid greens and ochre yellows. These vibrant colors, a cocktail of heavy scents, the swiftness of their arrival and their arrogant gait were overpoweringly, studiedly dramatic. Behind them followed three men, somberly dressed as though for a funeral, in jet black from their oiled hair down to their hand-made leather shoes.

Then the atmosphere changed as the faint, ethereal beat of clapping, palm just brushing palm, seeped through the silence. From one man came the sound of fingers sweeping across strings. From another emanated a deep and plaintive wail that soon flowed into a song. The rasp of his voice matched the roughness of the place and the ruggedness of his pockmarked face. Only the singer and his troupe understood the obscure patois, but the audience could sense the meaning. Love had been lost.

Five minutes passed like this, with the fifty-strong audience sitting in the darkness around the edge of one of Granada's damp *cuevas*, hardly daring to breathe. There was no clear moment when the song ended—it simply faded away—and the girls took this as their cue to file out again, rawly sensual in their gait, eyes fixed on the door ahead, not even acknowledging the presence of the foreigners in the room. There was an air of menace in this dark space.

"Was that it?" whispered one of the latecomers.

"I hope not," answered her friend.

For a few minutes, there was an extraordinary tension in the air and then a sweet continuous sound drifted toward them. It was not music, but a mellow, percussive purring: the sound of castanets.

One of the girls returned, stamping her feet as she paced down the length of the corridor-shaped space, the flounces of her costume brushing the dusty feet of the tourists in the front row. The fabric of her dress, vivid tangerine with huge black spots, was pulled taut across her belly and breasts. Seams strained. Her feet stamped on the strip of wood that comprised the dance floor, rhythmically *one*-two-*one*-two-*one*-two-three-*one*-two-three-*one*-two. . .

Then her hands rose in the air, the castanets fluttered in a deep satisfying trill, and her slow twirling began. All the while she rotated, her fingers snapped against the small black discs she held in her hands. The audience was mesmerized.

A plaintive song accompanied her, the singer's eyes mainly downcast. The dancer continued, in a trance of her own. If she connected with the music she did not acknowledge it, and if she was aware of her audience they did not feel it. The expression on her sensual face was one of pure concentration and her eyes looked into some other world that only she could see. Under her arms, the fabric darkened with sweat, and watery beads gathered at her brow as she revolved, faster and faster and faster.

The dance ended as it had begun, with one decisive stamp, a full stop. Hands were held above her head, eyes to the low, domed ceiling. There was no acknowledgment of the audience's response. They might as well not have been there for all the difference it made to her. Temperatures had risen in the room and those close to the front inhaled the heady mix of musky scent and perspiration that she spread in the air.

Even as she was leaving the stage, another girl was taking over. There was an air of impatience with this second dancer, as though she wanted to get it all over with. More black dots swam in front of the audience's eyes, this time on shiny red, and cascades of curly black hair fell over the gypsyish face, concealing all but the sharply defined Arab eyes, out-lined in thick kohl. This time there were no castanets, but the endlessly repeated, rattling of feet: *clack*-a-tacka tacka, *clack*-a-tacka tacka, *clack*-a-tacka tacka. . .

The speed of movement from heel to toe and back again seemed im-possibly fast. The heavy black shoes, with their high, solid heels and steel toecaps vibrated on the stage. Her knees must have absorbed a thou-sand shockwaves. For a while, the singer remained silent and gazed at the ground, as though to catch this dark beauty's eyes might turn him to stone. It was impossible to tell whether the guitarist kept up with her stamping or whether he dictated its pace. The communication between them was seamless. Provocatively she hitched up the heavy tiers of her skirt to reveal shapely legs in dark stockings and further showed off the speed and rhythm of her footwork. The dance built to a crescendo, as the girl, half whirling dervish, half spinning top, rotated. A rose that had clung precariously to her hair, flew out into the audience. She did not stoop to collect it, marching from the room almost before it had landed. It was an introverted performance and yet the most overt display of con-fidence they had ever seen.

The first dancer and the accompanist followed her out of the cave, their faces expressionless, still indifferent to their audience in spite of the applause.

Before the end of the show, there were another half-dozen dancers, and each one conveyed the same disturbing keynotes of passion, anger, and grief. There was a man whose movements were as provocative as a prostitute's, a girl whose portrayal of pain sat uncomfortably with her extreme youth, and an elderly woman whose seven decades of suffering were etched in her deeply furrowed face.

Eventually, once the performers had filed out, the lights came up. As the audience began to leave, they caught a glimpse of them in a small backroom, arguing, smoking and drinking from tall tumblers filled to the brim with cheap whiskey. They had forty-five minutes until their next performance.

It had been airless in the low-ceilinged room, which reeked of alcohol, sweat, and long-ago smoked cigars, and the crowd was relieved to emerge into the cool night air. It had a clarity and purity that reminded them they were not far from the mountains.

"That was extraordinary," commented Sonia to her friend. She did not really know what she meant, but it was the only word that seemed to fit.

"Yes," agreed Maggie. "And so tense."

"That's exactly it," agreed Sonia. "Really tense. Not at all what I imagined."

"And they didn't look particularly happy, those girls, did they?"

Sonia did not bother to answer. Flamenco clearly had little to do with happiness. That much she had come to realize in the past two hours.

They walked back through the cobbled streets toward the center of Granada and found themselves lost in the old Moorish quarter, the Albaicín. It was pointless to try to read a map; the tiny alleyways hardly had names and sometimes even petered out in sets of narrow steps.

The women soon got their bearings when they turned a corner and were confronted with a view of the Alhambra, now gently floodlit, and though it was already past midnight, the warm amber glow that bathed the buildings almost convinced them that the sun was still setting. With its spread of crenellated turrets that stood out against a clear black sky, it looked like something from *The Arabian Nights*.

Arms linked, they continued their walk down the hill in silence. The dark and statuesque Maggie reduced the length of her stride to match Sonia's. It was a habit of almost a lifetime between these two close friends, who were physical opposites in every way. They did not need to talk. For now, the crisp sound of their feet on the cobbles, percussive like the claps and castanets of the flamenco dancers, was more pleasing than the human voice.

It was a Wednesday in late February. Sonia and Maggie had arrived only a few hours earlier, but even as they were driven from the airport, Sonia had fallen under Granada's spell. The wintry sunset illuminated the city with a sharp light, leaving the snow-capped mountains that were its backdrop in dramatic shadow, and as the taxi sped into the city along the freeway, they caught their first glimpse of the Alhambra's geometric outline. It seemed to keep watch over the rest of the city.

Eventually their driver slowed to take the exit into the center and now the women feasted their eyes on regal squares, palatial buildings, and occasional grandiose fountains before he turned off to take a route through the narrow cobbled streets that spread through the city.

Even though her mother had been from Spain, Sonia had visited this country only twice before, both times to the resorts of the Costa del Sol. There she had stayed on the slick stretch of sparkling coast, where all-year sun and all-day breakfasts were marketed to the British and Germans who came in droves. Nearby plantations of matching villas, with ornate pillars and fancy wrought-iron railings, were so close and yet a million miles away from this city of confused streets and buildings that had been built over many centuries.

Here was a place with unfamiliar smells, a cacophony of ancient and modern, cafés overflowing with local people, windows piled high with small, glossy pastries, served by serious men proud of their trade, tatty shuttered apartments, glimpses of sheets hung out on balconies to dry. This was a real place, she thought, nothing ersatz here.

They swung this way and that, left and right, right and left and left again, as though they might end up exactly where they had started. Each of the small streets was one-way, and occasionally there was a near miss with a moped that was going the wrong way up the street and approaching them at speed. Pedestrians, oblivious to the danger, stepped off the pavement into their path. Only a taxi driver could have negotiated his way through this complex maze. A set of rosary beads suspended from the rear-view mirror clattered against the windscreen, and an icon of the Virgin Mary watched demurely from the dashboard. There were no fatalities on this journey, so she seemed to be doing her job.

The sickly, boiled-sweet smell of air-freshener combined with the turbulence of the journey had made both women feel nauseated, and they were relieved when the car eventually slowed down and they heard the grating sound of the handbrake being yanked into position. The two-star Hotel Santa Ana was in a small, scruffy square, flanked by a bookshop on one side and a cobbler on the other, and along the pavement was a row of stalls now in the process of being packed up. Smooth golden loaves and hefty tranches of flat, olive-studded bread were being wrapped, and the last remaining segments of some fruit tarts originally the size of wagon wheels were being stowed away in waxed paper.

"I'm ravenous," said Maggie, watching the stallholders loading up their small vans. "I'll just grab something from them before they disappear."

With typical spontaneity, Maggie ran across the road, leaving Sonia to pay off the taxi driver. She returned with a generous section of bread that she was already tearing into pieces, impatient to satisfy her hunger.

"This is delicious. Here, try some."

She thrust some of the crusty loaf into Sonia's hand and they both stood on the pavement by their bags, eating and scattering crumbs liberally on the stone slabs. It was time for the *paseo*. People were beginning to come out for their evening saunter. Men and women together, women arm in arm, pairs of men. All were smartly dressed, and though they enjoyed a stroll for its own sake they looked purposeful.

"It looks attractive, doesn't it?" said Maggie.

"What?"

"Life in this city! Look at them!" Maggie pointed at the café on the corner of the square, which was packed with customers. "What do you think they talk about over their *tinto*?"

"Everything, I expect," replied Sonia with a smile. "Family life, political scandal, football . . ."

"Look, let's go and check in," said Maggie, finishing her bread. "Then we could go out and have a drink."

The glass door opened into a brightly lit reception area that was given a sense of grandeur by a number of kitsch silk flower arrangements and a few pieces of heavy baroque furniture. A smiling young man behind a high desk gave them a registration form and, after photocopying their passports, told them the time of breakfast and handed them a key. The full-size wooden orange attached to it was an absolute guarantee that they would never leave the hotel without handing it in for replacement on the row of hooks behind reception.

Beyond the lobby, everything else in this hotel was tawdry. Nose to nose, they went up in a tiny box of a lift, their luggage balanced in a tower, and on the third floor emerged into a narrow corridor. In the darkness they clattered along with their suitcases until they could make out in large, tarnished figures the number *301*.

Their room had a view of sorts. But not of the Alhambra. It looked out onto a wall and, specifically, onto an air-conditioning unit.

"We wouldn't spend much time looking out of the window anyway, would we?" commented Sonia, as she drew the thin curtains.

"And even if there was a balcony with gorgeous furniture and far-reaching views over the mountains, we wouldn't use it," added Maggie, laughing. "It's a bit early in the year."

Sonia quickly threw open her suitcase, squashed a few T-shirts into the small bedside drawer and hung the rest of her things in the narrow wardrobe; the scrape of metal coat hangers on the rail set her teeth on edge. The bathroom was as economically sized as the bedroom, and Sonia, though petite, had to squeeze behind the basin to shut the door. Having cleaned her teeth, she tossed her brush into the single glass provided and reappeared in the bedroom.

Maggie was lying on top of the burgundy bedspread, her suitcase still unopened on the floor.

"Aren't you going to unpack?" inquired Sonia, who knew from experience that Maggie would probably spend the week living out of a suitcase that frothed over with bits of flirtatious lace and tangles of ruffled blouses, rather than actually hang anything up.

"What's that?" Maggie asked distractedly, engrossed in reading something.

"Unpack?"

"Oh, yes. I might do that later."

"What's that you're reading?"

"It was with a pile of leaflets on the table," Maggie replied from behind a flyer, held close to her face in an attempt to make out the words.

The low-voltage lighting lifted the gloom of the dark beige room only a little and scarcely provided enough illumination to read. "It's advertising a flamenco show somewhere called *Los Fandangos*. It's in the gypsy area, as far as my Spanish can tell, anyway. Shall we go?"

"Yes. Why not? They'll be able to tell us on reception how to get there, won't they?"

"And it doesn't start until ten thirty, so we could go and eat first."

Shortly afterward, they were out on the street, a map of the city in hand. They wound their way through a labyrinth of streets, partly following their noses, partly the orientation of the map.

*Jardines, Mirasol, Cruz, Puentezuelas, Capuchinas. . .*

Sonia remembered the meaning of most of these words from her schooldays. Each one held its magic. They were like brushstrokes, painting the landscape of the city, each one helping to build up a picture of the whole. As they got closer to the heart of this city, the street names clearly reflected the dominance of the Roman Catholic religion.

They were making for the cathedral, the city's central point. According to the map, everything emanated from here. The narrow alleyways seemed an unlikely way to reach it, but it was only when Sonia saw some railings and two women sitting begging in front of a carved doorway that she looked up for the first time. Towering above was the most sturdy of buildings. It filled the sky, a solid mass of distinctively fortress-like stone. It did not reach up to the light, like St. Paul's, St. Peter's or the Sacré-Coeur. From where she stood, it seemed to blot it out. Nor did it announce itself with a huge empty space in front of it. It lurked behind the workaday streets of cafés and shops and, from most places in these narrow streets, was unseen.

On the hour, however, it reminded the world of its presence. As the two women stood there, the bells began to toll. The volume was enough to make them reel back. Resoundingly deep, metallic clangs banged inside their heads. Sonia cupped her ears with her hands and followed Maggie away from the deafening noise.

It was eight o'clock and the tapas bars around the cathedral were already filling up. Maggie made a speedy decision, drawn to the place where a waiter stood outside on the pavement, smoking.

Once they were perched on high wooden stools, the women ordered wine. It was served in small stubby tumblers with a generous plate of *jamon*, and each time they ordered another drink, more tapas magically appeared. Although they had been ravenous, these small offerings of olives, cheese, and pâté slowly filled them up.

Sonia was perfectly happy with Maggie's choice of venue. Behind the bar, ranks of mighty hams hung from the ceiling, like giant bats suspended upside down in trees. Fat dripped from them into small plastic cones. Next to them were *chorizos*, and on shelves behind sat huge tins of olives and tuna. There were rows and rows of bottles just out of reach. Sonia loved this dusty chaos, the rich, sweet smell of *jamon* and the hum of conviviality that wrapped itself around her like a favorite coat.

Maggie interrupted her reverie. "So, how is everything?"

It was a question typical of her friend. As heavily loaded as the cocktail stick onto which she had speared two olives and a cherry tomato.

"Fine," answered Sonia, knowing as she said it that this response would probably not do. It sometimes annoyed her that Maggie always wanted to get straight to the heart of things. They had kept conversation quite light and superficial since they had met up at Stansted early that day, but sooner or later, she knew Maggie would want more. Sonia sighed. This was what she both loved and loathed about her friend.

"How's that dusty old husband of yours?" This more direct question could not be deflected with one single word, especially not "Fine."

Since nine o'clock, the bar had filled up rapidly. Earlier in the evening the clientele had been mostly elderly men, gathered in tight-knit groups. They were neat figures, Sonia observed, small and smartly jacketed, with highly polished shoes. After that, slightly younger people began to pack the place and stood chatting animatedly, balancing wine and plates of tapas on the narrow ledge that ran around the room especially for this purpose. The volume of noise meant that conversation was more difficult now. Sonia drew up her stool so close to Maggie's their wooden frames touched.

"Dustier than ever," she said in her ear. "He didn't want me to come here, but I suspect he'll get over that."

Sonia glanced over at the clock above the bar. Their flamenco show was beginning in less than half an hour.

"We really should go, shouldn't we?" she said, slipping down off her stool. Much as she loved Maggie, for the time being she wished to deflect her personal questions. In her best friend's view no husband was really worth having, but Sonia had often suspected that this might have been something to do with the fact that Maggie had never had one, at least not one of her own.

Coffee had just been served to them on the bar, and Maggie was not going to leave without drinking it.

"We've got time for this," she said. "Everything starts late in Spain."

Both women drained their rich cups of *café solo*, maneuvered their way through the crowds and went outside. The throng continued into the street and almost all the way to the Sacromonte where they soon found a sign pointing to "*Los Fandangos*." The *cueva* where they were going to see flamenco was set into the hillside, a white-washed, roughly plastered building. Even as they approached, they could hear the alluring sound of someone picking out chords on a guitar.

# CHAPTER 2

That night, back in the hotel bedroom, Sonia lay awake staring at the ceiling. As is the way with cheap hotel rooms, it was too dark in the day and too light in the night. Through the unlined curtains a beam of light from the lamp outside illuminated the beige pattern of hallucinogenic swirls on the ceiling, and her mind, still stimulated by caffeine, whirled. Even without the light and the coffee, the thin mattress would have kept her awake.

Maggie's rhythmic breathing in the next bed only a few inches away was strangely comforting. She mulled over the evening and how she had deflected her friend's questions. Whatever she said, Maggie would get at the truth sooner or later and would simply know how things were with her in spite of any words. She could tell merely from a shadow that flickered across a face in answer to the question "How are you?" what the answer should be. This was why James did not like her, and indeed why so many men shared his feelings. She was too perceptive, generally too critical of men and never gave them the benefit of any doubt.

James was, as Maggie so kindly put it, "dusty." It was not his age alone, but his attitudes. Dust had probably settled on him in the cradle.

Their wedding five years earlier, following a courtship of textbook romanticism, had been a vision of contrived but fairy-tale perfection. In this hard, narrow bed, so distant in every way from the expansive luxury of the four-poster where she had spent her wedding night, Sonia thought back to the time when James had appeared in her life.

They met when Sonia was twenty-seven and James was hurtling toward his fortieth birthday. He was a junior partner in a small private bank and for the first fifteen years of his career had worked an eighteen-hour day, ambitiously climbing his way up the corporate ladder.

Only weeks before his landmark birthday James "reprioritized." He needed someone to take to the opera, to dinners, to have his children. In other words, he wanted to be married. Though she was unaware of it for several years, Sonia eventually realized that she had nicely fulfilled an entry in his Filofax "to do" list.

Sonia remembered their first meeting very clearly. James's employer, Berkmann Wilder, had recently merged with another bank and had taken on the PR consultancy she worked for to rebrand them. Sonia always dressed provocatively for meetings with financial institutions, knowing that men who worked in the City of London usually had rather obvious taste, and when she was shown into the bank's boardroom, her attraction was not lost on James. Petite, blond, with a pert bottom well outlined by a tight skirt, and a neat bosom cupped in a lace bra just visible through a silk blouse, she satisfied several male fantasies. James's stares made her feel almost uncomfortable.

"Peachy," James described her to a colleague that lunchtime. "And quite sparky too."

The following week when she returned for a second meeting, he suggested a working lunch. The lunch led to a drink in a wine bar, and within the week they were what James called "an item." Sonia was being swept off her feet and she had no desire to feel the ground beneath them. As well as being quite handsome, he filled in all kinds of gaps in her life. He came from a large, terribly English, entirely conventional family. Such firm foundations had been lacking in Sonia's life and proximity to them made her feel secure. The two significant relationships she had been through in her twenties had ended disastrously for her. One had been with a musician, the other with an Italian photographer. Neither had been faithful to her and the appeal of James was his reliability, his prep school solidity.

"He's so much *older* than you!" objected her friends.

"Why does that matter so much?" queried Sonia.

It was the very fact of this age gap that probably gave him the resources for lavishly extravagant gestures. On Valentine's Day, he did not send a dozen red roses—he sent a dozen dozen, and her small flat in Streatham was overwhelmed. She had never been so spoiled or indeed so happy when, on her birthday, she found a two-carat diamond solitaire ring in the bottom of a glass of champagne. "Yes" was the only possible answer.

Although Sonia had no intention of giving up a job she enjoyed, James offered her long-term security and in return she brought a dowry of child-bearing potential and tolerance of a mother-in-law for whom no one was good enough for her son.

As she lay in her cramped Granada hotel room now, Sonia thought of their glorious white wedding. The marriage had taken place, two years after their first meeting, in the Gloucestershire village close to James's family home. There was a rather obvious imbalance in the congregation (representation on the bride's side was noticeably thinner than on the groom's, which swelled with second cousins, fleets of small children, and friends of his parents), but for Sonia the only really noticeable absence was her mother's. She knew that her father felt it too. Apart from that, everything was perfect. Sprays of freesias festooned pew-ends and scented the air, and there was a gasp as Sonia entered through the arch of white roses on her father's arm. In a full tulle gown that almost filled the width of the aisle, she floated down the strip of carpet toward her groom. Her hair crowned with flowers, the sun created a halo of light around her, and the silver-framed photographs in her home reminded her that she had looked translucent, other-worldly on that day.

After the reception (a four-course dinner for three hundred in a pink candy-striped marquee), James and Sonia left in a Bentley for a reception in a stately home, and by eleven the following morning they were on their way to an Indian Ocean paradise. It was a perfect beginning.

For a long while, Sonia had loved being petted, cared for. She enjoyed the way that James opened doors for her, came home from business trips to Rome with satin lingerie in silk-lined boxes, from Paris with perfumes packaged in boxes within boxes layered like Russian dolls, and with airport scarves from Chanel and Hermès that were not quite her.

On the surface of things, all looked rosy. They had everything: good jobs, a house in an affluent neighborhood that was steadily increasing in value, and plenty of space to begin a family. They seemed a solid couple, just like their home and the street where they lived. The obvious next stage in their lives was to become parents, but to James's irritation something held Sonia back. She had begun to make excuses, both to herself and to James, usually to do with it not being the right moment to take a career break. Admitting, even to herself, the real reason was not easy.

Sonia could not put a date on when the drinking had seemed to become a problem. There probably was not an exact moment, a particular glass of wine, a specific bar or an evening when James had come home and she felt he had had "too much." Perhaps the moment had been at a business lunch, or even at a dinner party, possibly the one they had given the previous week when the large mahogany table had been laid with their best china and cut glass, all gifts at their perfect fairy-tale wedding five years earlier.

She could picture her guests standing around sipping flutes of champagne in their comfortable shades of ice-blue drawing room, making conversation that followed a predictable pattern. The men had been uniformly dressed in suits, but the women had their own strict dress code too: floaty skirts and kitten heels and what at one time would have been called a twinset. Some kind of diamond pendant was de rigueur, too, and a set of fine jangly bangles. It was the smart-casual dress style of their generation: feminine, slightly flirty but steering well clear of tarty.

Sonia recalled how conversation had followed its usual pattern, and she remembered feeling almost at screaming point with the sheer predictability of the middle-class talk and with these people with whom she felt she had nothing in common.

That night, as usual, James had been eager to show off his huge collection of vintage clarets, and the husbands, tired after a long week in the City, had enjoyed knocking back a few bottles of 1978 Burgundy, though even after a glass and a half they began to get disapproving looks from their wives who now realized that it would be their job to drive home.

Cigars had made their appearance at midnight.

"Go on," coaxed James, passing around a box of pure Havana cigars, "guaranteed to have been rolled between a virgin's thighs!"

Though they had heard it said a thousand times before, the men all roared with laughter.

For conservative forty-six-year-old bankers like James, an evening such as this was perfect: safe, respectable, and just what his parents would have enjoyed.

That previous week, it had not been until well after midnight that the guests had all departed. Faced with the depressing aftermath of the dinner party, James had displayed a level of belligerence that had taken Sonia by surprise, given that it had been, as usual, his decision to fill their home with City colleagues and their shrill wives. It was not exactly her idea of fun either, dealing with glasses that were too fragile to go in the dishwasher, ashtrays full of smoldering dog-ends, tidemarks of soup now stuck to the bowls like green concrete, a tablecloth stained with splatters of claret, and white linen napkins covered with perfect lipstick kiss marks. Someone had spilled coffee onto the carpet and not mentioned it, and there was a splash of red wine on a pale armchair.

"What's the point of having a cleaner if we still have to scrub the dishes?" exploded James as he attacked a particularly resistant pan and sent a tidal wave of water flying over the edge of the sink. Even if his guests had limited the amount they had drunk, James had not.

"She only works during the week," said Sonia, mopping up the lake of greasy water, which lapped against James's feet. "You know that."

James knew full well that the cleaner did not come on Friday nights, but it did not stop him from asking the same question every time he found himself at the sink doing battle with stubborn stains.

"Bloody dinner parties," he swore, carrying in a third tray laden with glasses. "Why do we give them?"

"Because we get invited to them and you like them," Sonia replied quietly.

"It just goes round in bloody circles, doesn't it?"

"Look, we don't have to give another one for ages. We're owed lots of invitations."

Sonia knew not to pursue this line of conversation. It would be much better to button her lip.

By one o'clock, the plates were filed in perfect order, facing right in the dishwasher like a row of soldiers. They had had their usual argument about whether or not the sauce should be rinsed off the plates before stacking them. James had won. The smart Worcestershire china already gleamed inside the now humming machine. The pans were spotless too, and James and Sonia had nothing more to say to each other.

Retiring to bed in Granada was so different. She loved the solitude of this narrow bed and being alone with her own reflections. There was such peace in this. The only sounds she could hear were reassuring: a moped buzzing in the street below, a muffled conversation amplified by the acoustics of the narrow street, and the faintly rasping breath of her oldest friend.

In spite of the light that still streamed in from the lamppost outside, and even now a subtle brightening of the sky suggestive of dawn breaking, her mind finally shut down, like a candle extinguished. She slept.

# CHAPTER 3

Only a few hours later the insistent pulse of an alarm woke the women.

"Rise and shine," said Sonia with mock cheerfulness, peering at the bedside clock. "Almost time to go."

"It's only eight," groaned Maggie.

"You haven't changed your watch," replied Sonia. "It's nine and we're meant to be there at ten."

Maggie pulled her sheet up over her head while Sonia got up, showered and dried herself with a threadbare towel. By nine twenty she was dressed. She had come to Granada for a purpose.

"Come on, Maggie, let's not be late," she said coaxingly. "I'm going to nip down for some coffee while you get dressed."

While she breakfasted on a limp croissant and tepid coffee, Sonia studied the map of Granada and located their destination. The dance school was not far away, but they would have to concentrate on taking the correct turnings.

As she sat, Sonia mused on how things evolved. It had all begun with a film. Without that, the dancing would never have happened. It was like a board game—she had not known where the next move would take her.

One of the few things that James occasionally agreed to do on a weekday was to go to their local cinema, even if he was usually asleep well before the film's denouement. The local south London picture house resolutely refused to show blockbusters but had enough local clientele wanting to see high-brow, art-house films, to half fill it most nights. It was only a mile or so from where they lived, but the atmosphere was much edgier by the theater: Caribbean takeaways, kebab houses, and tapas bars competed with Chinese, Indian, and Thai restaurants, all a contrast with the glassy metropolitan restaurants closer to their home.

The side street into which they emerged after the film matched the hauntingly gloomy Almodóvar film they had watched. As they walked along, Sonia noticed something that she hadn't seen before—a brightly illuminated, flashing, Las Vegas–vulgar sign: SALSA! RUMBA! it shrieked in neon. In the dimly lit street, there was something reassuringly cheerful about the sign.

As they approached, they could hear music and see a suggestion of movement behind the frosted windows. They must have walked past this building on their way to the cinema but not even given it a second look. In the intervening two hours, the prosaic-looking 1950s hall, squeezed into the space where a bomb had fallen during the Blitz, had come to life.

As they passed, Sonia had taken in a smaller, illuminated sign:

**Tuesday—Beginners**
**Friday—Intermediate**
**Saturday—All Levels**

From inside came a scarcely audible but alluring Latin American beat. Even the faint suggestion of rhythm exerted a strong pull on her. The clipped sound of James's heels retreating down the street confirmed to her that he had not even noticed it.

Coming home from the office a few weeks later, she had, as usual, to force open the front door and push aside the embankment of paper that lay behind it. Leaflets clogged up the hallway as irritatingly as slush on winter roadsides—every type of takeaway and home delivery imaginable, catalogues for DIY shops that she had no intention of visiting, offers of carpet cleaning at half price, English lessons that she did not need. But there was one leaflet that she could not throw into the recycling bin. On one side was a photo of the neon sign that had winked at her all those weeks ago and the words: "Salsa! Rumba!" On the reverse were days and times for lessons, and at the bottom of the page, rather endearingly, the following words: "Lern to dance. Dance to live. Live to dance."

As a little girl, she had been taken to weekly ballet lessons and later on to tap dancing. She had given up dance school as a teenager but was always there until the bitter end at any school disco. Since they married, James had made it clear that dancing was not his "thing" so the opportunity rarely arose. The thought that there was somewhere she could take dance lessons less than ten minutes' drive from where she lived kept coming back to her. Perhaps she would pluck up the courage to go one day.

That day came sooner than she had imagined. It was a few months later. They had planned to see a film, and James had rung on her mobile just as she was arriving at the cinema to say that he was stuck in the office. Across the way, the neon lights of the dance school winked at her.

The hall was as seedy on the inside as it appeared on the outside. Paint peeled from the ceiling, and there was a waist-high tidemark all the way round the room as though it had once filled up with water like a giant fish tank. This might have explained the unmistakable smell of damp. Six bare lightbulbs hung down from the ceiling on irregular lengths of flex, and a few posters advertising Spanish fiestas were intended to cheer up the walls. Their tattiness only reinforced the general sense of decay. Sonia's nerve almost failed her, but one of the instructors spotted her in the doorway. She was given a warm welcome and was just in time for the start of a lesson.

She found that she soon picked up the rhythm. Before the end of the evening she discovered that the movement could turn into something as subtle as a twitch of the hips rather than a meticulously counted sequence of steps. Two hours later she emerged, flushed, into the chilly evening air.

For some reason that she could not have articulated to anyone, Sonia felt exhilarated. Even the music had filled her to the very top of her being. She was brimming—that was the only way she could describe it to her-self—and without hesitation she signed up for a course. Each week the dancing thrilled her more. Sometimes she could hardly contain her exuberance. For an hour or so after it had finished, the mood of the dance class remained with her. There was an enchantment about dancing. Even a few minutes of it could leave her in a state of near-ecstasy.

She loved everything about her Tuesday evening engagement with Juan Carlos, the stubby Cuban with the shiny, pointy-toed dancing boots. The rhythm and the momentum and the way the music reminded her of sunshine and warm places.

Over the following weeks, Sonia acknowledged that Tuesday was her favorite of all days, and her class the one unmissable commitment in her diary. What started as a distraction grew into a passion. Salsa CDs littered the boot of her car, and on her journeys to work she mind-danced as she drove. Each week, she returned warm and flushed from the exhilaration of her lesson. On the occasions when he was already in, James would greet her with a patronizing comment, bursting the balloon of her euphoria.

"Good time at your dancing class?" he inquired, glancing up from his newspaper. "How were all the little girls in their tutus?"

James's tone, though it pretended to be teasing, had a distinctively sarcastic note. Sonia tried not to be provoked but felt obliged to deflect his criticism.

"It's just like a step class. Don't you remember? I used to go to them all the time a couple of years ago."

"Mmm . . . vaguely," came the voice behind the newspaper. "Can't see why you have to go every week, though."

One day she mentioned this new interest of hers to her oldest school friend, Maggie. The two girls had been inseparable for the seven years they were at grammar school together, and two decades on they were still almost as close, meeting several times a year for an evening in a wine bar. Maggie was full of enthusiasm for Sonia's dancing. Could she come too? Would Sonia take her? Of course! It could only make it more fun.

In every way, their lives could not have been more contrasted: Sonia was an only child and her mother was already in a wheelchair by the time she started secondary school. The atmosphere in her tidy semi-detached house was subdued. Maggie, on the other hand, lived in a ramshackle house with four siblings and easygoing parents who never seemed to mind if she was in or out.

In their all-girls school, academic work absorbed little of their energy. Feuds, discos, and boyfriends were their main preoccupations, and confessions and confidences were the oxygen of friendship. When Sonia's mother was finally beaten by the multiple sclerosis that had been slowly destroying her for years, Maggie was the person Sonia cried with. Maggie more or less moved in with her, and both Sonia and her father appreciated her presence. She lifted the terrible gloom of their grief. This happened when they were seventeen. In the following year, Maggie had her own crisis. She became pregnant. Her parents took the news badly, and for the second time Maggie went to live with Sonia for a few weeks until they got used to the idea.

In spite of this closeness, they went very separate ways when they left school. Maggie's baby was born not long after—no one ever knew the name of the father, perhaps not even Maggie herself—and eventually she supported herself by teaching pottery part-time in a couple of colleges and at night classes. Her daughter, Candy, was now seventeen and had just started at art school. In a good light, with their big hoop earrings and quasi-bohemian style of dress, they could easily be mistaken for sisters. Though her long dark curls were almost identical to her daughter's, years of smoking had indented her sun-tanned face with lines that revealed her true age. They lived together in a slightly shabby area, close to a row of pound shops and the best Indian vegetarian restaurants this side of Delhi.

Sonia's lifestyle, a career in PR, an expensively upholstered home, and James were all very alien to Maggie, who had never hidden her concerns about her friend marrying such a "stuffed shirt."

Their lives might have gone in very different directions, but for nearly twenty years they had diligently remembered each other's birthdays and nourished their friendship with lengthy evenings over a few bottles of wine, when they told each other every detail of their lives until it was closing time, and then parted, not to be in touch again for weeks or even months.

For the first half of her introductory salsa class, Maggie sat out and watched. All the time she was tapping out the beat with her foot and rocking gently on her hips, never for a moment taking her eyes off the instructors' feet as they demonstrated that night's steps. Juan Carlos had the music turned up loud that night, and the insistent beat seemed to make the floorboards themselves vibrate. After the five-minute break, when everyone sipped water from their bottles and Sonia introduced her old friend to the other dancers, Maggie was ready to try the steps. A few of the regulars were skeptical that someone who had not been to the class before could join halfway through a term and expect to catch up; they feared that their own progress would be delayed.

The Cuban took Maggie's hand and, in front of the mirror, led her through the dance. The rest of the class watched, several of them hoping that she would flounder. Her brow might have been furrowed with concentration, but Maggie remembered every move and half-turn that they had been working on that night and was step-perfect. There was a ripple of applause as the dance finished.

Sonia was impressed. It had taken her weeks to get as far as Maggie had in half an hour.

"How did you manage that?" she asked Maggie over a glass of Rioja in the wine bar afterward.

She admitted that some years ago she had done some salsa on a trip to Spain and had not forgotten the basic technique. "It's like riding a bike," she said nonchalantly, "once learned, never forgotten."

Within a few sessions, her enthusiasm surpassed even Sonia's, and with few other commitments in her life, Maggie began going to a salsa club, dancing in the darkness with hundreds of others until five in the morning.

In a few weeks it was to be Maggie's thirty-fifth birthday.

"We're going dancing in Spain," she announced.

"That sounds fun," said Sonia. "With Candy?"

"No, with you. I've got the tickets. Forty pounds return to Granada. It's done. And I've booked us some dance classes while we're there."

Sonia could imagine exactly how badly this would go down with James, but there was no question of refusing Maggie. She knew for sure that her friend would have little sympathy for any kind of vacillation. Maggie was a free spirit and never understood how anyone could give up their liberty to come and go as they pleased. But most important for Sonia, she did not want to refuse. Dance already seemed like a driving force in her life, and she was addicted to the sense of release it gave.

"How fantastic!" she said. "When exactly?"

The trip was in three weeks' time, to tie in with the day of Maggie's birthday.

James's *froideur* was no surprise. If James had disliked his wife's new interest in dancing, his antagonism intensified when she had announced this trip to Granada.

"Sounds like a hen party," he had said dismissively. "Bit old for that kind of thing, aren't you?"

"Well, Maggie did miss out on the whole wedding thing, so perhaps that's why she's making such a celebration of a big birthday."

"*Maggie . . .*" As ever, James's contempt for Maggie was ill concealed. "Why didn't she ever get *married*? Like everyone else?"

He could see what Sonia saw in her university friends, her colleagues and the various acquaintances she had made within sugar-borrowing distance of their home, but his attitude to Maggie was different. As well as being part of his wife's dim and distant schooldays, Maggie did not fit into any boxes and he could not begin to see why Sonia kept in touch with her.

Far away from her husband, under the sympathetic gaze of a cheaply reproduced Virgin Mary in the breakfast room of the Hotel Santa Ana, Sonia realized that she had ceased to care what James thought of her unconventional friend.

Maggie appeared, bleary-eyed, at the doorway.

"Hi, sorry I'm late. Have I got time for coffee?"

"No, not if we're going to get there for the start of the class. We'd better go straight away," instructed Sonia, keen to obstruct any further procrastination that Maggie might be dreaming up. In the daytime, Sonia felt she was in charge. At night, she knew they would swap roles. It had never been any different.

They went out into the street and were taken aback by the pleasing fresh air. There were few people about: a handful of elderly folk with small dogs on leads, and the rest sitting in cafés. Most shop fronts were still hidden behind metal grilles, with only bakeries and cafés showing signs of life, the alluring fragrance of sweet pastries and *churros* scenting the air.

Sonia hardly looked up from her map, following the twists and turns of the alleyways and passageways to steer them to their destination. Every step of the way was guided by the blue lettering of the ceramic street signs. They crossed a recently hosed-down square, sloshing through puddles of water, and passing by a glorious flower stall that was set up between two cafés, its huge fragranced blooms luminous. The smooth slabs of the marble pavement were soft underfoot and the fifteen-minute walk seemed like five.

"We're here," announced Sonia triumphantly, folding the map into her pocket. "La Zapata. This is it."

It was a tatty building. Layers of small posters had built up over the years on the walls of its façade, one after the other stuck over the brickwork advertising flamenco, tango, rumba, and salsa evenings taking place all over the city. Every phone box, lamppost, and bus-shelter in the city seemed to have been used in the same way, informing passersby of forthcoming *espectáculos*, one flyer plastered over another often before it had even taken place. It was a chaotic kind of collage, but it represented the spirit of this city and the profusion of dance and music that was its lifeblood.

The inside of La Zapata was as scruffy as the exterior. There was nothing glamorous about it. This was not a place for performance but for practice and rehearsal.

Four doors led from the hallway. Two were open, two shut. From behind one closed door could be heard the sound of thunderous stamping. A herd of bulls charging down a street would not have made more noise. It stopped abruptly and was followed by the sound of rhythmic clapping, like the patter of raindrops after a thunderstorm.

A woman bustled purposefully past them and down an unlit corridor. Steel heel- and toecaps clip-clopped on the stone floor and music burst through a briefly opened door.

The two Englishwomen stood reading the framed posters advertising performances that had taken place decades earlier, slightly unsure what they should do. Eventually Maggie got the attention of a skeletally thin and tired-looking woman of about fifty, who seemed to run the place from a dark cubbyhole within the reception area.

"Salsa?" said Maggie hopefully.

With a perfunctory nod, the woman acknowledged their presence. "*Felipe y Corazón—allí,*" she said, pointing emphatically to one of the open doors.

They were the first in the studio. They put their bags in the corner and changed their shoes.

"I wonder how many of us there will be," mused Maggie, doing up her buckles. Her statement required no response.

A mirror ran across one end of the room and a wooden bar ran down another. It was a clinical space with high windows that overlooked a narrow street, and even if the glass had not been opaque with dirt, little daylight would have entered the room. A strong smell of polish seeped from the dark wooden floor worn smooth by years of wear.

Sonia loved the slightly musty smell of age and usage that emanated from the walls of this room, the way that the cracks between the boards had filled with dust, grime, and wax. She noticed the way fluff had mounted up between the segments of the ancient old radiators and saw silvery cobweb threads wafting gently from the ceiling. In each layer of dust there was another decade of the place's history.

Half a dozen other people drifted into the studio. There was a group of Norwegian students (mostly girls) all doing Spanish Studies at university, and then a few additional men in their early twenties appeared, all of them locals.

"They must be what are called 'taxi dancers,'" Maggie whispered to Sonia. "It said in the brochure that they hire them in to balance up the numbers."

Eventually, their instructors appeared. Felipe and Corazón were both raven-haired and as lean as young calves, but their weathered skin betrayed that they were well into their sixties. Corazón had evenly spaced rows of deep lines on her bony face, not etched there just by the passing of time but through expressiveness and the unashamed exaggeration of her emotions. Whenever she smiled, laughed, and grimaced it took its toll on her skin. Both were dressed in black, which accentuated their slimness, and against the whiteness of the room, they stood out like silhouettes.

The group of twelve had spread themselves out, all of them facing their instructors.

"*Hola!*" they said in unison, smiling broadly at the group lined up expectantly in front of them.

"*Hola!*" chorused the group, like a class of well-disciplined six-year-olds.

Felipe carried a CD player, which he set down on the floor. He pressed PLAY and the space they shared was transformed. The joyful sound of a trumpet introduction pierced the air. The class automatically mirrored Corazón's movements. It did not take a word from her; it was simply obvious that this was her intention. For a while the class warmed up gently, turning wrists and ankles, flexing heels, stretching necks and shoulders, and rotating hips. All the while they kept their eyes fixed on their teachers, fascinated by their pipe-cleaner bodies.

Though they had grown up in the flamenco tradition, Felipe and Corazón had seen which way the wind was blowing. In teaching terms, the Cuban-originated dance of salsa was more commercial and would appeal to an audience who might not be drawn to the dramatic intensity of flamenco. Some dancers of their age still performed, but Felipe and Corazón knew that they could not make a decent living out of doing so. Their strategy had worked. They had mastered salsa and created new choreographies, attracting many Granadinos as well as foreigners to their classes. They liked salsa; it was more superficial, less emotionally draining than their true passion, like a light Jerez next to a full-bodied Rioja.

Salsa instruction now began. It was Corazón who did most of the shouting. Her voice cut through the music and even the strident tone of jazz trumpet that blasted its way through the salsa tune.

"*Y un, dos, tres! Y un, dos, tres!* And! Clap! Clap! Clap! And! Clap! Clap! Clap! And . . ."

On she went. Repetition, after repetition, after repetition of the beat until it would haunt them and penetrate their dreams. Every turn their pupils mastered was greeted with huge encouragement and enthusiasm.

"*Eso es!*" That's it!

When it was time to move on, to try something new, Felipe would call out: "*Vale!*" OK! And a demonstration of the next turn, or *vuelta*, would commence.

"*Estupendo!*" the teachers would cry out, unashamed of the hyperbole.

Between attempts at each new move, the women would move round one partner, so that by the end of the lesson's first half, they had danced with all of the taxi dancers. Even if none of them could speak English, these young men were all fluent in the language of salsa.

"I love this," said Maggie as she passed Sonia on the dance floor.

There was a break when big jugs of iced water were brought in and poured into plastic cups. It had become stifling in the room and everyone drank thirstily while polite snippets of stilted conversation were exchanged between people of different nationalities.

Sonia and Maggie sauntered into the corridor and paused outside the studio, where framed posters jostled with each other. Felipe and Corazón appeared on one of them. The style of type dated it to around 1975 and it was advertising a flamenco performance.

"Look, Maggie, it's a picture of our teachers!"

"God, so it is! Hasn't age been cruel!"

"They haven't changed that much," said Sonia in their defense. "Their figures are pretty similar."

"But those crow's-feet—she didn't have them in those days, did she?" commented Maggie. "Do you think they'd show us some flamenco? Teach us how to stamp our feet? Give us a bit of a clatter on the castanets?"

Maggie didn't wait for an answer. She was already back in the studio, explaining and gesticulating to the teachers what she wanted them to do.

Sonia watched her from the door frame.

Finally, Felipe found some English words: "Flamenco can't be taught," he said gutturally. "It's in the blood, and only in gypsy blood at that. But you can try if you like. I'll show you some at the end of the lesson."

It was a statement designed to challenge.

For the next hour they repeated the movements from the first half of the lesson and then fifteen minutes before the end, Felipe clapped his hands together.

"Now," he said. "Flamenco."

He strutted over to the CD player, flicked swiftly through his wallet of music, and carefully extracted what he wanted. Meanwhile, Corazón changed her shoes in the corner, to a pair with heavy heels and steel-capped soles.

The class stood back, quietly expectant. They heard palms against palms and low drums. It was dark and very different from the happy-go-lucky sound of salsa.

Corazón strode out in front of the group. It was as though she no longer knew they were there. As a guitar played, she raised one arm and then another, her sinuous fingers fanning out like daisy petals. For more than five minutes, she stamped her feet in a complex sequence of heel and toe, heel and toe, that accelerated to a thunderous vibration before it stopped dead, with a final, decisive "BANG" of her hard shoe on the solid floor. It was a virtuoso display of strength and breathtaking technical prowess as much as a dance, somehow the more impressive because of her age.

On the very beat that she stopped, a wail emanated from the speakers and eerily wrapped itself around everyone in the room. It was a raw-throated male voice and seemed to express the same anguish that had shown on Corazón's face as she had danced.

Just before she finished, Felipe had begun and for a few seconds mirrored his wife's movements, proving to the audience that this dance was not pure improvisation but a well-rehearsed piece of choreography. Now Felipe took her place center stage. Narrow-hipped, his slim back arched into a C, Felipe briefly struck a pose before spinning himself around and beginning a series of floor-hammering steps. The sound of metal on wood bounced off the mirrored walls. His movements were even more sensual than those of his wife, and certainly more coquettish. It was as though he flirted with the class, his hands traveling up and down his body, his hips rocking one way and then another. Sonia was transfixed.

Almost competing with Corazón, he executed an ever more complex sequence of steps, time after time landing by some miracle on precisely the same spot, the music drowned out by the hammering of feet. The passion of it was extraordinary and it seemed to have come from nowhere.

Felipe's finishing pose, eyes to the ceiling, one arm wrapped around his back, the other thrown across his front was one of pure arrogance. From the back a quiet voice said "*Olé.*" It was Corazón; even she was moved by her husband's display, his total absorption in the moment. Then there was silence.

After a moment or two, Maggie broke it by applauding rapturously. The rest of the group clapped but with less enthusiasm.

Felipe's face broke into a smile, all traces of arrogance melting away. Corazón came out in front of the audience and challenged them.

"Flamenco? Tomorrow? You want?" she inquired, flashing her yellowing teeth.

Some of the Norwegian girls, slightly embarrassed by this display of naked emotion, turned to chat to one another; meanwhile the taxi dancers were looking at their watches to see whether their time as hired hands was nearly over. They did not plan to do overtime.

"Yes," said Maggie. "I want."

Sonia felt uncomfortable. Flamenco was so very different from salsa. From what she had seen in the past twelve hours, it was an emotional state of being as much as a dance. Salsa was carefree, an emotional escape route, and, moreover, it was what they had come to improve.

By now the rest of the class had dispersed and Sonia needed fresh air.

"*Adiós*," said Corazón, packing up her bag. "*Hasta luego.*"

CHAPTER 4

It was one o'clock. The dance studio did not have glamorous neighbors and the workaday side street in which they found themselves offered little more than a car-parts depot and a key cutter. As they walked to the end of the shadowy street and turned into the main road, the atmosphere changed and they were dazzled by the glare of sunlight and deafened by the crazed cacophony of lunchtime traffic brought to a standstill.

The bars and cafés were now crammed with builders, students, and anyone else who lived too far out of town to get home for their lunchtime siesta. All the other shops—greengrocers, stationers, and the plethora of hairdressing salons—were firmly shut up again, having opened for just a few hours since Sonia and Maggie had last passed. Their slatted metal grilles would not be raised again until sometime after four.

"Let's stop at this one," suggested Maggie, outside the second bar they came to. El Castilla had a long, stainless-steel bar and several tables down the side of the room, all but one occupied. The two Englishwomen quickly went in.

The smells were intense and mingled together to form a distinctive aroma of Spanish café life: beer, *jamon*, stale ash, the slightly sour smell of goat's cheese, a whiff of anchovies, and, wafting across it all, strong, freshly ground coffee. A row of uniformly blue-overalled manual workers sat up at the bar, oblivious to everything but the plates in front of them. Almost simultaneously they put down their forks, and clumsy hands reached for packets of strong cigarettes, generating a mushroom cloud of smoke as they lit up. Meanwhile the patron manufactured a row of *cafés solo*. It was a daily ritual for them all.

Only now did his attention turn to his new customers.

"*Señoras*," he said, coming to their table.

Reading from the board behind the bar, they ordered huge crusty *bocadillos* to be filled with sardines. Sonia watched the bar owner preparing them. In one hand he wielded a knife, in the other a cigarette. It was an impressive juggling act and she marveled as he ladled crushed tomatoes from a bowl and squashed them on to slabs of bread, fished sardines out of a bucket-sized tin, and all the while took regular drags on his Corona cigarette. If the process seemed unconventional, the end result was by no means disappointing.

"What did you think of the lesson?" asked Sonia, between mouthfuls.

"The teachers are wonderful," answered Maggie. "I love them."

"They're life-enhancing, aren't they?" agreed Sonia.

She had to raise her voice above the clatter of falling coins that erupted from a one-armed bandit next to their table. Since entering, they had listened to the perpetual warbling of the fruit machine, and now one of the café's customers happily scooped a handful of coins into his pocket. He walked away whistling.

Sonia and Maggie both ate hungrily. They watched as the workmen left the bar, leaving behind them a pall of smoke and dozens of tiny screwed-up paper napkins carelessly scattered on the floor like a snowstorm.

"What do you think James would make of it all?" asked Maggie.

"What? This place?" responded Sonia. "Too grubby. Too earthy."

"I meant the dancing," said Maggie.

"You know what he'd think. That it's all self-indulgent nonsense," replied Sonia.

"I don't know how you stand him."

Maggie always went for the kill. Her open dislike of James almost drove Sonia to his defense but she did not really want to think about her husband today and quickly changed the subject.

"My father, on the other hand, used to love dancing. I only discovered that a few weeks ago."

"Really? I don't remember anything about that when we were growing up."

"Well, it was all over by then anyway, because of Mum's illness."

"Of course it was," said Maggie, slightly embarrassed. "I forgot about that."

"When I last went to see him," continued Sonia, "he was so enthusiastic about my salsa lessons it almost made up for James's cynicism."

Sonia's father lived a mere thirty-minute drive away, in the outer suburbs on a characterless block of 1950s flats. Each visit, it seemed to take even longer before the buzzer went and the outer door, which let visitors into the pale green, uncarpeted communal hallway, opened. It was then a disinfectant-scented climb up to the second story of this building, and by that time Jack Haynes would be standing at his open doorway ready to welcome his only daughter in.

Sonia recalled that last visit and how the seventy-eight-year-old's round face had creased into a smile as she came into sight. She had embraced his stout frame and kissed the top of his liver-spotted head, making sure she did not disturb the few remaining strands of silver hair, which he had carefully combed back across his pate.

"Sonia!" he said warmly. "How lovely to see you."

"Hello, Dad." She hugged him tighter.

A tray with cups and saucers, a jug of milk, and a small plate of biscuits was already set out on a low table in the living room, and Jack insisted that Sonia take a seat while he went into the kitchen to fetch the teapot, which rattled noisily as he carried it through and set it down. Pale liquid slopped from the spout and splashed the rug, but she knew not to ask him whether he needed any help. Such a ritual as this preserved the dignity of old age.

As her father held the tea strainer above the cup and the brown liquid streamed through, Sonia began the usual line of questioning.

"So how—"

Her question was interrupted by the rumble of a train going past, only a few feet from the back wall, causing enough of a vibration to send a small cactus plant on the window-ledge crashing to the floor.

"Oh, what a nuisance," said the elderly man, struggling to his feet. "I'm sure these trains are getting more frequent, you know."

Once the dustpan and brush had been fetched and the scattering of gravel, dry soil, and spiny cactus limbs had been patiently reassembled and pressed back into the plastic pot, their conversation resumed. It covered the usual ground: what Jack had been doing in the past couple of weeks, what the doctor had said about his arthritis, how long he would have to wait for a hip replacement, how he had been to Hampton Court on a recent outing along with some of the other people who went to the day-care center, and a description of a funeral he had been to of an old National Service acquaintance. The latter seemed to have been the highlight of the month, the funeral wakes in village halls around the country providing welcome reunions for those who still survived, with hours of reminiscence and a slap-up tea.

Once her father had given her the headlines of his life in the past few weeks, it was Sonia's turn. She always found it hard. The machinations of the PR world would be incomprehensible to someone who had worked as a teacher all his life, so she kept talk of work to a minimum and tended to make it sound as though she was in advertising, which was a much easier world for an outsider to grasp. Her social life would have been equally alien to him. On that last visit, though, she had told him about the dance class she had begun to attend and his enthusiasm took her by surprise.

"What dances are you doing exactly? Who are your instructors? What sort of shoes do you wear?" he quizzed her.

Sonia couldn't believe that her father knew so much.

"Your mother and I used to dance a lot in our courtship and in our early married life," he told her. "In the fifties everyone did! It was as though we were all celebrating the end of the war."

"How often did you go?"

"Oh, at least twice a week. Always on Saturdays and then usually another night or two."

He smiled at his daughter. Jack loved it when she came to visit and knew it must be quite hard for her to fit these trips into her busy schedule. What he was always keen to avoid, though, was to talk too much about the past. It must be tiresome for children to have to listen to their parents reminiscing about days gone by and he had always been wary of it.

"But they always say that the best things in life are free, don't they?" he added, smiling at her, hoping that even with her lovely house and expensive car she still knew that.

Sonia nodded. "I just can't believe I never really knew," she said.

"Well, I suppose we stopped soon after you were born."

Although her mother had died when Sonia was sixteen, she was amazed that she had never known anything about this aspect of their lives. Like most children, she had not spent much time wondering what her mother and father did before she was there and her curiosity had never been much aroused.

"Don't you remember all the dancing you did yourself when you were little?" he asked. "You used to go every Saturday afternoon. Look!"

Jack had rummaged in the bureau and found some pictures. On top of the pile was a photograph of Sonia, pale and self-conscious in a white, ribbon-trimmed tutu, standing by the fireplace of her childhood home. Sonia was more interested in the other photos, which were of her parents at various dance events. One showed the pair of them, her father looking not unlike he did today though with more of his pale hair, and her mother, erect, elegant, her black hair slicked tightly into a firm bun. They were holding a trophy and on the reverse of the picture, in pencil, was written: "1953: Tango, 1st." There were several others, most of them taken at competitions.

Sonia held a picture in each hand. "Is this really Mum?"

In her memory, she was frail, semi-bedridden, and silver-haired. Here she was vibrant, strong, and, most arrestingly for Sonia, upright. It was hard to revise the image of her mother that she had had for so long.

"We all danced properly in those days," Jack assured his daughter. "We were taught the right steps and we danced *together*, not like people do nowadays."

These photos evoked such strong emotions for Jack, and as he gazed silently at this image of himself, memories of how he and Mary had not always performed according to the rule book returned to him. The rule of dancing is that the man leads, but for them this wasn't always the case. Within the subtlety of their movements, whether it was tango, rumba, or paso doble, Jack had known where Mary wanted to be led, and from the slightest pressure she exerted on his arm, they had developed a way of communicating this. She was totally in control of their movement. Having danced almost as soon as she could walk, until the moment when her legs began to lose the power to carry her, it could not have been any other way.

Jack found another envelope stuffed with photographs. Each one featured himself and his wife in a stiff pose and, on the back, the date and the dance for which they had won a prize.

"What happened to all those beautiful gowns?" Sonia could not resist asking.

"I'm afraid they all went to a charity shop when she stopped dancing," Jack answered. "She couldn't bear to have them in the wardrobe."

Though Sonia was amazed to have uncovered such a significant part of her father's life, and one that she had never been aware of, she knew without asking why they had really stopped dancing and why they had never talked about it. Her mother had developed multiple sclerosis during her pregnancy with Sonia and within a short time was confined to a wheelchair.

Sonia would have liked to spend the rest of the day asking her father more but could sense she might already have asked one question too many. He put the other photographs back in the envelope.

There was one stray picture that still lay facedown on his coffee table, and she turned it over before handing it back. It showed a group of children in hand-knitted cardigans. Two of them were sitting on top of a barrel and two others were leaning against it. They had stiff smiles. A group of tables in the background suggested it was taken outside a café, and the cobbles suggested somewhere continental.

"Who are these children?" she asked.

"Some of your mother's family," he answered, not volunteering any further information.

It was time for Sonia to go. She and her father embraced.

" 'Bye, sweetheart, it's been lovely to see you," he said, smiling. "Enjoy your dancing."

As she had made her way home that afternoon, Sonia's imagination had been filled with images of her parents gliding around the dance floor. Perhaps the discovery of their interest shed light on why she already could not imagine life without her dance lessons.

Sonia had been silent for a few minutes, chewing her way through lunch in the Granada café, tomato paste and crumbs spraying onto the table around her. When she looked up, her eye was caught by a series of cheaply produced oil paintings of women in long, extravagantly ruffled dresses. They were the clichéd image of Spain, but every restaurant and café in the city subscribed to the myth.

"Were you serious about wanting them to teach you flamenco?" Sonia asked Maggie.

"Yes, I was."

"But didn't you think it looked tricky?"

"I'd just like to learn the basics," said Maggie confidently.

"Whatever those are," responded Sonia.

It seemed to her that there could be nothing "basic" about flamenco. Surely it had an entire culture of its own, and she felt mildly irritated that Maggie had not recognized that.

"Why are you so down on it?" snapped Maggie.

"I'm not down on it at all," replied Sonia. "I'm just not entirely sure it isn't like being a Brit who comes on a cheap package holiday and asks whether he can learn how to be a bullfighter. It just doesn't look as though it can be done."

"Fine. But if you don't want to do it, it doesn't stop me, does it?"

The two women were rarely out of tune like this, and when it happened, it took them both by surprise. Sonia could not explain to herself why she felt so irritated by Maggie's attitude and by her assumption that she could penetrate the outer layer of this culture, but she felt it showed disrespect.

They finished eating in a silence that Maggie eventually broke.

"Coffee?" she asked, wanting to clear the air.

"*Con leche*," responded Sonia with a smile. They could not sulk with each other for long.

As the mid-afternoon sunshine was fading to an ochre glow, Sonia and Maggie returned to their hotel. The streets were now deadly quiet; the traffic had vanished and the shops remained firmly closed. They too would follow the Spanish pattern and take to their beds for a few hours of afternoon siesta. Sonia had slept very little the previous night and was now beginning to feel jaded.

Though the curtains filtered only a fraction of the light, nothing would have stopped Sonia falling into a deep sleep that afternoon. For several hours she was in a state of blissful unconsciousness.

When they woke, it was dusk, and light no longer streamed in. This was the major flaw in the siesta habit, having to get out of bed just as the dying light was telling your body and mind that it was time to climb into it.

Now it was Sonia's turn to have difficulty stirring and Maggie who bounced out of bed.

"Come on, Sonia, time to go out!"

"Go out? Where?"

She was half asleep, bleary-eyed, confused, and in a bemused state of semi-wakefulness in which she could not quite remember where she was.

"That's why we're here, isn't it? To go out dancing?"

"Dancing? Mmm . . ."

Her body was still heavy with a not-quite-fulfilled need to sleep. Her head throbbed. She could hear the sound of Maggie in the shower, singing, whistling, humming, her joie de vivre almost bursting through the bathroom wall. She could not face dancing tonight.

Maggie came back into the room, her hair wound up into a tall turban, a second towel tightly drawn across her breasts, her naked chest and shoulders dark against the whiteness. Sonia watched her. There was something majestic, even statuesque about this woman. Maggie continued to hum as she dressed, pulling on jeans and a white ruffled shirt and fastening a wide leather belt. Her face glowed from the warmth of the shower and the few hours of sunshine they had enjoyed earlier that day. She seemed lost in her own thoughts, and it was as though she had forgotten Sonia was there.

"Maggie?"

She turned round and sat on the end of her bed, fiddling with a pair of hooped earrings. "Yes?" she replied, her head tilted to one side.

"Would you mind if I didn't come out tonight?"

"Of course I wouldn't. But it seems a bit of a shame. We did come here to dance . . ."

"I know. I just feel completely wrung out. I'll come tomorrow, I promise."

Maggie continued to get herself ready, spraying on perfume, outlining her eyes in inky black, accentuating her long lashes with layers of mascara.

"Are you sure you'll be all right going on your own?" Sonia added anxiously.

"What's the worst that can happen?" Maggie laughed. "Everyone here is shorter than me. So I can always run away if I need to."

Sonia knew that Maggie meant it, and that she was a match for anyone. There was no need to give a moment's thought to her safety. Maggie was the most independent woman she knew.

Sonia continued to doze. At nine thirty, Maggie was ready to leave.

"I'm going to have something to eat on the way. Are you sure you don't want to come out with me?"

"No, really. I just want to catch up on sleep. I'll see you in the morning."

For a second night, Sonia enjoyed the tranquillity of her single bed. Though noises continued to float up from the street, there was a magical silence in the space of the room. She loved the knowledge that she was going to be here alone, that no one could dent her peace of mind.

It was so different from those nights when she went to bed early, tired out from a long day at the office and then lay, tense, wondering when James was going to arrive home. Perhaps once or twice a week he would stagger through the front door at three or four in the morning, and the stained-glass panes in the front door would shudder with the impact as it was slammed shut. He would then stumble up the stairs and collapse, fully clothed, onto the bed, his mouth breathing out the foul fumes of his evening excess. It was not the sex—fast, rough, and easily forgotten—that sometimes happened when he was in this state that repelled her most. It was the sour smell of stale alcohol that made her retch with disgust. It was a stench that revolted her more than any other in the world and she recoiled from this vast, dark hulk lying in the darkness next to her, rattling the stillness with his snores. On the mornings after these nights, there was no reference to his state of inebriation. James seemed to be able to rise at six without even a hangover, shower, dress in his City uniform, and leave for work with the same punctuality as he did on any other day. It was as though he was unaware that anything out of the ordinary had even happened. No one else was aware either. In the picture book of marriage, they were the perfect married couple. It was a story told for an audience.

Now, as she lay in the semi-darkness, she felt her stomach contract with the recalled nausea of it all. She rolled over onto her side and soon felt the chill of tears on her pillow. This was meant to be a peaceful night, one where she caught up on her sleep. It was not intended to be a night in which she tortured herself with recollection of all that was wrong. Occasionally she fell into a fitful sleep, and in the moments when she came to, she noticed that Maggie's bed was still empty.

At three o'clock in the morning, she was just dropping off to sleep when the sound of a key in the lock disturbed her.

"Are you still awake?" whispered Maggie.

"Yes," grunted Sonia. Even if she had been asleep, the noise of Maggie stumbling into the room would have woken her.

"I've had such a fantastic night," enthused Maggie, switching on the overhead light, oblivious to her friend's mood.

"I'm glad for you," Sonia answered, with ill-disguised annoyance in her voice.

"Don't be cross. You could have come with me!"

"I know, I know. I don't know why I didn't really, for all the sleep I've had."

"You're just afraid of letting your hair down," she said, tugging at the band that held her hair up and, as if to demonstrate her point, letting her thick, wavy locks tumble around her shoulders.

"We haven't got many nights here and you should come out. Why on earth didn't you?"

"There are hundreds of reasons why I didn't. I'm not good enough, for a start."

"That's complete rubbish," said Maggie. "And even if you aren't, you soon will be."

With this decisive statement she switched off the light and, now naked, threw herself onto her bed.

# CHAPTER 5

Despite her night of snatched, unsatisfactory sleep, Sonia rose early the next morning. The airlessness of the room had left her with a throbbing head and she yearned to get out. She was hungry too.

Their dance lesson was not until the afternoon, and since Maggie was clearly going to be comatose for a while, Sonia dressed quietly and crept out of the room, leaving her friend a note.

Turning right out of the hotel, she wandered up to the main street that ran like a spine through the center of the city. She soon realized that Granada was impossible to get lost in, so simple was the topography of this small city. Distant, toward the south, was a high wall of mountains; eastward the streets climbed toward the Alhambra; westward the roads sloped down toward a stretch of lowland. Even if she found herself in the maze of narrow alleyways that snaked around the cathedral, it would not be long before the gradient, a glimpse of mountain, or sight of that monumental building would tell her which way to turn. There was something liberating about this aimless meander. She could lose herself in these streets and yet never be fearful of being lost.

Every few turns brought Sonia to a new square. Many of them had grand, ornamental fountains, and all had cafés, each serving a handful of customers. One leafy, open space had four shops selling an almost identical range of tourist paraphernalia, comprising fans, dolls in flamenco costume, and ashtrays emblazoned with bulls. Outside another was a forest of a dozen postcard carousels. It seemed there were a million images of Spain that people would buy. Sonia chose quickly: a generic image of a flamenco dancer.

By the time she had wandered the streets for an hour, her head was clear. She was in the Plaza Bib Rambla and the flower market filled it with vibrancy on this rather colorless February day. It was nine thirty, and although the place still had the peace and quiet of a city out of season, a few more people were now wandering about. Sonia passed two Scandinavians with huge backpacks, chilly and slightly ridiculous in their optimistically chosen shorts, and a group of East Coast students being given a guided tour by a fellow American whose voice filled the otherwise peaceful space. There were several cafés to choose from, but one of them particularly appealed. Its tables were just catching the first rays of sunshine that were slanting across the rooftops, and standing outside it was a barrel overflowing with geraniums that had survived a cool winter.

Purposefully, she strode toward the sunniest table and sat down. She hastily scribbled the postcard to her father and then began to read her guidebook. It seemed that the city had much more to offer than the famed Alhambra and its gardens.

In what seemed like a matter of moments after taking her order, the elderly waiter served her with a creamy *café con leche*. As he did so, he looked over her shoulder. Her book was open at the page on Federico García Lorca, "the greatest of Spanish poets," as it described him. Sonia had been reading how he had been arrested in Granada at the beginning of the Spanish Civil War.

"He used to stay nearby, you know."

The waiter's words penetrated her concentration and she looked up. Sonia was surprised not just that he had looked at what she was reading but by the deeply serious expression on his handsome, lined face.

"Lorca?"

"Yes, he and his friends used to meet not far from here."

Sonia had once seen *Yerma* at the National Theatre. Oddly enough, she had gone with Maggie, because James had a last-minute business dinner, and she recalled her friend's verdict: "dull and depressing."

Sonia asked the man if he had ever met Lorca, and the waiter told her that he remembered seeing him once or twice.

"Many people here believe that part of this city died with him," he added.

The statement was both powerful and intriguing.

Sonia's knowledge of the Spanish Civil War did not extend much further than a couple of dimly remembered books by Ernest Hemingway and Laurie Lee; she knew that they had been involved, but little more than that. Her curiosity was aroused, given the way in which the disappearance of Lorca seemed to have touched this old man personally.

"What do you mean exactly?" she asked, aware that she must respond.

"When people realized what had happened to Lorca—that he had been shot in the back—it gave out the message to all liberal-minded people that it was not safe for anyone and that the war in Granada was as good as finished."

"Forgive me, but I don't really know very much about what happened in your Civil War."

"That's not surprising. Many people in this country don't know very much about it either. Most of them have either forgotten or been brought up in a state of near ignorance."

Sonia could tell that the old man disapproved of this state of affairs.

"Why did it happen?" she asked.

The waiter, who was small in stature like many Spaniards of his age, leaned forward and gripped the back of the spare chair at Sonia's table. His dark eyes stared at the red tablecloth so intently it seemed as if he was examining its weft and warp. Several minutes went by and Sonia wondered if he had forgotten that she had posed a question. Though his hair was still predominantly dark, Sonia observed that the skin on his chiseled face and hands was as creased as an autumnal leaf, and she guessed he could be in his eighties. She noticed too that the fingers of his left hand were badly deformed, she assumed with arthritis. Her father's mind often wandered like this so she was quite used to such a silence.

"Do you know something?" he answered finally. "I'm not sure I can tell you that."

"Don't worry," she reassured him, noticing that his eyes were red and watery. "It was just idle curiosity."

"But I do worry," he said, mildly agitated, now looking directly at her.

She suddenly realized that she had misinterpreted his earlier remark. There was a clarity in his look that told her that this man was as lucid as he had ever been.

He continued: "I worry that the whole terrible story will disappear, just like Lorca and so many other people."

Sonia sat back. The man's passion took her aback. He was referring to an event of nearly seventy years ago, and yet it was as though it had taken place yesterday.

"I can't give you one single reason why war broke out. The beginning of it all was so confused. People didn't really know what was happening, and they certainly had no idea at the time what it would lead to or how long it would go on for."

"But what triggered it all off—and why was Lorca involved? He was a poet, not a politician, wasn't he?"

"I know your questions sound so simple and I would like to give you simple answers, but I can't. The years leading up to the Civil War were not entirely peaceful. Our country was in turmoil some of the time, and the politics were so complicated most of us couldn't begin to understand them. People were going hungry, the left-wing government didn't seem to be doing enough and the army decided to take over. That's the quick way to explain it."

"That sounds fairly black and white."

"I can assure you it wasn't."

Sonia sipped her coffee. Her interest was engaged, and since he appeared to have no other customers, she was tempted to press the elderly man further.

A twelve-strong group of Japanese on a guided tour then arrived and were soon waiting expectantly for their orders to be taken. The elderly man moved away to attend to them, and Sonia watched him writing things on his pad. Without his patience it might have been a tortuous business given their lack of both Spanish and English, a language which he spoke with great fluency but a thick accent. No wonder so many menus here were illustrated with garish photographs of unappetizing-looking dishes and foaming milk shakes; at least that way foreigners could order just by pointing.

When he brought the drinks and pastries they had ordered, he also came out with another coffee for Sonia; she was touched that he had thought of her.

By now the café was filling up with people, and she could tell that the moment had passed for him to devote all his attention to her.

"*La cuenta, por favor,*" she said, using most of the words she knew to ask for the bill.

The café owner shook his head. "It's nothing," he said.

Sonia smiled. It was a simple gesture and she was touched. She knew instinctively that he was not in the habit of giving away drinks.

"Thank you," she said. "It was really interesting talking to you. I might go and look at Lorca's house. Where is it from here?"

He pointed down the street and said she must turn right at the end of it. It would not take her more than ten minutes to reach La Huerta de San Vicente, the Lorca family's summerhouse in the south of the city.

"It's pretty," he said. "And it's got some good mementoes of the man and his family. It's a bit cold, though."

"Cold?"

"You'll see."

Sonia could not ask him any more questions. He was busy now and had already turned his back to take another order. She rose from her seat, gathered her book, her bag, and her map, and edged her way past the other tourists.

As she walked away, the old man came after her, for a moment holding on to her arm. There was one more thing he was eager to tell her.

"You should go up to the cemetery as well," he said. "Lorca didn't die there, but thousands of others were shot up on that hill."

"Thousands?" she queried.

The old man nodded. "Yes," he said deliberately. "Several thousand."

It seemed a huge figure to Sonia, given the scale of this city. Perhaps the old man was a bit soft in the head after all, and telling a tourist to go and look at a municipal graveyard was fairly bizarre too. She nodded politely and smiled. Even if the house of a dead poet exerted some fascination, she had no intention of visiting a burial place.

Sonia followed the directions he had given her, taking the long straight road, Recogidas, toward the edge of town. Shops were now open, and snatches of music floated out onto the pavements that now began to fill with young women, arms linked, chattering, pristine carrier bags swinging at their sides. This was the street for youthful fashion, and alluring window displays of high boots, jewel-colored belts, and stylish jackets on blank-faced dummies drew these girls like children to sweetshops.

As she walked down the sunny side of a street, which pulsated with a sense that life had never been so good, the café owner's portrayal of a strife-ridden Spain seemed hard to imagine. Though she was intrigued by what he had told her of the war, Sonia was puzzled that so little evidence of it remained. She had noticed neither plaque nor monument that recorded the events of that period, and the atmosphere all around her did not suggest that these young people were burdened by the past. The historical buildings of the Alhambra might have been what drew most visitors to Granada, but a street such as this showed a Spain that was pressing on into the future, transforming buildings from the previous centuries into futuristic palaces of glass and steel. A few old shop fronts remained with their ornate fascias and the owner's name etched in gold on black glass, but they were a curiosity deliberately preserved for the sake of nostalgia, not part of this modern Spain.

At the bottom of the street where the shops ended and anonymous blocks of flats were planted in crop-like rows, Sonia could clearly see beyond the city to the green plains of the Vega, the lush pastureland beyond the city. Consulting her city map, she turned right and through some gates into a park. It extended over several acres and had been laid out in a style that was somewhere between dreary municipal and Elizabethan knot garden, with sandy pathways running between geometrically arranged borders and low box hedging. The plants had recently been watered. Moisture hung like crystal beads on velvety crimson petals and the heavy scents of rose and lavender mingled in the moist atmosphere.

As far as Sonia could see, the park was empty save for a couple of gardeners and two silver-haired men sitting on a bench, walking sticks propped against their knees. They were deeply engaged in conversation and did not even look up as she passed, nor were they remotely disturbed by the sound of a trumpet that pierced the air. The acoustics of the empty park amplified the sound of the lone musician, who was not busking (there would have been little point, given the paucity of passersby) but using the space to practice.

According to the guidebook, La Huerta de San Vicente was in the middle of the park, and through the dense foliage of a group of trees, Sonia could now make out the shape of a white, two-story dwelling. A few people were clustered outside waiting for the door to be opened.

The house was more modest than she had imagined for a place associated with such a grand name as Federico García Lorca. At eleven o'clock the deep green front door opened, visitors were permitted to file in and a smartly dressed middle-aged woman welcomed them in Spanish. Her manner was that of a housekeeper, thought Sonia, proprietorial yet reverential about the house she looked after. Visitors were expected to treat it like a shrine.

Sonia's Spanish allowed her to grasp a few things from the speech that the woman trotted out at the beginning of the tour: Lorca had loved this house and had spent many happy summers there—the house was as it had been the day he left in August 1936 to seek safety with his friends in the center of the city—after his death, the rest of his family had gone into exile—visitors were requested not to use flash photography—they had thirty minutes to look around.

Sonia got the impression that she expected visitors to know about the man and his work, just as a guide in a cathedral would assume tourists might know whom he meant by Jesus Christ.

There were interesting portraits on the walls and some of Lorca's the-ater set designs, but what it lacked was any sense of who this man was. It was a shell, an empty husk, and Sonia was disappointed. The old man in the café had spoken with such passion about him, and she was slightly be-mused by how little atmosphere remained in what had once been a family home. Perhaps it filled her with gloom because she had been brought here by the story of the poet's assassination.

She paused at the postcard display. Only here did something clarify itself. There were several dozen images of a man's face. Here was the man who had once filled this building with his presence. There was something astonishingly vivid and modern-looking about the face, chocolate-brown eyes meeting not just those of the photographer but of anyone who was standing at the postcard counter all these years later.

His hair was wavy, his brows thick, his skin slightly roughened by acne, and his ears stuck out more than he must have liked. He adopted many different guises. In one picture he played the role of uncle, and a niece, who resembled him so closely she might have been his own little daughter, sat on his lap learning to read, a stubby forefinger pointing to a single word. In another he was a sibling, cheerfully posing with his brother and sister, all of them appearing to suppress their laughter for the picture. The warmth of both the day and the affection between them made the image glow. Other pictures showed family groups and glimpses of a long-gone world when children were dressed in cotton pinafores and babies wore mobcaps, when women engaged in embroidery and men sat in striped deck chairs.

Whatever he was doing—playing the piano, giving speeches, lark-ing about, striking a pose—he was clearly a man who loved life, and a warmth and vitality emanated from these pictures that inspired Sonia in a way that the house itself had failed to. They provided glimpses of pre-cious carefree moments in a life that had been wiped out not long after. For that reason alone they were absorbing.

At the end of the row of postcards, which were ranked along the counter in neat wooden sections, there was one where he stood outside the front door of this very house, with a sharp shadow of bright summer sunshine behind him. Sonia wondered if it had been taken the summer of his arrest and death.

Sonia moved along the row, picking out one each of every image.

"Can I help you?" asked the girl on the cash desk.

She had been slightly bemused by the length of time this visitor had hovered. Sometimes the stock in here was pilfered, but that usually happened only when school parties came in, and this woman did not look remotely suspicious. When she saw the pile of cards in Sonia's hand, she leaned over toward a pile of books.

"If you want so many," she said, "it makes sense to buy this."

Sonia took from her the little book she held out and flicked through its pages. All the postcard images and more were contained in it, along with captions and quotes. With a dictionary, she might be able to translate them.

Her eyes rested on the last image of Lorca where he sat, white-suited, at a café table with a stylish-looking woman who wore a beret. A carafe of wine stood on the table in front of them, sunlight streamed down through the branches of trees in full leaf, and people sat back in their wicker seats at other tables. This was a portrayal of people at leisure, of Spain at peace.

Below the picture were a few words: "*Lo que más me importa es vivir.*" Sonia did not need a dictionary to translate them: "What matters to me most is to live."

The tragic irony of the words struck her forcibly. All these images of Lorca, in a turban, in an airplane, with friends, with family, showed him as a man with a huge appetite for life. It was unimaginable now that any poet could have been important enough to execute. The simple whitewashed farmhouse was an image of innocence, frozen in time, a memorial that had been left alone while all in its immediate surroundings had been swept up in a new, forward-looking Spain. It was like a gravestone without a corpse.

She handed over some pesetas for the book and left.

Soon she was back in the hotel. As she pushed the button for the lift, Maggie stepped out of it, radiant after ten hours of uninterrupted dreams.

"Sonia," she gushed, "where have you been?"

"Just having a wander. I did leave you a note."

"Yes, I saw it. I just wasn't sure when you'd be back."

"I'm going up to grab my shoes," Sonia said through the narrow gap between the closing doors of the lift.

In the claustrophobic box of the lift, she began to feel slightly faint and realized she should have had something to eat. In the glow of sepia light, she caught a glimpse of herself in the mirrored wall. Compared with the vision of Maggie's bright face, she felt hollow-eyed and sunken-cheeked. Half-moons of darkness hung like eclipses below her eyes, and her hair looked mousy with grease. She acknowledged to herself that it did not matter to her what she looked like, but she knew she would still feel the age-old pangs of resentment when men cast admiring glances at Maggie and she became her invisible friend. Having spent years practicing this role, it was an all-too-familiar feeling.

Back in their room, she swiftly brushed her hair, defined her eyes with kohl pencil and smeared on some lip gloss. In the descending lift, her spirits lifted slightly as she observed the improvement.

Soon they were outside in the street, and the two women propelled each other along, both equally excited by the prospect of their dance lesson.

It was Maggie's birthday, and that night Sonia willingly went out dancing with her friend. Just before midnight, she found herself ducking to enter a low stone archway and descending a narrow staircase into a dimly lit basement. There was a small bar at one end, with a row of stools in front of it, and the two couples who were dancing were enjoying the luxury of having the whole dance floor to themselves. At this stage of the evening, the flamboyance of their twists and turns was almost acrobatic.

Sonia soon saw the reason for her old friend's insistence that they should come here. Hardly had they reached the foot of the stairway, when a handsome, stocky, figure emerged from the shadows near the bar and made his way toward them. Above the conversation-stifling noise of the music, Maggie introduced Paco, and although the three of them mimed frantically, little was communicated. The problem was not so much the relentlessly thudding beat as much as Paco's lack of English and theirs of Spanish. He did, however, show an attentiveness toward Sonia that allowed her to appreciate his charm, buying drinks for both women until, with a gesture of apology, he eventually led Maggie away to the dance floor. Sonia could see his appeal. Though she towered over him, there was something alluringly sexual about Maggie's new man.

Sonia watched, mesmerized by the way in which Paco's hand spread against the small of Maggie's back like a star, as he guided her firmly about the floor with deft, understated moves. She was perched on a stool, a glass of cold beer in her hand, and a strong sense of déjà vu overwhelmed her. How many times had she watched from the sidelines as Maggie danced? It happened when they were fourteen, and it was still happening more than twenty years on.

No one stayed a spectator for long, though—the collective enthusiasm for dance meant that everyone was going to be involved. The club was now filling up, and soon Sonia was approached. There was no question of saying no, even had she wanted to.

She recognized the music. It was one of the tracks that they had danced to that afternoon, and the familiarity of its rhythm gave her confidence. It was neither too slow nor too fast. The five minutes that followed were intimate, energetic, enlivening, and physical. Almost immediately she felt the welcome synchronicity between mind and body as her feet began to move without instruction. It was as though the invisible ropes that kept her anchored to the ground had been severed. On the final beat of the music, the encounter was over. The dance was an end in itself. All she noticed was that her partner took her through the steps as if he had danced for his whole life. It was as natural to him as breathing.

On her third or fourth dance, each one with a new stranger, Sonia began to feel less inhibited. She was no longer telling her feet which way to point, and her mind no longer counted a beat. She had experienced a fleeting sense of what this might be like once before, watching the Cuban instructors back in London and seeing the expression on their faces that showed they were dancing with their souls not their minds. Sonia recalled the way in which the hairs on her neck had stood on end. Now she knew what that felt like. The enchantment of dance had buried itself deep inside her.

Between dances, she had gravitated back toward the bar. Occasionally, Maggie and Paco stepped off the dance floor and came to find her. Maggie glistened. Her white shirt, luminous in the fluorescent lighting, was transparent with perspiration, and tiny droplets beaded her hairline like a tiara.

"Are you okay, Sonia?" she asked. "Are you having a good time?"

"Yes. I'm having a great time," she responded, and there was no edge to her answer.

She had no idea at what hour her head finally sank into her pillow. It was another sleepless night but not, this time, because she was anxious about Maggie, whose bed in the twin room remained empty. Tonight, it was the endorphins coursing through her body that kept her spinning round till sunrise.

# CHAPTER 6

Not long before midday, Sonia turned the taps to COLD and gasped as the water sputtered from the showerhead, covering her in waves of shocking iciness. It was what she needed to feel fully awake and with the day. Her next thought was for coffee, and for that there was only one destination. She slipped out of the lobby, knowing that she would be too late anyway for the paltry hotel breakfast of shrink-wrapped, long-life croissant, whose only chance of being brought to life was to be dipped into the weak coffee.

By some kind of homing instinct she retraced her route to the pretty square where she had been the previous day. It was not just the excellence of his *café con leche* that drew her back but the sense that some of her conversations with the kind waiter were yet to be concluded. It was chilly, and none of the other tables outside was occupied when she arrived, so she went inside. For more than five minutes, she sat there and no one came. Her sense of disappointment was out of proportion to the situation. There were plenty of other cafés close by that would serve decent coffee, she told herself.

While she was waiting, she took the time to observe that the busier the café, the more it seemed to attract additional customers. She was about to follow the trend and take her business elsewhere when she heard a friendly voice behind her.

"*Buenos días, Señora.*"

She turned. There was the café owner, smiling, evidently pleased to see her.

"I thought you must be closed."

"No, no. I'm sorry, I was on the telephone. What can I bring you?"

"*Café con leche, por favor.* And something to eat? A pastry?"

Some minutes later, both arrived.

"You had a late night?" commented the man. "If it's not rude to say it, you look very tired."

Sonia smiled. She enjoyed the café proprietor's honesty and knew she must look terrible, with smudges of yesterday's mascara and all the other signs of sleep deprivation.

"Was it a good night?"

"Yes, it was," she replied, smiling. "I went dancing."

"You liked that? You found some *duende*, perhaps?"

Sonia was unfamiliar with the word. It sounded rather like "duet," so perhaps he was asking if she had found a partner. For the first time in the last twenty-four hours, her thoughts turned to James. How would he have liked it here? Would he have appreciated the jaded décor of the dance school? The relentless exertion of the dancing lessons? The decibel level in the nightclub? The answer to all of these questions was "No." Perhaps he might have enjoyed the grandeur of the architecture, she thought as she glanced at the upper stories of the strong, rather magnificent buildings that constituted even this unimportant square. A spark of guilt passed through her when she realized that she had not even thought to ring James, but, on the other hand, he had not rung her either. He would be frantically involved in some deal at the bank, she was fairly certain of that, and would not be missing her.

"I had a fantastic time," she answered simply. "*Fantástico.*"

"*Bueno, bueno,*" he said, as though he got some personal satisfaction from the fact that his customer had had a good night out. "People will always dance. Even when we were living under a tyrannical regime, people continued to dance. For many of us, the priests had destroyed our religion, but many people simply had another one ready-made. Dancing became a new religion for a few people, a way of rebelling."

"It was for dance classes that I came here, really," said Sonia. "I just enjoy it, but I don't really see it becoming my religion," she added, laughing.

"No, I don't suppose it will. But things are different today. Granada is full of dance now and people do it freely."

As on the previous day, the café owner seemed to have more time on his hands than customers to fill it, though Sonia could imagine that in the high season this would not be the case. She was in no hurry either, and this smiling elderly Spaniard clearly wanted to make conversation with her.

"Do you dance?" asked Sonia.

"Me? No," he replied.

"So how long have you had this café?" she asked.

"Oh, for years now," he replied. "I took over in the mid-1950s."

"And you've been here all that time?"

"Yes, I have," he said quietly.

To stay in one place, in one job, for all those decades was almost beyond the reach of Sonia's imagination. How could anyone tolerate the sheer tedium of such stubborn continuity?

"Things were still in a state of upheaval then. It was all to do with the Civil War. It changed everything."

Sonia was embarrassed by her ignorance of Spanish history, but she felt she had to give an adequate response.

"It must have been awful for—"

The man cut her off. She saw that he suddenly had no wish to pursue this line of conversation.

"But you really don't want to hear about it. It's such a long story, and you've got dancing to do."

He was right. There had not been any other customers since her arrival, so he was still in no hurry for her to leave, but she did have a dance class to go to. Even though she loved sitting here passing time in this café with its kind owner, she could not miss her dancing. She glanced at her watch and was amazed to realize how much time had passed—it was one thirty in the afternoon. The lesson was at two o'clock.

"I'm so sorry," said Sonia. "I have to leave soon."

"Tell me before you go—did you go to Lorca's house?"

"I did. I saw what you meant about it being cold. It's hard to put your finger on it, isn't it? But somehow you can sense that it all ended badly there, and that's the reason that no one has lived in it for all those years."

"Did you like the park?"

He genuinely wanted her views and was interested in what she had to say.

"It was a bit formal for my taste. It's quite hard to make a garden gloomy, but they had managed."

Sonia felt she had been inadvertently rude about this man's city and was relieved by his reaction.

"I completely agree with you. It's not a nice place. Lorca himself would have hated it. I know he would. It's just the kind of stiffness and lack of imagination that he was opposed to."

The elderly man was suddenly aroused from his gentle state into one of ire. She could not help contrasting him with her father, in whom gentleness and patience was the entire man. Nothing budged Jack Haynes from his mood of quiet acceptance. The café owner, however, was different. She caught a glimpse of something steely in his look, a glint that suggested he was not a gentle old man through and through. There was another side to him. It made her reflect that the stereotype of the fiery Spanish personality had something in it after all. That hard look was very different from the kindness she had associated with him until now. It was a hint of anger, not with her, but with something that had gone through his mind. The creases around his mouth had hardened, and his eyes had ceased to twinkle with the warm smile that she had already grown to recognize.

"I really must go," she said. "Thanks for my breakfast. Or was it lunch? I don't know really, but thank you."

"I have enjoyed talking to you. Enjoy your dancing."

"I'm not going home until the day after tomorrow," she said. "So I might come back for breakfast if you're open."

"Of course I'll be open. Except for the occasional day off, I have been open every day since I can remember."

"I'll see you tomorrow then," said Sonia brightly.

Sonia smiled, partly at the prospect of seeing him again but also at the evident pride he took in this café, which was clearly his life's work. There appeared to be no one else involved. No wife. No son to follow in his footsteps. She slung her bag over her shoulder and got up to leave. It was less than five minutes until the start of her dance lesson.

# CHAPTER 7

The next morning, for the first time, Sonia understood why the nearby mountains were called the Sierra Nevada, the snowy mountains. Although the sky was bright, there was an icy freshness in the air, and when she pushed open the door of the hotel to leave, it was like stepping into a fridge.

Today was their last full day in Granada. Sonia was already feeling nostalgic about her visit, though it was not yet over. There was still one more dance lesson and one more chance to emerge from a nightclub as dawn was breaking.

The sun would struggle to appear above the pale turrets of the Alhambra today and would cast a golden glow only briefly on the squares before it sank behind the mountains. The owner of her favorite café, El Barril, as she had now noticed it was called, knew that few of his customers would sit outside when the temperatures had plummeted so had not bothered to put any chairs out that day. Sonia entered the dark interior, and gradually her eyes adjusted to the dimness.

The old man was behind the bar polishing glasses, and he emerged to greet her. He did not need to ask what she wanted to drink, and there was soon the shriek of the coffee grinder as he began to prepare her coffee with all the diligence of a scientist conducting an experiment.

Even he was finding it difficult to operate in the gloom, and he crossed the room to switch on the lights. The place was transformed by the sudden illumination. It was much larger than Sonia had realized, a big square room with perhaps thirty round tables, each with two or three chairs, and at the back of the room several dozen more piled up to the ceiling. There was nothing remarkable about the furniture or the décor, but what caught Sonia's eye were the walls. Every square inch of them was covered.

On one wall were several dozen *corrida* posters. Sonia had seen something like these in the prints sold all over Spain, customized with the tourist's name, so that people could imagine themselves famed toreadors. The posters on the walls here were not souvenirs, though. They carried the patina of age and authenticity. Sonia rose to read them.

The fights advertised by these posters had taken place in bullrings all over the country: Sevilla, Madrid, Málaga, Almería, Ronda . . . The list went on. The venues were all different, but one name was common to them all: Ignacio Ramírez.

Sonia walked slowly along the row of prints, taking in detail, like an art critic at a gallery opening. The posters eventually gave way to a montage of black-and-white pictures of a man, presumably Ignacio Ramírez. Some of the pictures were stiffly posed portraits, and in each one he wore a different bullfighting costume: tight, embroidered breeches, a short, heavily brocaded bolero jacket, and a tricorn hat. He glowered, violent, handsome, an arrogance burning through the picture. Sonia wondered whether this was the same look he gave the bull in order to terrify him into submission.

Another set of pictures showed him in action, apparently doing that very thing. There he was, facing the bull, only a few meters from five hundred kilograms of untamed fury. In several, the swish of his cape was a passing blur, just captured by the photographer's lens. In one picture, the animal passed close enough to brush the matador's body and his horns seemed wrapped up in the cape.

By now, a cup of the deepest black coffee, along with a jug of steaming white foam, had been set down on a table close to where Sonia stood. She stirred in a drop of milk and sipped slowly, hardly taking her eyes away from the pictures. The café owner stood next to her, almost poised to answer a question.

"So who was Ignacio Ramírez?" she asked.

"He was one of the boys who once lived here and a star bullfighter."

"And was he eventually killed by a bull?" asked Sonia. "He looks slightly too close for comfort here."

"No, that wasn't how he died."

They stood in front of a picture that showed the bullfighter with arms raised, sword held high, and the bull only feet away. It captured the dramatic pause right before the matador plunged his weapon between the animal's shoulder blades. Man and bull looked each other in the eye.

"That," said the café owner, "is '*la hora de la verdad.*'"

"The hour of . . . ?"

"Well, you would translate it as 'The moment of truth.' It's the moment when the matador must make the kill. If he gets his timing wrong or doesn't do it cleanly, then that's the end of him. *Terminado. Muerto.*"

It was only when she had studied every single one of the pictures and gazed into the impenetrably dark eyes that stared out at her, that she noticed the massive head and shoulders of a bull on the wall at the far end of the bar. He was as black as coal tar, with shoulders nearly a meter across and, even in death, a look of terrifying ferocity. Underneath, though almost too high to read, Sonia could make out a date: "3 de Septiembre 1936."

"That was one of his best kills," said the old man. "It was here in Granada. The bull was a beast and the crowd went completely wild. It was a stupendous day. I can't even begin to describe to you the excitement in the bullring. Have you ever been to a *corrida*?"

"No," said Sonia, "I haven't."

"You should," said the old man with passion. "Even if it's just once in your lifetime."

"I'm not sure I could sit there. It looks so brutal."

"Well, the bull usually dies, it's true. But there is much more to it than that. It's like a dance."

Sonia was unconvinced but knew it was not the moment for a discussion on what she imagined to be a cruel sport. She wandered to the wall opposite, which was covered with equal density by dozens of photographs, mostly of young women in flamenco costume. In some of them, there was a man too.

At first glance they looked like a series of shots of different girls, but on closer examination Sonia saw that they were in fact all of the same person, metamorphosing from child to adult, from little girl with puppy fat in polka dots to glowering, voluptuous beauty in lace, from ugly duckling to elegant swan complete with feather fan. In each one, her hair was different, coiled, plaited, or knotted into a chignon, and in some an enormous comb stood up from the back. The outfits varied too. There were dresses with extravagant ruffled trains, sometimes a fringed shawl or a knee-length skirt, and even one with trousers and a short jacket. But in all of the photos she had the same provocative, fiery expression, what Corazón would have called *actitud*.

"That was Ignacio's sister," said the old man, volunteering the information.

"What was her name?"

"Mercedes Catalina Ramírez López." He spoke the name slowly, as if reciting poetry.

"That's quite a name."

"It's a fairly typical one here. Her family all called her Merche."

"She was beautiful, wasn't she?"

"Yes, she was . . ." For a moment he seemed lost for words. " . . . very beautiful. Her parents doted on her, and her brothers nearly ruined her with the way they spoiled her. She was a rebellious child, but everyone adored her. She was a dancer, you see, a flamenco dancer—and a very good one, a very, very good one. She was famous in the region."

"Where did she dance?"

"She danced at all the local fiestas, at *juergas*, which are private parties, and sometimes in the bar. From about the age of three, she would amuse everyone by pretending to be a flamenco dancer, endlessly practicing the moves as though she was a wind-up doll. On the day she turned five, Mercedes had her first proper lesson up there in the Sacromonte, and for her birthday she was given her first pair of proper dancing shoes."

Sonia smiled. She was touched by the formal manner in which the old man spoke. His was the careful English of an elderly foreigner, and she could tell he enjoyed recounting the minutiae of the past.

"She sounds very determined about it all. Did her mother dance?"

"No more than most women here," replied the old man. "Everyone in Granada grows up seeing people dancing flamenco. It's part of the city. You can't avoid it, at fiestas, at parties, up in the Sacromonte, and most girls at some point have a go, but not to the extent of that little girl."

"Who accompanied her? Did her father play the guitar?"

"He did a little. But one of her brothers was very musical, so she always had someone willing to play for her. She gave her first performance when she was about eight years old, right here in the bar. Emilio, the musical brother, was playing and she got a fantastic reception, not just because everyone in the audience had watched her growing up—they weren't patronizing her, I promise. It was more than that. When this little girl danced, she took on some other dimension. It was like magic. Even when people had got used to seeing her dance, she could still pull in a crowd every time she performed."

The elderly man was silent for a few moments as he gazed at the photographs, and Sonia thought she saw his old eyes water. He coughed, as if to clear his throat. She could tell that he had something else to say.

"She had *duende.*"

There was that word again. She remembered him using it the previous day and had not really understood it then, but today, in this context, she did. It was something otherworldly, as far as she could understand it, like the power that made hairs stand on end.

They both stood in front of the wall of photographs for a few minutes, and Sonia looked at this woman. Yes, she could imagine that this woman had *duende.*

She said farewell and promised the café owner that she would come and see him if she ever returned to Granada. In their brief acquaintance, Sonia had grown fond of the old man, and she kissed him on both cheeks as she left. How unlike Maggie she was. This was the closest she had come to a holiday romance. And she did not even know his name.

# CHAPTER 8

They took their final class that day, and on the dance floor that night Sonia felt the air beneath her feet. It was as though they did not touch the ground. Everything she had learned that week fell into place. Some part of her had always struggled with the notion that the woman was meant to be in an entirely responsive role. But tonight the paradox made sense to her: being passive did not mean being subservient. Her power lay in how well she chose to respond. There was no subservience involved. It was subtle, and for a moment she thought of James and imagined how impossible he would find it to understand.

All night, she was whisked, whirled, and wound like a spring. At four in the morning, she could finally dance no longer, but as she thanked her last partner, her face beamed with pleasure. She had neither trodden on his feet nor tripped him up, and she was dizzy with exhilaration.

It had not been such a satisfying evening for Maggie. Paco had not appeared, and for the first time in a few days, she returned to the hotel with Sonia.

The streets were still full of life when they emerged from the nightclub; couples coiled together in doorways and youths engaged in furtive exchanges of drugs and money. Almost overpowered by cheap brandy, Maggie leaned heavily on her friend, and as they staggered along the cobbled streets, it took every ounce of Sonia's strength to hold her upright. She was considerably smaller than Maggie, and several times they both nearly lost their balance. Sonia was reminded, once again, of their teenage years and how little distance they seemed to have come.

She managed to get her friend into bed, tucked the sheets firmly around her, and set a glass of water on her bedside table. Maggie would wake up with a raging thirst.

The following morning, a thick head was the least of Maggie's troubles. She was inconsolable that Paco had turned out to be as unreliable as any other man she had ever met.

"But you were going home today anyway." Sonia tried to reason with her.

"That's not really the point," said Maggie nasally. "He never said goodbye."

On the journey to the airport, Maggie was silent, partly stupefied by the miniatures from the minibar that she had consumed in place of a more substantial breakfast. Sonia tried to lift her out of her despair.

"You really haven't changed since we were sixteen!" she teased gently.

"I know." Maggie wept quietly into a sodden tissue and continued to stare out of the car window. Occasionally she made a kind of drowning noise as she gulped down her sobs.

Sonia rested her hand on her friend's arm as a gesture of comfort, and she reflected on the irony of a supposedly cheerful birthday celebration that had begun with her own tears and ended with Maggie's. Perhaps women were hard-wired to weep.

The taxi traveled at terrifying speed along the motorway, dodging in and out between cars and huge semis that transported the products of Spain's now rich, poly-tunneled farmland toward the markets of northern Europe. Both women were silent for the next half-hour, and eventually Maggie's outburst of grief and self-pity began to subside. She had exhausted herself.

"I should stop myself getting carried away," she said eventually, tears welling up again in her eyes, "but I'm not sure I can."

"It's hard," said Sonia comfortingly. "It's so very hard."

Their charter flight to Stansted was delayed by four hours, and by the time they landed and crossed London, it was after eight o'clock in the evening. They shared a taxi from Liverpool Street to Clapham, and before it dropped Maggie off, the women gave each other the warmest embrace.

"Take care, Maggie," called Sonia out of the window.

"And you. I'll ring you."

As the cab moved off, Sonia glanced out of the rear window and saw Maggie fishing in her bag for a key. Litter and leaves swirled together in the gutters. Two figures in hooded jackets loitered close by. The dimly lit Clapham Street seemed nothing but forlorn.

Though it was only a further five minutes in the cab, Sonia's neat street, with its clipped hedging, perfect tesselated paths and polished door furniture was a world away from Maggie's, where every house had a row of bells and a front garden crowded with bins.

Despite Maggie's misery, which she knew from experience would probably not last forever, Sonia was determined to hold on to the sense of well-being that these past few days had given her. She rang the gleaming doorbell, but no one came, which struck her as odd since James's car was parked outside. After waiting a few more seconds, still expecting to see his shadowy outline appear behind the stained-glass panes, she began to rummage for her key.

Once inside, she dumped her bags on the hall floor and pushed the door shut with her foot. Amplified by the harsh acoustics of the hallway's high ceiling and polished tiles, the sound of the door slamming shut was like the crack of pistol fire. She winced. It was a noise that James hated.

"Hello," she called out. "I'm back."

Sonia could see through a crack in the door that James was in an armchair in the sitting room. He waited until she entered before answering.

"Hi," he grunted, as though she had just returned from work rather than almost a whole week away.

The coolness of his tone suggested that he was not really interested in an answer. The flat monosyllable conveyed no enthusiasm, and nothing was going to be added. She echoed his tone with her own crotchet-beat response.

"Hi." And then with some hesitation: "How have things been here?"

"Fine, thanks. Just fine."

The newspaper, which had briefly been lowered, now moved up in front of him again like a sash window. Sonia could just see the top of his head and the shine of his just-beginning-to-be-bald pate.

The staccato delivery of James's last words carried more than a hint of irritation, and the pages of his newspaper made a snapping sound as he pulled them straight and resumed his perusal of the previous day's share movements. Sonia turned to leave the room, desperately in need of something to quench her thirst, and heard James's sarcastic tone of voice calling out to her retreating back: "Don't worry too much about dinner. I had a big lunch."

The words brought Sonia's spirits crashing down hard. She was reminded of the feelings of despair that she had experienced in the hotel room only four days earlier. Granada already felt a million miles away.

*I wasn't going to worry actually*, she thought as she retreated to the kitchen. "Okay then," were the words that came out. "I'll see what I can knock up."

James had evidently eaten out every night while she was away. Nothing in the fridge had been used up; the cheese was moldy and the tomatoes bearded. At the back was some smoked salmon just past its sell-by date, which she was sure would not poison him, and a couple of free-range eggs. Enough to make a meal, of sorts.

As Sonia stood in her kitchen, which squeaked with antibacterial cleanliness, the sterility of the environment crawled over her like a damp sheet. An empty glass stood next to the sink, the ring of water around it the sole blot on the otherwise perfect landscape of the work surface. The oak kitchen cabinets with their glass insets were some kind of attempt to emulate an old cottage style, but these units would not weather with age. They would never even acquire a little characterful dust in the corners of the moldings, such was the scrutiny of the cleaner's lightly dampened cloth.

It was James's house when they married, and somehow she still thought of it that way. It had already been gutted and decorated before she arrived, and there had never been any question that anything should be modified to her taste.

At that moment James appeared, casting a cursory glance at the ingredients that sat on the kitchen worktop.

"I've had second thoughts," he said. "I'm going to turn in. Got an early meeting. 'Night."

Before Sonia had had the opportunity to respond, James had gone upstairs. She ran the tap until it turned icy cold and filled her glass, drinking the water in one long draft until her head tipped back and her face was turned upward to the ceiling. One of the spotlights had gone. The little black hole in the ceiling held her attention for a moment.

Once, her interest in the minutiae of her home would have driven her immediately to the cupboard under the stairs, and the dead bulb would have been prized from its cavity and a new one put in. Not now. It no longer seemed to matter.

She had sometimes stood in this kitchen and asked herself the one question that really mattered: "Is this really it?" She was less certain than ever before that it was.

James's coolness toward Sonia continued. He worked late at the office and so did she, catching up on various crises that had brewed in her absence.

Almost a week passed before they sat down and had a meal together, and when they did, conversation was stilted. What could they talk about? Sonia knew James would not want a detailed description of her time in Granada and would certainly not want to hear that Maggie had fallen in love.

Conversation was kept very general until, halfway through a second bottle of wine, James said, "You've had a postcard from some greasy dago."

At this point he rose, staggered over to the kitchen dresser, where they always left that day's post, and picked up a postcard. It was of the Alhambra.

"Dear Sonia," he read aloud, "I enjoyed our talks. If you ever come to Granada again, come and see me. Miguel."

The postcard had been addressed to the hotel and forwarded to Sonia. It was a sweet gesture from an old man, and she wondered how he had known her name.

James held out the postcard to Sonia, as though it was burning his fingertips, and she took it from him.

"I imagine it's from the waiter I talked to a few times," she said. "His name must have been Miguel."

"I suppose it must," snorted James with derision.

"I went to his café every morning. He told me a bit about Granada's history," said Sonia defensively.

"I see," said James, leaning back in his chair and emptying the last of the bottle into his glass. "A *waiter*," he added.

"Surely you don't have a problem with that. He was ancient, James!"

"You expect me to believe that? You really expect me to believe that? For God's sake, Sonia, I'm not an *idiot*."

He leaned toward her now and shouted this last comment into her face. She felt a droplet of red-wine spittle land on her mouth and was repulsed. Sonia did not want this argument, but she did want the last word.

"I'm not sure about that," she said as she turned on her heel, leaving the room and the debris of their dinner still on the table.

She slept in the spare room that night and the ones that followed. As usual, James left for work at the crack of dawn and returned when she had gone to bed. It was strange, Sonia realized, how easy it was to live in the same house as someone and never see him, and she wondered how long they could keep this up.

Even if some kind of confrontation had been inevitable, she would never have imagined that a slightly limping, elderly man, who lived a thousand miles away, would be the catalyst. That much had surprised her.

# CHAPTER 9

Sonia and James had not spoken for some days now. She was not naïve enough to expect an apology from him, especially as he still believed that the sender of the postcard was some kind of holiday romance, but she had desperately hoped for a thaw in the atmosphere.

Maggie rang her a few days later.

"Meet me at The Grapes at eight thirty?"

Maggie had only one thing she wanted to talk about that evening, and Sonia guessed what it was going to be the moment she came through the door that evening. She radiated contentment. The last time she had seen her friend, her eyes had been swollen with tears. Tonight they shone with excitement.

"So, what's happened?" Sonia asked expectantly.

She had already bought a bottle of wine and now poured a glass for Maggie, who picked it up and clinked it against Sonia's.

"Well . . . Paco rang on Saturday. Apparently his car broke down that night and he couldn't get to the club . . . And he couldn't get a signal on his mobile. He was genuinely, really, really sorry."

"That's good. So he should have been, given how upset you were."

"But there's more than that. He wants me to go out there again—to stay with him this time."

Sonia hesitated. Though she knew that good sense never played much of a part in Maggie's decision making, she felt it was occasionally her role to suggest it, to voice caution.

"Do you really think that's such a good idea?"

Maggie looked slightly quizzically at her friend. "I can't really think of a good reason why I shouldn't go," she said. "In fact, I'm thinking of giving everything up and going out there to live. It's been on my mind for ages."

"But what about Candy?"

"Candy wants to move into a flat with some friends from art school, so she won't miss me too much."

"And your work?"

"It's all freelance. I could give it up tomorrow. And Spain is fantastically cheap to live in. I've got a bit saved up."

"It all seems a bit speedy to me."

"Yes, but let's face it, Sonia, what do I have to lose?"

Maggie was right. The boundaries of her life were fluid. Though Sonia might have been anchored down to the last detail, Maggie was tied by very little. Her daughter was already independent, and she had no financial commitments.

"Even if things don't work out with Paco," she said, swirling the wine round in her glass, "at least I'll be in a country that I love."

As far as Sonia was concerned, there were only two reasons for telling Maggie not to go: first, that she would miss her friend and, second, that she doubted the sincerity of the Spaniard.

She voiced neither. At the end of the evening, it became clear that Maggie already had her flight booked, confirming what Sonia had half suspected, that her opinion was not being sought at all.

Maggie was so full of her own exciting plans that Sonia only got around to telling her about her problems with James at the end of the evening.

"So you fell out pretty much as soon as you came home? Because he decided you'd been having an affair with some waiter?"

"That's about the sum of it," admitted Sonia sheepishly.

"But it's so ridiculous. He really is an idiot, if you don't mind me saying so."

"No, I don't mind. It's not as though you haven't always thought that." Sonia laughed.

They drained the bottle of wine and finished the meager little bowl of olives that they had ordered to remind themselves of being in Spain.

On the pavement they hugged each other.

"Take care, Maggie," said Sonia. "You'll call me when you get there, won't you?"

"Of course I will. You'll be coming out to see me. If you don't visit, I'll come and drag you over there."

Ten days later, the various threads of her life all tied up as neatly as they ever could be, Maggie left to pursue her infatuation.

# CHAPTER 10

Sonia counted up the weeks since she had visited her father. Nearly two months had passed since she had last seen Jack, and a wave of the unshared guilt of the only child passed through her.

Croydon. If ever there was a place more antithetical to Granada, it was this gray suburb. Its lack of romance, magic, and beauty must be unparalleled in the Western world, thought Sonia to herself. It hurt the very soul to drive down its gray streets. She wondered if the architects of the 1960s ever came back to view the way their work had aged. Had they ever imagined the pale concrete streaked with jagged stains and the huge panes of dark, smoked glass opaque with dust? Why on earth would those who designed it ever return? It was, however, the place that her father loved, and even though he had seen it change beyond recognition, he saw only the ghost of how it once had been. It was where his heart was.

The ritual was the same as ever. That Saturday afternoon in his flat, Jack Haynes had set out some Nice biscuits on a plate decorated with now-faded flowers.

"How is your dancing going?" he asked.

"It's going really well." Sonia smiled. "I'm so enjoying it."

"That's good. I wish I could still do it." He chuckled. "I could have taught you some of our favorite steps. Though I expect you'd find them too old-fashioned now."

"I'm sure I wouldn't," responded Sonia kindly. "Dance is dance, isn't it?"

"Well, I don't know about that. But anyway, I'm so pleased that you are still doing it."

"I can't imagine ever giving it up."

"And how was Spain?" he asked. "I got your postcard. Did Maggie have a nice birthday?"

Sonia had rung her father just before she went, to tell him that she was going away with her old school friend.

"It was fabulous," Sonia told him, sipping from the fine china cup. "We took some dance lessons while we were there."

"How lovely. And where did you stay?"

"Granada . . ."

Hardly had the word left her lips when she heard her father repeat it, softly under his breath.

"*Granada?* Your mother was born in Granada."

"*Was* she?" exclaimed Sonia. "I don't think I ever knew that. I *loved* it."

After that came a barrage of questions from Jack. He wanted to know all about the city, what it looked like, what and where she had eaten, and whether she had visited any of the monuments. At the best of times, he was always interested in her life, but today he seemed hungry for information.

She described the networks of cobbled streets, the wonderful tree-filled squares, the grand boulevards, and the way in which snow-capped mountains formed a backdrop of almost film-set unreality to the city. She enthused about the warm, red-hued Alhambra and the atmospheric Moorish quarter just below it, unchanged for centuries and still unspoiled by cars. He listened with rapt attention, but, more than anything, he was eager to hear about the dancing.

She described the school, the teachers, and the nightclub where they put it all into practice, and the kinds of dancing they had done.

"We did salsa, merengue, and even a little flamenco," she told him.

Jack poured himself some more tea. As usual, a goods train rumbled past and their cups rattled gently in their saucers.

"Granada is such a beautiful place. Why on earth did Mum leave?" asked Sonia.

Stirring in some sugar, Jack Haynes looked up at his daughter. "It was something to do with the Civil War. Lots of people left about that time, I believe."

"But didn't she ever want to go back?"

"I don't think so. Anyway, she met me." He smiled, his old face creasing into as many wrinkles as his years.

"Of course she did," responded Sonia. "And I can't imagine you ever living in Spain."

It was not easy to imagine her father in a foreign country. He was uncomfortable in the heat, disliked eating anything but plain food, and had no grasp of any language apart from his own.

"But didn't she have relatives to visit?"

"I don't believe there was any family left there."

Her father sounded sufficiently vague for Sonia to realize that there was little point in asking too many questions, but they began to reminisce about Sonia's mother. Usually, Jack never dwelled on the subject of Mary for long. Though he had lived with her infirmity and nursed her for fifteen years, when death came it had been a shocking blow for him. Strangers who met him usually assumed that her mother had only recently died. It still seemed so raw. Today, though, she was emboldened to pursue the subject.

"I do have a vague memory of something from when I was about ten or eleven," she mused.

"What was that?"

"That Mum was very disapproving when people started to go to Spain on holiday. And that when one of my friends from school came back and said how fantastic it was, she hit the roof."

"Yes, I remember that too," said Jack quietly.

"And one summer I asked if we could go there."

Jack recalled it vividly. Though Mary Haynes was physically frail, her reaction to the suggestion had been violent. Occasionally she displayed traces of a fierce Mediterranean temper, and he could remember almost to the syllable the words she had used, each one spat out with venom.

"I would rather have my fingernails pulled out than set foot in that country . . . until that Fascist is dead and buried," she had said.

At the time, Sonia had no comprehension of who her mother meant by "that Fascist." At first she wondered if she had simply been insensitive, asking for a trip to a faraway place when her parents could scarcely afford any kind of holiday at all. Later on, though, her father had explained the problem to her.

"Franco is still in charge," he had told her when her mother was out of earshot. "He brought about the Civil War that was the reason for your mother leaving Spain. She still hates him."

It was 1974 and a year later Franco died. Even then, Sonia's mother had shown no desire to return and never mentioned Spain again.

They drank more tea, and Sonia ate one of her father's sugary biscuits.

"It's so sad that she never saw Granada again," reflected Sonia. "Did she keep up her Spanish?"

"Not really, after a while. In the very beginning she couldn't speak a word of English, but I remember the morning when she woke up and realized that she no longer dreamed in her native tongue. She wept."

Jack Haynes did not want his daughter to dwell on the sadness of her mother's exile from her homeland. As far as possible, he wanted her to have a positive image of her mother and he pulled himself up sharply.

"Look," he said, "I have a few pictures of your mother from when she was in Granada." He opened the heavy desk drawer and burrowed under some papers before finding a dog-eared envelope.

As he settled himself back into his armchair, a few pictures fell out onto his lap and he passed them to Sonia. There was one picture of Mary taken outside a church, perhaps at her First Communion, but it was the second and third that arrested her. In one, her mother was wearing traditional flamenco costume. The eyes were playful, teasing, flirtatious, but nearly half of her face was tantalizingly concealed behind a fan. If she had not known this was Mary Haynes, it would have been difficult to identify her. What was hard to imagine was that the woman in this picture could really be one and the same person as the frail woman of her memory. In this photograph she was raven-haired, majestic, unmistakably Andalusian.

Then Sonia looked at the next. For a moment she simply stared. Her mouth went dry. In this one, Mary was totally unrecognizable as her mother, but she reminded Sonia of someone else. She bore a striking resemblance to the girl in the pictures in the bar. It was a notion that Sonia knew she should dismiss as absurd but one she could not entirely put out of her mind.

She could tell that these pictures were well thumbed, and she always suspected that her father spent more time leafing through his past than he would ever have allowed her to know about. The last thing she wanted to do was to upset him with more unnecessary questions.

The woman behind the fan could have been any girl with characteristic Granadino features, she told herself sternly, but when her father went to the kitchen to refill the teapot, Sonia slipped a couple of photographs into her handbag. She stayed for one more cup of tea and then kissed her father goodbye.

The stalemate with James could not continue. Sooner or later they had to speak.

Sonia knew that it would be her job to instigate some kind of rapprochement, as James was even more stubborn than she. She left him a note on the kitchen table one night before she went to bed, suggesting they have supper together the following day, but the following morning when she came down to breakfast, she saw that the note had not even been touched. She went up to their bedroom. Though James always neatly made the bed, she could tell he had not made it that morning. The laundered shirts that their cleaner had left in a pile on the middle of the bed the previous day had not been moved. James had not been home.

That evening, Sonia met him in the hallway. She said nothing about his absence the previous night.

"I think we should eat together tonight," she said.

"Okay. If you want."

"I'll do some pasta," she offered as James brushed past her into the bathroom.

They never got as far as eating the *tagliatelli putanesca*. Before Sonia had even finished preparing the sauce, James was draining the first bottle of wine. The touch paper had already been ignited.

As she poured herself a glass from a second bottle, which was already uncorked and standing on the table, she could sense James's aggression.

"So, been dancing lately?" he slurred.

"Yes," Sonia replied, trying to keep herself calm, neutral.

"You must be a bloody professional by now."

She sat down, playing with the stem of her glass and took a deep breath. The wine had emboldened her too.

"I'm starting lessons on Fridays now," she said.

"Fridays . . . That's kind of the weekend, isn't it?"

In spite of herself, she began to trickle oil onto the flames. "It's the day that they hold intermediate lessons. I'm not really a beginner now," she continued.

"Yeah, but Fridays will be a pain in the arse. It'll bugger up Friday nights, Sonia."

James's tone to her now was friendly but slightly mocking, and she found this strange mix mildly threatening.

James poured himself another glass and slammed the bottle down on the table.

"It's a fucking *nuisance*, Sonia!"

"You don't need to put it like that, James."

"Well, tough! That's the way I see it," he slurred. "This dancing thing just doesn't fucking well fit with our life, Sonia."

Our life, thought Sonia, turning this pair of words over in her head. *Our* life?

The words sounded alien to her. She couldn't identify with them any more than she could picture an existence without dance. There was a degree of menace in a six-foot drunk, even one sitting at his own kitchen table in a pinstripe suit. He rocked back on his chair and glared at Sonia. Wine splashed onto his yellow silk tie, and she watched the spreading stain. She wanted to avoid confrontation at all costs.

The pasta was cooked. Sonia switched off the gas, and just as she lifted the pan she heard James roar, "*WELL?* Are you going to give it up or not?"

The volume of his voice almost made her drop the pan. Scalding water splashed across the floor, and realizing that her hands were shaking violently, she put the pan down on the draining board.

"Look, I don't really feel like eating at the moment," she said. "I'm going to have an early night."

She had genuinely lost her appetite and left the room, nauseated with fear and shocked by the realization that she was married to someone who now instilled such terror in her.

It looked as if the new "normality" of sleeping in separate rooms would continue. A knot tightened in her stomach. She had never imagined it would get to this.

The next afternoon she received a text from Maggie asking her to come out to Spain for a few days. It took Sonia less than a second to write her three-letter answer. There was nothing pressing in her diary, and another trip to Granada would be a welcome escape. She could do with a few days to mull things over, and she would visit the old man at the bar. It was just the opportunity she had wanted.

# CHAPTER 11

Neat rows of olive trees, strong vines, and ripening vegetables checkerboarded the fields. High in the mountains, snows had gently melted through the last few weeks of March and into April, supplying steady streams of moisture for germination, and now the rich soils were dense with crops. Sunshine, growing in intensity almost by the day, began to ripen strawberries and tomatoes from green to scarlet. Craggy mountains, rolling hills, smudges of white-washed pueblos dotted among them, and great spreads of cultivation—through the murky airplane window, Sonia peered at this landscape, transformed since she last saw it by the early summer warmth.

The air-conditioned aircraft left her unprepared for the blast of heat that greeted her as its doors were opened. She blinked as she emerged into the late-afternoon sunshine, gusts of warm air circling around her on the tarmac as though a giant hair dryer was targeting her with its hot blast. In that moment, she felt herself begin to thaw. The icy English weather of the past few months had chilled her to the core.

A taxi whisked Sonia into Granada's city center, giving her a glimpse of the Alhambra as she passed. The driver was in a hurry, swerving between other cars in the rush-hour traffic, impatient to return to the airport for another flat-fare passenger.

Maggie was living in the Albaicín, the old Arab quarter where the winding cobbled streets were barely wide enough for pedestrians, let alone cars, so the taxi driver peremptorily dropped Sonia off in the Plaza Nueva.

She stood in the square and looked about her. One side was lined

with cafés, all of them now crowded with people, mostly tourists refresh-
ing themselves with soft drinks and ice creams in a forest of colorful
umbrellas advertising beer or Coke. Following Maggie's directions, she
walked up to the church at the far end and climbed some broad stone
steps to the side of it.

The wheels of her bag rattled noisily on the cobbles as she made her
way along the Calle Santa Ana, hugging a slim strip of shade. She rang
the doorbell to flat 8, at number 32. Beyond the ornate ironwork and the
glass of the outer door she could see a hallway tiled from floor to ceiling
with bright blue and white tiles. High above her, she heard her name. She
stepped away from the doorway and looked up.

Almost dazzled by the brightness of an azure sky, she saw a silhouette.
It was Maggie, leaning precariously over a balcony.

"Sonia!" she called. "Here! Catch!"

A bunch of keys landed noisily on the stones.

"It's the silver one! I'm on the fifth floor!"

Sonia let herself in and began to climb the stairs.

By the time she reached the right floor, she was panting. Maggie stood
in the doorway, smiling, exotic in a bright printed kaftan, eyes luminous
in her tanned face.

"Sonia! It's lovely to see you," she cried, taking her friend's suitcase.
"Come in."

After the brightness of the tiled stairwell, the flat seemed dark. A
low-voltage lightbulb in the hallway gave out a dim glow, and Sonia's eyes
struggled to adjust to the gloom.

Maggie's sitting room was decked out in Moorish style, with rugs and
throws, Arabic lanterns and mobiles of colored glass that jangled in a
breeze that blew lightly through the apartment. Sonia was as charmed by
it as by the view, out of the huge floor-to-ceiling windows, of the River
Darro, which ran just below the building, carving a divide between the
clustered buildings of Granada's oldest *barrio*.

"It's heavenly," said Sonia. "How on earth did you find a place like
this?"

"Through a friend of a friend of this gorgeous man I met when I went into the estate agency to find somewhere to rent."

"Gorgeous man?" inquired Sonia, immediately picking up on something in Maggie's tone of voice.

"Oh, yes, Carlos," she replied, not quite blushing. "He owns the estate agency."

"But what about Paco?"

"I'm sure you can guess. He came to meet me at the airport when I arrived, and we spent a couple of nights together. And then, after that, it was excuses, excuses, excuses. But really, in the end I didn't mind," she said. "I sort of owe it to him for making me come out here."

"So it's okay, is it?" Sonia asked.

"Okay?" exclaimed Maggie breathlessly. "It's so much more than okay. They really know how to live life here. It's quite exhausting, though, going to bed at three in the morning when you have to get up to work. But I love it. I absolutely love everything about it."

"And what about this Carlos?" asked Sonia teasingly.

"Well, he seems quite keen. We've seen quite a lot of each other. And he likes dancing . . ." Maggie mentioned the latter as though it was the most important of all.

For several hours they lounged on low, bright cushions and drank mint tea. They had so much to tell each other, having spoken only once on the telephone since Maggie had moved to Granada. Sonia confessed James's worsening drink habit and his resentment of her dancing, but she did not reveal how fragile things had become.

The sun had gone down by the time they went off into the city in search of tapas.

Later that evening, leaving Maggie to meet her new boyfriend, Sonia went to El Barril. She hoped to catch Miguel before he closed for the night. She smiled to herself as she thought of the conclusion James had jumped to when she had received that postcard all those weeks ago.

It was almost eleven thirty when Sonia turned up there, and she decided to go inside to find him. She could see on his face an immediate flash of recognition.

"Yes, yes!" he exclaimed. "You are the beautiful English lady. You have come back!"

"Of course. And thank you for the postcard."

"It reached you!"

"How did you know my name?" she said, holding out her hand for him to shake, which he did with great enthusiasm.

"I caught a glimpse of your signature when you were writing a postcard," he admitted guiltily. "It stuck in my mind."

"Oh!" she said, rather surprised.

He seemed to have slowed down a little in the weeks since she had been there. She was warmed by his welcome and settled herself onto a stool at the bar. All the other customers had gone.

"Are you here to do more dancing?" he asked. "You must want coffee—and a brandy?" Before Sonia had replied to either question, steam was gurgling noisily through a jug of milk and conversation was temporarily precluded.

While Miguel was busy, she got up and strolled as nonchalantly as she could toward the display of pictures on the wall. There they were, just as before, the proud bullfighter and, next to him, the dancer. Sonia went up close and stared into the girl's eyes. No, she could not be absolutely certain. The features were similar to those of the woman in the photo she had squirreled away in her wallet, but they did not appear identical. The dress in her own photo was reminiscent of those in the framed pictures, and yet not exactly the same.

Miguel came up behind her with her coffee and handed it to her.

"You like these pictures, don't you?" he said.

Sonia hesitated. "Like" wasn't really adequate to describe the effect they had on her, but she couldn't tell Miguel the truth. It would sound so farfetched.

"I'm fascinated by them," she said. "They're real period pieces."

"They are certainly that," agreed Miguel.

"Perhaps it's because they're in black and white," she said hastily. "It makes them seem from a distant era. They couldn't have been taken last week, could they?"

"No, that's right. They capture a particular time," responded Miguel. "A very specific moment in history."

His statement seemed heavily loaded, and Sonia sensed that the pictures meant as much to Miguel as they might to her. She could not help pursuing the conversation.

"So," she said casually, concerned not to betray the depth of her interest, "tell me how Granada has changed."

She was sitting at the bar. She picked up a slender sachet of sugar from a glass dish and poured it into her coffee. Miguel was polishing glasses and lining them up neatly.

"I took the bar over in the 1950s," he began. "It was quite rundown then, but in the late twenties and early thirties it had been a great focal point. Everyone from workmen to university professors came here. People didn't invite each other into their homes; they met in bars and cafés instead. There weren't many tourists to speak of in those days, just the occasional intrepid Englishman, perhaps, who had heard stories of the Alhambra."

"You make it sound like a golden age," commented Sonia.

"It was," he said, "throughout the whole country."

Sonia then noticed a picture at the end of the wall. "They look like the Ku Klux Klan," she exclaimed. "They're really sinister!"

The image showed a group of several dozen figures clad in white robes, with small round eyeholes cut out of their pointed, witch-like headdresses. They were processing down a street, some of them engaged in the labor of carrying a cross.

"That's a typical Holy Week procession," said Miguel, folding his arms.

"It's very dramatic," said Sonia.

"That's right. It's just like theater. Today you're spoiled for entertainment, but we didn't have very much in those days and we loved it. I still do. Every day in the week before Easter these huge icons of the Virgin or Christ are carried around the town. Have you ever been in Spain for that week?"

"No, I haven't," replied Sonia.

"It's in a few weeks' time. It's an unforgettable experience, if you haven't seen the *pasos* before. You should stay."

"That's a lovely thought," said Sonia, "but I'll have to come back for Easter another year."

"The icons are huge, and it takes over a dozen men hidden underneath to carry each one through the streets. They're accompanied by the brotherhood from their church and a band."

Sonia peered at the photograph. "*Semana Santa 1931*," she read aloud. "Was that a special year?"

The old man paused.

"Yes. The king left just after Easter of that year, and the country got rid of its dictatorship. The Second Republic was declared."

"That sounds like a major event," said Sonia, now more ashamed than ever of her ignorance of Spain's history. "Was it violent?"

"No," said Miguel. "It was bloodless. There had been plenty of unrest beforehand, but for most people this marked a new beginning. There had been eight years of dictatorship under Miguel Primo de Rivera, and throughout that time we had retained the monarchy. It was the worst of all worlds. As far as most people were concerned, the dictatorship had done nothing to benefit ordinary people. All I can really remember is my parents moaning about some of the laws they passed, like banning crowds and making cafés close early."

"I can imagine that was unpopular!" interjected Sonia. It was hard to imagine Spain without its bars and cafés being open all hours.

"And anyway," continued Miguel, "the dictatorship had done nothing to help the poor, so when King Alfonso XIII left and the Republic began, millions of people knew life would improve. There were big celebrations that day, and the bars and cafés were overflowing with people."

The excitement in Miguel's voice could not have been greater if these events had happened only the day before. The memory of them was vivid.

It was almost poetic, Sonia thought, the way he talked about it.

"It was a magical moment," Miguel said. "Everything seemed full of promise. Even at the age of sixteen, I sensed that. We were breathing the fresh air of democracy, and from then on there would be many more people who would have a say in how the country should be governed. The power of the landlords who had subjected millions of peasants to a life of poverty was reduced at long last."

"I can't believe those things were still going on in the 1930s!" exclaimed Sonia. "It sounds so primitive—peasants . . . landlords!"

"That's a good word for it," said Miguel. "Primitive."

He had poured two generous brandies, explaining he always had one at the end of each day and was happy to have company.

"There's one thing I remember very vividly. Everyone seemed to be smiling. They were so happy."

"Why would that have stuck in your mind?"

"I think some people had gone through a time of great hardship and anxiety. As children, we probably just accepted the way things were, but I think our parents' lives had been tough."

Miguel glanced at the clock and registered some surprise. "I'm so sorry," he said apologetically. "I hadn't realized the time. I really should be closing up."

Sonia felt panic rising inside her. Perhaps she had missed the moment to ask him more questions about the pictures on the wall and might never be given another opportunity to solve her nagging doubt about the photograph tucked away in her bag. She said the first thing that came into her head, anything to detain the old man for a little longer.

"But you still haven't really explained what happened," she said quickly. "Why did you end up taking over the café?"

"The shortest answer I can give you is this: the Civil War." He held his glass to his lips but, before taking another sip, lowered it again, and his eyes met her expectant gaze. "But if you want, I'll give you a longer version."

Sonia beamed at him. "Would you?" she said. "Do you have time?"

"I'll make time," he said, nodding in affirmation.

"Thanks. I'd love you to tell me more. And will you tell me more about the Ramírez family?" she asked.

"If you like. Most people just aren't interested in the old days. But I'll tell you what I can. My memory is better than most."

"And will you tell me about the dancer and the bullfighter?" she asked, trying to conceal her enthusiasm.

"I could even take you around the city if you'd like. I do sometimes close on Wednesdays at this time of year. I need the occasional day off at my age."

"It's really kind of you," said Sonia, now slightly hesitant. "But are you sure?"

"Of course. I wouldn't have offered if I didn't mean it. Why don't you meet me, *mañana* . . . ? Tomorrow at ten. Outside here."

It was an enchanting prospect, to be shown the city by someone who knew it so well. She knew that Maggie had no interest in Granada's history or culture, even if she now had encyclopedic knowledge of its tapas bars.

Sonia said good night to Miguel and went back to the flat. She needed a good night's sleep.

Sonia was there to meet Miguel at precisely ten o'clock the next morning. It was strange to see him out of context and without his apron. Today he was dressed in a smart olive-green jacket and highly polished leather shoes. She looked at him slightly differently and realized for the first time that he must once have been extremely handsome.

"*Buenos días*," he said, kissing her on both cheeks. "Let's go somewhere for a coffee before I take you on a tour. I have a favorite place."

A few minutes' walk away was a small square, dominated by the statue of a woman.

"It's Mariana Pineda," explained Miguel. "I'll tell you about her later, if you are interested. She was a feminist heroine."

Sonia nodded.

The café where Miguel took her was much bigger than his own and more crowded, but he was warmly welcomed by the rival patron and teased for being with a *señora guapa*. Most of the other tables were occupied by dapper elderly men chatting with each other while several businessmen stood at the bar, all of them perusing copies of *El País*. Strong cigarettes smoldered in a row of ashtrays. The bar staff worked earnestly and swiftly, preparing *tostadas* with olive oil, tomatoes, or jam, or noisily drying cutlery. Fresh *churros* gleamed beneath a glass dome.

Two well-dressed women, mid-fifties, chestnut hair stiffly coiffed, were getting up to leave as Miguel and Sonia arrived and they slipped quickly into their seats. It was a busy café and space was at a premium. While clearing away two brandy glasses, their rims red with lipstick, the waiter took Miguel's order, and within moments they were served; his speed and efficiency were as pleasing as a dance.

"Where shall I begin?" asked Miguel rhetorically.

Sonia leaned forward expectantly. She knew he was not waiting for an answer.

"I think I'll tell you a little more about the time just before the Civil War," he said. "There was the half-decade I mentioned between the end of the dictatorship in 1931 and the beginning of the Civil War in 1936. It was known as the Second Republic, and there was relative content for the Ramírez family during those years. Yes, I think that would be a good place to start."

# PART II

# CHAPTER 12

Monumental fountains played in Granada's squares, and elegant nineteenth-century buildings dominated the center of the city. Their tall windows and graceful wrought-iron balconies contrasted with the ramshackle irregularity of the older Arab quarter, whose red-roofed buildings, with their confusion of triangular and trapezoid tiles, nestled into a tight space at the foot of the hill. The entire city was dominated by the Alhambra, its majestic towers watching over the city from the top of the hill.

Many of the roads were rough and stony, and in spring, rain turned them into rivers of mud. Beasts of burden were used to carry goods around the city, and live animals were herded through the streets. In winter, there was always a whiff of dung in the air, and on a hot day in summer, the whole city reeked. The River Genil would sometimes burst its banks when the snows on the mountains high above Granada began to melt but by August might almost have dried up. Its bridges were meeting places for friends and lovers throughout the year.

The Ramírez family lived above El Barril. It had been in the family for three generations, and Pablo Ramírez had been born in the same bedroom where his wife had given birth to their children. Pablo had married his wife, Concha, when she was eighteen, and their first child, Antonio, was born a year later. By the time she was twenty-six, they had four children, and the once curvaceous Concha was lean with hard work and worry. Her beautiful face was still round, but she looked more than her age. Pablo, who was several years older than his wife, was small and dark, a typical Granadino.

Though they rarely had a moment of relaxation, it was a secure existence, and a comforting sense of continuity more than made up for their limited income. Always there was someone coming or going through the bar and into the apartment above it, and though Pablo and Concha were usually busy, the family still managed to eat together every day at three. It was a ritual that they both insisted on, and all the children made sure they were there. When they were younger, they had all felt their father's slipper for being late. Love and respect for their parents was the one thing they all had in common.

El Barril sat at a meeting point between Granada's various different cultures. Living on the edge of the Albaicín, the children were equally at ease in the atmosphere of the Arab quarter, where the air rang with the rhythms of blacksmiths beating on metal, as in the Sacromonte, where the gypsies lived in their homes hollowed out of the hillside. And the plaintive wail of *gitano* song was as much a part of everyday life as the deep tones of the cathedral bells and the calls of stallholders in the flower market. From the rooms on the top floor they could see the green meadows outside the boundary of the city, and the Sierra Nevada beyond.

Like all Granadino children, Antonio, Ignacio, Emilio, and Mercedes Ramírez had grown up playing in the streets and socializing in the squares. They mostly stayed quite close to the Plaza Nueva where their parents' café was situated and, when they were small, amused themselves with games of pitch and toss, and paddled in the River Darro beneath the Albaicín. The latter was an area where many of their friends lived, and though it was one of the poorer *barrios*, its poverty did not prevent it from being one of the most cheerful and lively.

Brothers, sisters, parents, and classmates were the population of their world. They were friends with whole groups of siblings, so if Concha Ramírez was curious about where one of her children might be, the information was never hard to find.

"Oh," she would be told, "Emilio is playing with Alejandro Martínez—his brother just told me." Or, "Paquita's mother told me to tell you that Mercedes is going to the fiesta with them tonight."

In that way, the city seemed a very small place. They were free to wander about, and there was more of a threat from being trodden on by an irritable mule carrying firewood in from the countryside than being knocked down by one of the few cars that drove about in the city. In daylight hours, Pablo and Concha Ramírez never gave a second thought to their children's whereabouts. It was a city without danger, somewhere impossible to get lost in, and the influence of the outside world remained firmly at bay. They had very little experience of anywhere but this city. Once, a long time back, there had been a visit to the seaside, but it was never repeated. The only journey they made on a regular basis was to a village up in the mountains north of Granada where Concha's sister, Rosita, lived.

In 1931, when the Second Republic began, Antonio was twenty, Ignacio eighteen, Emilio fifteen, and Mercedes twelve. Pablo and Concha Ramírez loved them all equally and unreservedly.

Antonio, the eldest, was broader than his father, and like everyone in his family he was dark. Behind his spectacles glittered earnest chestnut eyes. He had been a serious child, and the fully grown young man was no different from the boy. Listening to adult conversation had always been his favorite pastime, and growing up in a café had exposed him to plenty. Pablo and Concha were always nagging him to play with his peers, but he lost interest in childish games at an early age. He did, however, have two very close friends, both known to him since early childhood.

One of them was Francisco Pérez, whose family lived on the corner of Calle Elvira and Plaza Nueva. In this confined world of theirs, the Ramírez and Pérez families were as close as blood relatives. Luis and María Pérez lived above their locksmith business, which had been set up many generations before, with their two sons, Julio and Francisco. When he was not behind the counter in his shop, Luis was always in El Barril, and in more than four decades of friendship he and Pablo had never run short of conversation.

The second of Antonio's close friends was Salvador. "El Mudo" they called him, unabashed by the bluntness of the nickname. The mute boy. Over the years, Salvador's good friends had become fluent in sign language, and the three of them would sit for hours engaged in discussion. Naturally Salvador, who had been both deaf and dumb since birth, was the most eloquent and graceful of them all in the way he communicated: crocheting the air with his hands, making patterns that built into expressions of humor, joy, anger, and concern. Some of the time, his feelings would be greatly exaggerated, and at other times a subtle shrug or movement of his fingers would be all that was required.

When the Second Republic was declared, one of the new government's priorities was to make sure that everyone had the opportunity to learn to read, and they launched a campaign to stamp out illiteracy. Antonio had just qualified as a teacher, which had always been his ambition, so the aim of the Second Republic to provide education for all met with his approval. He relished being part of something bigger than just the day-to-day work in a classroom. He saw that illiteracy made slaves of people and that every *analfabeto* taught to read was one less person to be an underpaid servant to the capitalists. He knew that education was a powerful liberating force.

After 1931, Señora Ramírez tried to persuade him not to go to political meetings. She regarded them as more dangerous than bullfights. It was ironic really, but she was not entirely wrong. At least in a bullfight, the struggle is occasionally balanced and the fighter and the animal have an equal chance. In politics, this was not always the case.

Ignacio was the most colorful of them all. Although he was the most conceited person imaginable, he was also exciting company to be in. With ebony hair and eyes, he had a bewitching effect on people, particularly women. They could not leave him alone, and that often made his life complicated. He only had to look in their direction and they were smitten. It was often like that for many men in this macho world of the *torero*—they were put on the same pedestal as movie stars.

The bullfighting obsession had begun very early. From the age of three, a café tablecloth had doubled as a cape while Ignacio practiced his turns, his *verónicas*. Before he could even form sentences he knew what he wanted to do when he grew up.

Ignacio often performed his miniature *corrida* in front of a willing audience in the café, where drinkers would cheer and gasp as he killed his imaginary bull. When cajoled, both friends and brothers would play the bull's part for him. It was done with reluctance, given they knew it would probably mean feeling the bruising thrust of his wooden sword between their shoulder blades. For Ignacio, there was no acknowledgment of the boundary between fantasy and violence.

"*La hora de la verdad!*" he would cry in triumph, a bloodthirsty grin on his face. He was emulating "the moment of truth," when the matador is poised to plunge the blade into the bull. With the charging animal now close, he had no time for hesitation, and he knew, even as a child, that the cleaner the kill, the safer the man and the more impressed the spectators. As he held the toy sword aloft, it was as though he heard the crowd's collective intake of breath and the uncanny hush of a vast mass of humanity held in pure suspense. Who knows how many times he performed this dress rehearsal for what would become reality so many years later? When he was five, his grandmother had made him a little costume for his birthday and he wore it until all the seams frayed and finally split.

At the age of fifteen, Ignacio had left school. He had kicked his heels and just about everything else since he was born, and his parents found him hard to control. The classically perfect measurements between oval eyes, strong nose, and a mouth such as only a painter would devise, made him seem untouchably divine. His behavior was far from godlike, though. It was not even human some of the time. As a child, he often acted like an animal, and indeed he had the strength of an ox, making him a good match for the bull when he eventually went into the ring to fulfil his inescapable destiny.

Sturdy but slim-hipped, he could not have had a more perfect form for the bullfighter's costume: the jeweled jacket known as a *traje de luces*, and the leg-skimming hose that clung to buttocks, thighs, and calves. He had earned the title "El Arrogante" by the time he was nine, and it would follow him into adulthood and around the *corridas* of Spain. He had spent the past three years almost continuously shadowing one of Granada's matadors, watching him fight and observing him rehearse his turns with an imaginary bull, just as he himself had done as a child.

If he had ever had a nickname, Emilio's might have been "El Callado," the silent one. He could not have been more different from his swaggering, self-aggrandizing older brother, Ignacio, but occasionally when he did break his long silences, there was no mistaking the strength of his passions. His horizons were the nearby meadows of Granada's Vega in one direction and the Sacromonte in another, and he felt no need to know what was happening beyond them. His world was contained within the smooth and shapely body of his prized possession: a honey-colored flamenco guitar.

Emilio was taller than his brothers. He was also the palest and the frailest. Like a tree reaching upward to find the light, Emilio outgrew the other men in his family in height if not in width or weight.

Unlike Ignacio, who had been constantly out in the street, playing football and occasionally disappearing until very late at night with his friends, Emilio was usually in the attic room of the apartment. There he would sit for hours at a time, his back grazing the roof tiles, doubled like a hunchback over his guitar, his strong fingers picking out the notes of some forlorn tune. There was no question of him needing the light to read the notes on a printed page. The music was entirely in his head, and in the gloom of that attic room, he would shut his eyes tight to block out any remaining chinks of light.

If anyone was drawn by his playing to the top of the narrow staircase, he rarely noticed their presence. He would carry on plucking his strings, enveloped by the enchanting waves of sound, locked inside his own rapturous music-making. He needed no one. Anyone who did eavesdrop would soon slope away, feeling guilty that they had intruded on his private world.

Emilio was not ambitious like Antonio and Ignacio, which was just as well really, as his parents were eventually going to need someone to work in the bar and he had anticipated doing that job since he had been able to see over it. He wanted nothing more than to stay in Granada. The guitar was his real passion. He had been taught by one of the customers in the bar, an old gypsy type called José, and though the old man died before Emilio was even twelve, the boy had already learned the basic techniques of flamenco. He worked on those until he was nearly as good as the stars of the Sacromonte.

He was already playing for his sister quite a bit when her parents allowed her to perform. Indeed, the only person Emilio acknowledged when they climbed the laddered stairway was his little sister. Mercedes could not keep away from the sound of her brother's playing, and he tolerated the girl's interest in a way he would not have done with anyone else.

Like many little girls, Mercedes could dance flamenco from the age of five. Before this, it was discouraged, as a child's bones were considered too soft to cope with the heavy pounding. So at a very early age, she would steal up to the attic and in the claustrophobic darkness beneath the sloping roof, she would find the rhythm with her palms, at first sitting down on the floor by Emilio's feet. Later she would rise to her feet and begin to stamp and twirl, and by now Emilio might even open his eyes to show her that he did not mind her being there. These were their private fiestas.

It was common to see little girls, knee-high to their fathers, performing in private homes at local *juergas*, and their precocious brilliance was a spectacle that quickly drew an audience. Even if her mother worried about those soft bones, Mercedes was not a child to be told what to do. In that tiny space she learned to snap her fingers, twist her body and click the castanets. There was no one teaching her; she simply emulated the *señoritas* that she had seen, picking up their haughty demeanor, watching their steps and absorbing the sound and the fury of their movements. It seemed to come completely naturally to her, even if she was not of gypsy blood.

Concha was always surprised that Emilio did not find Mercedes' presence an irritation, and then, one night when she stood at the bottom of the stairs listening, she realized why. Mercedes added to his music. The beat of her heels on the wooden flooring and the clapping together of palms gave it percussion.

People in the street below sometimes heard the quick pattering of her feet, and they would look up to see if they could detect the source of the sound. It was as fast and as smooth as the sound of someone rolling their Rs, as rapid as the vibration of a tongue against the roof of the mouth.

At the age of twelve, there was a strength and sturdiness about Mercedes that within a few years would bloom into voluptuousness. She had the same heart-shaped face as her mother, with dimples in her cheeks and chin, and the furrow on her brow was beginning to deepen. The glossy waves of black hair that flowed down her back were long enough for her to sit on.

She had a best friend, Paquita Maneiro, who lived in the Albaicín. The pair of them were often found sitting in a courtyard watching Señora Maneiro spinning and weaving. The woman's fingers did not stop from morning until night, and even then she seemed able to see in the dark, working on her rugs in the flickering candlelight. It looked like a hard way to make a living, but it had been a conscious choice. Her husband had died five years earlier, and she could easily have taken to the streets to earn her living. It would have been a quicker way to make a few pesetas than the back-breaking work she now did. While she wove, the two girls would dance in front of her, their steel toecaps catching the edges of the rounded cobbles. Like Mercedes, Paquita loved flamenco, but she struggled to dance with the same fluency.

As the only girl in the family, Mercedes was doted on by her brothers to the point of being spoiled. She always seemed to get what she wanted, and none of them liked to provoke her bad temper, which could easily be stirred. The haughty expression of the flamenco dancer came naturally to her.

The Ramírez family lived a relatively contented existence, even if peace did not always reign domestically. Their children were strong individuals, and this was something their parents celebrated, but on the days when doors slammed and arguments raged, it was something they bemoaned. Ignacio was usually at the center of the troublemaking and did not seem to be happy unless he was arousing one of his brothers to anger.

He loved to provoke his generally patient older brother, Antonio, and to wrestle with him to prove his own superior strength, and there was nothing that entertained him more than to goad the shy Emilio to a fight. But Ignacio never argued in any way with Mercedes. He teased and danced and flirted with her. Only she could diffuse the poisonous atmosphere that sometimes existed between her brothers.

Though their lives had been happy and content even during the 1920s, the Ramírez family celebrated when the Second Republic arrived. It was like a sweet springtime breeze for Spain. Someone had found the key, unlatched the door and thrown open the windows. Fresh air coursed through, lifting the dust and blowing the cobwebs away. Though most in the city had been well enough fed, many people in the countryside around it had been living hand to mouth. Landowners had kept their laborers on the breadline, feeding them just about enough to ensure that they were capable of working the land for them. Some of the customers at El Barril came in from outside and told stories of the hardship that people were enduring in rural areas. Concha's own sister had relatives who had been subjected to this harsh regime.

Concha was thrilled by the new liberty that the Second Republic was bringing, especially to women. Though Pablo would never have used it to suppress her, the repeal of the *código civil*, the civil code that gave men precedence over their wives, was of huge significance. There were many women, less fortunate than Concha, who were treated like chattel.

"Listen to this, Merche!" Concha said with excitement. Though her daughter was only twelve, she could see how much impact some of the changes being made could have on her future. She was reading out of the newspaper. "This is what it used to say:

"'The husband owes protection to the woman and the wife obedience to her husband. . . . The husband is the representative of the wife. She cannot, without his permission, appear in court.'"

Mercedes looked rather blankly at her mother. With such devoted parents as hers, it was unsurprising that the child failed to see the implications. The old law effectively precluded women from divorcing their husbands.

"And this is what it says now," Concha continued, excitedly:

"'The family is in the safekeeping of the state. Marriage is based on equal rights for both sexes and can be dissolved by mutual agreement or by demand of either party.'"

This was not legislation that directly affected the Ramírez family, but a new equality in marriage was emblematic of the kind of changes taking place under the Republic. Now there was education for all, and culture of all kinds flourished, with elitism looking as though it might be a thing of the past.

As well as the excitement of these political developments, the other huge event for the Ramírez family in 1931 was Ignacio's first venture into the bullring. He was one of the banderilleros, the team of men who, with the use of their capes and sharp blades, goad and wound the bull before the matador arrives to make the final kill.

After all his years of childish play and fantasy, it was time for Ignacio to feel the heat of the bull's breath.

Bullfighting was popular in Granada, and for a while there were even two bullrings in the city, the old and new, both of them in use. The Ramírez family had all been to the Plaza de Toros many times, but to see one of their own emerging into the ring would be a historic event for them. They were all there to witness the moment, except Emilio, who was disgusted by the whole idea of an innocent animal being murdered in front of a cheering crowd. For Mercedes it was the first time she had been permitted to go. She could hardly contain her excitement.

It was a hot June day, the kind that gives everyone a glimpse of what the summer will hold, teasing everyone with an early blast of the intense heat that will be the average in July and August. The atmosphere was one of excitement, of fiesta.

"Why do you keep fanning yourself?" asked Mercedes. "We're in the shade."

For the first time since they could remember, the family were in the better seats, out of the glare of the sun.

"I didn't realize I was," said her mother, flicking her fan back and forth. "I just wish they would start." Clearly she was agitated.

There was a trumpet fanfare and the crowd fell silent for a moment. Then began the parade. From the gateway marched the three matadors and their teams of mounted lancers—the picadors—banderilleros and a *mozo de espada*, the sword bearer.

"Is that really our son?" whispered Concha into her husband's ear. Tears pricked her eyes.

A group of uniformly movie-star-handsome young men paraded around the ring, dazzling the audience in the late afternoon sunshine with the sparkle of metallic embroidery that embellished their costumes. The shameless femininity of their rhinestone-encrusted, candy-colored outfits in mauve, pink, pistachio green, and ochre yellow made them appeal more than ever to the adoring crowds of women. For this day of days, Ignacio had picked a vibrant turquoise that made him stand out from the crowd, and with the skin-tight knickerbockers, the unashamedly vivid outfit only accentuated his glorious masculinity.

Their hats deferentially held in the right hand and their heavy pink capes supported in their left, they bowed low in front of the dignitaries in the presiding box. Already they enjoyed the adulation of the crowd. The matador who was at the top of the bill that day acknowledged the cheers of his fans with a grand sweep of his arm, and then the entire troop processed out again. Ignacio's matador was the second on the bill.

The first kill was a dull affair. The bull was slow and presented little challenge to anyone in the *cuadrilla*. As his corpse was dragged around the ring by the team of horses, there was little reaction, just a desultory ripple of applause.

Moments later there was another trumpet blast. The gates swung open and a bull thundered in. He was a massive animal. Deep, chocolate brown, with a thick neck and wide shoulders, his curved horns appeared needle sharp.

"What a beauty," breathed Pablo Ramírez.

"He's huge!" exclaimed Mercedes with excitement.

Usually the best of the six bulls to be killed that day was kept until last. It was hard to imagine that any would be finer than this.

For the initial stage, the second of the matadors and his banderilleros, which included Ignacio, toyed with the bull, testing his grit with their capes, confusing him, twisting him this way and that to start the process of trying to tire him out. At this stage, bull and man seemed on equal terms. The bull was not yet maddened, but as they continued to play with him, the animal began to sense their contempt and his anger grew. He could lower his head and charge faster than a man can run. For one moment at least, he was king of the ring.

Unlike most, this bull could almost pivot, and seemed agile, given his weight. The matador had to work out how best to challenge him, noting if he charged by instinct to left or right. Once he had done this, they all withdrew from the ring. Concha breathed a sigh of relief. Ignacio was still alive. She gripped Mercedes' hand and the girl felt the clammy chill of her mother's anxiety.

Next, the picador entered the ring, his horse weighed down with padding, its eyes blinkered. Within seconds, the man's job was done. He had plunged his lance deep down into the muscle that stood erect on the bull's neck. Blood oozed until the crimson had spread across his back like a blanket.

The bull was to have his revenge, though. His head bowed low, he barged into the horse and lifted it up with his horns, goring the unprotected part of its stomach. He tossed it aloft as if it weighed less than air, and the picador struggled to keep his balance as his mount tumbled beneath him. Its vocal cords severed, the wounded creature was unable to make a sound.

"The poor horse!" squealed Mercedes, horrified. "Will he die?"

"I think he probably will, darling," replied her mother. This was no place for anything other than realism.

The Ramírez family watched as Ignacio re-entered the ring with the other banderilleros to lure the bull away from the dying horse and the stranded picador. It seemed to Concha the most dangerous and unprotected role on the stage, and the eyes of twenty thousand spectators would be on her son as the banderilleros stood with just a length of pink cloth and no other weapon to defend themselves against six hundred kilograms of confused and angry beast.

As the first of the banderilleros in this group, Ignacio left his cape and now had his longed-for opportunity with his knives. He wanted to show the crowd that he could provide more excitement than the matador himself and was determined to bring them right to the edge of their seats. His aim was to be the one whose name was celebrated in the bars that night.

Legs straight, arms stretched up with the two blades held aloft, he stood his ground against the bull, which charged at him from one side of the ring to the other. At the moment when the horns seemed only a hand's width from his chest, he sprang into the air to get the trajectory he desired for his daggers. In one seamless movement he plunged the sharp points of the banderillas deftly into the neck muscle and jumped from the bull's path. The knives had dug deep into the shoulder muscles, and their tasseled ends waved in the air. Ignacio had aimed close to the wound already inflicted by the picador, and blood now seeped out to form a shiny saddle of red.

Ignacio's split-second timing could have been construed as simple folly, but the crowd were excited now. They gasped and cheered in one breath. This was exactly the sort of entertainment they wanted: a strong sense of risk and the chance to see human blood.

Ignacio had fulfilled his ambition. He had thrilled the crowd and won their adulation by making them marvel at his bravery and gasp at how close to the edge he had come.

No one who saw Ignacio would ever doubt the link between this sport and the bull-leaping of ancient Crete. For the briefest moment this lithe banderillero appeared to take off. Another few centimeters and he might have jumped right over the charging animal. It was pure acrobatics. At this point, he stood without cape, without sword, without dagger, and there was nothing between him and the bull, which now turned round to look at his assailant.

"I can't even look," said Concha, burying her head in her hands, convinced of her son's imminent death.

Antonio gently took his mother's arm and held it. "He'll be fine, Mother."

Antonio was right. Ignacio could walk across the ring in front of the bull now and come to no harm. The bull's energy was flagging. The danger had passed. Within a moment he had retreated into the *callejón*, the passage that ran behind the ring's wooden barricade.

This bull was finished off by the matador, but the important work had been done by the three banderilleros. Perhaps they had been over-efficient, since the bull was virtually on his knees by the time the matador appeared with his red cape. The animal scarcely had the energy to follow the sweep of the scarlet *muleta* as the gold-clad figure of the matador executed his turns. The final moment when the sword pierced his heart thrilled no one.

The animal's finale was a farewell lap around the ring, dragged by the horse team. They used him like a brush to paint a perfect circle of crimson in the sand. It was his final humiliation.

Ignacio's second outing that afternoon was as impressive as the first. El Arrogante's career had been magnificently launched. The *aficionados* had noticed him.

For days after, the menus in the city's restaurants were dominated by stew made from *rabo de toro*—oxtail—and platters of braised cuts from these delicious beasts who had spent their innocent lives in rich pastures. The meat market in Granada was full of *toro*, and everyone in the Ramírez family enjoyed it, with the exception of Emilio, who would not have it near his plate.

Concha realized then that watching her son in the ring was not going to get any easier and that, however many times she did it, she would always have a premonition of her beautiful slim-hipped boy being gored to death. She tortured herself with this. Occasionally Pablo attempted to reassure her with statistics on how few fighters were ever killed in the ring, but he could not allay her fears.

# CHAPTER 13

A few months after the arrival of the Republic, a certain amount of disillusion began to set in. Conversation in El Barril soon turned to the rumors that divisions on the left were beginning to develop and there were mutterings that the socialist-dominated Republican government were not bringing the swift end to poverty that they had promised. Even before the end of 1931 there were clashes between security forces and protesting workers who felt their interests were not being represented.

There were plenty who yearned for a return to rule by the wealthy and privileged, and many loathed the new liberalism, blaming it for a wave of permissive behavior that they found hard to stomach. Over the next few years they opposed the Republic at every possible opportunity. The new government had swiftly made itself unpopular among conservatives by interfering with the Catholic Church and restricting its religious processions and celebrations. This was seen as a severe threat to a traditional way of life. The power of the Church had also been weakened by the opening of new schools that were not religiously affiliated. The Church united with the landed and the wealthy in resenting the new regime, bemoaning the removal of their unchallenged power.

Even within the government itself divisions began to open up, a situation exploited by those who were keen to bring it down. At the beginning of 1933, as part of a wave of violence in the province of Cádiz, a group of anarchists besieged the Civil Guard post in the town of Casas Viejas and declared the arrival of libertarian communism. Inevitably, fighting broke out.

"But aren't these people meant to be on the same side?" commented Concha. "I don't understand it. If they start fighting each other, we might as well go back to a dictatorship!" She was looking over Antonio's shoulder at that day's newspaper headlines.

"That's the theory," he responded. "But I'm sure these workers don't feel as though the government is on their side. Most of them have been unemployed for a year."

Antonio was right. These starving "revolutionaries" had been living on the edge of desperation, eking out a living by begging, poaching, and hoping for the occasional hand-out. The announcement of an increase in bread prices had finally spurred them to action.

Within days the news worsened. Civil Guard and Assault Guard reinforcements arrived from Cádiz to put down the insurrection. They surrounded the house of a six-fingered anarchist known as Seisdedos, and orders were eventually given for the building to be burned down. As well as those who died in the flames, other anarchists who had previously been arrested were shot in cold blood.

"That's brutal!" commented Ignacio, when he saw the report that a dozen men had died in this repression. "What does the government think it's doing?"

Ignacio was not someone who naturally sided with peasants and revolutionaries, but for those like him who did not support the Republican-Socialist government that was in power, it was an opportunity to criticize the Prime Minister, Manuel Azaña. The incident had shocked the country, and the right wing saw a situation that could be exploited to its own advantage, quickly accusing the government of barbarism.

"I think the days of the coalition might be numbered," Ignacio said in the innocent but knowing tone that he knew would annoy his older brother.

"We'll see, shall we?" responded Antonio, determined not to lose his temper.

The two brothers were often at loggerheads, and politics became a growing source of contention. In Antonio's view, Ignacio had no firm political beliefs. He just liked trouble. Sometimes he was just not worth arguing with.

In elections held late in 1933, Antonio desperately hoped that the liberals would stay in power. To his dismay, a conservative government was elected, and any reforms that the left had brought in were now threatened. Rumblings of anger erupted into explosions of discontent. Strikes and protests were staged. Both the socialists and Fascists had burgeoning youth movements and the highly politicized young men of Antonio's generation were in the vanguard, on both sides.

The situation worsened the following year, and in October 1934 there was an abortive attempt by the left to stage a general strike. It failed, but an armed rebellion in Asturias, the northern coal-mining area, continued for two weeks, with far-reaching consequences. Villages were bombed and coastal towns shelled.

The center of the action was a long way from Granada, but the Ramírez family followed events closely.

"Listen to this," said Antonio, his tone one of outrage as he read that day's newspaper. "They've executed some of the ringleaders!"

"Why does that surprise you?" Ignacio responded. "They can't have that sort of thing happening."

Antonio decided not to react.

"Serves those leftists right for burning down churches!" Ignacio continued, determined to provoke his brother.

The Spanish foreign legionaries brought in to deal with the situation had not only executed some of the leaders; they had also killed innocent women and children. Large areas of the region's principal towns of Gijón and Oviedo were bombed and burned out.

"Mother, look at these pictures."

"I know, I know, I've seen them. They say everything . . ."

The destruction of the buildings was not the last revenge. The people were now brutally repressed. Thirty thousand workers were imprisoned, and torture was commonplace in the jails. The socialist presses were silent.

The atmosphere in the country changed. Even in El Barril, where Pablo and Concha did what they could not to seem biased toward any political party, they could feel distrust between people beginning to set in. Some of their customers openly supported the socialists; others clearly welcomed the conservatives into government, and at times there was animosity between them. There was a subtle shift of ambience in the bar. The halcyon days of the Republic seemed to be coming to an end.

Whatever the changes and upheavals going on in politics, Concha was concerned that any of the privileges that had been won for ordinary people were being eroded. Most important, she would lament the disappearance of any improvements for women. For the first time in Spain's history, women had been getting into public office and participating in politics. Thousands of them were now going to university, too, and taking part in sports, even bullfighting.

Concha and her friends flippantly called the new freedoms for women "liberation and lingerie" because of the exciting new undergarments that they now sometimes saw advertised in the newspapers. Having moved out of rural poverty herself when she married Pablo, she wanted to see Mercedes improve her life, too, and had been pleased at the prospect of her daughter growing up in a society full of opportunity. With women now in professions such as law and medicine and reaching positions of power and influence, Concha hoped that life for Mercedes would have more to it than polishing glasses and lining them up neatly along the bar. Though Mercedes seemed to think of nothing but dance, her mother regarded it as something of a childish pastime.

She did not worry about her sons. They had already-evolving careers and their futures looked promising.

"Granada is full of opportunities," she said to Mercedes, "so imagine what it must be like in the rest of Spain!"

Mercedes had only a limited idea of what the rest of her country was like, but she nodded with agreement. It was usually the best thing to do with her mother. She knew that Concha did not take her dancing seriously enough. As the months and years passed by, she vowed it was all she would ever want to do, but it was hard to convince her parents. All of her brothers appreciated this ambition of hers. They had watched her dancing from the days of her first flamenco shoes, the smallest anyone made, to the present time when she was a match for anyone in Granada, and Mercedes knew that they understood her desire.

When tales had begun to filter through from Concha's family in the countryside that landless farm workers were once again being ill treated, she lectured her family on the unfairness of it all.

"This is not what the Republic was meant to stand for!" she would rant. "Is it?"

She expected a response from her children, even if her husband remained studiedly neutral. Pablo found this by far the best position to take, given that his business relied on the need to welcome anyone who cared to come in the door. He did not want El Barril to be too firmly identified with politics of any color, unlike several bars in Granada that had become meeting places of very specific cliques.

Antonio muttered in agreement. He was more keenly aware of the political shifts taking place than anyone else in his family. He was following events in the Spanish parliament, the Cortes, closely, and read the newspapers voraciously and retentively. Though the city of Granada had a strongly conservative bias, Antonio, like his mother, was naturally drawn toward the left. The family could have remained unaware of this but for the fights he used to have with Ignacio. The two boys lived on the edge of conflict.

As children, they had fought over practically everything from toys and books to who should have the last piece of bread in the basket. Ignacio would never acknowledge that age and precedence should have any connection. Now the disagreement between them extended into the more serious business of politics, and though with fewer physical bruises and scratches than before, it was with hatred that they fought.

Emilio always remained silent when his brothers argued. He did not want to get drawn in, knowing that Ignacio was more than likely to pick on him. Mercedes occasionally interjected. The vehemence of their arguments upset her. She wanted them to love each other, and for her this dislike seemed an unnatural state of affairs between brothers.

Another reason for their current polarization was Ignacio's entrenchment in the bullfighting crowd. The people who were drawn to this sport—or, rather art, as so many people thought of it—tended to be the most conservative of Granadinos. They were the landowners and the wealthy, and Ignacio happily adopted their attitudes and even voted for the Right like most members of this well-heeled set. Pablo and Concha accepted these inclinations and hoped that maturity might make him see that reason lay more in the middle ground. Meanwhile, Antonio found Ignacio's swaggering hard to stomach and never bothered to conceal his disdain.

The household seemed to relax only when Ignacio was away for a *corrida*. His days as a banderillero were behind him now, and he had completed his apprenticeship as a *novillero*, a period during which he could fight only young bulls. He was now a fully fledged *matador de toros*, and at his *alternativa*, the ceremony where this transition was formalized, the experts noted his prodigious talent. Wherever he went, not just in Granada, but in Sevilla, Málaga, and Córdoba, too, Ignacio's reputation grew with every appearance.

As Emilio grew up, he began to develop an antipathy to his brother that surpassed even Antonio's. They were instinctively polarized on all matters. Ignacio taunted Emilio on several counts: for his passion for the guitar, for his lack of interest in women, and that he was not, as his older brother described it, "a real man." Unlike Antonio, who could spar with words even better than Ignacio, Emilio would retreat into silence and then into his music. His lack of desire to retaliate and to fight back with Ignacio in one of the ways he understood, through fists or a clever turn of phrase, infuriated his brother all the more.

Although she was a much more sociable creature than her brother, Mercedes was immersed in the solipsistic world of music and dance. Nothing much had changed for her from the age of five to fifteen. She still spent much of her time in the attic listening to her brother or visiting her favorite shop behind the Plaza Bib Rambla, which made the best flamenco dresses in the city, talking to the owner, fingering the fabrics and feeling their folds, letting the extravagant ruffles run through her fingers, as though she was a soon-to-be-bride selecting her trousseau.

The shop, run by Señora Ruiz, was her private paradise. Racks of dresses hung from the ceiling in both adult and child sizes, and there were even tiny costumes for babies who could not yet walk, let alone dance. All of them were made with the same attention to detail, and their tiers of ruffles edged with ribbon or lace were all meticulously starched. Every single one was different and no two fabrics repeated. There were simple skirts for lessons and plain white shirts, embroidered shawls with silky tassels, hair combs and rows of shiny castanets. Boys were not forgotten and there were suits in every size, from toddler to adult, with black hats to complete the outfit.

Mercedes' favorite dresses were those with wired lower hems that would move in perfect wave motion as a dancer rotated. These were the ones she yearned to own, but they cost many pesetas and she had to make do with fantasy. Though she had three costumes sewn by her mother, she still wanted what she called a "real" dress, and the shopkeeper never tired of discussing quality and cost of fabric with her. For her sixteenth birthday, her parents had promised to grant her wish.

People had been marveling at the way she performed since she was eight. It was common for girls to start dancing in public at that age, and it was never considered unsuitable or precocious. From the age of eleven, she had been going up the hill into the Sacromonte, which was where the gypsies lived in their dank homes hollowed out of the hillside. Though she had several friends in the area, the real reason she went to the Sacromonte was to see an old *bailaora* known as La Mariposa.

Most people thought her a mad old witch. Indeed, María Rodríguez had lost some of her reason, but she still had the memories of her great dancing days. They were as clear to her as if they had been yesterday. She saw in Mercedes a glimpse of her younger self, and perhaps in her elderly mind she thought that she and the child were one and the same as she relived her dancing through the adolescent girl.

Mercedes did have friends her own age, but it was at this woman's crumbling home that her mother would always look for her first. It was her retreat and the place where her obsession grew.

Señora Ramírez was worried about Mercedes' schoolwork, and reports from her teachers were unimpressive. She wanted to see her daughter take advantage of what this changing world might offer.

"Merche, when are you going to stay at home to do your studying?" she demanded. "You can't spend your entire life spinning around. It'll never make you a living."

She tried to make it sound light-hearted, but she was serious and Mercedes knew that. The girl bit her tongue to prevent herself from answering back.

"There's no point arguing with Mother," Emilio told her. "She will never see your point of view. Like she never sees mine."

Concha's view was that without gypsy blood Mercedes could never be a "proper" dancer. She believed that the *gitanos* were the only ones who could dance, or play flamenco guitar, for that matter.

Even Pablo disagreed with her. "She's as good as any of them," he would say defensively to his wife when they watched her at a fiesta.

"Even if she was," responded Concha, "I would rather she was doing something else. That's how I feel."

"And she 'feels' that dancing is the right thing for her to be doing," interrupted Emilio bravely.

"This is nothing to do with you, Emilio, and we'd rather you didn't egg her on quite so much," snapped Concha.

Her father had always encouraged Mercedes' love of dancing, but he was now beginning to worry about it, though not for the same reasons as his wife. Since the conservative government's win in the elections and the unrest in the north, the Civil Guard were beginning to tighten the screws on those who were not seen to conform. Anyone who fraternized with the gypsies, for example, was now regarded as a subversive. The amount of time Mercedes spent in the Sacromonte was beginning to worry even Pablo.

One afternoon Mercedes came running back from La Mariposa's and burst through the door of El Barril. The place was empty except for Emilio, who was behind the bar drying cups and saucers. He was working almost full-time in the café now. His parents were resting in the apartment, Antonio was at school teaching his last lessons for the term, and Ignacio was away in Sevilla for a *corrida*.

"Emilio!" she said breathlessly. "You have to take the evening off. You've got to come out with me!"

She came up to the bar, and he could see droplets of perspiration on her forehead. She must have been running hard and her chest was heaving from the exertion. Her long hair, sometimes neatly plaited for school, was disheveled and hanging loose about her shoulders.

"Please!"

"What for?" he asked, continuing to dry a saucer.

"A *juerga*. María Rodríguez just told me that Raul Montero's son is coming to play. Tonight. We are invited to go—but you know I can't go on my own . . ."

"What time?"

"About ten o'clock. *Please*, Emilio! *Please* come with me." Mercedes gripped the edge of the bar, wide-eyed, pleading with her brother.

"All right. I'll ask our parents."

"Thanks, Emilio. Javier Montero is meant to be nearly as good as his father."

He could see that his sister was excited. The old lady had told her that if Javier Montero was even a fraction as handsome as his father or one tenth as accomplished on the guitar, then he was worth going to see.

Javier Montero was not exactly a stranger because many of the *gitanos* knew of him. He had come at their invitation from his home in Málaga. Musicians often came in from the outside, but this one had excited local anticipation more than most. Both his father and his uncle were among the biggest names in flamenco, and that summer night in 1935, El Niño, as he was known, was to play in Granada.

When they entered the long windowless room, a seated figure was already quietly playing a *falseta*, a variation on the piece that he would eventually open with. All they could see of him was the top of his head and a mass of glossy black hair that hung down and entirely screened his face. Bent lovingly over his guitar, he appeared to be listening, as though he believed it was the instrument itself that would give him his melody. Someone was subtly rapping out the rhythm on the tabletop nearby.

For ten minutes, while people were still coming into the room, he did not look up. Then he raised his head and gazed into the middle distance toward a point that only he could see. It was an expression of pure concentration, the pupils of his dark eyes just registering the outlines of the few figures already seated. With the light behind them, their faces were in the shadows, their silhouettes haloed.

The young Montero was spot-lit for all to see. He looked younger than his twenty years, and his dimpled chin gave him an unexpected innocence. There was something almost feminine about him, with his copious, glossy tresses and features that were finer than most gypsy men.

From the moment she saw him, Mercedes was transfixed. She thought he was extraordinarily beautiful for a man, and when his face disappeared once again behind the shroud of his mane, it was like losing something. She willed him to look up so she could resume studying him. He continued idly moving his fingers across the strings, vain enough to want a bigger crowd and clearly not planning to start his performance until the room was filled to capacity.

More than half an hour later, and without apparent warning, he began.

The effect of his playing on Mercedes was physical. At that very moment, it was as though her heart expanded. The powerful beating that resounded in her ears as loudly as a drum was entirely involuntary. On the low uncomfortable stools on which they sat, she hugged herself in an attempt to still her shaking body. In her life, she had not heard anyone play like this. Even the older men who had been playing for half a century did not produce such an exquisite sound.

This *flamenco* was at one with his guitar, and the rhythms and melodies that he could draw from it passed through the audience like an electric current. Chords and melody emanated from his instrument along with percussive taps on the *golpeador*. It was as though a third invisible hand was at work, and the sureness of his technique and the originality of the music astounded them all. The rise in room temperature was palpable and the murmured utterance of "*Olé*" was passed around the room like a hat.

Beads of sweat streaked Javier Montero's face, and for the first time, as he tipped his head back, the audience could see that his features were distorted with concentration. Rivulets of moisture coursed down his neck. The drummer took over for a few minutes, allowing him to rest, and once again he stared out blankly across the heads of the audience. He did not engage with them even for a moment. From where he sat, they were a single, amorphous mass.

There was one further piece and then, twenty minutes from the start of the performance, he gave a brief nod of his head, rose from his seat, and edged his way past the applauding crowd.

Mercedes felt the edge of his jacket brush her face as he went past and caught the sweet-sour scent of him. Something akin to panic seized her now. It was as strong as pain, and her heart resumed its earlier violent beating. In one thunderclap instant, the postured gestures of love and grief that she had copied from other flamenco dancers over the years became real. The playacting had been a dress rehearsal for this moment.

The anguish, the despair that she might never again set eyes on this man, almost made her forget herself and shout aloud: "Stop! Don't go!" Reason and reticence could not hold her back, and she got up and slipped away, leaving Emilio discussing with others in the *cueva* what they had all just witnessed.

Such heightened atmosphere was not uncommon in these performances, but even so, the player had been a cut above the best of them, they all agreed, and their slightly rivalrous envy of his brilliance gave way to admiration.

As the fresh air hit Mercedes, she nearly lost courage. Just outside the door, in the shadows, was the figure of the *guitarrista*. The fiery glow from a cigarette gave away his presence.

Suddenly her boldness seemed almost shameful.

"*Señor*," she whispered.

Montero was used to such advances. The allure of a masterful player invariably proved irresistible to someone in the audience.

"*Sí*," he replied. The lack of depth in his voice was a surprise.

Mercedes was set on a course of action, and in spite of a very reasonable fear of rejection, she continued. She was on a tightrope with an obligation to move forward or backward. Having come this far, she had to speak the words she had rehearsed in her head.

"Will you play for me?" Overwhelmed by a sense of her own audacity, she braced herself for rejection.

"I *have* just played for you . . ."

There was a weariness in his voice. For the first time he bothered to look at her. He saw her features picked out in the lamplight. So many women approached him like this, seductive, available, aroused by his playing, but when he saw them in the light he could see they were old enough to be his mother. Sometimes, though, high on the adrenaline of his performance, it did not deter him from an hour or so of intimacy with them. Being the object of worship never failed to have some appeal.

This girl was young, though. Perhaps she genuinely wanted to dance. That would make a change.

"You'll have to wait," he said roughly. "I don't want a crowd."

He had done enough performing for the day, but the thought of seeing what this girl wanted from him was quite intriguing. Her audacity was enough to persuade him, even without her pretty face. He lit another cigarette and remained in the shadows. The minutes passed and the crowd drifted away.

Mercedes, hovering out of sight, saw the willowy figure of her brother slope down the narrow cobbled street and out of sight. He would assume that she was already at home. Only the *cueva* owner remained, eager to lock his doors for the night.

"Could we have just a moment inside?" Javier asked him.

"All right," he said, recognizing Mercedes. "If you like. But I need to go in ten minutes. No more."

Mercedes switched the light back on. Javier resumed his position, head bent, listened to the intervals between the strings, adjusted two of the pegs, and then looked up. Now he was ready to engage with this *señorita*.

Until this moment, he had taken in little about her, merely her youth, but now, watching her, poised and ready to dance, he saw that she was no coy child. She had everything of the haughty madam about her: the poise, the "attitude," a sense of drama.

"So what do you want? Some *alegrías*? *Bulerías*?"

In a simple full-skirted summer dress and flat shoes, she was not properly attired for dancing, but this did not deter her.

"A *soleá*."

She amused him, this girl. He smiled at the confidence she displayed in front of him. It flowed out of her before she had uncoiled so much as a fingertip.

Now his attention was fully on her, like a beam of light. She tapped her palms together to take up his beat, and once she could feel that his rhythm and hers were perfectly synchronized, she began to move. She hammered out a pattern of beats on the floor, quite slowly at first, then raised her arms above her head and coiled her hands, folding them back almost flush against her wrists.

Then her feet began to move, faster and faster until they began to purr. There was not a breath between them, one step followed so swiftly after the other. To begin with, Mercedes danced shyly, a respectful distance between herself and accompanist. He watched her closely, skilfully reflecting her movements in his playing, just as Emilio always did.

This dance continued for five or six minutes, and she twirled and stamped, always returning to the same spot with her feet. The outline of her muscular body was visible to Javier through the thin cotton of her dress. Dancers tended to move the folds of their dresses as part of the choreography, but the fabrics were often heavy and Mercedes found the flimsiness of her frock a liberation. On the final beat she stopped, breathless, and her body continued to sway from the exertion.

"*Muy bien.*" He smiled for the first time. "Very good. Very, very good."

She had not so much as glanced at him during the dance, but he had not taken his eyes off her. It seemed to him that she had undergone a transformation between the opening and closing bars.

He had forgotten the pleasure it could be to accompany a dancer. For some years he had avoided it. He so rarely came across a dancer that he wanted to be with. They were rarely good enough.

Now it was his turn to choose the music.

"Next the *bulería*," he announced.

Mercedes found this a much harder dance, but she had no trouble picking up his rhythm. The moment he began, she sensed the beat and the pace and her feet moved almost automatically. The dance was just for him now, and it was her task to respond. She turned slowly through three hundred and sixty degrees, her pale, extended fingers reaching out but never touching him.

It was a longer piece and she gave everything this time. There would not be another after this. As she turned, her black curls flew out like a blanket and her hair clip clattered to the floor. Her arms seemed both to lead and to follow her rotations until, like a gyroscope, she finally slowed and ended the dance in one last stamp that timed with his final chord.

She was breathless and soaked with perspiration; strands of damp hair trailed across her face. She looked as though she had been running through the rain.

Pulling a chair toward her, Mercedes sat down. The silence was overpowering, unnerving after the noise they had been making. To break the tension, she busied herself by leaning down to retrieve her hairpin.

A few minutes passed. Javier studied this young woman who had turned into someone else while she danced. Quite unexpectedly, she had moved him. Perhaps once before in his life he had been ignited by a *bailaora*, but more often he had felt like a packhorse bearing a burden. A long time ago he had made the decision not to be an accompanist. With this girl it had been a duet.

"Well . . ." said Javier ambiguously, watching her as she fastened her hair back.

She felt uncomfortable in the spotlight of his gaze. Trying to hold her breath to hear what he might say next, while still panting, made her feel as though she might burst.

" . . . was that what you wanted?"

His question was not what she had anticipated, but she had to answer.

"It was more than I had hoped for," was all she could think of to say.

The *cueva* owner had returned and was jangling his keys. This musician might be fêted in other places, but that did not stop the proprietor wanting to lock up and go home.

Javier replaced his guitar in its case and snapped it shut.

Outside, he turned toward Mercedes. The temperature had dropped, and in her sweat-soaked dress she shivered with cold. He could see her shaking, and it seemed natural to take his jacket off and put it around her shoulders.

"Look, you take this. I'll come and get it in the morning before I leave," he said gently. "How will I find you?"

"My father's café. El Barril. Just off the Plaza Nueva. Anyone will direct you."

Under the flickering light of the gas lamp, he took a long look at this creature and was puzzled by his own reaction to her. She was a curious mix of child and woman, an adolescent on the brink of adulthood, naïve and yet worldly. He had seen many young flamenco dancers like her, virginal and yet lacking in innocence. Usually their extravagant sexuality vanished the moment they stopped dancing, but with this girl it was different. She exuded a sensuality, the memory of which would keep him awake that night.

Mercedes arrived home and could immediately sense she was in trouble. Emilio had returned an hour before, expecting her to be there, and was now sitting at a table in the bar with his parents. Girls were never allowed out at night unaccompanied, and Concha and Pablo were furious, both with their son for not performing his role of chaperone and also with their daughter. She knew that it was not worth explaining that she had been dancing. It would only provoke the usual lecture on how dancing was going to get her into trouble one day. It was something she did not want to hear.

"And what exactly are you wearing?" demanded Pablo. "That's not yours, is it?"

Mercedes absentmindedly fingered the lapels of Javier's jacket.

"What do you think you are doing, going around wearing a man's jacket?" There was indignation in her father's voice.

She drew the jacket around her. It was suffused with the smell of the *flamenco*, and she breathed deeply, taking its intoxicating fragrance into her lungs. Her father held out his hands, expecting her to remove the offending item of clothing, but she darted past him and ran to her room.

Concha pursued her up the stairs and banged furiously on her door. "Merche! Come out at once!"

The girl knew that she could safely ignore her mother's summons. Everyone was tired and soon they would retire to bed. They could argue again in the morning.

Though it was a warm night, she slept with the jacket wrapped around her, inhaling deeply on the memory of the man who owned it. If she never saw him again, at least she would have this. She would never let it go.

The next morning Javier strolled into the café. It was Saturday so there was no school and Mercedes had been hanging out of her window since she woke up, hoping he might come.

He had lain awake almost the entire night. He could not stop thinking about that young dancer. When he shut his eyes, she was there, and when he opened them, she stayed with him. Such sleeplessness was unusual for him. Most nights he retired to bed exhausted, full of whiskey and cigars.

Unless he was actually in the company of women, he did not spend much time thinking about them. But this girl haunted him. He was glad of the excuse to go and find her again the next day.

He rather hoped that in the daylight she might not be as he remembered. He was mildly irritated with himself. He certainly did not need his life complicated by love. Perhaps the half-light of the previous evening had helped create a fantasy. In either case, he had to get his jacket back. It was his best.

A young man was making coffee at the bar when he went in. It was Emilio. Before Javier had time to speak to him, Mercedes rushed in. She was holding out his jacket. In the daylight, her charm seemed all the greater. Any trace of shyness that had been there the previous night had gone, replaced with the most open and enchanting smile he had ever seen.

Emilio observed them. He had recognized Javier.

"Thank you for lending me this," Mercedes said, holding out the jacket.

How could she keep him there for a moment longer? She was desperate for inspiration.

"Was my dancing all right?" she asked impulsively.

"You are the best non-*gitana*, the best *payo*, that I have ever seen," he answered truthfully.

It was a statement of such extravagance that she found it hard to believe. She blushed, not knowing whether he was teasing or telling the truth.

"If I ever come back, will you dance for me again?"

Her words dried in her throat. The question needed no reply.

They stood, a meter apart, breathing each other's air.

"I have to go now."

Though the desire was there, he could not peck her on the cheek or touch her arm. He knew that such actions were unacceptable, and in any case, he was aware of the watchful gaze of Emilio, who was noisily piling up plates behind the bar.

A moment later, Javier was gone. To her own surprise, Mercedes found that she was not sad. She knew with absolute certainty that she would see him again.

For weeks she waited, thinking of nothing else and trying to retain the memory of his smell.

Eventually a letter arrived. Javier had written to Mercedes via her teacher, La Mariposa. He was returning to Granada and wanted her to perform with him. They could rehearse at the old *bailaora*'s house.

Mercedes agonized. This man was a total stranger to her family, he was half a decade older than she, and, most unacceptably of all, he was a *gitano*, a gypsy. She knew what her parents would say if she asked them. For her there was only one course of action, and that was to do all of this behind their backs. She was prepared to take any risk to dance with Javier again.

Mercedes confided in Emilio, knowing that he would not betray her. He continued to play while she sat on his bed, bubbling over with news of this invitation.

"I will tell our parents," she promised. "But not straightaway. I know they'd only stop me."

Emilio did his best to conceal his resentment. He knew he was being left behind.

Mercedes was insensitive to the implications for her brother and carried on excitedly: "You will come and see us perform, won't you? Even if I can't ask our mother and father, it won't be the same unless you come . . ."

The first time she took her dancing shoes up the hill to María Rodríguez's house to meet Javier, her trembling legs could hardly carry her. How was she going to dance when they shook so much she could scarcely walk?

She reached the old woman's house and, as she always did, lifted the latch without knocking. The interior was dark, as usual, and it would take her eyes a few minutes to adjust. María normally appeared a few moments later, alerted to her arrival by the sound of the door.

Mercedes sat on the old chair by the door and began to change her shoes. Out of the shadows came a voice.

"Hello, Mercedes."

She almost jumped out of her skin. Assuming that she would be the first there, she had completely failed to notice that Javier was already in the room.

She did not even know what to call him. "Javier" seemed too familiar. "Mr. Montero" seemed absurd.

"Oh, hello . . ." her voice said quietly. "Did you have a good journey?"

It was the kind of neutral conversation that she had heard adults having so many times.

"I did, thank you," he replied.

Just then, as if to diffuse the awkwardness of the moment, María came into the room.

"Ah, Mercedes," she said, "you're here. So shall we see some of this dancing? It sounds as though Javier was quite impressed with you last time he came to Granada."

They repeated the *soleá* and the *bulería* from their first meeting, and then Javier played a sequence of other dances for Mercedes. As the hour went by, almost without a break, she relaxed. They almost entirely forgot the presence of María Rodríguez. Occasionally she quietly joined in with the *palmas*, but she did not want to distract them.

Eventually Javier stopped.

"I think that's probably enough for today, isn't it?" the old woman said.

Neither of them seemed to have anything to say.

"So I think another rehearsal, same time next week, and you should be ready to perform together. I'll work on a few things with you, Mercedes, meanwhile. Thank you," she said to Javier, smiling. "I'll see you both next week."

"Yes . . ." said Mercedes. "See you next week."

She looked across at Javier, who was packing away his guitar. His eyes met hers and he seemed to hesitate. There was no doubt that he was on the point of saying something, but he changed his mind.

A moment later he was gone. Within minutes, having changed her shoes, Mercedes, too, was outside on the cobbled street, but Javier had already disappeared. Their contact had been so intimate and yet so distant.

Mercedes' stomach churned with anxiety and confusion. She thought of nothing but Javier and counted not the hours but the minutes until she would see him again. She confided in her friend Paquita.

"Of course he isn't going to think of you in that way," said Paquita. "He's five years older than you! He's nearly Ignacio's age!"

"Well, I don't think of him as a brother," said Mercedes.

"Just be careful, Merche. You know the reputation of those *gitanos* . . ."

"You don't know anything about him," answered Mercedes defensively.

"But neither do you really. Do you?" teased Paquita.

"No. But I know how I feel when I am dancing with him," she said very seriously. "It is as though the whole world is contained in María's small house. Nothing outside it exists or matters."

"And when will you see him again?"

"He's coming back in a week's time. I can't sleep. I can't eat. I can't think of anything else. There *is* nothing else."

"Has he kissed you?" asked Paquita inquisitively.

"No!" exclaimed Mercedes, almost affronted. "Of course he hasn't!"

They were in the courtyard of Paquita's home. Both sat silently for a while. Paquita could not doubt her friend's sincerity. She had never heard her talk in this way. They had both spent many hours of their lives hanging about in the city's squares exchanging flirtatious words and glances with boys their age, but these feelings Mercedes had for Javier Montero appeared to have nothing to do with such childish crushes.

For Mercedes, the days passed with agonizing slowness until the next rehearsal. Concha noticed the dark shadows beneath her daughter's eyes and her listless manner. She also became concerned about the uneaten food on her plate.

"What's the matter, *querida mia?*" she asked. "You look so pale!"

"It's nothing, Mother," she replied. "I had to finish some schoolwork last night."

It was an explanation that satisfied Concha. She had, after all, been nagging Mercedes to take her studies more seriously.

The day for the second rehearsal arrived. Mercedes was almost overcome with nausea when she woke that morning. At five o'clock she went to La Mariposa's house. She was not due there until six, but she wanted to be the first there this time.

Mercedes put on her shoes and warmed her wrists by rotating them round and round and back again, tapping her feet as she sat there to create a rhythm: *one* two, *one* two, *one* two, one two *three*, one two *three*, one two. . .

Still María had not appeared. Mercedes stood up, and her feet resumed the rhythm of the *seguiriya*. She began to turn, and her steel heel-caps hammered on the floorboards of this tiny house. There was only just enough room for her hands to stretch upward without touching the ceiling, and the walls could scarcely contain the volume of noise that she was making. As she twirled, Javier's playing filled her imagination.

Though Mercedes was oblivious to the racket she was making, it was audible in the street outside. For a few moments, Javier stood watching her through the window. What he could see was a young woman entirely lost in her own world, almost hypnotized by the rhythm of her own movements. What he could not see was the vision of himself that filled Mercedes' imagination.

In her mind he sat on the low chair in that room almost shredding his fingers with the passion of his playing.

Perhaps five or six minutes went by as she performed her private, solemn dance. He was transfixed not merely by the sight of the raw emotion she expressed so openly and so unreservedly; but by the lack of inhibition that was only possible in one who was dancing unobserved. What also held his attention was this combination of technical virtuosity with something that seemed almost wild. As she spun round and round and round again, she was like a creature possessed. Javier knew that to make those disciplined, precisely practiced steps appear improvised was almost impossible. This girl was achieving it, and watching her thrilled him to the core of his being. Such *duende* was so rare. It was like an electric current passing through him.

A moment before Mercedes stopped dancing, he felt a tap on his shoulder. María Rodríguez. He had no idea how long she had been standing there and whether she had observed him spying on Mercedes. He did not ask. He felt like a voyeur.

"Let me take that from you," he said, taking her basket of shopping to cover his embarrassment. "It looks heavy."

"Thank you," said the old woman, acknowledging his gesture.

"I don't know where she gets this fury from. It just rages up from inside her. And then she channels it into her dancing. You clearly recognize that this girl is exceptional."

He nodded. Her comments were enough to indicate to Javier that María knew he had been watching her young protégée.

When María opened her door, Mercedes was still panting from the exertion of the dance. She was virtually steaming. She gave a shy smile, which for Javier seemed at odds with the overt sexuality that he had witnessed through the windowpane.

Mercedes had thought obsessively of this *guitarrista* in the past week, and it seemed natural that he should be back there, sitting on the low chair tuning his guitar. It was as though neither of them had moved from this very room in seven days.

They exchanged a few polite words of greeting, and María Rodríguez took a seat in the corner of the room, ready to listen and observe.

"What would you like me to play?" asked Javier.

"A *seguiriya*," she said firmly.

Javier bent his head low over his guitar and smiled to himself.

Mercedes picked up the rhythm from his introductory chords and soon she was dancing.

Whenever Mercedes glanced at Javier, he was utterly absorbed in his playing, and when he looked up to watch her, she seemed far away. They were unaware of each other's interest.

This time, as Javier looked up to observe, he noted that her movements were crisp and her timing exact. Her *zapateado*, the quick toe, sole and heel movements, were as faultless as before, but she held something back this time. She seemed more reserved, shy, like her smile. When he glanced across to where María had been sitting, he saw that she had disappeared from the room. He stopped playing, emboldened by the absence of their chaperone.

"Come and sit down," he instructed her gently, indicating the empty chair next to his.

Mercedes was surprised by the sudden cessation of his playing and his invitation. They had never sat so close to each other before. She did not hesitate for a moment. Even if she did not always do what she was told, she was used to being given instructions by adults.

Once she was sitting down, he reached out and took her hand. It trembled violently against his own. He suddenly realized that he had nothing in particular that he wanted to say and that it was purely for the opportunity to hold her hand that he had stopped her dancing.

"You dance so beautifully, Merche."

It was all he could think of to say.

He held her hand tightly, and then, in a moment that seemed one of madness even to himself, he brought it to his lips and kissed not the back of it but the palm. Even for someone who had bedded dozens of women, it was a gesture of surprising intimacy.

Instinctively, Mercedes gave him her other hand and Javier held them both in his. They sat like this for a moment, their eyes meeting for the first time, and nothing needed to be said.

When María came back into the room, Mercedes got to her feet. Javier resumed his playing, and within the hour they had gone their separate ways once again. In spite of his gypsy blood, Javier knew where the boundaries lay.

Their first performance together was the following week, but in the meantime there was an important date in Mercedes' diary.

Three days before she was due to meet Javier again, it was her sixteenth birthday. Her family celebrated, and as she had long been promised, a large, soft parcel was waiting for her on the café table at breakfast time that day.

She tore the paper open, and as she did so, folds of a magnificent flamenco dress billowed out. It was a classic design, black spots on a red background, exactly the one she had always dreamed of having, and she held it up to herself and twirled round. For a moment after she had come to a stop, the wired tiers seemed to have a life all of their own and continued to bounce from side to side and up and down.

"Thank you, thank you!" she cried in appreciation, hugging both her mother and the dress.

It was warming to see and feel her daughter's excitement, but Concha silently rued Mercedes' passion for her dancing. She had noticed that her daughter was spending even more time than ever with María Rodríguez.

Before their first performance, Mercedes and Javier were to meet at María's house. It was a few steps from the *cueva* where a crowd was already gathering. Most of them were drawn by the *tocaor*'s reputation, but some of them were intrigued by the combination of the great man from Málaga with this local girl.

As Javier arrived, Mercedes appeared from María's back room where she had been changing.

The dress fit perfectly around every curve of her body, closely following the contours of breasts and hips. It was a stunning transfiguration, and she was fully aware of the impression she made on Javier as she entered the room swathed in scarlet, her cheeks flushed with excitement.

"You look . . . wonderful," he said.

"Thank you," she replied, knowing that it was true.

She came up close to him now, full of courage and eager anticipation for their performance.

Without hesitating, he reached out and stroked her hair, and as she

took another step toward him, she felt his fingers touch her chin. Instinctively, she tilted her head upward.

Javier's kiss shocked her with its strength and intensity. Mercedes had
been kissed only once before on the mouth, and it had been a disappointment. This was an embrace that surged through her, body, mind, and
soul. Whether it lasted for minutes or only seconds had no relevance.
It was powerful enough to feel as though her life now divided into two:
before and after the feel of his soft lips on hers.

It was time for them to go. María Rodríguez, who had known what
had to happen between these two before they did, walked up toward the
*cueva* with them.

No one was disappointed. Mercedes danced with more intensity than
ever before. The *guitarrista* and *bailaora* were perfectly paired.

At a second performance, the *cueva* overflowed. Emilio was there to
see them this time, and even he, predisposed to criticize this man who
had usurped his role, could see that this was a remarkable partnership. At
times, the spark between Mercedes and Javier could have ignited a blaze.
Emilio slipped away before the applause died down. The last thing he
wanted was for his sister to notice he had even been there, and even less
so for her to see his reaction.

While Pablo and Concha thought their daughter was in her room
finally getting round to doing some schoolwork, she was dancing with
Javier Montero in the Sacromonte. It was only a matter of time before
someone mentioned it to them, and sure enough they did.

"You are only just *sixteen*!" shouted her father, when she returned
that night. She had hoped her parents would already be in bed, but she
found them sitting waiting for her. Pablo's anger made an even greater
impact because it was so rare.

"All I'm doing is *dancing*!" she defended herself.

"But how old is this man? He should know better," continued Pablo.

"You've been very deceitful," reprimanded Concha.

"You're a disgrace!" Ignacio, who had arrived home moments earlier,
joined in. "Dancing with a bloody *gypsy*!"

Mercedes knew it was pointless trying to defend herself. She was under attack from all sides.

Emilio was the only person who understood this compulsion of hers, but he had sensed the brewing storm and withdrawn to his room. Because he had been displaced by an outsider, his own resentment continued to brew. Filial love had been swept aside by the infatuation that now dominated his sister's every waking moment.

"Just go to your room. And don't come out," ordered Pablo.

Without argument, Mercedes did exactly as she was told. Javier had traveled back to Málaga that night so there was no reason to leave it.

For two days Mercedes stayed upstairs, and Concha left meals outside her door. An hour later she would return to find them untouched.

Eating was the very last thing Mercedes felt like doing. She lay on her bed and wore herself out with weeping. In one move, her parents had taken away the two things that were at the center of her life: dancing and Javier. If she could not dance with her *gitano*, she was not going to dance at all. And if she could not dance, she could not bear to live.

Emilio knocked at her door late one afternoon and went in. Mercedes sat up when she saw him. Her eyes were swollen with crying.

He stood at the end of her bed, his arms folded. "Look," he said, "I understand how you feel."

Mercedes blinked at him. "Do you?" she asked quietly.

"Yes," he said. "And I am going to talk to our parents. I've seen you dancing with Javier, and that sort of performance doesn't happen every day."

"What do you mean?"

"It was . . . um . . ." Emilio struggled. He suddenly felt awkward in front of his sister.

"It was what?"

"It was . . . perfection. Or something close to it. Between you and . . . him."

Mercedes did not know how to react to her brother's clumsy compliment. She could see how much it had cost him to say it.

Emilio was true to his word. He took his father to one side, knowing that, of the two of them, Pablo was less vehemently against Mercedes' dancing than Concha.

"You can't just put a stop to something like this," he said to his father. "Nothing can stand in its way."

Emilio's representations on Mercedes' behalf made Pablo reconsider. Even his description of the way Mercedes danced made her father proud, and, within a few days, Concha, albeit reluctantly, had agreed to meet Javier.

CHAPTER 14

During the few weeks while these negotiations were going on, Mercedes' obsession with dance had increased. There was nothing else in life that she wanted to do.

Letters were exchanged, and one day Javier arrived at El Barril. For an hour he talked with Pablo.

In spite of himself, Señor Ramírez warmed to this young man. There was no doubt that he was a serious member of the flamenco scene, and Pablo's view of the situation began to shift. Javier Montero had played not just in Granada and Málaga but in Córdoba, Sevilla, and Madrid. He even had forthcoming engagements in Bilbao, the home of his celebrated *guitarrista* uncle.

Eventually Concha appeared and introductions were made. She was not predisposed to liking Javier, but it was impossible to do otherwise. There was a sincerity in his manner that shone out and, sometime later, when she eventually heard him performing, she knew that it was this same quality that gave his playing such power.

Mercedes was not allowed to leave her room while Javier was there. Maternal fury was not so easily dispelled.

Javier was bold. He made it clear that he wished to continue playing for Mercedes in Granada, but he wanted more than that. He wanted to take her to other cities. He did not tell Mercedes' parents as much, but he felt his whole life was held in limbo. As far as he was concerned, his future was in their hands, dependent on whether or not Mercedes could continue to dance for him, and he to play for her.

After an hour or so, their meeting came to an end. Speaking for himself and his wife, Pablo agreed to consider Montero's request.

Concha was very concerned. Having Mercedes dancing with Emilio was safe, but this was another matter altogether.

"How do we know where all this will lead?" she said to Pablo. "She's only just sixteen and he's almost five years older!"

Since he had now met Javier, Pablo's views had changed. He smiled.

"And what is the age difference between *us*?" he inquired wryly.

Concha did not reply. It was at least a decade.

"What is the subject of this conversation?" asked Pablo. "Are we just talking about dance? Or do you think there is something more?"

Concha thought of her daughter's hollow eyes and uneaten meals. Hard as she tried, she found it difficult to attribute these things to a ban on dancing. She was not a heartless woman and had once known that same intense, all-consuming love herself, even if it had grown quieter with the years.

"What is it that worries you more?" asked Pablo. "Our daughter's love of dancing or the possibility of her falling for this man?"

"Well, we can't ask her that," said Concha flatly.

"And anyway, the two things might be bound up together," mused Pablo.

"You know I wanted her to expand her horizons," lamented Concha, "but not quite in this way."

"Is there really a choice? If we don't let her dance with Javier, what else do you think she is going to do? Sit in her room like a good student?"

Antonio had come in.

"What do you think?" Concha asked him.

"Are you sure you want my opinion, Mother?"

His mother nodded. He hesitated to take sides in a dispute between his parents, but clearly a casting vote was needed.

"My view is this. One of the reasons her dancing affects people is that they witness this extraordinary determination," he said. "And that same determination will never allow anyone to get between her and this *flamenco.* You're fighting a losing battle if you try to stop her."

Her mother was silent for a while as she reflected on what Antonio had just said.

"Well, as long as you chaperone her, Pablo, I suppose I shall have to put up with it."

A while later, Mercedes came downstairs. The girl was pale. She knew her future had been discussed that afternoon.

Her parents were both in the bar.

"We met Javier today," said Pablo, telling her something she already knew. "And we liked him."

"But can I dance with him again?" she asked impatiently. It was all she wanted to know.

Mercedes was overjoyed when she heard of her parents' decision.

A week later, she packed her bag. A crisp new flamenco dress spilled out. Antonio had given her some money to buy it.

"I think you'll need a spare," he had said, kissing her on the forehead.

Mercedes and her father traveled on a bus to Málaga. They were to be away for three days. It was the farthest distance she had ever traveled, the longest time she had ever been alone with her father, and the first time she had danced away from her home city. Even without the prospect of seeing Javier, everything about this trip to the bustling friendly city of Málaga was an adventure. They rented a room close to where Javier lived, and on the first morning he collected them for a rehearsal, which was to be in the backroom of the café where they were to perform that night.

Pablo was amazed by the transformation in his daughter's dancing. He sat, mesmerized, as they went through their repertoire of tangos, fandangos, *alegrías*, and *soleares*. This was a different Mercedes from the one he had seen dancing at a fiesta only a few months before. The little girl had become a young woman.

That night they were on a stage set up in the café and the audience was receptive. Javier was familiar to them, as was his father, Raul, who played at the beginning of the evening.

Mercedes was more nervous than she had even been in Granada. Everything was so unfamiliar. She was sure the audience would not like her, but the performance went as well as the rehearsal. No one failed to appreciate the grace and energy of her dancing, the fineness of her hand movements, the love, the fear, and the fury that she expressed through them all.

Neither of them could stop smiling, an expression that was so at odds with the mood of much of the music and dancing. They could not stop themselves. Mercedes felt euphoric and, when she saw the pride on her father's face, was unafraid to show it.

At the end of the evening, a photographer wanted to take pictures of them, together and separately. The following morning when Javier came to meet Mercedes, he had a set of portraits for her.

"You can show them to your mother," he said. "You look beautiful in them!"

"But there isn't one of you!" she protested. "I want a photograph of you!"

"I'm sure your mother doesn't!" he teased.

"It isn't *for* my mother," she said.

"I'll swap you a photograph," he said. "I want one of you as well."

In every photograph, the subjects beamed almost from ear to ear.

The second night's performance was in Málaga's movie theater. It was a much bigger room than the café, and the stage was higher. As she waited in the wings behind some thick red curtains, Mercedes' anxiety almost got the better of her.

Javier took her hand gently and lifted it to his lips.

"You will be fine, my sweet, you will be fine. Don't worry. They will love you."

His tender concern gave her courage. After only a minute or so on stage, she heard a murmured *"Olé"* and knew that the audience was with her. There was no playacting of emotion in her dancing. In her mind, she merely re-created the anguish of separation from Javier, and the passion she required to dance poured out of her.

It was another magnificent performance. The local paper described it as a "triumph," and their photographs appeared on the front page.

Pablo was persuaded to travel with his daughter on some future engagements and Mercedes' career and reputation grew. As did her devotion to the *guitarrista*. Their love was absolutely mutual, as equal as their limelight on the shared stage. When they were apart, both of them counted the days until they would be reunited.

Emilio tried to hide his sense of rejection. He stayed at home playing his guitar much less now that he did not have his sister's encouragement. When he was not working, he did not want to hang around in El Barril, especially when Ignacio was about.

A favorite haunt of his was the Café Alameda in the Plaza Campillo, a place much frequented by artists, writers, and musicians. Without ever having the nerve to join his table, Emilio and his friend Alejandro would sit on the periphery of Lorca's circle, a coterie known as El Rinconcillo, simply because it usually occupied the "corner" of the room.

Lorca was a regular visitor to Granada. He spent as much time as he could with his family on the outskirts of the city, and his arrival there was considered significant enough to be mentioned in the local papers. Drawn there by the anguish and mystery of Andalusian culture, Lorca embraced flamenco as an embodiment of everything the region stood for. He had friends who were flamenco dancers and *gitano* companions who were guitarists and taught him to strum in the gypsy style. For Lorca this place felt like home, and the way in which people lived there inspired his work.

Emilio's admiration of Lorca was little short of hero worship. He was happy to be in the shadow of his shadow, and on the occasions when Lorca cast a dazzling smile in his direction, Emilio felt as though his glowing heart might burn right through his shirt. He loved everything Lorca produced, from his poetry and plays to his music and drawings. But perhaps what he admired above all was his openness about his sexuality. *Perhaps I shall have the same nerve one day*, he thought to himself.

Ignacio used his brother's attachment to the Café Alameda as an excuse to goad him. During the long winter months when Ignacio had no cause to be away in other cities for bullfights, he would spend long nights of drinking with his banderillero friends and return belligerently drunk. With too little to occupy them, some of these boys became indolent in the cold months. Like a few of the others, Ignacio was waiting for his next chance in the bullring.

Emilio would wince when he heard the characteristic slam of the door, long after El Barril itself had closed. If he heard whistling, too, it was a bad sign. It was his brother's way of feigning nonchalance before he made trouble, and Ignacio was in the mood to do so on this particular night.

"How is El Maricón today then?" asked Ignacio, using a derogatory expression to refer to Lorca. In the snide way he phrased the question, he managed to call his brother a "fag," too, knowing that he would not retaliate.

This taunting of Emilio made Antonio hate Ignacio more than ever.

"Why don't you just leave him alone?" shouted Antonio. His anger was not only for the way he abused his brother. Ignacio's hatred of homosexuals represented a more general bigotry that was common to many on the right wing of politics. Theirs was a narrow, macho, and intolerant vision.

The country's politics continued to be troubled, and Antonio was glad when he heard that there was talk on the left wing of a coalition. The appalling events in Asturias eighteen months earlier had made the left realize they needed political unity to get back into power. They wanted to give themselves a fresh start and put social justice at the top of their agenda to appeal to the average voter. It had been a tense few months in the Ramírez household, not just because of the personality clashes between the brothers but because of their political differences too.

Elections were held in February of 1936, and across the country as a whole, the socialists gained the majority of votes. In Granada, things were not so simple. The right-wing party won, but following claims of intimidation and infringements of the law, the results were annuled. Clashes broke out between right-wingers and trade union members, and antagonism between the parties intensified. In Granada churches were gutted, newspaper offices were wrecked, and the theater was destroyed by fire. The way Ignacio reacted, anyone would have thought that Emilio had personally struck the match.

Concha tried to calm the storm that raged in her own household, but the situation both inside their home and in the wider world did not improve. That summer a sequence of events triggered an outbreak of widespread violence. After a police lieutenant was gunned down by four Fascists outside his house in Madrid, the leader of the right-wing monarchist party, Calvo Sotelo, was killed in revenge. A shoot-out followed between police Assault Guards and Fascist militia near the cemetery in the capital city where both funerals were taking place, and four people were killed. The political temperature was high and tensions even higher.

Mercedes was preoccupied with her next flamenco engagement and counting the days until she next saw Javier. Now that she had left school, their performances could have been more frequent, particularly with the number of requests that they received, but Pablo was only prepared to leave El Barril for a few days each month. She had ceased to notice the growing dissent between her brothers and was unaware of the turbulence in the country as a whole. A series of performances was scheduled in Cádiz for July, and she was busy mastering some new steps, spending hours each day cocooned with María Rodríguez, enveloped in the warm anticipation of seeing Javier again in a week or so.

Alone in her room, Mercedes would gaze at the photograph of her *guitarra* propped against her bedside lamp. His strong cheekbones and the shock of straight glossy hair, a slim strand of it across one eye, seemed more beautiful to her every time she looked at the picture. The camera lens had captured so well the directness of his gaze, and the power of those smiling eyes reached down into the depths of her.

Meanwhile, the rest of her family watched the gathering storm. They had heard the distant rumbles, but none of them had foreseen its scale.

# CHAPTER 15

July 17, 1936 was a typical summer's day in Granada. The heat was blistering. Shutters were down to keep out heat, light, and dust. There was listlessness in the air. No one knew what to do with themselves.

Concha and Mercedes sat outside the café under the shade of the awning.

"It's even warmer outside than it is indoors," said Señora Ramírez. "There's nothing cooling in that breeze."

"It's just too hot to do anything," responded Mercedes. "I'm going to lie on my bed."

As Mercedes rose, her mother noticed that her daughter's dress was transparent with sweat. She got up, too, and gathered their glasses onto a tray. There were no customers that afternoon. The square was devoid of life and the leaves on the trees crackled in the breeze, so dried out in these oven-hot temperatures that some had already begun to fall.

The city's siesta was as deep as a coma. Mercedes was almost unconscious until well beyond six o'clock that evening, when the mercury fell for the first time since midday. Even for Granadinos these were soaring temperatures. In a feverish sleep, she had a vivid dream that Javier and she were dancing in the bar downstairs, and when she awoke, there was a moment of sadness at realizing he was a hundred kilometers away in Málaga.

The next day, customers coming into El Barril each reported a different version of the rumors that military movement was taking place across the water in North Africa. There was some confusion at the time, with one radio broadcast announcing one thing and another contradicting it, but the truth soon became apparent. A group of army generals were rebelling against the government and staging a *coup d'état*.

Under the leadership of General Francisco Franco, the Army of Africa, comprising foreign legionaries and a fighting force of Moroccan mercenaries, were to be transported across the strait from Spanish Morocco to mainland Spain. Once they had landed, generals in army garrisons across Spain were to stage a rising in their own towns and cities and proclaim a state of war.

Granada melted in 100 degrees of heat, cobbles burned through shoe leather, and the mountains disappeared in a shimmering haze. That morning, the local paper, *El Ideal*, had carried an announcement on the front page that they could not bring any general news "owing to forces beyond our control."

In the café, Pablo was agitated. "Something's really wrong, Concha, I know it is," he said, pointing to the headline.

"It's nothing, Pablo. Probably a strike or something. The government isn't going to lose control. Don't worry so much." She tried to reassure him, but he was unconvinced.

Pablo's sense of ill-ease was well founded, as both of them really knew. The government's claim that on the mainland business was as usual, in spite of a military *pronunciamiento* in Morocco, did not reassure them.

It seemed at odds with the rumor that a certain General Queipo de Llano had seized command of the garrison in Sevilla and, with only one hundred or so soldiers, had swiftly taken over the city.

"So how can they tell us that everything is normal?" Pablo said to anyone listening.

Like those in many other towns, the people of Granada felt vulnerable. They demanded weapons from the government, but to everyone's dismay, the Prime Minister, Casares Quiroga, had forbidden the distribution of arms to the people and was absolutely adamant that what had happened in Sevilla did not affect the rest of the country. He maintained that everywhere else, the army remained loyal to the government.

On a different radio wave, the voice of General Queipo de Llano could be heard shrieking his victorious message. Except for Madrid and Barcelona, he raved, the whole of Spain was now in the hands of Nationalist troops. Neither of these contradictory messages was accurate, and they left the people of Spain in total confusion.

In Granada, there was considerable alarm. Rumors were spreading that, in Sevilla, people opposing army rule were being massacred and thousands more were being detained. Suddenly, neighbors who had seemed to support the Republic came out against it. Pablo and Concha could feel it in the café, even on the morning of the eighteenth. Customers did not know whether to trust each other, or even whether to trust Pablo and Concha themselves. The ground had shifted beneath their feet.

The fate of individual towns and cities seemed to depend on whether their army garrison remained loyal to the Republican government. In Granada, a new military commander had arrived in the city only six days earlier. General Campins was staunchly loyal to the Republic and firmly, if naïvely, believed his officers would not rebel and join Franco's cause. The workers were not so confident, but when they asked to be armed in case the army rebelled, their civil governor, Torres Martínez, followed government instructions and refused to distribute weapons.

Most of the Ramírez family was still awake at two o'clock on the morning of the nineteenth. No one had any intention of sleeping, even if the stifling heat of the day had allowed them.

"But why won't they give us any weapons? Who's to say that those soldiers aren't going to turn on us?" Antonio demanded of his father.

"Come on, Antonio!" his father urged him. "That's exactly the point. What good will it do to have all you young men running about in the city brandishing guns that you don't even know how to use? Eh? Tell me what good it would do!"

"Try not to be so anxious," urged his mother. "We must keep calm and just see what happens."

"But listen!" bellowed Antonio, disappearing to turn up the dial on the radio they kept in the cramped office behind the bar. "Listen to this!"

The voice of Queipo de Llano echoed around the bar, as he bellowed his list of towns where the Nationalists were already victorious.

"We can't just sit here and let this happen, can we?" As he appealed to his parents for even the slightest sign of agreement or support, Antonio's eyes filled with tears of frustration.

"Perhaps Mother is right," suggested Mercedes. "It's probably best not to get too worked up about it. Everything seems to be all right here so far, doesn't it?"

Antonio's reaction was not just born out of the youthful desire to wield a weapon. He had heard that it was not only the military that should be causing anxiety to Martínez. There were two other key players in this unfolding drama: the blue-uniformed Assault Guard and the green-clad Civil Guard.

Though both of these gendarmeries theoretically owed allegiance to the civil authority, their loyalty to the Republic also turned out to be questionable. The disloyalty of the Civil Guard to the government in most places was unsurprising, but the support of the Assault Guard, which had been formed and organized under the Republic, might have been expected. Antonio had heard that in Granada a conspiracy against the Republic was brewing in both these forces. In the Civil Guard, Lieutenant Pelayo was plotting, as was Captain Álvarez of the Assault Guard.

Even if Martínez and Campins had not fully grasped the situation, the workers sensed that something was afoot, and that night a huge group gathered in one of the city's most central squares, the Plaza del Carmen. Granada was like a pressure cooker with its contents almost at boiling point. At any minute it seemed as if the lid could be thrown sky-high by the force of an explosion.

They were mostly manual workers and, without the lethargy-inducing heat, their anger would have tipped them into earlier action. People were desperate for weapons. Anything would do. In order to arm themselves, men wiped dust from the oldest of pistols. Soon the streets were full of boys and men ready to fight, and even those who had never given more than a passing nod to politics found themselves whipped up into a frenzy of sympathy for the Republic.

Antonio and his two friends Salvador and Francisco went to the Plaza del Carmen to see what was going on. Everywhere they looked they saw men brandishing weapons, even up on the rooftops. At this point, the troops were still confined to their barracks. No one knew where the power lay or what was going to happen, but the city was brimful of tension and fear.

In the early hours of July 20, the plans for the rebellion in Granada were finalized. Captain Álvarez committed the support of his Assault Guards to the leader of the rebels within the army garrison.

Right up to that very afternoon, the members of the civil government had been unaware of what was brewing. Martínez was meeting with some of his supporters, including Antonio Rus Romero, Secretary of the Popular Front, and also the head of the Civil Guard. At some point, a message came through to Romero that the troops were lining up in the barracks and getting ready to march. Campins received a phone call telling him the situation and was incredulous. He maintained that the troops had sworn they would be loyal, but he would visit the barracks immediately to see for himself. When he arrived, he was shocked to find that not only had the artillery troops rebelled but the infantry regiment, the Civil Guard, and the Assault Guard had also come out against the Republic.

Campins was now a prisoner and, worse, was forced to sign a document drawn up for him that declared a state of war. The papers also outlined the punishments for anyone who did not comply with the new regime, crimes ranging from possessing firearms to gathering in groups of more than three people.

The citizens of Granada had no real information, but late in the afternoon, when the city was quiet and all the shops were still shut for siesta, some trucks trundled through the sleepy streets carrying stern-faced army troops with eyes focused neither to right nor left. Behind them came artillery. Some people misunderstood the reason for their presence in the street, believing them to have come out to fight against the Fascists, and a few in their ignorance saluted them.

It was the sound of these trucks and the grating of their gears that disturbed Concha's siesta. She was dozing in her darkened bedroom over-looking the street, and immediately awoke Pablo. They opened one of the shutters just enough to observe what was going on below their window and stood close enough to feel each other's hot breath in the dark room. If the soldiers looked up, they would have seen them, though the roar of the engines would have drowned out the sound of Concha's voice.

"Holy Mary," she whispered, her fingers tightening around her hus-band's arm. "It's happening. It's really happening."

Something was taking place in front of them that had been rumored for days. Concha felt panic rise inside her.

"Where are the children? Where are they? We need to find them."

Concha's immediate response was to gather her family together, and her anxiety was scarcely concealed. The sight of these armed brigades, whoever they supported and whatever their orders, meant that no one's safety was guaranteed.

"Antonio is out somewhere—maybe Ignacio too. But the others are in their rooms, I think," Pablo replied, running out onto the landing to begin checking the bedrooms.

Though the children were all stronger and sturdier than their parents, the need to know the whereabouts of their offspring was primitive and compelling for Pablo and Concha. They ran from room to room, waking both Mercedes and Emilio, before they found Ignacio's bed was empty.

"I can tell you where he is . . ." muttered Emilio sleepily, stumbling down the stairs from his attic room.

"Where? *Where* do you think he is?" asked his mother anxiously.

"With that Elvira woman probably."

"I don't want to know that, Emilio. Now isn't the time for talking like that about your brother."

Elvira was the wife of one of Granada's most celebrated matadors, Pedro Delgado, and Ignacio's long afternoons with her had been the sub-ject of much gossip. According to Ignacio, the older man was as aware as anyone of the situation, and when he was out of town, he more or less left her to be taken care of by his protégé, the young Ramírez. This did not validate the situation. Before marrying, Elvira had been a prostitute, albeit a high-class one, and whatever else Concha Ramírez thought of her son's behavior, this was what appalled her most.

"All right then," answered Emilio snappily. "But that's where you'll find him if you want to."

Even with Fascist troops beginning to fill the streets, Emilio could not allow an opportunity to denigrate his brother slip by.

Antonio was not at home either. No one had seen him that day.

They all gathered around the narrow gap between the long shutters in the master bedroom. Mercedes stood on the bed, a hand on each of her father's shoulders to balance, eager to catch a glimpse of what was happening down in the square. The last of the troops had gone by, and now it seemed unnervingly still.

"What's going on, Emilio? Are they still out there?" Mercedes' voice was all too audible in the silence. "I can't see. I can't see!"

"Ssh, Merche," said her father, gesticulating that she should keep her mouth shut.

He had made out the sound of muffled voices only a few doors up the street from them, and now they all heard the unmistakable sound of gunshots.

One-two-three.

Inwardly, they all counted the rhythmic, even, bullet beats. At that moment, their world began to alter. The sound of firing would punctuate their waking hours and penetrate their sleep for a long time to come.

Voices came from down in the street right below them, outside the café itself, but unless they leaned out, it was impossible to identify the speakers. Before long, their curiosity was satisfied. Two men were marched out across the square, arms raised in the air.

"They've come from the Pérez house. It's Luis and one of the boys! It's Luis and Julio!" gasped Concha. "My God. Look, they're taking them away. They're actually taking them away . . ."

Her voice trailed off. It was hard for all of them to take in the sight of innocent men under arrest and being led away by soldiers. It was with some disbelief that they faced the significance of this moment.

"They've done it, haven't they? The army have taken over," said Emilio flatly.

It was a situation that those who had been unimpressed by the Republican government had long since hoped for, but for supporters of a democratically elected party it was almost beyond belief that the rule of law should have been overturned before their very eyes.

With horror, the Ramírez family watched their friends being marched away. Once they were out of sight, the family withdrew from the window and stood around in the semidarkness.

Concha closed the shutters and sank onto the bed. "What are we going to do?" she asked, looking around at the silhouetted forms of her husband and children.

The question was rhetorical. There was no action they could sensibly take, apart from staying in their home and waiting to see what happened next.

Not long afterward, Antonio returned. He listened with disbelief as they described how Luis Pérez and his son had been taken away.

"But why have they arrested them? On what grounds?"

"Who knows?" answered his father. "But we had better go round and see María and Francisco later."

"Are you sure that's wise?" asked Concha, a note of cautious self-preservation creeping in.

Antonio then told his family what he had seen out on the streets that day, and especially of the moment when he realized that the army had rebelled.

Along with Francisco and Salvador, he had been in the crowd that had amassed in the Plaza del Carmen. He described the moment of confusion when news had reached them that the troops were out of their quarters and marching toward the square.

"We assumed that the soldiers coming in our direction were there to ensure public order and defend the Republic," he said. "But we soon realized our mistake."

The intentions of the military became all too clear. With a cannon and machine guns now in position in front of the town hall, the crowd had had two options: to disperse or to be fired on.

"We just weren't ready to face anything like that," Antonio continued. "Francisco thought we were a bunch of cowards running away, but we wouldn't have had a chance!"

"So what happened?" asked Mercedes.

"We fled down a side street, and then all we heard was the sound of gunfire."

"I think we probably heard it too," Emilio said.

"And now," concluded Antonio, "there are artillery batteries occupying every strategic point around the town: the Plaza del Carmen, the Puerta Real, and the Plaza de la Trinidad. And you didn't believe me this morning, Father! If only we'd been given some weapons, we could have stopped all this!"

Both his parents shook their heads.

"It's awful, it's awful," said Pablo, looking at the floor. "We just didn't think it could really happen."

Antonio told them everything else that he had heard. Torres Martínez was apparently under house arrest—"If he had been more on top of the situation," grumbled Antonio, "we might not be in this mess"—and Valdes had taken over the post of Civil Governor. All of this seemed to have been achieved without the slightest resistance. Antonio had also heard the rumor that the town hall had been taken over, and the mayor, Manuel Fernandez-Montesinos, who was Lorca's brother-in-law, had been dramatically arrested during a meeting with fellow councillors and locked up.

They sat and puzzled over what the humble locksmith, Luis Pérez, and his son had in common with the well-connected socialist mayor of the city, but people from all walks of life were being marched from their homes for arbitrary reasons. Intellectuals, artists, workers, and freemasons were among the six thousand or so of those arrested in the first week. Being a known left-wing supporter or a member of a trade union now put a person's life in danger. Antonio decided to keep to himself what he knew about the politics of Francisco's older brother, Julio. Even Luis himself might not have known of his son's membership in a communist organization.

"The worst thing of all," declared Pablo, "is that both the Civil Guard *and* the Assault Guard are now on the rebels' side."

"You keep saying that, Pablo, but I don't believe you," Concha protested.

"I'm afraid he's right, Mother. I've seen a few of them out there in the street talking to groups of soldiers. They certainly didn't look as though they were on different sides," confirmed Antonio.

Antonio now sought to reassure his mother about what seemed to worry her most of all: that Ignacio was safe.

"He'll be back soon," he told them. "I'm quite sure of that."

At around midnight, when everyone but Concha had fallen into a fitful sleep, Antonio was proved right. Ignacio arrived home.

"You're back," said his mother, appearing at her bedroom door. "We've been so worried about you. You wouldn't believe what's been going on today—here in this very street."

"Everything's going to be fine," said Ignacio blithely, taking his mother into his arms and planting a kiss on her forehead. "Really it is."

Though he could not see it in the darkness, her face registered some confusion. Had Ignacio been so entwined with his lover that the events of the day had passed him by? She did not have the chance to ask him. He had taken the stairs two by two and closed his door behind him. There was always the morning, she thought to herself. Nothing would have changed by then.

# CHAPTER 16

Next morning, the streets were deserted. Shops and cafés kept their doors locked, and the tension inside every home spread eerily into the empty streets.

The takeover of Radio Granada gave the Nationalist cause a perfect medium to broadcast their version of the previous day's events. *El Ideal* reinforced the same news stories and gloated over the easily won success of the rebel army forces and the fact that so many middle-class citizens of Granada had come out in support of Franco.

The Ramírez family stayed indoors, the café doors firmly bolted and the wooden shutters fastened. They took turns watching from the first-floor windows, and the day was broken up with the passing of truckloads of troops and the regular sound of a voice crying out: "Long live Spain! Death to the Republic!"

Emilio sat on his bed strumming chords. Although he was apparently indifferent to the events going on outside, his stomach nevertheless churned with fear. He played until his fingers were sore, drowning out the sound of gunfire with his passionate *seguiriyas* and *soleares*.

Even Antonio, usually patient with his brother, was dismayed by Emilio's convincingly feigned lack of interest in the military coup.

"Doesn't he know what this could mean?" he pleaded to his father as they toyed with lunch that day, a meager meal of cheese and olives. They had decided not to risk a potentially fruitless and dangerous outing to find bread. Emilio was not hungry and had stayed in his room.

"Of course he doesn't," sneered Ignacio. "He's in his own little *fairy-tale* world as usual."

Everyone in the family but Ignacio turned a blind eye to Emilio's homosexuality so no one reacted to his jibe. Just once, a few months before, Concha and Pablo had finally discussed their concerns with each other. Even in the more liberal climate of the early days of the Republic, attitudes to homosexuality had not changed in Granada.

"Let's just hope he grows out of it," Pablo had said.

Concha had nodded. Her husband assumed this was in affirmation and the subject was never raised again.

Like everyone on the side of the Republic in the city, they had lost their appetite for food, if not for news. On the radio they picked up that the airfield at Armilla had been taken and that the big explosives factory on the road to Murcia was now in the hands of the Nationalists. Both were considered of huge strategic importance, and those who wanted life to revert to normal now began to resign themselves to the idea of a new regime in their city.

Mercedes opened her window at dusk that day and leaned out to catch a breath of air. Swifts crossed the sky in front of her, and bats darted to and fro. The events of the previous night—the sounds of gunshots and the sight of their neighbors being taken away—lingered with her, but her thoughts were elsewhere.

"Javier, Javier, Javier," she whispered into the night. The yellow light from the gas lamp below her window flickered with the gusts of warm air, and a moth twirled in its momentary brightness. She yearned to dance and could think of nothing except when she might see her *guitarrista* again. Five weeks had passed since she had seen Javier, and only the memory of their last kiss sustained her. If only this emergency could end so that they could be together, she thought.

Faintly, escaping through the roof tiles and into the creamy atmosphere, she could hear the sound of Emilio's playing. She climbed the stairs for the first time in a while, drawn to the comforting sound of his music. Only now did it occur to her that he might have felt abandoned when she had started dancing with Javier, and she was unsure whether he would welcome her intrusion.

He said nothing when she entered the room but continued to play, which had always been his way when, as a little girl, she had first invaded his privacy. The hours passed. Dawn broke. Mercedes woke to find herself lying on Emilio's bed. Her brother was asleep in his chair, his arms still wrapped around his guitar.

Concha opened up the café the next day. After a day of having the doors and shutters tightly closed, it was a relief to throw them open again and replace the stale air.

There seemed no particular reason not to open up, and the bar became the focus of intense discussions about what might happen next. Stories abounded about people being brutalized in order to betray friends or neighbors, and everyone had seen arrests taking place. Arrests were being made for a huge range of so-called crimes. What was lacking was hard information and knowledge of the bigger picture of the country as a whole. Uncertainty and fear mingled.

In Granada there was one area that was still resolutely holding out against Franco's troops—the Albaicín. From their café on the edge of this old quarter, the Ramírez family now had good cause to fear for the fabric of their own home and livelihood.

Theoretically, this *barrio* should have been able to defend itself. It occupied a steep hillside and even had a moat, in the form of the River Darro, running along its lower boundary.

Barricades had been erected to block entry into the Albaicín, and from their superior vantage point the inhabitants there were in a strong position to defend their "castle" against the troops. For several days there was incessant fighting, and the Ramírez family watched many members of the Civil Guard and several Assault Guards being carried away wounded.

Radio Granada gave regular warnings that anyone resisting the Assault Guard would be fired on, but still the siege continued. There was no doubt in anyone's mind that the determination of those holding out in the Albaicín would win over.

They might have had a better chance if the army had not already occupied the Alhambra, which loomed above them. One afternoon, as

Concha watched from her window, it was as though mortars rained from the heavens. Ammunition poured down on the Albaicín, blasting roofs and walls. After the rebel soldiers had wreaked this comprehensive destruction, the dust settled briefly. Moments later, the low moan of an airplane was then heard and aerial bombardment began. The people of the Albaicín were sitting targets.

For some hours, resistance continued, but then Concha saw a stream of people starting to emerge from the still-rising dust. Women, children, and elderly men, all with bundles of clothing and handfuls of possessions that they had rescued from their homes, began to descend the hill. It was hard to hear much above the noise of the machine-gun fire that now sprayed the rooftops, and the thud of artillery, but every so often between the silences, the sound of children crying and the soft moan of the women could be heard as they hurried toward the barricades.

The last few men, as they ran out of ammunition and realized the game was up, climbed onto rooftops and waved white sheets to signal their surrender. They had put up a brave struggle but knew that the Fascists had enough ammunition to raze every home in their *barrio* to the ground.

The most fortunate managed to escape toward Republican lines, but the majority were caught.

Antonio appeared that afternoon, pale with anxiety, his hair peppered with the dust that seemed to hang in the still air.

"They're just shooting them," he said to his parents, "anyone from the Albaicín that they catch—just shooting them. In cold blood."

Coming to terms with their own powerlessness was a terrifying moment for them all.

"They're completely ruthless," said Concha, almost inaudibly.

"I think they've well and truly proved that," agreed her husband.

Although the initial takeover had been accomplished with impressive stealth and bloodless efficiency, the days following it brought a wave of resistance and violence. There was continuous shooting that night, and machine guns were in action from dawn till dusk.

Five days after the initial takeover of the garrison, and once the bombardment of the Albaicín had come to an end, it became quieter. The workers were now on strike, which was the only safe means to register immediate protest against events.

With bread and milk easy to obtain, no one was going hungry, and El Barril could be run reasonably normally. The Ramírez family stayed close to the café, with the exception of Ignacio, who came and went with a smile on his face.

Elvira Delgado's husband had been in Sevilla when the army had taken over there, and his firmly held right-wing position made him fearful of moving across the territory in between, which was still held by the Republic. His absence from Granada made Ignacio even more jubilant about the military coup than ever. He had bought a copy of *El Ideal*, which he left behind on a table in the bar and, with its references to "Glorious General Franco," there was no doubting its politics. Emilio came downstairs and saw it there, its taunting headline an offense to anyone who supported the Republic.

"Fascist bastard!" he said, hurling it across the room, its pages separating out across the floor like a carpet.

"Emilio, please!" shouted his mother. "All you do is make things worse."

"They couldn't be worse than they already are, could they?"

"But once things settle down, General Franco might not turn out to be such a bad thing," she responded. Emilio knew as well as she did that these were words neither of them believed.

"I'm not talking about Franco, Mother. I'm talking about my brother." He picked up one of the loose sheets of newsprint and waved it in front of his mother's face. "How dare he bring this filth into the house?"

"It's just a newspaper." Even if it was looking unrealistic in the country as a whole, Concha's yearning for peace in her own family obliged her to try to be conciliatory. Emilio knew that his mother hated what Franco was trying to do as much as he did.

"It's not just a newspaper. It's propaganda. Can't you see that?"

"But it's the only one on sale now, as far as I know."

"Look, Mother, it's about time you faced up to something about Ignacio."

"Emilio!" said Pablo, drawn into the room by the sound of raised voices. "That's quite enough. We don't want to hear any more . . ."

"Your father's right. There's quite enough fighting going on outside, without everyone in here shouting at each other too."

By now Antonio had appeared too. He knew that the old-established dislike between his two younger brothers had intensified. It was linked with the conflict that was rumbling like an earthquake across their entire country. The divisions of politics had entered their home. The hard-line conservative attitudes of those who wished to take over the country were a serious personal threat to Emilio, and the hatred between these two young men was now as real as that between the Republicans and the Fascist troops that patroled in the streets of Granada.

Emilio stormed out of the room, and no one spoke until the sound of his feet thumping up the stairs to the attic had receded.

News reports on the radio and in the newspapers were often no more accurate than rumors on the street, but the overall picture was becoming clear: Franco's troops were not having the success they had hoped for throughout the region, and though some towns had surrendered, many others were putting up fierce resistance and were able to remain loyal to the government. The country carried on in a state of uncertainty.

In Granada, as though to force men to declare which side they were on, the Nationalists now asked for people to sign up for guard duty. These volunteers wore blue shirts and became part of the tyranny. There were numerous other ways to show support, and shirt color indicated which particular right-wing group you were affiliated with—blue, green, or white. The right wing loved the discipline and order of uniform.

By the end of July, Antonio could see the resistance was effectively all over in Granada. The strike came to an end, and for a short while it was as though nothing had happened. Taxis stood in their usual positions; shops opened; cafés rolled out their awnings. The sun still shone, and the heat was not as fierce as it had been the previous week.

Everything appeared the same, but everything had changed. Even if much of the country was fighting back, Granada was now undisputedly under martial law. Civilians were forbidden to drive vehicles, the right to strike was abolished, and the possession of firearms was banned.

Concha was still in her nightgown one morning, sipping her early morning coffee, when Ignacio came in through the front door of the café.

"Hello, my darling," she said, relieved to see him and refraining, as usual, from asking where he had been all night.

He bent down, kissed her on the top of her tousled hair, and wrapped his arms around her neck. The unmistakable smell of a woman's perfume almost overwhelmed her. It was lily of the valley, or was it damask rose? She could not quite tell as it was all mixed up with the familiar smell of her son's body and perhaps a cigar or two that he had smoked the previous evening.

He pulled out the chair next to her, sat down, and took her hands in his. For years, Concha had been the practice ground for her son's now-famed charm. She did not have a favorite son, but she did have one whose ability to win her over far surpassed that of the other two.

Ignacio had been due to appear in a number of bullfights that summer; for a while at least, the season was suspended and this meant he was a man at leisure. He seemed positively at ease with life and with himself.

"It isn't going to be so awful, is it?" he said. "What did I tell you?"

"I wish I believed it, Ignacio," she said, holding him at arm's length and looking into his eyes. His dark, seductive pupils swam with affection.

A week or so of this conflict had been more than enough to fray her nerves right to the very edge, and even the sound of a door banging was enough to make her jump out of her skin. She was still haunted by the sight of their neighbors being dragged away from their home. The previous day they had heard that both Luis and Julio had been shot, and the Pérez home was looted on the same night. Poor María now lived in fear of her life and would not leave her apartment. Concha had visited every day since the arrests of Maria's loved ones, and that morning the woman had been beyond consolation. Francisco was too angry to be able to comfort his mother, and Antonio spent the day with him trying to keep the lid on his friend's fury. Now Ignacio was trying to tell Concha that things were not going to be "so awful."

In some ways, their nerves had yet to be tested. First thing in the morning on July 29, an aerial bombardment of Granada began that was to last on and off until the end of August. The worst thing about it was not the wanton destruction of their city. It was the fact that many of them were on the same side of this conflict as the Republican planes now bombing them.

Occasionally, the bombers' targets met the approval of those who still supported the legal government.

Antonio was out on the street one morning with his father and saw Republican planes flying overhead. They opened their machine-gun fire on the cathedral tower. Though it was the most beautiful and celebrated of holy places, the damage to Isabella and Ferdinand's great edifice and burial place did not stir either of them. Like most people who supported the rightful Republican government, they had long since stopped kneeling down in front of the altar, so disgusted were they with the collusion of the priests in this rebellion. Right from the beginning, the Catholic Church had sided with the army in this coup.

Newspapers continued to play their role in stirring up aggravation in the Ramírez household.

"It's that Fascist rag again," said Emilio, casting a disdainful look at the newspaper that lay on the bar. "Why does he have to bring it here?"

On that morning it provided detailed coverage of a victory for the Nationalist troops. The Republicans had landed some of their planes at Armilla, not realizing that it had already been taken by the army. When they descended from their planes, they were taken prisoner and the Fascists gleefully celebrated the "delivery" of some magnificent new aircraft.

"What a gift for Franco," commented Antonio, under his breath.

Such stories did nothing for the morale of anyone who supported the Republic. Though they were battling to retain their ground, it seemed that things could still go either way.

For the next few days, Granada continued to be bombed from the air and more innocent people died, their houses collapsing around them. Sirens sounded the alert, but even though the arrival of planes was advertised, there was no real place of refuge. Occasionally a member of the Civil Guard might be buried in the rubble, but it was mostly the innocent citizens of Granada who were terrorized by the daily routine of bombs that seemed to increase in destructive power as each day went on.

On August 6, a bomb fell close to the café in the Plaza Nueva. One of the upstairs windows shattered, spraying the room with shards of glass, and everything in the building was violently shaken. Glasses fell off bar shelves and bottles crashed to the ground; brandy flowed across the floor in a dark river.

Concha cleared up the mess, helped by Emilio and Mercedes. For the first time in their lives they saw their mother weep and were disconcerted by the sight of her despair.

"I hate all this," she began tearfully.

Her children exchanged glances. They could see that she was about to launch into one of her occasional tirades.

"Our country's a mess! Our city's a mess—and now our café . . . just look at it!" she cried.

There was no doubt that these catastrophes were all linked, but the only one they could resolve was the one in front of them.

"Look, we'll all help clear this up," said Emilio, balancing on his haunches to pick up the jagged remains of a dozen or so bottles. "It's not as bad as it looks."

Mercedes went to find a broom. For the first time in weeks, something had distracted her from thinking of Javier. He had occupied the central-most part of her mind for almost every waking moment since the coup, but the proximity of the bomb had jolted her.

But as she swept the floor, even the musical jangling of the shards of glass brought her mind back to the man she loved. What had dominated her mind before she met him? She hated this wretched conflict for separating them.

Antonio appeared and made his mother sit down. He was now pouring her a drink from the only surviving bottle.

"I don't know how long we can carry on . . ."

"What do you mean?" asked Antonio, anxious to calm his mother down.

" . . . running the café. It's all so . . ."

Antonio could tell his mother was tired, but they all needed to keep going. Each day everyone looked for signs that the situation in the city might be getting more stable, and there was a determination on Antonio's part to ensure that some part of their lives continued without disruption. At this point, food supplies were still relatively plentiful in the city so there was no difficulty feeding their customers; fish was the only thing that they could not get hold of as the city was cut off from the coast at present, but meat, bread, vegetables, and fruit were easy to obtain.

"Look, we need to try and carry on as normal; otherwise they really have won, haven't they?" he coaxed his mother.

She nodded with weary resignation.

Bombs had fallen on the Plaza Cristo and on the Washington Hotel, close to the Alhambra, where people had taken refuge from machine-gun fire. Nine people died in the city that day, the majority of them women, and there were numerous serious casualties. At the same time as the deaths of these innocents, other equally blameless people were being tried. The rumble of Republican bombers passing overhead had only increased the resolve of the Fascists to pass sentence on those who still supported the government. Even before the ink dried on the signatures authorizing these deaths, their executions were carried out.

The first people to stand trial were the Civil Governor, Martínez, the president of the local council, a lawyer named Enrique Martín Forero, and two trade unionists, Antonio Rus Romero and José Alcantara. From their appearance in front of a jury on July 31 to their court-martial, sentence and execution at dawn against the cemetery wall, it was a mere four days. For these men and for their families and friends, these were days of fear and disbelief that such unlawful decisions could be happening in the name of justice.

In the days that followed, numerous other key figures in Granada faced the firing squad—politicians, doctors, journalists. The news of these deaths horrified the Ramírez family.

"It means that no one is safe," said Pablo. "Absolutely no one."

"If they can justify killing those men, then you're right," said Antonio, who had always sought to reassure his parents.

Even he had now lost hope that this conflict might reach a swift conclusion once the parts of the army that had remained loyal to the Republican government had retaliated and gained control. The ruthlessness of the troops who were carrying out Franco's orders was breathtaking and without compromise. Idealists like Antonio were only just beginning to realize the nature of their enemy.

By the second week of August, both the heat and the bombing had intensified, but the former now ceased to be a topic of conversation. It was strange how one day, a whole building could be devastated and everyone would emerge miraculously unscathed, and then the next day a single explosion could kill half a dozen people in the street. Such an ill-fated group were the women who died when the Calle de Real Cartuja was targeted. Their deaths were as random as the roll of dice.

For over a fortnight now, Granada had been an island of Fascism in a sea of loyal Republicanism. Antonio had held on to the hope that this relatively small area of land could be taken back, but he was losing faith. News began to drift in of Nationalist successes in various other places including Antequera and Marbella.

The Nationalist force had now organized its defense against air bombardment of Granada. German cannons were in strategic positions to deter Republican planes, so air raids stopped.

Once the bombs ceased to drop, the streets of Granada were again full of activity. There were more people around than was usual for the time of year. Many would normally have left the city for the duration of the summer but had been afraid to do so because of the uncertainty of the political situation. Combined with the influx of people from surrounding villages, the population had swelled.

The atmosphere was clearly not one of celebration, but at certain times of day, the teeming streets and squares were redolent of fiesta. The cafés were full. People sat close to share precious shade, and young women moved about between the tables collecting coins for Red Cross hospitals that had been set up around the city to treat the wounded.

Cinemas were open as usual but were obliged to endlessly repeat the few films that they had in stock, and entertainment-starved audiences had no choice but to tolerate the repetition and to watch the newsreels, which were alarming, whichever side of the political spectrum they were on.

Ignacio continued to antagonize his family with his own reaction to events. About the total domination of the city and nearby villages by the Fascists, he did not bother to hide his triumphalism, but as time went on, he would also rant and rave about atrocities reported to have been committed by those defending the Republic in towns such as Motril and Salobreña.

"They dragged women into the sea," he shouted at Antonio and Emilio, who listened silently to their brother, "and murdered their children!"

Whether this was true or merely rightist propaganda, they were not going to give Ignacio the satisfaction of a reaction.

"And presumably you know they've destroyed the harvest—and killed the flocks!" he added.

Their silence infuriated him. He came right up to his brothers, and Antonio could feel the heat of Ignacio's anger as he spat his next words right into his face: "If we all starve, it won't be Franco's fault!" he said, almost nose to nose with Antonio. "It'll be the fault of you Republicans! Can't you see it's all over? The Republic is *finished*!"

Everywhere Granadinos sat huddled around radios. Fingers were yellow with nicotine, and nails were bitten down to the quick. Anxiety, tension, and heat made the city rank with sweat. Rumors of mass executions in other parts of the country intensified the terror.

People feared those who lived on the same street and even those who lived under the same roof. Across the country, families were being torn apart.

# CHAPTER 17

Ignacio's reports of Republican troops abandoning their weapons and fleeing from their positions in the villages up in the hills had more substance than the rest of his family wanted to admit. The effectiveness of Franco's army in and around Granada had been swift and absolute.

"I just can't believe it!" said Concha one morning, ill-concealed disgust in her voice. "Have you been out this morning?" Her question was addressed to Antonio and Emilio. "Go down the street and look! Take a walk down to the cathedral. You won't believe your eyes."

Emilio did not react, but Antonio got up and left the café. As he turned right, down Reyes Catolicos, he saw immediately what it was that had vexed his mother so much. Near the cathedral, the streets were decked in red and yellow bunting. It must have been put up very early that morning and now the city was dressed as for fiesta.

It was August 15. In another year, the date might have meant something to him, but now it was meaningless. It was the Feast of the Assumption, the celebration of the day that the Virgin Mary was taken up to heaven, and for the hundreds of faithful that gathered around the cathedral doors, trying to hear the Mass that was being sung inside, this was one of the most revered days of the Church calendar; there simply was not enough room inside to accommodate them all.

From within came the sound of clapping. The ripple of applause spread into the square, and soon the crowd joined their hands in response. The appearance of the Archbishop's procession at the main door was greeted by the perfectly timed blast of a military fanfare.

Now blocked in by the densely packed flock, Antonio struggled to extricate himself. This blatant display of military and ecclesiastical co-operation sickened him and he pushed his way out of the square. As he turned back onto the main street and up toward the Plaza Nueva, he almost collided with a troop of legionaries, marching down toward the cathedral, their hard, chiseled faces streaked with sweat. His own step almost turned to a run as he sped back toward home. He was scarcely aware of the groups of elegantly dressed people standing on their flag-bedecked balconies, though some of them noticed him, a sole figure moving against the steady tide of soldiers.

When he arrived back at the café, his parents were sitting together at a table. Pablo smoked, gazing into space.

"Antonio," said Concha, with a smile for her eldest son, "you're back. What's happening out there now?"

"People celebrating, that's what," he said, almost choked with disgust. "Catholics and Fascists. It's awful. I can't stand it. That smug, fat-arsed Archbishop . . . God, I'd like to run him through like a pig!"

"Ssh, Antonio," said his mother, noticing that a few people were coming into the café. Mass was over and the bars would now fill with people. "Keep your voice down."

"But why, Mother?" he hissed. "How can a man who is head of the Church here ignore all this killing . . . this *murder*? Where's his compassion?"

Antonio was right. Monsignor Agustin Parrado y García, Cardinal Archbishop of Granada, was one of many senior members of the Catholic Church who sided wholeheartedly with Franco. These people saw the insurrection of the army generals as a holy crusade, and for that reason alone would not intervene to save the lives of anyone falsely imprisoned and sentenced by the Nationalists.

Concha had tied her apron and was soon behind the bar, followed by her husband, and by the time they had taken orders, Antonio had disappeared out the door.

It may have been no real comfort to Antonio, but Franco soon began to make demands on those who supported him, to the tune of tens of thousands of pesetas. There were subscriptions for the army, the Red Cross, and for the purchase of aircraft, and some supporters even had to share their homes with senior army officials. The cost of war was not cheap for anyone, and the banks themselves were in crisis. No one was depositing money. They were only making withdrawals, and the vaults were being drained of their reserves.

Pablo and Concha listened to the grumbles of their few wealthy customers. The café had always had a mixed clientele, and the couple had worked hard to maintain their image of absolute neutrality. Anything else would have been suicidal in this climate and atmosphere.

"They took away my husband's Chrysler last week," said one well-coiffed woman of about fifty-five.

"How dreadful," responded her friend. "And when do you think you'll get it back?"

"I'm not sure I'd want it now," she replied, the disdain evident in her voice. "I saw it only this morning—crammed full of Assault Guards. You can imagine what a filthy mess they'll be making of it. It already has a big dent in the door!"

Both sides were feeling the cost of this conflict. Many people had relatives in other cities, and for some time now communication between Granada and the outside world had been restricted. No amount of brandy that they served could fully calm the anxiety of people who sat in the café fretting about the well-being of sons or daughters, uncles and parents in Córdoba, Madrid, or distant Barcelona, from whom they had received no word. Mercedes was becoming desperate for news of Málaga.

Now that Granada was firmly in their hands, the Nationalists were sending out troops to other towns. Antonio and his friends were heartened to hear that many of them were putting up strong resistance. Although the narrow passage between Sevilla and Granada was held by the Nationalists and heavily guarded, much of the rest of the region was still holding out against Franco's troops, and fierce combat went on even in small towns that they had assumed could be taken without a fight.

The sinister task of keeping watch over people in Granada was now shared with members of the Fascist Falangist youth party, who happily participated in denouncing and persecuting anyone they suspected of being Republican. Crimes against the new regime could consist of anything from having communist propaganda daubed on your walls, which the Falangists might have put there themselves to stir up trouble, to having voted for the socialist party in previous elections. The terror of arbitrary arrest and imprisonment was intense.

For Emilio, the day after the Feast of the Assumption, August 16, was the worst of the conflict so far. Within twenty-four hours, both his close friend Alejandro and his hero, Lorca, were arrested. The poet had traveled to Granada to stay with his family just before the coup, but realizing the danger he might be in because of his socialist sympathies, he left his home and took refuge with a Falangist friend. Even being with someone who supported the right did not protect him. His detention took place on the same day as the execution of his brother-in-law, the Mayor, Montesinos, who was shot against the cemetery wall.

The news of Lorca's arrest got round quickly, and for three days his family and all of those who loved him waited anxiously. He belonged to no political party so there was slim justification for his detention.

Emilio was working in the café when he overheard two customers talking. At first, he thought he must have been mistaken, when he realized who they were talking about.

"So they shot him in the back, did they?" asked one of the men.

"No, in the backside . . ." the other murmured. "For being a homosexual."

They were unaware that Emilio was listening to their every word.

A moment before, Ignacio had come downstairs. He had caught the last words and could not resist joining in.

"Yes, that's exactly what happened—they shot him in the arse for being a queer, a *maricón*! There are too many of his type in this city."

Everyone in the room went completely silent. Even the ticking clock sounded embarrassed, but Ignacio could not resist another stab. This captive audience was irresistible.

"We need *real* men in this country," he challenged. "Spain will never be strong while it's full of fairies."

With those words he strode through the bar and disappeared into the street. His was a sentiment shared by many on the right. Manliness was a prerequisite for the true citizen.

For a while no one spoke. Emilio stood, frozen to the spot, tears flowing down his face. At one point he wiped them away with his cloth, but still they came. When Concha appeared, she took her son's arm, led him into the office behind the bar, and shut the door. The muffled sound of sobbing was drowned out as customers resumed their discussions. Pablo appeared to take over at the bar. There had been no news of Alejandro, and Emilio felt the situation could not get any worse.

The death of Lorca was a landmark event in this conflict. Any residual belief in fairness and justice was destroyed. People across Spain were horrified.

At the end of August, just when people in Granada were beginning to feel safe from airborne attack, Republican army planes reappeared. Some thirty bombs were dropped on the city, the antiaircraft cannons doing absolutely nothing to prevent them. Although their action brought renewed fear and terror to everyone, including those who supported them, it showed that the Republican cause was not yet a lost one.

"You see," said Antonio, appealing to his parents the next day, "we can still fight to restore the Republic!"

"We all know that," interrupted Emilio, "apart from Ignacio, of course."

Concha sighed. This bitterness between her sons, which had brewed for so many years, now wearied her. She had struggled so hard not to take sides and to be even-tempered and even-handed.

When the air strikes ceased, the city once again put on a display of normality.

One day, at the end of the month, Ignacio came in looking more satisfied with life than ever.

"There's going to be a bullfight next week," he announced to the family. "My first here as a *matador de toros*."

Antonio could not resist a tart comment. "It'll be good to see a bull-ring put to its proper use," he said. They all knew to what he was refer-ring.

Earlier in August, in the bullring at Badajoz, a town in the southwest, instead of the blood of bulls the huge ring of sand had soaked up the blood of thousands of Republicans, socialists, and communists. They had been herded toward the neat white *plaza de toros* and through the gate, where the parade usually entered, and into the ring. Machine guns were lined up for them, and eighteen hundred men and women were mowed down. Some of the bodies lay for days until they were dragged away and their blood turned black in the sand. Reports mentioned that passersby had retched at the sickening smell of spilled blood and that the only thing the victims were spared was the sight of their town being ransacked and looted.

"Whatever happened in Badajoz," retorted Ignacio defensively, "those *rojos* probably deserved it."

He pushed past Antonio and put his hands on his mother's shoulders.

"You will come, won't you?" he asked imploringly.

"Of course I will," she said. "I wouldn't miss it. But I'm not sure your brothers will be there."

"I wouldn't expect them to be," he said, spinning round to look at Antonio. "Especially him upstairs."

The mood in the bullring the following week was euphoric. The stands hummed with excitement as the spectators, dressed in their best finery, talked animatedly and waved to friends across the crowd. For the pre-dominantly conservative *aficionados* of this sport, the reopening of the ring symbolized a return to some form of normality, and they savored the moment.

Pablo and Concha were there that afternoon to watch their son. Anto-nio, Emilio, and Mercedes had chosen to stay at home.

From where they sat on this late afternoon, securely enclosed in the perfect circle of the Plaza de Toros, the devastation that had taken place in parts of their city was out of sight. What mattered to the majority of people there at that moment was that they could enjoy the resumption of their old way of life, a sense of their élite position, a re-establishment of the old traditions and hierarchy. Even the choice of seat, in the sun or the shade, *sol o sombra*, reflected social standing in the city.

"Whatever happens in the next few months," went one conversation overheard by Concha, "at least we've got rid of those awful lefties in the town council."

After that she tried not to listen to the two elderly men next to her, who clearly had no idea how brutally and thoroughly some of the socialist town councillors had been eliminated, but snatches of conversation kept drifting across to her and they were hard to ignore.

"Let's pray that the nation will see the light and give in to General Franco," said one of them.

"We live in hope," responded the other. "It would be much better for everyone. And the sooner it happens the better."

"Try not to listen to them," said Pablo, overhearing too. "There's nothing we can do about the way these people think. Look! The parade is going to start . . ."

The pageantry seemed more scintillating than ever, the men more handsome, the costumes more vivid. For the past hour, Ignacio had been preparing himself in his dressing room. He was laced into his trousers, and his hair was dressed and pinned before he put on the smooth felt *montera* hat. He admired himself in the mirror and lifted his chin. The gleaming white of his costume accentuated his dark hair and tanned skin.

As he emerged into the ring with the others and they bowed before the fight director and the local celebrities who sat in the box, he wondered how life could possibly get better than this.

And everything is yet to come, he reflected, basking in the sheer joy of anticipation.

Ignacio was the third of the matadors to make his entrance in the ring.

Though they had been polite, the crowd had been unimpressed by the other fighters. The second had a false start when his first bull rammed the wooden barricade and smashed his horns. The creature's carelessness earned him his freedom and a return to the rich pastureland where he had been reared. This matador played his next bull deftly before making a swift, clean kill, but there had been no showmanship, nothing that thrilled the crowd.

They hoped for more drama with Ignacio. Many of them had seen him perform before, and his reputation for deliberate, breathtaking near-misses with the bull had received plenty of coverage in the pages of the local newspapers.

The crowd was ready for something that captured the imagination, and they always expected the best to be last. For many, the amount of death and violence they had witnessed in the past month or so had merely whetted their appetite for more. They had seen plenty of blood spilled that afternoon, but the twin pleasures of danger and catharsis had so far been lacking. These bulls had not yet presented any real risk to these young men.

The cruelty of the crowd was palpable. They did not want the bull to die too soon: the stages of his degradation before the final decisive blow must be slow and painstaking and his suffering must be drawn out.

Most of the arena was now in shadow and the day was finally cooling. A shaft of low, late afternoon sunlight caught the dazzling gold embroidery of Ignacio's jacket. This was the best time to fight.

The bull thundered toward him, and as its horns came into contact with the cape, its forelegs left the ground. Despite the wounds from the picador and the banderilleros, the animal still had plenty of energy. The *muleta* cape brushed its back as Ignacio executed a deft flick.

After he had executed his first few simple turns, Ignacio became more daring. He dazzled the crowd with the elegance of a "butterfly" pass, sweeping the cape behind his back, and then to their astonishment, he knelt on the ground.

"What absolute gall!" they gasped. "What confidence!" "What nerve!"

The bull's head was lowered. Would Ignacio get away with such an audacious maneuver? Seconds later, the crowd would have their answer.

Ignacio got to his feet and acknowledged their applause. His back was turned to the bull now, a further demonstration of his supremacy over the animal. The gesture was almost contemptuous. If the bull had it in him, he might have gored the perfect, rounded buttocks of his pert derrière, but the beast was already losing his will.

The *faena* was nearly completed now. There were some more *verónicas*, when he twirled the cape above his head as he pirouetted. On the final one, the wounded bull brushed so close to Ignacio's body that his pure white jacket was painted crimson with the animal's blood.

"Now I understand why he wore that color," said Concha to herself.

Ignacio touched the left horn as he passed. It seemed almost affectionate, as if he was stroking the bull, thanking him for the opportunity to prove himself.

The build-up had all the grace and elegance of a dance seen in slow motion, and now the bull came before him, almost on bended knee, worshipful. Ignacio raised the sword and plunged it deep, reaching the animal's heart. As they watched the last twitch of the defeated beast, the crowd were on their feet and waving their handkerchiefs. Ignacio's confrontation with the bull was as near perfection as a bullfight could be.

Apart from joining with the occasional gasps uttered collectively by the crowd, Ignacio's parents had remained silent for the duration of the fight. Once or twice Concha had gripped her husband's arm hard. It was difficult for a mother to see her son facing a charging bull and not experience a moment of pure terror. Only when the dead weight of the animal's corpse was being dragged on its final circuit by the team of horses could she allow herself to breathe again. Then Pablo was up with the rest, awash with pride at the sight of his son basking in the crowd's adulation.

The fanfare sounded. Ignacio returned, parading before the crowd, arms aloft to acknowledge the cheers. Sensual and provocative, these slim-hipped youths strutted a single circuit of the ring, dazzling in their purples, pinks, and blood-stained white.

Concha rose to her feet. She too was proud of Ignacio, but she hated this place, its atmosphere sickened her, and she was glad when they could leave.

The bullfight seemed to bring about a brief renaissance of the old Granada. Everyone flooded out, the bars filled up, and into the small hours the streets thronged with people. Civil Guards kept a wary eye, alert for trouble, but anyone who felt uncomfortable about the underlying sense of right-wing triumphalism stayed indoors that night.

Ignacio was the man of the hour. In the smartest bar near the bullring he was fêted by his entourage and dozens of wealthy landowners and *aficionados* who queued up to shake his hand. There were dozens of women all keen to catch his eye, too, and the party went on late into the night. Everyone in this coterie shared similar views on the current situation in Spain, and the drunken toasts and songs reflected this.

> *Lovely Lorca, what a bore!*
> *NOW we bet your arse is sore!*

They chanted the words over and over again, thrilled with the double entendre.

"You should have seen my brother when he heard about Lorca," said Ignacio laughingly to the group he was standing with. "Devastated!"

"So he's a poofter too, is he?" said one of the more vulgar men through a thick cloud of cigar smoke.

"Well, let's put it this way," answered Ignacio conspiratorially, "he doesn't share my taste for girls . . ."

One of the more voluptuous women in the bar had sidled up to Ignacio during this conversation, and his hand had slipped around her waist as he carried on talking to his male friends. It was an almost unconscious gesture. At three in the morning when the bar would eventually shut, they would stroll together to the nearby Hotel Majestic, which always kept a few rooms back for the stars of the bullfight.

During the days that followed, Ignacio was irrepressible. He could scarcely contain his jubilation. The family were given the head of his magnificent kill. Somewhere in a dark corner of the café, it hung for some years, its staring expressionless eyes looking out at customers as they came in to El Barril.

But even while Ignacio was celebrating, the violence continued. Lorca was only one of hundreds who had disappeared.

About a month later, there was a horrendous banging on the glass panel of the El Barril's door at three o'clock in the morning. The violence of the knocking was almost enough to break it down.

"Who's that?" yelled the elderly Señor Ramírez out of his third-floor window. "Who the devil is making all that noise?"

"Open up, Ramírez. Now!" It was a harsh voice, and its owner, in using Pablo's last name, clearly meant business.

By now, every inhabitant of the street was out of bed. Shutters were open, women and children leaned out of windows, and a few courageous men had come out onto the pavement and were now face to face with the dozen or so soldiers in the street. Dogs barked and the strident sounds of their yapping ricocheted off the walls, creating a deafening cacophony in the narrow streets. Even as the bolts were being pulled across, the hammering continued to rain down on the glass. Only when Pablo opened the door did it cease, and then even the dogs were silent. Five of the soldiers pushed past him into the café and the door banged behind them. The others remained in the street, loitering, smoking, indifferent to the resentful glares of the civilians around them. The street was quiet. Perhaps two minutes or twenty passed. No one could say.

Eventually the door was thrown open. Silence was replaced by the sound of screams. It was Señora Ramírez.

"You can't take him away! You can't take him!" she wailed. "He's done nothing wrong! You can't take him!"

There was a sense of desperation and helplessness in her voice. She knew that no protestation of hers could stop these men. The fact that they had no legal warrant to make an arrest mattered not a fraction of a peseta.

There were no streetlights so it was hard to see exactly what was going on in the shadows, but everyone could see that it was Emilio who was standing in the street. He was still in a nightshirt, which glowed supernaturally white in the gloom, his hands were tied fast behind his back, his head was downcast, and he was perfectly still. One of the uniformed men shoved him in the stomach with his rifle butt.

"Get going!" he ordered. "Now."

With that, Emilio seemed to come to life. He stumbled away from his home like a drunk, almost losing his balance on the uneven cobbles.

Then there was the sound of Señor Ramírez, trying to calm his wife: "We will get him back, my dear. We will get him back. They have no right to take him."

Half a dozen soldiers trooped down the street behind Emilio, two of them regularly jabbing him between the shoulder blades to steer him in the right direction. Soon they disappeared around the corner and the metallic click of military footsteps faded. Now the street was full of people, neighbors in huddles, women comforting Concha, men both furious and fearful.

Antonio and Ignacio stood nose to nose.

"Come on," said Antonio. "We have to follow them. Quick."

It had been a long while since Ignacio had responded to any instruction from his brother, but for now at least they had a common purpose. Concern for their own flesh and blood, particularly their mother, briefly united them.

It was only a minute or two before they caught sight of the uniformed group and then followed them stealthily for half a mile, retreating into dark doorways and archways every time they paused. If they were spotted, it would do no one any good, least of all Emilio. The real surprise to Antonio was that their route took them to the government building. Less

than a month earlier, Granada had been ruled from there to the benefit
of the people.

There was another jab in the back for Emilio as he fell over the threshold, and then the door banged firmly shut. By now it was beginning to get
light, and the two brothers would not be able to hang around in the street
for long without being seen. They squatted in a doorway, unable even to
light a cigarette in case a burning match drew attention to them, and for
ten minutes or so remained huddled like this, arguing over what to do.
Stay? Go? Hammer on the doors?

The decision was soon made for them when, shortly afterward, a car
rolled up to a side door and two soldiers got out. Some unseen figures
admitted them into the building, and within a few moments they re-
emerged. This time, there was another figure between them. They were
supporting him because he was unable to walk, but it was not a humane
gesture. The man was bent double with pain, and when they opened the
door of the vehicle and bundled him in, it was obvious that there was no
kindness intended. He was being treated like a package. As he fell into
the car, both Antonio and Ignacio caught a glimpse of the still-gleaming
white nightshirt and knew beyond doubt that the person they had seen
was Emilio.

The car roared off into the night, and they had to accept that they
could not follow.

Antonio's heart was heavy. Men can't cry, Antonio repeated to himself.
Men can't cry. His face was locked in a spasm of grief and disbelief, his
hand held fast over his mouth to stifle the sound of his sobs, but his eyes
overflowed with tears. For some time the brothers stayed crouched low in
the doorway of some stranger, who even now slept soundly in his bed.

Ignacio was getting agitated. It was nearly light now, and they had to
get away from this place and back home. Their parents would be waiting
for news.

"What are we going to tell them?" whispered Antonio, his voice choked.

"That he's under arrest," said Ignacio bluntly. "What's the point of
telling them anything else?"

They walked in silence, slowly through the empty streets. Antonio longed for some comfort from his younger brother, but he would receive none. Ignacio's sangfroid about the situation puzzled him for a moment. He knew that Ignacio hated Emilio, but he could not allow himself to suspect that he was involved in his own brother's disappearance.

As the older brother, it would be his duty to tell their parents what had happened. Ignacio would remain in the background, his views of the matter as shadowy as the street.

It was more than a month since the Nationalists had taken over in Granada, but the number of people being arrested daily and taken off in trucks to the cemetery to be shot was still rising. It seemed unbelievable that this could happen, least of all to someone so close to them.

"Perhaps they just want to question Emilio about Alejandro," offered Mercedes helpfully, desperately clinging to a straw of hope. There had been no news of Emilio's best friend since his arrest.

Concha Ramírez's grief overwhelmed her. She could not contain it. An active imagination and the terror of the unknown filled her mind with visions of what might be happening to her son.

Pablo, however, refused to accept that he might never see Emilio again and talked as though his son might appear again at any moment.

Sonia and Miguel had long since drained their second and third coffees, and from time to time the waiter approached to see if they needed anything more. Two hours had passed since they arrived.

"They must have been so distraught," said Sonia.

"I think they were," murmured Miguel. "It meant that these terrible events were not just happening to other people but to them. And the arrest of one family member meant they were *all* in danger."

Sonia looked around. "It's getting quite smoky in here. Do you mind if we get some fresh air?" she asked.

They paid the bill and wandered out. Miguel continued to talk as they strolled across the square.

# CHAPTER 18

For days Concha prayed for her son's return. She knelt at his bedside, her hands clasped in supplication, muttering to the Virgin to have mercy. She had little faith that anyone was listening. The Nationalists had claimed God, and Concha was sure He could not be answering prayers on both sides of this conflict.

The room was in the same state as it had been the night Emilio was torn out of his bed. His mother had no plans to rearrange anything. The sheets were rumpled, swirled like cream on the surface of coffee, and the clothes he had been wearing the day before his arrest were carelessly slung across an old chair. His guitar lay on the other side of the bed, the sensuous curves of its lovely body so like a woman's. It struck Señora Ramírez as ironic that this might be the closest Emilio had ever got to having something so feminine and voluptuous in his bed.

On the second morning after Emilio's arrest, Mercedes found her mother in his room, crying. For only the second time in weeks, she thought about something other than Javier, and possibly for the first time in her life, she began to emerge from her childish introspection.

Over eight weeks had now passed since Mercedes had seen Javier, and she had not smiled since that day. As far as she knew, Javier had been at home in Málaga when the rebel soldiers took over Granada, and there was no reason for him to risk his skin coming back. Even for her. So she was torn between anxiety that something terrible had happened to him and growing irritation that he had not contacted her. She did not know what to think. If he was safe and happy somewhere, why had he not contacted her? Why had he not come? For Mercedes, it was a curious state of uncertainty and made her sad and dissatisfied, and just about everything in between, but the sight of her mother's tears shocked her into the realization that people around her might be suffering as much as she was.

"Mother!" she said, putting her arms around Concha.

Unaccustomed to such tenderness from her daughter, Concha wept all the more.

"He'll come back," whispered the girl into her mother's ear. "He'll come back."

Feeling her mother shuddering in her arms, Mercedes felt suddenly afraid. Perhaps the loving, gentle brother with whom she had shared so much was not going to return.

A few days passed in this state of unknowing. Pablo buried himself in the business of running the café. It was as busy as ever, and now he did not have Emilio helping him out. Though he felt heavily weighed down with anxiety, a whole day would pass where he could keep his mind occupied with other things. From time to time, the sharp recollection of Emilio's absence came almost like a physical blow, and when this happened, he could feel a lump rising in his throat, and tears, such as his wife could shed so freely, had to be fought back.

On the fourth morning after Emilio's arrest, Concha decided that this stalemate in their lives could not continue. She had to know the truth. The people who might hold some records were the Civil Guard.

She had always regarded these sinister individuals, in their ugly patent leather hats, with great suspicion, and since the conflict had begun, her dislike of them had intensified. They always lurked on the edge of treachery and betrayal in this city.

She went alone to the Civil Guard offices. Tremblingly she gave Emilio's name, and the guard on duty opened the ledger on his desk to find the log for the past few days. He ran his finger down the list of names and turned several pages. Concha's heart lifted. Her son's name was not there. Perhaps this meant he had been released. She turned to leave.

"*Señora!*" he called out in a tone that might have sounded friendly. "What did you say your surname was?"

"Ramírez."

"I thought you said Rodríguez . . ."

For Concha Ramírez, the world stood still at that moment. Her hopes had been held so high, but now she knew by the tone in his voice that they had been in vain. It was almost an act of deliberate cruelty that he had raised them, and now they were to be crushed, like an insect beneath his boot.

"There is an entry for a Ramírez. Yesterday morning. Sentence has been passed. Thirty years."

"Where is he?" she asked in a whisper. "Which prison?"

"I can't give you that information yet. Come back next week."

In turmoil, she just managed to get to the door before she fell to her knees. The news had winded her like a physical blow. She gasped for air, and it was some moments before she realized that the animal howls she could hear were her own cries. In the echoing vestibule of the Civil Guard offices, the sound of her anguish reverberated from the high ceiling. From behind the counter, a bespectacled man regarded her with total lack of concern. He had seen several other weeping mothers already that morning, and their troubles elicited little sympathy from him. The only reaction they provoked was one of irritation. He did not like "scenes" and hoped that this woman, like the others before her, would get out of here soon.

Once in the street, Concha had just one purpose: to make her way back home to share this news. As she stumbled along, the familiar buildings provided her with much-needed support as she took each clumsy step toward her destination. Passersby took her for a drunk woman and steered clear as she staggered from one shop doorway to the next. She hardly recognized the roads of her own city but, by instinct, through the haze of her own tears, made her way to the familiar frontage of El Barril.

There was little need to tell Pablo what was wrong. He could see from the look on her face as she pushed open the café door that the news was bad.

For nine nights they lost sleep, and each day Concha sought confirmation of where Emilio had been taken. She was now a familiar figure at the government offices. Eventual confirmation that her son was in a prison close to Cádiz brought a strange sense of relief. The prison was more than two hundred kilometers away, but at least they knew something for certain.

Concha's first thought was to make the journey to see her son. If she could take him some food, at least he would not starve.

"But it's a ridiculous distance to travel," said Ignacio. "Particularly on your own."

"I have no choice," said Concha.

"Of course you have a choice!" insisted Ignacio.

"One day you will understand," she responded patiently, "when you have your own children."

"Well, God help you. That's all I can say."

The journey there took her two days. Despite the papers she had, which were meant to allow her safe conduct, the frequent checks by soldiers and Civil Guards were often carried out with aggression, and on several occasions she was certain she would have to turn back to Granada.

When she eventually arrived, Concha's request to see her son was denied.

"He is in solitary," barked the officer on duty. "He has currently lost all his privileges."

Quite what those "privileges" might be in this awful place, she could not imagine.

"How long will that last?" she asked, numb with disappointment.

"Could be two days, could be two weeks. Depends."

She did not have the heart to ask what it depended on. In any case, she would not have any faith in the answer.

The basket of food was left. She had no idea if it would ever reach him. Inside one of the walnuts she had packed in the bag, she had concealed a note. It was just a mother's letter, with superficial news of family life and messages of love sincerely meant, but when it was found, his time alone in a cell was increased by a week.

Tales of conditions inside prisons reached Pablo and Concha from many sources. Occasionally someone succeeded in escaping, but the more common stories were of the daily firing squads and the arbitrariness of the lists of victims.

While Concha was preoccupied with the personal drama of her son's imprisonment, mothers were losing sons all over the country. Sons were losing mothers too.

By the autumn, Nationalist bombers were terrorizing the defenseless people of Madrid, and nobody was safe. Even mothers queuing for their children's milk were blasted to eternity. The capital was Franco's real goal, and Nationalist troops had reached the outskirts of the city. Leaflets had been dropped warning the population that unless they handed the city over, it would be wiped off the face of the earth. The relentless air raids were beginning to wear the population down. They were sitting targets.

Everyone, whether they supported the Republic or Franco, followed what was taking place in Madrid. What happened to the capital city could determine the outcome of this conflict for the whole country.

At the beginning of November, the first Russian planes arrived and counterattacks began. Though the Republic was now doing better in the air, the Nationalists began to have some success on the ground. That same month they took one of the city's suburbs, Getafe, which gave them hope that they were on their way to complete victory.

Antonio studied the newspapers more closely than ever and often read out extracts to his mother as she dried the glasses in the morning.

"'In spite of bombardment from Republican troops the Nationalist army has taken the area of Carabanchel and significant bridges have been gained, which could allow access to the inner city,'" Antonio read. "'Hand-to-hand combat has been taking place on the streets and losses run into thousands on both sides. Franco's troops have pushed through Republican lines into the University City.'"

Antonio did not know that his mother was already well abreast of events from listening early each morning to a banned radio station broadcasting from Málaga.

"It could be the end of it all," said Antonio. "Perhaps Franco is about to get his way."

Ignacio, who had come into the café and heard Antonio's comment, saw the opportunity to comfort his mother. "Well, Mother," he said, "as soon as Franco can declare victory, you might have your Emilio back."

"That would be a relief," she said, smiling at the thought. "But doesn't it depend what the charges against him are?"

"I suppose it might. I'm sure they weren't serious, though."

It sometimes suited Ignacio to take a conciliatory position with his mother. It assuaged his occasional pangs of guilt that his indiscreet talk over his brother's homosexuality might have led to his arrest. If he had anticipated the severity of his brother's sentence and the grief it would cause, he might have been more careful, however much Emilio sickened him.

Franco's victory in Madrid was not as imminent as Ignacio thought. The exhausted citizens of Madrid saw uniformed soldiers marching past them and assumed these men were battalions of Nationalist troops. With some astonishment and much joy, they soon realized their error. The strains of their revolutionary songs and the distinctive tune of "The Internationale" told them that these were *Brigadistas*, members of the International Brigades, who had come, as if by magic, to their rescue. Among them were Germans, Poles, Italians, and English, and it was said that, to a man, they were going fearlessly to the frontline.

Members of the anarchist movement, who were strong believers in freedom, even if not always the most disciplined of fighters, were also arriving to help defend Madrid against Franco, and there was further fighting in the University City, including an attack on the hospital, held by the Nationalists. The area was soon back in Republican hands and the frontline once again redrawn.

Later in November 1936, Ignacio was browsing through that day's right-wing newspaper, getting the latest on what was happening in Madrid. Unlike the rest of his family, who could not bear to read the biased reports of the right-wing press, Ignacio ostentatiously did so, and his muttered remark that it was a pity that Franco had given up the fight for Madrid at this stage was too much for his normally phlegmatic father to take.

"Ignacio," Pablo said, finally losing his temper, "do you really think it's right for soldiers to kill innocent people?"

"Which innocent people?" Ignacio did not conceal his scorn. "What do you mean by 'innocent'?"

"The ordinary people of Madrid, of course! Women and children who are being blasted to bits. What have they done?"

"So what about all those prisoners then? They hardly deserved to die, did they? Don't talk to me about *innocence*! There's no such *thing*!" Ignacio slammed the table with a fist.

Ignacio was referring to the execution of a thousand Nationalist prisoners earlier that month. Madrid had been a city of mixed sympathies, both Republican and Nationalist, and when the army coup took place, many Nationalists who were trapped inside the city were forced to go into hiding. In spite of this, many had been flushed out and imprisoned. When it had looked as though the Nationalist army might be on the point of taking Madrid in early November, there was serious concern that the army officers now in prison might join the invading force. To prevent this from happening, several thousand prisoners were evacuated and shot in cold blood outside the city by Republican guards who were eager to join the defense of their capital.

Pablo was silenced. Even diehard supporters of the Republic were ashamed of what had happened. He walked away. Sometimes this was easier than pursuing an argument with his son, and though he totally disagreed with him, Ignacio's final words rang almost too true. In this conflict it was sometimes hard to say who was completely without blame.

The horror continued in Granada. One afternoon in December, when the streets were dark by early afternoon and the cobbles shone like metal under the streetlamps, two Nationalist soldiers came into the bar. This time there was no need for them to hammer on the glass. The bar was open and still full of customers having coffee after their lunch.

"We'd like to take a look around," one of the soldiers announced to Pablo, in a manner that was too friendly for comfort.

The café owner made no attempt to get in the way of their search, knowing that it would only incite them to unnecessary aggression.

Behind the bar was a small kitchen and, off that, a small office not much bigger than a cupboard where Pablo did his ordering and kept his chaotic inventory of goods. As well as a desk, there was an old wooden chest of drawers that spewed out papers even before the Fascist vandals set to work ransacking it. They turned each drawer over until the contents of the chest emptied, not pausing to read even one piece of paper. They were like children, grinning to each other as the mess in the room worsened, enjoying the blizzard as they tossed papers in the air. It looked just like a game. They were not in the slightest bit interested in the bills for bread and ham.

Pablo continued to serve at the bar. "Don't worry," he said bravely to his wife. "We'll clear the mess up later. We've got nothing to hide, and I'm sure they'll soon be gone."

Concha sliced carefully through a huge slab of *manchego*, arranging it with more than usual care on a plate, successfully making herself look busy and at ease. Inside, her stomach churned with fear. Silently she and Pablo agreed that a pose of complete innocence was the best approach to the situation.

Customers continued to drink and talk in quiet tones, but the tension in the room was palpable. People in Granada were accustomed now to such intrusions, and though it was hard to talk naturally in this atmosphere, they were determined to hold on to the small routines of their lives, such as the ritual of visiting a bar or café at least once a day.

The two intruders were not really there to search. Once the room was blanketed in white, their attention turned to the real reason they had come. It was the radio that interested them. The rest had been a charade. With a triumphant look on his face, the taller of the two soldiers reached for the dial, turned it on and stood back. There was no need to tune it.

A signal was already being picked up, and a voice now filled the room. It was the unmistakable tones of the communist radio station that regularly broadcast its updates on the current state of events across the country. He turned up the volume so that the sound carried out of the room and into the bar. There was a definite smirk on the face of the younger soldier as he appeared in the café. The radio now blared around the room. Pablo and Concha immediately ceased their activities, and behind the barrier of the bar, they clasped hands. All eyes focused on the Fascists who stood, arms folded, perfectly calm.

Concha always listened to the radio in the very early hours of the morning, when Pablo had cleaned up the last of the ashtrays and glasses and the rest of the family had retired to bed.

The higher ranking soldier cleared his throat. He would need to project his voice to make himself heard above the sound of the radio. Concha loosened her tight grip on her husband's hand and moved slightly forward. She would not give this pair the satisfaction of an interrogation. She would give herself up now and save everyone time. It was not to be so easy, however. She could feel her husband's hand locked around her upper arm, and then, a moment later, he had pushed her almost roughly to one side and now stood in front, partially blocking her view of the soldiers.

There was a fraction of a second in which she might have protested, but then the moment had passed. Pablo held out both wrists, was handcuffed, and seconds later was being led out into the street and away. His look silenced his wife. She knew what it meant. If she spoke up then, they would take not just him but her as well. This way they only got one of them.

She was racked with guilt, but shock allowed her to carry on with her day's work in a dream state.

Mercedes walked into the café about an hour after the soldiers had left with her father. She had spent the morning with Paquita and her mother, helping them to organize things in their new apartment. The fabric of her friend's home in the Albaicín had proved to be unstable after the summer bombardment, and for safety's sake they had been obliged to find somewhere else to live. For the first time in a while, Mercedes wanted to dance, and she hoped to find Antonio at home. He could just about pick out a tune, and her need was strong enough for her to overlook the fact that he was a poor substitute for Javier or Emilio.

Concha was in the office reordering the last of the strewn papers when her daughter appeared. She knew immediately that something was wrong. She had not seen her mother so pale since the night that Emilio was taken away. Moments later, Antonio returned home from school and Concha calmly informed them both of what had taken place. They were distraught, but there was nothing to be done.

Ignacio returned late that night, unaware that anything was amiss. His mother was locking up for the night, and his reaction to his father's arrest was one of anger. It was not directed against those who had arrested him but against his own family, in particular, Concha.

"But why did he have to listen to that radio?" he protested. "Why did you let him?"

"I didn't let him," she explained quietly. "It wasn't him listening to it."

"It was Antonio!" he shrieked, his voice cracking with anger. "That *rojo* brother! The stupid bastard—he'll be the death of all of us, you know. He doesn't care—you do realize that, don't you? He doesn't care!"

His face was almost up against his mother's. She could feel his hatred.

"It wasn't Antonio," she said quietly. "It was me."

"You . . . ?" His voice was quieter now.

She explained that it was she who had really committed the crime.

Ignacio was furious with both his parents. His father should have stopped her from listening in to subversive radio stations, and she should not have made herself an object of such suspicion by campaigning for Emilio's release.

"You should have kept a low profile," he raged at her. "This is already branded the *café de los rojos*, even if Father didn't realize it!"

But there was nothing that could be done. Some days later they heard that Pablo Ramírez was in a prison not far from Sevilla.

When first arrested, Pablo had been locked up, along with hundreds of others, in the cinema of a nearby town. Many prisons were makeshift at that stage. The Nationalists were arresting so many thousands of people that the ordinary prisons were overflowing. Bullrings, theaters, schools, and churches all became places to lock up the innocent, and the irony was never lost on the Republicans that places of pleasure, entertainment, education, and even worship now became venues for torture and killing.

In the cinema where Pablo found himself, afraid, disoriented, and in the dark for twenty-four hours a day, people slept in the foyer, in the aisle, and slumped in the uncomfortable wooden seats. This had lasted a few days before a group of them was transferred to a prison two hundred kilometers north. No one bothered to tell them its name.

The prison had been built for three hundred inmates but now held two thousand. At night they lay tightly packed in rows without so much as a finger's width in which to turn and with nothing to cushion them from the stone floors. It was a cold hell. If one man coughed, the whole cell was woken, and their proximity to each other meant that a single case of tuberculosis could spread like a forest fire.

Pablo was moved to several different prisons during this period, but the routine was the same in all of them. The day began even before dawn broke, with the menacing jangle of keys and the thunderous sound of metal bolts being slid across to release the prisoners from their cages. There was a breakfast of thin gruel, enforced attendance at religious services, the singing of Fascist patriotic songs, and long hours of pure tedium and discomfort in the icy, lice-ridden cells. Dinner was like breakfast but with a handful of lentils tossed into the liquid, and it was at this stage of the day that fear began to stir their bellies.

After their evening meal, a few men began to mutter prayers to a God they hardly believed in. Sweat broke out on every temple and hearts palpitated. It was time for the execution list to be read out in the dull monotone of the prison governor. They were obliged to listen, dreading the sound of each first syllable in case it was the beginning of their own name. The condemned would be taken away that night and shot the following dawn. The list seemed arbitrary and appearance on it could be a matter of chance, as though the warders had sat around a brazier drawing lots to pass the time.

For most there was a mixture of nausea and relief at realizing they would live another day. Always, one or two who had heard their names lost their self-control, and their raw, helpless grief jolted the others from complacency. It could easily be them tomorrow.

Occasionally, Concha visited Pablo. She would leave early in the morning and return at midnight, racked with anxiety at the conditions he was living in and her fear that Emilio would be facing the same horror. She still had not seen her son.

Apart from those visits, Concha's every waking hour was now spent running the café. Recognizing that her mother was cracking beneath the strain, Mercedes now offered to help and learned that keeping busy was one way to take her mind away from the absence of so many people she loved.

They had been informed that Emilio had been moved to a prison near Huelva, which was an even more difficult journey than the one to Cádiz, but the following month Concha was finally able to visit him. She had packed a basket with food and supplies and was half excited about seeing him and half fearful of the state he might be in.

When she arrived at the prison, the officer looked at her with disdain.

"Your rations for Ramírez won't be required," he said icily.

She was handed the death certificate. It stated that Emilio had died of tuberculosis. For so long she had clung to a last shred of hope, but it was now replaced with the uncompromising certainty of death.

Concha had no recollection of her journey home. Numbness and shock allowed her to function mechanically for the many hours it took to get back to Granada.

Ignacio had become an increasingly rare presence. The fragmentation of his family should have concerned him, but his main interest was one of self-preservation, so as usual only Antonio and Mercedes were there when their mother arrived home. The pallor of her skin and the colorlessness of her lips told them everything. They put her to bed and quietly sat with her through the night. The following day she silently showed them the death certificate. It told them only what they already knew.

When her mother was away visiting her father, Mercedes ran the café single-handedly, but on other days, when she had some time, she went up to the Sacromonte. Dancing was the only part of her life that had any meaning now. She took a risk to do so, given that there were new restrictive rulings on behavior in Granada. Women were obliged to dress with modesty, to cover their arms, and to wear high collars, but, more significantly, "subversive" music was banned, as was dancing. The tight tourniquet of the regime made Mercedes want to dance all the more. It was an expression of freedom that she would not allow them to take away.

María Rodríguez had limitless patience and an inexhaustible range of footwork sequences to show Mercedes, and she was the first to appreciate that this girl had added new layers to her dancing. The absence of Javier, the death of Emilio, and the atmosphere of grief that saturated her home meant that little was required of her imagination when she had to express pathos and loss. It was as real as the floor beneath her feet.

In Antonio, preoccupied and distant, there was no trace of the smiling older brother that Mercedes remembered. He was now the acting head of the household and was always concerned about Mercedes' welfare, especially when she returned late from the Sacromonte. This was now a city where dancing was not considered desirable.

In the shuttered nocturnal gloom of the apartment, the discreet click of a closing door penetrated the silence. To the crime of being late, Mercedes had added the sin of trying to conceal her surreptitious homecoming.

"Mercedes! Where in the name of God have you been?" came a harsh whisper.

Antonio emerged from the shadows into the hallway, and Mercedes stood facing him, her head bowed, hands concealed behind her back.

"Why are you so late? Why are you doing this to us?"

He hesitated, suspended in the uncertain space between total despair and uncompromising love for this girl.

"And what are you hiding? As if I couldn't guess."

She held out her hands. Balanced on her flattened palms was a pair of scuffed black shoes, the leather as soft as human skin, their soles worn to transparency.

He took her wrists gently and held them in his hands. "Please, for the very last time I am asking you . . ." he implored.

"I'm sorry, Antonio," she said quietly, her eyes now meeting his. "I can't stop. I can't help myself."

"It's not safe, *querida mia*, it's not safe."

# CHAPTER 19

Antonio and Ignacio's rift grew deeper every day. Francisco Pérez, his close friend, had put it into Antonio's head that his brother might have had something to do with the betrayal of his father, Luis, and brother, Julio. It had seemed an outrageous accusation at the time, but Antonio had never been able to dismiss it entirely. Ignacio's close connections with the right-wing element that now held the power in the city certainly left no doubt in anyone's mind that he was in Franco's camp. He was a celebrity mascot for some of the city's most vicious perpetrators of injustice and violence.

Antonio knew he had to exercise the most extreme caution. In spite of their blood kinship, he was aware that his views and friendships with active socialists made him vulnerable with his brother.

Though Granada was in Nationalist hands, there remained a strong undercurrent of support for the legal Republican government, and there were many people prepared to resist the tyranny under which they were now forced to live. This meant that the atrocities of war were not only perpetrated by supporters of Franco. Murders of people suspected of collaboration with Franco's troops were commonplace, and there were frequently signs of torture to be found on their corpses.

Some of these incidents began as little more than street brawls, with name-calling, pushing, and shoving. Within moments they might turn into full-scale fights between young men who, in many cases, had grown up together kicking a ball in the street. The same maze of narrow streets, with their sweet-sounding names, Silencio, Escuelas, Duquesa, once the location for endless childhood games of hide and seek, became the scene of terrifying pursuit. Doorways, momentary hiding places in those happy times, might now provide refuge and the difference between life and death.

On a night late in January 1937, Ignacio and three of his friends had spent most of the evening drinking in a bar near the new bullring. It was in the area frequented by supporters of the new regime and a hang-out of the bullfighting crowd, so if Republican sympathizers showed their faces it was likely to lead to trouble. There was a small group of drinkers in the corner who were not known to most of the regulars, and a scent of trouble hung in the air. Even if no one turned to stare, they were all aware of the quartet of slightly scruffily dressed youths, and the barman served them with careful formality, not wishing to engage in conversation.

Around midnight, the strangers got up to leave. As they walked by, one of them gave the seated Ignacio a hard shove in the shoulder. In any other circumstances it might have been construed as a friendly gesture, but not in these times and not in this bar. It was Enrique García. He and Ignacio had been at school together and had not been the best of friends even then.

"How's Ignacio?" Enrique asked. "How's Granada's number-one matador?"

The last comment was taunting, and Ignacio was quick to pick up the innuendo. García's insinuation that he was involved in the executions that had been taking place in the city infuriated him. For Ignacio, there was a distinction between what he regarded as being a casual informer and actually being an assassin. His own blood lust he saved for the bullring.

He knew that he should not react. If García was here to pick a fight, this would give him just the excuse he needed.

García towered over Ignacio. Like a picador on horseback, the man had a clear advantage. Rarely did Ignacio feel so vulnerable, and he hated this man's proximity and the menacing way in which he leaned over him, as if poised to plunge a *pica* into his side. If Ignacio was to control his hot-blooded temperament, he had better get out of here. Fast.

"Right," he said quietly, looking around at his circle of friends. "I think it's time for me to go."

A murmur passed around the group. It was relatively early for them to be leaving, but they could see that Ignacio needed to be on his way. There was unspoken acknowledgment between them that if they accompanied him outside, it might be taken as a sign of aggression. It was clearly preferable for Ignacio to slip away. There was a chance that the situation might defuse itself if he did so.

Within seconds he was on the street. In spite of the hour, there was no one else around. Hands in his pockets, he sauntered up San Geronimo toward the cathedral. It was a damp night, and the cobblestones glinted in the light of the dim gas lamps. He was not going to hurry. Thinking he heard the sound of another footstep, he turned his head, but there was no one there and he walked on, stubbornly determined not to hasten his step. Close to the top, he turned a sharp right toward one of the city's busiest streets.

It was there on the corner that he felt a sharp pain in the side of his neck. Whoever delivered the blow had been waiting for him in a doorway, knowing that his victim would be taking this route to get home. The shock sent him reeling into the gutter. He bent double with pain; his vision blurred and his stomach churned with nausea. A second blow was dealt between his shoulder blades. With trepidation, his greatest fear being that his handsome face might be struck, he raised his head and saw three more men approaching him. They had appeared from the street parallel to San Geronimo, Santa Paula, and he realized that he had walked into some kind of carefully laid trap.

There was only one course of action now, and that was to try to escape. Fueled by a surge of adrenaline, Ignacio began to run. His fitness for the bullring had never been put to such good use. He turned blindly, left and right, losing himself in these streets that he had known so well since boyhood. His sight was still blurred, but he kept his eyes to the ground, watching his feet so that he did not trip. A sensation of dampness spread across his body.

To get his breath back, he crouched in a doorway. He saw that it was not sweat that saturated his shirt but blood, copious and crimson. He had his own weapon, a bone-handled knife he always carried with him, and though he had not yet had the chance to use it, he now reached inside his jacket to check that it was there. His only thought was to get home, but as he tried to get to his feet, his legs gave way beneath him.

He knew now he was the hunted beast, with little chance of getting away unscathed from his adversaries, who were no doubt armed with sharper blades than his. Perhaps he could remain concealed until they called off the chase. In a moment of rare leniency, the director of a bullfight will grant a reprieve if he thinks that the bull has showed an outstanding degree of bravery. Ignacio prayed that these *rojos* might think that he had succeeded in shaking them off and leave him be. Perhaps this was the optimism that a bull carried with him right through to that final moment with the matador: that there will be a last-minute chance of salvation.

When he had gone into the bar earlier that evening, he had been as unaware of what was to come as a bull entering the ring. Those lefties had planned it all, he now realized, and they thought they knew the outcome, like the ticket-holders at the *corrida*. The whole evening had taken him through the stages of the bullfight, and as he crouched in that dark doorway, his body was tensed to withstand the final blow that was surely to come. Those moments of truth for the beasts he had brought to their knees passed before him, and he knew then the inevitability of his end. There had never been a shred of doubt about the result of this ritual. He had been as trapped as a bull in a ring from the moment of García's first passing shove to the wounds he had sustained.

Perhaps this was the last of Ignacio's coherent thoughts before he began to slide into unconsciousness, his body now slumped so a passerby might have mistaken him for a sleeping beggar. Dimly, he saw two figures approaching. In his blurred vision of a now fast-fading world, their heads seemed haloed in the lamplight. Perhaps these were angels coming to his rescue.

On a street called Paz, García seized him by the jacket and swiftly delivered one last knife thrust. This final stab was an unnecessary gesture. You cannot murder a dead man.

They dragged him by the ankles into the middle of the road so that in the early hours of daylight his body would be discovered; such a killing was as important for its propaganda value as for being a specific act of revenge. From a niche in the wall of a nearby church, a saint gazed down at Ignacio's body. A broad red trail marked the route from where he had hidden, and a trickle of blood found a course between the cobbles and wound its way through them. The rain would have washed it all away by morning.

Inside the church, an effigy of Christ appeared to drip with blood through his neatly pierced side; outside, the life of a real man had ebbed swiftly away through a crude gash in his neck.

As it was getting light, a message arrived at El Barril. For Concha the sound of hammering on the door immediately evoked the terrible memory of Emilio's arrest. She had scarcely slept since that night almost six months before, and even when she did, she was roused by the slightest sound, the bang of a shutter in the next street, the stirring of one of her remaining children in his or her bed, a creak on the stair, a stifled cough.

Antonio was sent to identify the body. It was not as though there could be any doubt. Though he had been savaged with stab wounds, Ignacio's handsome face was unblemished.

Dressed in his finest *traje de luces*, Ignacio was taken from the morgue and driven by horse and carriage up to the cemetery on the hill overlooking the city. Antonio led the funeral cortège. His sister put what little strength she had into supporting her inconsolable mother, bearing her meager weight against hers.

For Concha Ramírez, each step was an effort, as though she carried the burden of the coffin herself. At the approach to the cemetery gates she suddenly felt the full force of the irrefutable: that two of her sons were dead. Before this moment, she could cling to some small vestige of hope that none of this was real. It was not a destination she cared to reach. Friends walked silently behind them, heads bent, staring at dirty shoes on the damp road.

A sizable crowd turned out for this funeral. Along with the family ap-

peared every bullfighting *aficionado* within a hundred miles of Granada
and the outlying areas. Ignacio's may not have been a long career, but it
was a distinguished one, and in a short time he had established a large
following. This included a good number of women; some of them were
simply nameless admirers in his crowd, but just as many were girls who
had been loved by him, whether for a few days or just for one night. His
mistress, Elvira, was there, too, along with her husband, Pedro Delgado,
who had come to pay his respects to one of Andalusía's finest young fighters. He tried to ignore the copious tears that rolled unchecked down his
wife's cheeks but then noticed that she would have been alone among the
women if she had not been crying.

A stone marked the spot. *"Tu familia no te olvida."* There may only
have been one corpse, but the grieving was more than enough for two.
The Ramírez family shed bitter tears. Concha wept for the loss of not just
one but two of her fine sons and mourned them fiercely and equally. Both
Emilio and Ignacio had tested the limits of their parents' tolerance, but
none of that seemed important now.

The grief of losing Emilio was as raw on this cold January day as it
had been on the day he had been taken from their home, and it seemed
as though Concha's state of mourning might have no end without the
presence of a body. This funeral served as a double ceremony for both
second- and third-born.

Though both Antonio and Mercedes were devastated by the loss of
their brothers, it was the scale of their mother's grief that overwhelmed
them. For days she did not eat, speak, or sleep, and it seemed that nothing would bring her out of this catatonic state. For a long while she was
beyond their reach.

To lose loved ones on both sides of this conflict was a double misfor-
tune for the Ramírez family, and they were bewildered that they had been
dealt this blow. They survived the following weeks in a state of disbelief,
oblivious to the fact that similar events were now taking place all over
their country. For the present it was no consolation that theirs was not the
only family enduring such unforeseen horror.

# CHAPTER 20

The crisp days of January had now given way to the damp days of February that wrapped a gray blanket around the city. The sun scarcely penetrated the clouds, and the Sierra Nevada had disappeared into the mist. It was as though Granada had no connection with the world outside.

Eventually, the acute grief in the Ramírez family lessened, and the day-to-day business of surviving in a country at war with itself began to distract them. The café had begun to look neglected. Concha's attempts to keep the place clean and swept were woefully inadequate. Even if she could have managed all alone, anxiety for her husband exhausted her, and a lingering sense of loss over Ignacio and Emilio continued to sap her energy.

Food shortages were becoming increasingly common, and it was a daily struggle to get supplies for her family as well as provisions for the café. El Barril was her children's inheritance, and its survival was now her sole preoccupation. Concha tried not to resent the portly girthed owners of the grand homes in the Paseo del Salón who always seemed to have plenty to eat when for many it was a period of queues and malnourishment.

Over the past few months, Mercedes had become progressively less self-centered, and now helped her mother without needing to be asked. In her own mind, however, she felt overwhelmed by the futility of it all. Serving people coffee and small glasses of fiery cognac sometimes seemed so utterly pointless, and occasionally she could not help expressing this to her mother.

"I agree with you, Merche," said Concha. "But it reminds people of normal life. Maybe that's enough for the present."

Brief moments of social intercourse in a busy café were the only link with earlier days of peace and what they would soon describe as "the old days." For Mercedes everything seemed bleak. Naked trees stood like skeletons in the streets and squares. The city was gradually being stripped bare of everyone she cared about. She had still not received any news from Javier. It had been more than six months.

One morning, Concha was watching her daughter sweep the café floor, slowly and meticulously moving crumbs, ash, and scraps of paper napkin into the center of the room. She observed how her daughter drew perfect invisible arcs on the floor and how her hips rolled in a circular motion as she worked. The sleeves of her knitted cardigan were rolled up and the muscles of her sinewy arms were taut as she gripped the broom. Concha had no doubt that, in her imagination, Mercedes was in some other place. Dancing no doubt. Listening to Javier.

Mercedes had lived in a dream world since she was a small child, and now it was only her fantasies that made life bearable. Sometimes she wondered if it would be like that until she died. It was certainly the only way to survive these cursed times. She looked up, feeling her mother's gaze.

"Why are you staring at me?" she demanded sulkily. "Isn't my cleaning good enough?"

"Of course it is," replied her mother, feeling the strength of her resentment. "You're doing a very good job. I do appreciate it, you know."

"But I hate it. I hate every second, of every minute, of every hour of every day," she retorted petulantly, sending the broom clattering across the room.

She pulled out one of the wooden chairs from a nearby table and for a moment her mother shrank back, thinking that she was about to throw that too.

Instead, Mercedes sank down onto it, exhausted. She rested her elbows on the table and held her head in her hands. Even if Mercedes had dealt bravely with her losses during the last few months, her ability to hide her feelings suddenly left her.

The young woman had more than enough to weep about. Two of her beloved brothers had died, her father was in prison, and Javier, the man who had ignited greater feelings of love than she had ever imagined possible, had vanished. Even Concha could not expect her daughter to be content with what remained. This was the moment to lament what had been taken away. Gratitude and the counting of blessings could wait.

One of their regular customers appeared at the door and then retreated; he could see that it was not a good moment for his daily *café con leche*.

Concha drew up a chair close to her daughter and put her arm around her. "My poor Merche," she whispered. "My poor, poor Merche."

Mercedes scarcely heard her, so loud was her keening.

Though their circumstances were not of Concha's making, she felt profoundly guilty about the way her daughter's life was turning out. It was as though the essence of it had been ripped out, and she sympathized with her frustration and sadness. Though they went about their lives as normally as possible, strain was etched on the faces of everyone who lived in Granada. Fear of the Civil Guard, of the Nationalist soldiers, and even of the wagging tongues of their neighbors haunted them. The tension in this city was affecting them all.

Concha's instincts were to lock her daughter away and to protect her from everything outside this dark, wood-paneled room. Now that her husband and her son had been seized from these four walls, home no longer seemed to offer the same security they had once taken for granted. Both women knew that the warmth and safety it appeared to offer were merely an illusion. For this reason she found herself speaking words that were contrary to every ounce of maternal instinct.

"You must find him."

Mercedes looked up at her with surprise and gratitude.

"Javier," Concha said emphatically, as though there could be any doubt about who she meant. "You must see if you can find him. I suspect he is waiting for you."

It took Mercedes no time to prepare, and within minutes, she was ready to go. Her eagerness to see Javier again overcame any hesitation about setting off alone. Up in her room, she grabbed her coat and a scarf. She tucked the photograph of her *tocaor* into her purse and then, at the last moment, noticed her dancing shoes just poking out from under her bed. I can't go without those, she thought as she bent down to pick them up. When she found Javier, she was quite likely to need them.

As Mercedes came downstairs, Concha was in the bar finishing the cleaning.

"Look, I know your father would disapprove of me letting you go . . . and I'm not sure it's the right thing . . ."

"Please don't change your mind," Mercedes appealed to her mother. "I'll be back soon. So . . . wish me good luck."

Concha swallowed hard. She could not show Mercedes her anxiety. She hugged her briefly and handed her some money, a lump of bread and some cheese wrapped in waxed paper, knowing that her daughter had not eaten yet today. Neither could bring herself to say the word "goodbye."

Just as the bells of the nearby church of Santa Ana were clanging twelve, Mercedes hastened out of the café.

Concha carried on. Anyone would have thought it was business as usual.

Concha had been so preoccupied with the mechanics of keeping the café running that she had ceased to monitor Antonio's comings and goings. With all her other anxieties, her first-born son seemed one of the few people about whom she did not need to worry. School was functioning again, and Concha assumed that his late nights were being spent at school preparing lessons. But, in fact, all his free time was being spent with Salvador and Francisco, his close childhood friends.

Silence had never meant solitude for El Mudo. Expressive eyes and perfect features drew people to this boy. Young women drawn into his embrace were never disappointed by his lovemaking, and his gentle instincts for a woman's needs were all the more sensitive for his lack of speech and hearing. They adored him all the more for the fact that they never left his bedroom with declarations of love echoing in their ears, their hopes vainly raised in the heat of the night. His two friends were in awe of his success.

Often the trio felt itself the object of curiosity. Strangers were fascinated by the spectacle of their sometimes wild gesticulations. Outsiders, who mostly assumed that all three of them were unable to hear or speak, found the boys as entertaining as mime artists and were intrigued by the silent world they inhabited. To local people, the sight of Antonio, Francisco, and Salvador all rocking with silent mirth in the corner of the café was part of an everyday scene. When only two of them were together, they always played a game of chess.

They met most days in the same café where they had licked ice creams as children and had grown up to believe in similar ideals. Their socialist beliefs now bonded them more closely than ever. The blood loyalty they had sworn to each other when they were eight years old had never wavered and for all three of them, socialism was the only possible route to a fair society. They knew some of the radicals in the city, left-wing lawyers and a smattering of politicians, and they tended to go to the bars they frequented, hovering on the edge of any group where politics was being discussed.

That evening, they had already gone over the same old ground, discussing for the hundredth time what was happening in Granada, where supporters of the Republic were still being randomly arrested. Salvador suddenly gestured to his companions that they needed to be watchful of two men in the corner of the bar. Being deaf, he could read more than most into a minor change of facial expression, which had led some to suspect him of supernatural mind-reading powers. In truth, he did what anyone could do: he observed the finest nuances of facial expression and learned to detect the merest hint of discomfort. His judgment was unerringly accurate.

"Be careful," he signed. "Not everyone in here shares our views."

Generally they could communicate with each other in complete privacy, but occasionally Salvador would sense an unfriendly scrutinizing stare. Now was one of those moments. He was not, after all, the only *sordomudo* in Granada and there were others who might know the language.

"Let's go," said Antonio.

They would have to continue their planning elsewhere, and all three rose to leave, tucking a few pesetas under the ashtray for their beers.

Within minutes they were back in Salvador's apartment. With an ear pressed close to its heavy door, even a determined eavesdropper would have struggled to hear more than the occasional rustle. Salvador was currently living alone. His mother and grandmother had been at an aunt's *cortijo* outside the city when the coup had taken place and had not returned. His father had died when he was eleven.

Salvador cleared the table of a variety of cups and plates, and they sat down. He set a pan of water on the gas stove and found a small bag of coffee. Francisco was already using a dirty plate as an ashtray, and the smoke coiled its way up to the high ceiling, clinging to the yellowing walls.

They were gathered at the table to make plans together, but there was a sense of unease, not only because the neighbor, a thin-faced book-keeper, had opened his door to peer at them when they had passed but because resentment was simmering between them. The air had to be cleared.

Like all of those who opposed Franco, the three of them had accepted that there had never been any real means of resistance to the coup in Granada. The city's strongly conservative heartland had received the Nationalist troops with almost open arms, and it was too late to do anything about it now, since to show yourself an enemy of the new regime was tantamount to suicide.

Though Franco's men were firmly in charge of Granada, it did not mean that all those who opposed the *alzamiento*—the uprising—were apathetic. Francisco had certainly not been idle. He now knew that the charges against his father and brother had been the mere possession of trade union cards and had lost no time in seeking revenge for their deaths. He did not care how. His only desire was for the sour smell of Nationalist blood. Although the Fascists held the city of Granada with a firm fist, their grip on many of the surrounding rural areas was still tenuous. Francisco had become part of a campaign of resistance and subversion. In some places, Civil Guard garrisons that had betrayed the Republic were easily overcome, and once they were out of the way, there were plenty of young men like Francisco overflowing with anger to unleash against the landowners and priests who supported Franco.

Land workers and trade unionists had then set about collectivizing some of the great estates, and the storehouses of the landowners were broken open. Malnourished peasants waited outside, desperate for anything with which to feed their families. Bulls, which had been bred and grazed on the finest pastures, were slaughtered and eaten. It was the first meat that many of them had tasted in years.

It was not only the blood of the bulls that Francisco spilled. Violence was perpetrated against individuals too. Priests, landowners, and their families paid the price that many of those who supported the Republic felt they deserved.

Antonio, who clung on to the ideals of justice and fairness, balked at these random and uncoordinated acts.

"It does more harm than good," he said bluntly, churned up with a mixture of disgust and admiration at what his friend was capable of. "You know what your priest-killings and your nun-burnings mean to the Fascists, don't you?"

"Yes. I do," responded Francisco. "I know exactly what they mean to them. They show them we mean business. That we're going to run them out of the country, rather than stand by and let them stamp all over us."

"The Fascists don't care about those old priests and a few nuns—but you know what they do give a damn about?" he said.

For a moment Antonio had abandoned the use of sign language. He sometimes found it hard to express himself that way. Salvador put his finger to his lips, urging his friend to keep his voice down. There was every danger that someone could be listening at the door.

"What?" said Francisco, unable to contain himself to a whisper.

"They want support from outside Spain and they use your actions for propaganda. Are you too stupid to see that? For every priest that dies, they probably win a dozen more foreign troops. Is that what you want?"

Antonio's blood was raised as well as his voice. He could hear himself sounding like a schoolteacher, didactic, patronizing even, and yet, just as when he was in the classroom, he was completely certain of his rectitude. He had to impress this on his friend. He sympathized with Francisco's thirst for blood and for action, but he wanted his friend to make good use of this passion, in a way that was not counterproductive. Reserving their energies for a united onslaught against the enemy was how Antonio felt it should be done. It was the only chance any of them had.

Francisco sat in silence, and Antonio carried on haranguing him, ignoring the appeals of Salvador to leave him alone but reverting now to signing.

"So how do you think they react in Italy? What does the Pope say when they tell him what's happening to priests here? No wonder Mussolini is sending troops to support Franco! Your actions are giving us *less* chance of winning this war, not more! It's hardly winning sympathy for the Republic."

For his part, Francisco had no regrets. Even if his friend Antonio was right and retribution followed, his sanity had been saved by the momentary release he felt when he pulled a trigger. The satisfaction of seeing the target of his well-directed bullet folding over and sinking slowly to the ground was immense. He had needed ten such moments to feel that his father and brother were avenged.

In spite of these words to one of his oldest friends, a small part of Antonio despised his own inaction. His family was fragmented, his brothers killed, his father imprisoned, and what had he done? Though he disapproved of the way in which Francisco had gone about it, he quietly envied that he had enemy blood on his hands.

Salvador added his support to Antonio's appeal. "And the massacre of all those prisoners too," he signed. "They've hardly helped our cause either, have they?"

Even Francisco had to agree with this. The execution of the Nation-alist prisoners in Madrid had been an atrocity, and he conceded that it was not a moment for them to be proud of. Most important for Antonio's argument, the event had been used by the Nationalists to illustrate the barbarism of the left and had cost the Republicans dearly in terms of the support they so desperately needed.

Whatever the differences of opinion that might have existed between these three friends, there was one thing that now united them: they were all ready to break out of the prison that Granada had become, not to take part in isolated acts of barbarism but to join a more coordinated campaign.

"Whatever we agree or disagree about, we can't hang around here, can we?" urged Francisco. "It's too late for Granada, but that's not the whole of Spain. Look at Barcelona!"

"I know. You're right. And Valencia and Bilbao and Cuenca . . . And all the rest. They're resisting. We can't just sit here."

In spite of everything, there was a wave of optimism sweeping across Republican territory trapped under Fascist control that this uprising could be crushed. The resistance met by Franco's troops was only just the beginning. Given time, they could organize themselves.

Salvador, listening, involved and gesticulating agreement, now signed the word that had not yet been stated: "Madrid."

Antonio had left this off his list. This was the place to which they must go. The symbolic heart of Spain that must be fought for at all costs.

Four hundred kilometers north of where they sat in the semi-darkness of Salvador's apartment, Madrid was effectively under siege and if any-where needed to resist the Fascists, it was the capital city. A popular army had been established the previous autumn to unite the portion of the army that remained loyal to the Republic along with volunteer militia to form some kind of unified force with a central command. All three friends yearned to join the action and to be part of the struggle. Unless they went soon it might be too late.

For some months, with the volume turned so low that the listener had to sit with his ear pressed up against it, Antonio had been using the radio in Salvador's apartment to pick up news of the situation in Madrid. The capital city had been suffering bombardment by Franco's troops since November but, with the help of Russian tanks, had held out. Madrid continued to put up stronger resistance than the Nationalists had expected, but there was now a rumor that another great battle was about to begin.

Antonio and his friends may have stood by and watched their own city fall into Franco's hands, but the significance of allowing Madrid to go the same way was not lost on any of them. This had to be the moment, and the compulsion to leave was irresistible. Franco had to be stopped. They had heard that there were young men coming from all over Europe: Britain, France, and even Germany, to help the cause. The notion of this war being fought for them by foreigners spurred them to action.

Throughout the previous few days Antonio had thought only of Franco's growing dominance in Spain and the way in which his troops seemed to be spreading unstoppably throughout the region. The fact that they were meeting substantial resistance in the north of the country gave those that supported the Republic some hope. If he and his friends did not join the fight against Fascism, they might forever regret their inaction.

"We must go," said Antonio. "It's time."

Resolute, he set off home to make preparations for departure.

# CHAPTER 21

By the time Antonio went to tell his mother he was leaving, Mercedes had been on the road for some hours. From Granada, she took the mountain road rather than the main route south, thinking she would meet fewer people that way. Though it was February and the snow was still thick on the mountaintops around her, she had taken off her thick woolen coat. She walked for five hours that day, and but for the extremities of her gloveless fingers, she was almost too warm.

For a short distance between Ventas and Alhama a farmer gave her a lift on his cart. He had just sold two dozen chickens at market and now had space to accommodate a passenger. The smell of livestock hung heavily about him, and Mercedes tried hard not to show her revulsion at the odor of him and the mangy dog that sat between them. There was a comforting normality about riding along next to this weatherbeaten man whose hands were raw with cold and crisscrossed with deep tears and scratches.

Mercedes had regularly spent part of her summertime in the countryside outside Granada, and visits to her aunt and uncle in the sierras had been a happy aspect of her childhood. She was familiar enough with the landscape when the trees were in leaf and the meadows flirtatious with wildflowers, but in winter it was chilled and bare. The fields were a grayish brown, waiting for spring crops to be sown, and the road was stony and rutted. The mule's hoofs regularly slipped on loose shale, which slowed its already lazy pace. The weak afternoon sunlight provided no warmth.

Mercedes knew to trust no one and made little conversation, answering the old man's questions in monosyllables. She came from Granada and was going to visit her aunt in a village outside Málaga. That was about all she volunteered.

He was no doubt equally untrusting of her and gave little information about himself.

Once during the journey they were stopped by a Civil Guard patrol.

"Purpose of journey?" the interrogator demanded.

Mercedes held her breath. She had prepared herself for this, but now that she was faced with the moment, her mouth dried.

"My daughter and I are on our way back to our farm in Periana. We've been to market in Ventas," the farmer said cheerfully. "Chickens were fetching a good price today."

There was nothing to suggest that he was lying. An empty cage, the faint whiff of chicken excrement, a girl. They waved him on.

"Thank you," she said quietly when the patrol was well out of earshot. She looked down at the pattern of the road's rough surface as it moved under the big wooden wheels. She told herself she must still not trust this man and should stick to her fictitious story even if he now appeared to be a friend and knew that she needed some protection.

They traveled on for another hour or so until it was time for the farmer to turn off. His farm was up in the hills; he indicated somewhere in the direction of a wooded area on the horizon.

"Do you want to stop with us for the night? There would be a warm bed for you, and my wife makes a decent enough supper."

In her exhausted state, she was, for a moment, tempted. But what did that invitation convey? Though he had been kind to her, she had no idea who this man was and, wife or no wife, she suddenly felt the full force of her vulnerability. She must keep going toward Málaga.

"Thank you. But I should press on."

"Well, have this anyway," he said, reaching behind his seat. "I shall be enjoying my wife's cooking in an hour or so. I won't be needing it."

She now stood in the road beneath him and reached up to take a small burlap bag. She could feel the reassuring bulk of a small loaf inside and knew that she would be grateful for this the next day. She had nearly run out of the supplies she had stashed away in her pockets and was grateful for replenishments.

Clearly he had not been offended by her refusal of his invitation, but she knew it had been better not to be open with him. Gone were the days when you could feel entirely sure of those you knew, let alone strangers. They wished each other well, and in moments he had disappeared out of sight.

Once again she was alone. The farmer had said that she was about five kilometers from the main road that would lead her to Málaga, so she decided to keep walking until she reached it before having a rest. If she did not set herself these goals, she might never reach her destination.

It was about six in the evening and dark by the time she got to the junction. Hunger was beginning to hammer at her stomach. She sat down by the roadside, leaned against a large stone, and reached into the small sack. As well as the loaf, there was a lump of cake and an orange.

She tore off a wedge of the now dry and crumbly bread and chewed it slowly, washing it down with swigs of water, for a while oblivious to her surroundings and absorbed entirely in sating her hunger.

Uncertain of the distance to the next village and whether she would be able to buy anything to eat there, she hoarded the cake and the orange for later. Protected from the wind, she closed her eyes. Against the dark screen of her closed eyelids, an image of Javier appeared. He was perched on the edge of a low chair, his back curved over his guitar, his eyes cast upward toward her through the dark mop of his fringe. In her imagination, she felt the warmth of his breath and daydreamed that he was only a few yards away, waiting for her to dance. The temptation to step into the dream began to seduce her. In spite of knowing that she should keep walking and that with each passing hour she might have less chance of finding the man she loved beyond measure, Mercedes lay down and slept.

When Antonio retured to the El Barril, there was one dim light still burning behind the bar. He leaned over to reach the switch, and as he did so, a voice startled him.

"Antonio."

He could make out the silhouette of a familiar figure. Obscured in the inky shadows at the back of the café, his mother was seated alone at a table. There was enough light filtering in from a gas lamp in the street for him to cross the room without stumbling into tables and chairs. As he looked at Concha sitting there alone, his heart pounded with fear and sorrow at what he had to tell her. Could he deal her such a blow?

"Mother! What are you doing down here so late?"

Now that he was close, he could see a large glass on the table in front of her. This was very unlike Concha. It had always been his father's job to do the final clearing up in the bar, and he knew that Pablo always sat over a drink at the end of the evening and usually had a few cigarettes too. But not his mother. She was always so desperately tired in the late evening that she would simply bolt the door and ignore the last glasses on the tables, knowing that Mercedes would make it her first job to clear them away in the morning.

There was no reply from Concha.

"Mother—why are you still up?"

There would be a good reason for his mother's change of routine, but he was fearful. Everyone lived on edge in this city.

"Mother?"

Though she was scarcely visible, he could see now that her arms were folded across her body and that she gently swayed. It was almost as though she were rhythmically rocking a baby.

By now Antonio was crouched down next to her, his hands on her shoulders, gently shaking her. Her eyes were closed.

"What is it? What has happened?" His voice was insistent.

Concha tried to reply, but her speech was cloudy with cognac and tears. The effort of speaking made her weep all the more. She was incomprehensible with grief. Antonio held her tight, and when she was reassured by the firm embrace in which he now held her, the spasm of her crying subsided. Eventually, when he let her go, she lifted her floral apron to her face and noisily blew her nose.

"I told her to go," she said falteringly.

"What are you talking about? Who did you tell to go?"

"Mercedes. I told her to go and find Javier. She will never be happy unless she goes to him."

"So you have sent her to Málaga?" responded Antonio with a note of disbelief.

"But if she can track down Javier, they can go somewhere together. She couldn't stay here pining like that. I was watching her every day, aging with grief. This war is awful for all of us, but at least Mercedes has a chance of being happy."

In the darkness, Concha did not see the color drain from her son's face.

"But they're shelling Málaga," he said, his mouth dry with anxiety. "I just heard."

Concha did not seem to hear her son.

He held his mother's hands between his own. It was pointless castigating her at this moment, though he knew his father would not have hesitated.

"We're forced to live with our enemy here," she continued. "At least she's given herself the chance of getting away from them."

Antonio could not disagree. His own view matched hers, almost too closely. He knew that she was right about the sense of impotence that reigned in Granada. Though there had been considerable bloodshed and destruction in the days that followed the coup, the city had been taken over with relative ease and many of its inhabitants regretted that they had not been ready to fight back. Other towns and cities were putting up a much stronger defense.

"So when did she go?"

"She packed a few things this morning. She was gone by lunchtime."

"And if she's challenged, what will her story be?"

"She'll say that she has an aunt in Málaga . . ."

"Well, that much is almost true, isn't it?"

" . . . and that the aunt is sick and she is planning to bring her back to Granada to nurse her."

"It's plausible enough, I suppose," said Antonio, wanting to reassure his mother that she had done the right thing in encouraging his sister to go, though he knew that the whole venture was fraught with potential danger.

In his current role as head of the family, he felt that he should express more anxiety, if not anger, over his sister's irresponsible behavior. They sat in silence for a while, and then Antonio went over to the bar and poured himself a generous tumbler of brandy. He tipped his head back and swallowed it in a single gulp. The sound of his glass landing on the bar startled his mother from her reverie.

"Will she come back if she can't find him? Did she promise?"

Antonio watched his mother's eyes widen with surprise.

"Of *course* she'll come back!"

He wanted to share Concha's optimism, and now was not the time to fill her with doubt.

He put a protective arm around his mother and swallowed hard. Now was not the right time to reveal his own plans either, but he could not delay for long. He was going to need the protection of a dark night, and tonight's cloudy sky and new moon would have been perfect for their departure.

In the very early hours of the following day, woken by the cold dawn, Mercedes made some headway along the main road. It felt open and exposed, but it was virtually a straight line to Málaga from here.

That afternoon, up ahead in the far distance, she saw a small cloud of dust on the horizon. It moved like a slow, small whirlwind. There had been nothing on the road going in the other direction for some hours, and all she had seen was an occasional bare tree along the way.

As the distance between them diminished, Mercedes could make out human shapes. There were a few donkeys, some of them pulling carts, and their pace seemed painfully slow. They were moving no faster than the most cumbersome float in a Holy Week procession.

Their approach was inexorable though, and she began to wonder how she would pass. This human tide formed a barrier between herself and her destination. It was nearly an hour later, when the distance between them had diminished to a few hundred meters and she could hear the uncanny silence in which they walked, that she asked herself the question, "Why?" Why were all these people on the road, on a chilly February afternoon? And why were they so quiet?

It became clear that this was a convoy, a caravan train of people and carts on the move. It was mystifying; they were like a procession that had taken the wrong turn at the *feria*, or pilgrims making a religious journey from one city to another to carry a precious icon. And even as they neared, Mercedes' mind could not make sense of what she saw. It was as though a whole village full of families had decided to move house, all at once, and had piled themselves up with everything they owned: chairs, mattresses, pots, trunks, toys. Mules almost disappeared under the weight and bulk of it all.

Once she was face-to-face with the people who led the way, their silence was unnerving. No one seemed to speak. They looked right through her as though she did not exist. They were like sleepwalkers. She stood aside to let them pass. One by one they went by, old, young, the lame, the wounded, children, pregnant women, eyes staring ahead or fixed to the ground. One thing they all shared, apart from a look of fear, was a sense of resignation. There was vacancy in their expression, as though all emotion had been wiped out of them.

For a while Mercedes watched them pass. It was strange to be unnoticed, and it did not occur to her to stop anyone to inquire where they were going. Then she noticed a woman who was sitting on her haunches, resting by the side of the road. A child sat close by, mindlessly drawing circles in the dust with a stick. Mercedes saw her opportunity.

"Excuse me . . . can you tell me where everyone is going?" she asked gently.

"Going? Where they're going?" The woman's voice, though feeble, conveyed her incredulity that anyone could be asking this question.

Mercedes rephrased her inquiry. "Where have you all come from?"

The woman answered without hesitation. "Málaga . . . Málaga . . . Málaga." Each time she spoke the word, her voice grew fainter until the final syllable disappeared into a whisper.

"Málaga," repeated Mercedes. Her stomach contracted. She knelt down beside the woman. "What has happened in Málaga? Why have you all left?"

Now that they were on the same level, the woman looked at Mercedes for the first time. The quiet crowd continued to file past. No one gave the two women and the grubby child a second look.

"You don't know?"

"No, I've come from Granada. I'm on my way to Málaga. What's going on there?" Mercedes tried to suppress her anxiety and impatience.

"Terrible things. Such terrible things." There was a catch in the woman's throat, as though she feared to recount them.

Mercedes was caught between the desire to know the truth and the dread of it too. Her first thought was for Javier. Was he still there? Was he in this vast crowd, making his way out of the city? She needed to know more, and after a few minutes of sitting in silence with this woman, she plied her with another question. She might be her only source of information, since nobody else seemed to be stopping.

"Tell me. What's happened?"

"Do you have any food?"

Mercedes suddenly realized that there was only one thing that preoccupied this woman. Neither the events of the past few days nor her unknown future interested her. It was the stomach-gnawing ache of hunger and the nagging whine of her little son desperate for something to eat that crowded her thoughts.

"Food? Yes, I do. When did you last eat?" Mercedes was already reaching into her bag to find the cake and the orange.

"Javi!"

The small boy glanced up and within a second was upon them, grabbing the cake from his mother's hand.

"Stop!" she snapped at him. "Not all at once! Don't snatch!"

"It's all right," said Mercedes calmly. "I don't need it."

"But I do," said the woman weakly. "I'm so hungry. Please leave some for me, Javi."

Her appeal was too late. In his desperation, the child had consumed every last crumb, and now his cheeks were almost bursting, leaving him unable to respond.

"It's been so hard for him to understand why we've been desperately short of food for a few weeks," she said tearfully. "He's only three."

Mercedes felt annoyed with this little boy for being greedy. Now she held the orange firmly in her hand and handed it to his mother.

"Here," she said. "Have this."

The woman peeled it slowly. Each segment was offered first to her child and then to Mercedes, and when they declined, she put it in her own mouth, maintaining the discipline to consume it slowly and carefully and to enjoy every drop of juice that trickled down her parched throat.

No one else stopped. The crowd just kept passing. The woman was visibly strengthened.

"I think we should move on now," she said generally to the space around her.

Mercedes hesitated. "But I don't think I am going your way," she said.

"Which way are you heading then? Not to Málaga!"

Mercedes shrugged. "That was my plan."

"Well, if I tell you what has happened there, it might change your mind."

They stood face to face at the edge of the road.

"Tell me then," said Mercedes, trying to conceal her own distress.

"Málaga didn't have a chance," the woman began, her face close up to Mercedes'. "The port was being bombed, but that wasn't the worst bit. It was when they arrived in the city—thousands of them. Maybe twenty thousand, that's what they said."

"Who? Who arrived?"

"Moors, Italians, Fascists, and more trucks and weapons than we had in the whole of our city. It's been smashed to bits—from the sea, from the air, on the ground . . . And there we were—defenseless. No one had thought to dig any trenches! They were raping the women and hacking off their breasts; they were even killing our children."

The horror of it all was almost too much for her to describe. The legionaries who arrived were the most vicious of all Franco's troops and contemptuous of death itself. Most of them had been brutalized by the war in Africa.

"There were thousands seized," she continued. "Innocent men like my husband were executed, their bodies left unburied. They mutilated the dead. There was no choice. We had to get out."

The woman's description was delivered in rapid bursts and under her breath. She did not need to broadcast the information to those who filed past them. They had all been there and so had her son, who did not need a reminder of the horror of the past days.

There were further atrocities to catalogue, and once the woman had begun, she seemed determined to tell Mercedes the whole story. She told it without emotion, recounting the facts dispassionately, numb with shock.

Many of the legionaries were already fugitives and criminals when they were recruited and then, further dehumanized by the ferocity with which they were expected to fight, behaved like animals toward their victims. "*Viva la muerte!*" they chanted. "Long live death!" Even among those who fought on the same side, they instilled fear and disgust.

"The city is on fire. Everything is under threat apart from the Fascists' houses, of course. There is nothing left for anyone there now. Many of these women are now widows. Look at them! Look at us! We have nothing but the clothes we're standing in—and the chance to escape."

Mercedes surveyed the pitiable crowd as they passed. From where she sat at the side of the road, all she saw were countless legs and feet passing in front of her. She did not look at their faces but at the lines of boots, so worn and broken down they might have already walked a thousand miles. The disintegrating leather of old soles provided little protection for blistered flesh. Toes protruded from the remnants of threadbare, rope-soled shoes. One woman appeared to be shod in crimson shoes, but when

Mercedes looked closely, she saw that they were just stained the color of her own blood. It had saturated the canvas.

Mercedes gazed. She was mesmerized. Old calves bulged purple with varicose veins, young feet were horribly misshapen by swellings and blisters, and from stumps of feet tightly bound, traces of blood seeped through the folds in bandages. And dozens had limping gaits, their weight supported by sticks or crutches.

She stood dry-mouthed. If she stayed with these people, she would probably be safe. She wondered again if Javier might be somewhere in this great moving mass of people and convinced herself that she might find her beloved if she asked around enough and showed everyone she met his photograph. If she went to Málaga, it sounded as though she would probably be killed. Her decision was made. With a deep intake of breath, Mercedes turned and faced east.

Night was beginning to fall, but people did not break their journey just because of darkness. They feared that the Fascists would not be content with driving them from their city and would be pursuing them relentlessly even now.

The meager moonlight kept the road in front of them just visible. There were another one hundred and fifty kilometers to go before they reached Almería, which was their destination, and even for the youngest and fittest, it would be many days before it would even be in sight.

Mercedes walked with the woman, who seemed grateful for some company.

"I'm Manuela," the woman eventually told her. "And my little one is Javi."

The child's diminutive form of her lover's name had already endeared the little boy to her. He had ceased to grizzle now that he had eaten and, for a time his mother took him on her shoulders. Mercedes was amazed at her strength, given that her clothes hung from her emaciated body like a shroud and her cheekbones almost pierced her colorless skin. After a while, seeing that Manuela was exhausted, Mercedes took a turn. Javi's mother had removed his worn boots and the child's soft feet bounced on her chest as she walked. Just as she remembered her father doing to her, she held them to make him secure and found much comfort in their warm little pads. She was happy when she realized that his head had slumped on top of hers. He was asleep.

That night, Concha was exhausted, too, and desperate for the solace of her bed. The past twenty-four hours had exhausted her. The last of her customers had just gone home, and briefly she had propped the door open to dissipate the dense pall of smoke that hung in the air. The temperature had plummeted that night, and her breath came out in white plumes as she gave each table a swift, circular wipe.

With the door already open, she was unaware of her son's entrance, and he had to cough to ensure that she was not taken by surprise.

"Antonio! You're home early . . ." Her voice trailed off as she saw the grave look on his face.

He came quickly to the point. "Look, I have to go away, Mother. I'm hoping it won't be for long."

All the things he had had in his mind to say about it being for his father's sake went unsaid.

"That's just what you should do," Concha said, disarming her son with her immediate, measured response. "I'm glad you told me. I always imagined that you might just slip away into the night."

For a moment Antonio was lost for words. His mother's strength astounded and inspired him.

"I could never have done that. How would you have known what had happened to me?"

"But that's what people are doing, isn't it?" replied Concha. "It means that when the Guards come to interrogate the parents, they can say: 'Gone? Has he? Well, I don't know where he has gone . . .' with complete innocence."

Concha felt, as did anyone of Republican leanings, that a crucial point had been reached in this conflict and that Franco's advance had to be stopped.

Antonio was amazed by his mother's understanding but questioned whether it might just be the prospect of losing another of her sons that numbed her. Could she differentiate between departure and death, or were the two simply blurring into a general abyss of loss?

"I don't want you to tell me anything," she pleaded. "I don't want to know—then nothing can be forced out of me. I mustn't be made to betray you."

"Well, I don't know where we will end up anyway."

"We?"

"Francisco and Salvador are coming with me."

"That's good. There's strength in numbers."

Both of them weighed up the ambiguity of Concha's words. They both knew that it was not in manpower where the Republicans lacked strength but in weaponry. While substantial supplies of arms were coming in to Franco's forces from Germany and Italy, those fighting for the Republic were deficient in ammunition, not in men.

There was silence for a moment.

"When are you going?"

"Tonight," he said almost in a whisper.

"Oh . . ." Her voice was small, her breathing shallow now. She tried to make light of her son's imminent departure. "Can I pack you something to eat?"

It was a mother's natural first thought.

Half an hour later he was gone. The air in the room was now crisp and clear, and only then did Concha shut the door. She shivered with cold and dread. Though Antonio had kept it to himself, his mother had a good idea of his destination. She would, though, have endured the slow pulling out of her fingernails before revealing it.

# CHAPTER 22

The thin sliver of moon cast little light on the trio as they left the city a few hours later, allowing them to avoid the keen-eyed attention of the Civil Guard. Getting out of the city without being challenged required a degree of luck and had to be done in the dead of night. They carried just enough food to last until the end of the following day and no keepsakes to undermine the pretense that they were farm laborers in search of work. If they were searched, their story would have to be watertight, and even the smallest token—a memento, a photograph—might be used against them. Spare clothes would certainly arouse suspicion and provide enough evidence for arrest.

For most of that night they walked, wanting to put as big a distance as they could between themselves and Granada before day broke; wherever they could, they branched off onto small roads where they were less likely to encounter Nationalist troops.

In the early hours of the following morning they hitched a ride with a truckload of militia; these men were fired up by the prospect of victory over Franco and were certain this could be achieved. The ragged crew they had joined amused themselves with Republican songs and to passersby raised their clenched fists in salute. Within a few hours, Antonio, Francisco, and Salvador were being treated like brothers. Now they really felt they were on the move.

Like them, the militiamen were aiming to join the efforts to protect Madrid and had heard that a battle was being fought to the southeast of the capital in the Jarama Valley.

"That's where we want to be," said Francisco. "In the thick of things, not here in this truck."

"We'll get there soon enough," muttered Antonio, attempting to stretch his legs.

They trundled for one uncomfortable kilometer after another across the open, empty landscape. In some areas there was little to indicate that this was a country at war with anyone, least of all itself. The open sierra seemed undisturbed. Early crops had been sown by some farmers, who were all but oblivious to the political storm that raged around them, but there were other areas where landowners had not bothered and the naked soil lay uncultivated, germinating the hunger that would eventually bite back at them.

Salvador, buffered by Antonio and Francisco, lip-read the conversation around him but took no part in it. No one commented on his silence. Some of them in the truck were half dead with exhaustion. They had come from towns near Sevilla, where they had been engaged for months in a campaign of heavy but fruitless resistance, and did not even register his presence, let alone that he was different. This was how Antonio and Francisco planned it; if anyone suspected Salvador was deaf, he would not be allowed to fight, but they knew how much it meant to him to be there.

For most of the other twenty-one men, there was palpable excitement at the idea that they might now have a purpose. They were riding into Madrid to lift a siege, and they sang songs of victory before it had been won.

For a few hours each night, they climbed down from the back of the truck, limbs weary from inaction, aching from the discomfort and continual vibration on the unending, uneven road. Once the bottle had been passed around and the singing had faded, there were a few hours of fitful sleep with nothing between the gravelly earth and their heads but prayerful hands. They could not afford the luxury of using a jacket as a pillow. They needed every layer they had around them if the blood was not to freeze in their veins.

Francisco coughed incessantly in his sleep but disturbed no one. At four thirty, Antonio rolled a cigarette and lay in the dark, watching the smoke curl away into the damp air. It was the clank of tin mugs and the faint whiff of something that resembled coffee that stirred them. Their necks stiff, their stomachs hollow with hunger, rested in neither body nor mind, they stretched their limbs. Some got up and wandered off to urinate in the nearby bushes. This was the low point of the day: the colorless dawn, a bitter chill that might not lift until midday, and the prospect of another day of discomfort and hunger. Only later on, as their bodies were warmed by the proximity of one another, did their spirits rise and the songs begin again.

Antonio and his friends were well on their way northward when Mercedes began her second day's trek with the refugees from Málaga. Though people mostly walked in silence, there was the occasional frantic cry of a mother looking for a child. In this great crowd it was easy for people to become separated, and there were several children to be seen aimlessly wandering, their faces shiny with snot and tears and panic. Their distress always upset Mercedes, and her grip on Javi's hand would tighten. No one wanted this unnecessary grief, and great efforts were made to reunite those who were separated.

Though most continued to walk at night, exhaustion and hunger forced some to stop for an hour or so, and there were always small mounds at the side of the road. Families huddled together, a blanket pulled over them for warmth and protection, now making use of the mattress that they had dragged from their home to create a small private tent for themselves, a miniature home.

The chill of the night contrasted with the sudden intense flashes of sunshine that would beat down on them at midday. The warmth never lingered, but for a brief while children would be bare-armed as though for a summer picnic.

In the vanguard of this procession, there were mostly women, children, and the elderly, and these were the ones that Mercedes walked with. They had been the first to leave Málaga, desperate to escape from the city's captors. Farther toward the back of the procession trudged the surviving men and exhausted, defeated militia who had stayed in the city to put up a final show of resistance. Even if they walked night and day, the journey to Almería could take five days. For the old, sick, and injured it might be many more.

A few cars and trucks had set out at the beginning of this exodus, but almost all of them had now been abandoned by the wayside. Along with these was the scattered debris of domestic life. Household chattel hastily taken from kitchen cupboards to form the basis for a new life now lay by the roadside. There were other, more surprising objects: a sewing machine, an ornate but chipped dining plate, an heirloom clock, all now discarded and worthless, along with the optimism with which they had been carried out of their homes.

For the first half of the route, there were many donkeys piled high with bedding, buckets, and even furniture, but most of these were eventually to buckle under the weight of their burdens, and their corpses became a common sight on the side of the road. At first a few flies gathered round their eyes, but once their bodies began to decompose, they arrived in swarms.

Though generally they walked in a silence punctuated only by the sound of their own footsteps and the gentle rattle of their belongings, from time to time Mercedes told Javi a story. Much of the day, she carried him, and they both sucked on sugarcane pulled from the fields. It was all that remained to give them energy now that their food was gone, and when exhaustion overcame them, they would take a fitful nap by the roadside.

Mercedes noticed a trunk that lay open in the middle of the road, its contents spilling out. A few garments had blown into a nearby bush and were now caught on its thorns: a bright white communion dress, an embroidered baby's nightgown, a wedding mantilla. They were spread out on the bush like advertising posters, almost taunting those who saw them with reminders of when those items had last been worn, of a time when life had been peaceful and when baptism and marriage could take place.

Everyone filing past had the same thought. Those rituals now seemed long-ago luxuries.

From time to time they passed through a small town or village that had been evacuated. Nothing remained. A few people ransacked empty homes—not for valuables but for something useful, like a bag of rice that might sustain them for a few more days.

Though Mercedes and Manuela occasionally spoke, there was generally little conversation among the one hundred and fifty thousand that walked. The only sounds were the scrunch of a shoe on the loose surface of the road and the occasional whimper of a baby, some of them newly born by the roadside.

When they were close to Motril, the halfway point of their journey, the two women heard a low grumble. It was late in the afternoon. Mercedes mistook it for the sound of trucks, but Manuela immediately recognized it as aircraft noise and stopped to look up. Nationalist planes were passing low overhead, cumbersome, noisy, and graceless.

People watched them and wondered. No one spoke. Then the bombardment began.

During the months since this conflict had begun, Mercedes had never experienced the feelings of absolute terror that gripped her now. Her mouth filled with the metallic taste of fear, and for a moment the sound of her heart pounding drowned out the cries of alarm that went up around her. Her instinct was to run as hard and fast as she could, but there was nowhere to hide—no cellars or bridges or underground train stations. Nowhere. There was Javi to worry about, in any case, and his mother. She stood rooted to the spot as the planes passed directly overhead, her hands over her ears against the deafening roar.

Mercedes grabbed Manuela, who clasped Javi. They stood locked in this embrace, eyes closed against the world and the horrifying scene unfolding around them. Mercedes could feel the woman's sharp bones through her clothes. It was as though she might snap. They had nothing to protect them and, like most of the inhabitants of Málaga, so recently traumatized by the horrors of shelling and machine-gun fire in their own city, Manuela was briefly paralyzed by the fresh onslaught of Fascist aggression.

"Let's get off the road," shouted Mercedes. "It's our only hope."

The irony was that the only places to hide along this unwelcoming stretch of road were the craters left in the fields by bombs that had exploded earlier. Many people cowered in them, petrified. At least the bombers had supplied some shelter for their terrorized victims.

Soon bodies lay everywhere like broken dolls.

To the horror and disbelief of everyone on the road that day, there was an even more terrifying method of attack to come. When the bombers had finished their work, fighter planes appeared to claim their next wave of victims. In order to instill more terror, they strafed the roads and then the people themselves. There were blinding flashes all around as bullets drew two lines of flaming dots among the screaming crowd. It was not a challenge for the pilots of those planes; they could have blown their targets apart with their eyes shut.

Mothers whimpered like babies when they saw their own children toppled like skittles. Some were mothers of four or five, and there was no protection that they could offer. In any case, a careful aim could wipe out several people in a single burst.

On one occasion, a two-seater plane came so low that Mercedes caught a glimpse of the pilot and behind him the gunner. People scattered, thinking that they might outrun his bullets, but their action was futile. The gunner could easily maneuver his machine gun to maximum devastation. The pilot's face dimpled into a smile as he mowed them down.

Then everything went quiet. The minutes went by and the airplanes did not return.

"I think they've gone now," Mercedes said, trying to reassure Manuela. "We need to be on our way. We don't know when they might come back."

The air was filled with the moans of the injured and bereaved. The problem for many now was whether to make an attempt to bury their dead or to continue toward the sanctuary of Almería. The ground was hard and burial was not easy, but some made the attempt. Others just covered the bodies with the only blankets they had and moved on, taking the guilt and the grieving with them. If it was a mother who had been killed, their children were immediately adopted by others and shepherded onward and away from the gruesome sight of a parental corpse.

In the previous forty-eight hours, there had not been a moment when the man she loved did not occupy the central-most place in her mind. It was only when the bombs came crashing around her that she was jolted out of this reverie. Then, for the first time on her search, he had been far from her mind. Even the possibility that the man she loved might be somewhere in this diminishing crowd temporarily seemed of no importance to her. Getting this fragile creature, Manuela, and her son to safety now became her main concern.

Many were maimed, not killed, and a fresh wave of walking wounded was added to those who had limped from Málaga. The journey had to continue and the direction remained the same. There was no turning back and they could not stand still.

Manuela did not speak. For a moment she seemed paralyzed by fear, but Mercedes' firm arm and the feel of her son's hand pulling on hers brought her to her senses. They resumed their journey.

Where the route turned toward the sea, the waves could be heard bashing against the rocks. The rhythm of nature was oblivious, and once or twice Mercedes saw people lying on a beach and was uncertain whether they were dead or alive. Either way, the sea would sweep them away sooner or later if they did not move. Donkeys lay beside humans, also dying. Swollen tongues protruded from their mouths.

On the fifth day that she had been walking, there was a moment when the sun briefly blazed and the water sparkled. Mercedes found Javi tugging at her skirt and pulling her toward the sea. It seemed to him as though it must be time for play, to toss pebbles into the waves, to dabble his toes into the water.

His childhood would eventually resume but not yet. It would be too macabre to play among corpses.

"No, Javi, not now," Manuela snapped, picking him up.

"We'll go and play in the sea another day," said Mercedes, "I promise."

On a day when even the distant sight of a bird aroused terror in her, evoking memories of the planes that had massacred so many of them, she had only one aim: to reach her destination. Her mind was once again turned toward Javier. The thought of him sustained her as they walked these last kilometers, but she needed a new plan to find him.

Some people never made it to Almería. There were the wounded who fell by the way, but also some who took their own lives. Those such as Mercedes, who had gradually slipped toward the back of the exhausted human flow, saw the bodies of those who had shot themselves and others who had hanged themselves from the trees. They had come this far, but desperation had finally overcome them. Many times Manuela had to hide Javi's eyes.

On reaching Almería, Mercedes was almost overwhelmed with tears of relief at the sight of the buildings and the promise of refuge. They had all walked far enough to deserve a feast, and her first thoughts were of something to eat. She had daydreamed of fresh bread.

For many people, exhaustion now swept over them. The streets of Almería seemed such a safe place to sleep after the exposed unsheltered road, and the pavements were like mattresses after the rough terrain of the week before. Most people sank down gratefully with whatever family they had left, and some dozed in broad daylight, the buildings around cocooning them like the walls of a room.

As soon as they arrived, Mercedes and Manuela began queuing for bread.

"Why don't you go back to Granada to find your family?" asked Manuela as they were standing together in a line. "Javi and I don't want to lose you, but if we had somewhere else to go, we would. You don't have to be here."

Mercedes did not want to return to Granada. It was the least safe option of all. Her family was a marked one. And Javier was not in Granada. It was this single fact that determined her decision. Her only real chance of survival was to stay away, and the only possibility of happiness was to find the man she loved. There was every chance that he would have survived. Javier was younger and stronger than most of the people that she saw around her. If they had escaped from Málaga, would he not have done so too?

"Half of my family aren't even in Granada any longer," Mercedes reminded Manuela, "and I need to carry on looking for Javier. If I don't keep searching, I'll never find him, will I?"

Javi was scratching at the ground with a stick, making a zigzag pattern in the dust, oblivious to the conversation going on between them. Mercedes looked down at the top of his dark head and stroked his hair. All she could see from above were his long lashes and the little splayed cushion of his nose. She picked him up from the ground and stroked his soft cheek. Even after all these days without bathing, the child's skin had a sweetness about it. Holding him was an extraordinary comfort.

"Well, you know you're welcome to be with us, don't you?"

"I know, I know . . ."

She did not want to be blunt, but her only desire now was to find Javier. The woman whose corpse she had seen hanging from the tree a few miles back had run out of purpose. Mercedes had not.

Once she had helped to settle Manuela and Javi safely in the doorway of a boarded-up shop where they would all sleep at least for the coming night, she went off to explore.

She continually stopped people to ask them whether they had seen Javier, and her picture of him was retrieved from her pocket a hundred times. Once or twice she found someone who thought they had seen him. The *guitarrista* was well known in Málaga, and several people were sure they had caught sight of him before they had fled, even if they had not seen him since. At one point her hopes were raised when someone helpfully offered that they had just seen a man with a guitar. Mercedes hastened off in the direction he indicated and soon saw the figure that had been described to her from the back. Her heart missed a beat. Seeing the slim outline of a man carrying a battered guitar case, she hastened after him. She called out and the man turned around. As he did so, she realized that this man bore not the slightest resemblance to Javier. She found herself face to face with a man of more than fifty. She apologized and let him walk away. Tears of disappointment almost choked her.

She retraced her steps to where her companions were. Even with their small number of possessions, they had made a neat, open-fronted home around them. Javi was already asleep, sprawled across his mother's lap. Manuela dozed, her head leaning back against the wooden door frame. They looked peaceful together.

Mercedes wandered off to see if she could find some more food for them all. She joined two queues, only to be disappointed when what was being sold had run out before she had reached the front. Procuring a few grams of lentils at the end of a third was a triumph.

Almería had once been a beautiful city, but she was too tired to notice and was completely unaware of the route she had taken. By the time she had stood in a few queues she had lost track of time. She did not possess a watch, and the sunless afternoon sky gave her no clues. She had been away for perhaps two hours.

As she was beginning to retrace her steps toward the center of the city, she heard the distant sound of a siren and shortly after that the thud of an explosion and then another, closer this time. A shiny silver airplane passed overhead. Surely not here too? Their safe haven had been a very short-lived one.

When she got closer to the main square, she could smell burning and sense the chaos, and as she turned the corner, she found herself going against the tide, just as she had on the day when she met the procession filing out of Málaga. This time she must fight her way through. Panic rose inside her. In all the time since she had left Granada, she had not felt such fear. She was even more terrified than when they had been bombed on the road. The fleeing crowd were pushing her away, back in the direction she had come from, but she fought against them, maneuvering herself toward the edge of the street so that she could stop and wait for the stampede to go by.

Eventually this first wave passed, and then came the casualties. Some were supported; others were carried; many were lifeless. It was an unnervingly silent parade. Eventually they all passed, and but for a few stragglers, dazed and dusty with particles of fallen masonry, the street was quiet again. Mercedes trembled with fear. Though she had pictured what she would see when she turned the corner into the square, her anguish was no less intense when she saw the reality.

One entire side was bombed to oblivion, and every building had collapsed. Not a single wall or pillar remained standing. It was a jumble of angled metalwork, twisted frames, and blackened wood. Everything was charred or razed to the ground. Mercedes recalled that the shop that had briefly been Manuela's home was in the far corner, and she could see the empty space that it once occupied.

"Holy Mary, Mother of God . . . Holy Mary, Mother of God . . ." she muttered through her tears. She crossed the square quickly and recognized, even from its charred remains, the fragments of the deep green shop front where she had last seen her friends. There was nothing there now except fallen masonry and twisted metal girders.

Mercedes stood motionless. The absence of the two people that she had briefly known but intensely cherished dug a huge hollow inside her.

Someone came up behind her and tapped her on the arm.

She started and swung around. Manuela!

But it was not. It was an old woman.

"I saw them. I'm sorry. They didn't have a chance when that beam came down."

If their shelter had been close to the center of impact—and the crater nearby suggested it—they might not have suffered. This was Mercedes' first thought. Javi at least might have been sound asleep. She desperately hoped that this had been the case.

"Were they your family?"

Mercedes shook her head. She was completely incapable of speech.

There was nothing to say, even if her contracted throat had allowed it. She simply stood there and stared numbly at the place where her friends had once been.

More than a dozen had been killed in this single raid. Very few of the victims were residents of Almería; the majority were those who, like Manuela and Javi, had trekked for two hundred kilometers, only to perish in a strange city. The Fascist bombers had been efficient. They knew that the streets would be swollen with refugees, sitting targets on the streets, defenseless.

Mercedes looked around. She saw a woman standing in the wreckage of her home. She had watched it fall and now fruitlessly sifted for possessions in the remains of charred wood and snapped-off banisters that had once been on the floor above. If she did not retrieve what she could now, it would not be there for long. There were plenty of the desperate and destitute ready to scavenge dangerous and derelict properties.

Mercedes had considered herself lucky to have avoided machine guns, shells, and aerial bombs on the long walk. She wondered why she had been spared in this latest onslaught as well.

In the pockets of her coat were the only possessions she now had: a bag of lentils and half a loaf of bread in one, and in the other her dancing shoes.

# CHAPTER 23

Several days after leaving Granada, Antonio and his friends reached the outskirts of Madrid, approaching from the eastern side where Republican militia were in control. The sight of what had happened to the capital was shocking, and the hollow, bombed-out buildings stirred them to anger. As their truck passed by, small children looked up at them and waved and women raised the *puño*, the Republican fist. The arrival of every new Republican supporter refreshed the hope that the Fascists could be kept out of their city.

As they queued to sign up for the militia, along with the men with whom they had traveled, they learned more about the situation in the capital city.

"At least there's the promise of rations if we join up," said one of their companions. "I'm looking forward to some decent grub."

"I wouldn't hold out your hopes," said another. "There might not be much going here . . ."

Since September, Madrid had been full of refugees. Many of the towns surrounding it had been captured, and their terror-stricken populations had descended on the capital, swelling the population to many times its usual size. It was encircled by the enemy, but the ring was not so tight-knit that it could not be broken through, thus sustaining the citizens' belief in freedom. The people of Madrid and the thousands of refugees with their possessions tied in rag bundles hoped that this awful situation would soon be over. They could not live on bread and beans forever.

In the previous November, optimism in Madrid had wavered. More than twenty-five thousand Nationalist troops had planted themselves in the western and southern suburbs and were reinforced within a few weeks by troops from Germany. The starving people of Madrid could feel the clamp around them tightening, and with food becoming scarcer by the day, belts were drawn in too.

Then rumors circulated that the Republican government had evacuated from Madrid to Valencia. In the abandoned government offices, papers fluttered at empty desks and portraits kept watch on empty corridors. Birds flew in through half-opened windows, and drops of pale excrement were now splashed across dark leather chairs. The move was supposedly temporary. Filing cabinets remained half-filled, and walls of books were undisturbed, dust already gathering around their elaborately tooled spines and along the fine beading of the wood-paneled walls. High windows prevented the population from seeing inside these silent rooms, but they could imagine them and some were full of despair.

The majority in Madrid realized, though, that the absence of their government did not mean that the city had to fall to Franco, and there was renewed determination among them. Men, women, and children would join the fight, and from the beginning that was what they did, with small children running errands to the front and a few brave women swapping their brooms for guns.

The now-departed government's fears that the Fascists were about to enter Madrid were not immediately realized. Franco was held up in Toledo, and meanwhile aid finally arrived from the Soviet Union, as did anti-Fascist volunteers from all around the world. Along with the communists, who had been ready to take over the defense of the city when the government left, these International Brigaders helped in the city's defense.

"*Salud!*" they cried.

"*Salud!*" the foreigners replied.

There was no common language, but this gesture of solidarity and a single word was understood by them all.

Antonio found himself in conversation with a man who was a father of seven children.

"Until recently, you could let the children play in the streets. Sometimes things could seem quite normal for a few hours," he said ruefully. "That's all changing now."

Antonio looked around and saw how the buildings were scarred from mortar-fire and pockmarked with bullets. Panic and disorder was instilled by the regular crack of gunfire and the crump of shelling. It was obvious to Antonio that the sweetness of normal life, when things could be taken for granted, had been snatched away and replaced by the constant, stomach-tightening sensation of fear. Morale-boosting propaganda posters were peeling away from the walls, as frayed as their hopes.

"And you can imagine how much the children enjoyed the first few days when they couldn't go to school," the father continued.

The children already yearned for the old routine, as did their mothers. Their well-ordered lives were like neatly stacked carts of fruit that had been overturned, their contents spilled into the gutter.

Standing in the streets, anxious to fight for these people, Antonio could see how crucial the deceptive guise of normality had become. Between air raids, shoeshine boys could still make a meager living. Mothers and grandmothers walked through the streets in their best winter clothes, their children in velvet-collared coats, either lagging too far behind or running in front to vex their elders. Men in felt hats with scarves around their necks to keep away the February blasts sometimes still took their evening stroll. It might have been the hour of *paseo* on an ordinary day during peaceful times.

At the sound of the siren, women would tighten their grip on the hands of their children, and if they had too many to keep an eye on, strangers would stop and help. The great temptation was to look upward to the sky, to see the planes and even to watch the battle that might take place above them. This was the instinct of children, and many were pulled reluctantly into the darkness of the subway, to be hidden before the bombs fell around them screaming. In former times, the subway had been a way of getting from one side of the city to the other. Now, for some, station platforms had become a place of refuge and for others even a permanent home.

Eventually, terrified of what was happening above them but fearful of remaining for too long below, people would come up into the light, emerging into a street where buildings had been dissected like cakes with a carving knife. Perfect cross sections of precious homes were revealed, their treasured interiors now on display for the world to see. Plates and dishes were stubbornly unbroken and waiting to be used, even though their owners might be dead.

Eyes looked up into the privacy of strangers' lives, to see clothes wafting in the breeze, neat beds unmade by the wind, a dining table teetering on the edge, its checkered cloth still held down with a bowl of artificial flowers, pictures askew, bookcases empty, their contents spewed across the floor, a ticking clock that measured the passing of time before the next bomb blast or the days until this apartment block would be demolished for safety's sake. A mirror often hung on the back wall, reflecting the destruction. In some places, only the façades of buildings remained standing, as fragile as cheap movie sets.

On their first day in the city, the trio from Granada were caught up in the chaos of such an air raid and nearly choked on the dust of shattered masonry, which did not settle until long after they had emerged from the claustrophobia of the airless, underground shelter.

When they had arrived in Madrid, the very worst of that winter's chill was over, but the hunger continued. The constant nagging of an empty stomach was enough to encourage some men to join up with the militia, since it meant at least the promise of rations, and as Antonio queued up with his friends to sign up, he realized that he too was looking forward to a decent plateful of food. It was days since they had eaten more than a bowlful of watered-down lentils.

The mood here in Madrid was very different from that in Granada, where there were so many restricting new rules. Here was an almost revolutionary atmosphere, relaxed, casual, and even sensual by comparison. Hotels were taken over for the soldiers, many of whom had never seen such grand paneling and fine gilding. The buildings themselves were cracked like old china.

The foreigners were a novelty to the Granadinos. They enjoyed the camaraderie with strangers from countries they could not even picture but found it odd that their own private conflict was now being played out on an open stage.

"Why do you think they're here?" Francisco asked his friends, baffled by the foreigners' presence. "They know as well as we do what will happen if Franco invades this city."

"They hate Fascism as much as we do," answered Antonio.

"And if they don't help stop it in our country, it will only spread to theirs," added Salvador.

"It's like a disease," said Antonio.

International Brigaders were hungry for action and mostly unafraid of what might happen to them. The people of Madrid could not have wished for better friends.

It was Antonio and his friends' first night in the poster-daubed city, a bigger and more sophisticated place than the one they had grown up in. The three of them were sitting up at a bar in one of the old hotels, and Antonio caught sight of himself in the tarnished glaze of the old mirrors that lined the walls behind the bar. Though the reflection was murky, their faces seemed happy and relaxed, as though they were just three young men, out for the night, carefree, shirts slightly crumpled, their hair slicked back, a little the worse for wear. The dim, sepia glow of the room flattered them and obscured the cavernous shadows under eyes that were hollowed out by hunger and exhaustion.

Antonio lost interest in his own reflection. His attention was drawn away by a group of girls who stood talking by the door. While he was merely observing them in the mirror, they remained unself-conscious, but he knew that would change as soon as they knew they were noticed.

He nudged Salvador and realized that he had been similarly mesmerized. After the days of being packed in a truck like livestock, and the prospect of battle, the allure of these women was almost irresistible.

These girls were among the few people in this city for whom life had improved with this conflict. From the arrival of the first militia regiment, and now all the young men from foreign countries as well, business had boomed. Demand greatly exceeded supply, and though there were women who in peaceful times would have died rather than sell their bodies, some were now hungry enough to compromise.

When the three girls sauntered toward the bar, Francisco turned and smiled. He, too, had been watching them. They carried with them the cloying smell of cheap scent that was more intoxicating to these young men than the best Parisian fragrance worn by the smart women of Granada. Conversation began and the women introduced themselves as dancers. Perhaps they had been once. Drinks were bought and the chatter continued, with all of them shouting above the sound of a hundred other voices and the insistent music of an accordion player who moved about between the tables. There was only one thing on all their minds, though, and within the hour they were in a rundown brothel a few streets away, drunk on cheap brandy and succumbing to the powerful anesthetic of sex.

The following morning, renewed after the deepest of sleeps, the friends from Granada were dispatched to the front line. The battle at Jarama, southeast of Madrid, had been going on for ten days now. It was where these young men wanted to be and the reason they had come. Antonio did not dread the crack of gunshots, the thud of a shell landing close by, the deep groan of an imploding building. The Granadinos were now officially part of the untrained militia unit they had traveled up with from the south. The Republic had lost such a huge part of its trained army that it welcomed any willing fighters such as these. Their enthusiasm and innocence obscured even the thought of death—it had barely entered their heads—and they posed with the other soldiers for lighthearted photographs that were unlikely to reach home.

At Jarama, Nationalist troops were aiming to seize the highway that ran to Valencia and had surprised the Republicans with their attack on February 6. With the support of German tanks and planes, forty thousand troops, including many foreign legionaries, who were the most ruthless of them all, Franco had begun his offensive. Before the Republicans had time to organize themselves, strategic hills and bridges had been seized. Soviet tanks slowed the advance a little, but the Nationalists had begun to move forward, and huge losses had already been sustained when the Granadinos arrived.

When they reached the site of the battle, they expected to go into action immediately. They stood around the lorry that had brought them and surveyed the landscape. It hardly looked like a battleground. They saw neat vineyards and rows of olive trees, low hills, and clumps of gorse and wild thyme.

"There doesn't seem to be much cover . . ." commented Francisco.

He was right, and before they had the opportunity to use their guns they found themselves part of a team dispatched to dig trenches. A pile of old doors had been salvaged from the shattered remains of a nearby village and were to be used to strengthen the trench walls. Francisco and Antonio worked together, standing in the ditch while others passed the doors down to them. Many still had their smooth brass handles; some had the faded paint of a door number.

"I wonder what happened to the people who lived behind this one," Antonio mused. It had once guarded the privacy of its owners, but now their home must be standing open to the winds.

Dug down into the olive groves on the hillside above the River Jarama, they waited for their first taste of action. By now they had done more than their fair share of trench reinforcement, and this conflict had provided nothing but boredom. The dampness of the ground was bad enough during the day, but at night it gave them no sleep, and here for the first time they picked up the lice that were to plague them for many months to come. The inescapable, continual need to scratch, both day and night, was torture.

"How much longer do you think?" muttered Francisco.

"For what?"

"This. This sitting here. This waiting. This nothing."

"God knows . . . but we can't make things happen."

"But we've been doing *nothing* for days. I can't stand it. I was more useful in Granada. I'm not sure I want to hang around here."

"Well, you'll have to. You'll get shot by our own men if you try and leave. So don't even think of it."

Playing chess or writing letters to relatives kept them occupied only for a while.

"It seems a bit pointless writing letters," said Antonio with uncharacteristic glumness, "when the person you're writing to might not even be alive by the time the letter arrives."

He was addressing his letter to his aunt Rosita, in the hope that she might keep it for Concha. It was too incriminating to send a letter directly to his mother. He hoped that she was safe and wondered whether she had managed to visit his father. He prayed that Mercedes would have found Javier or made her way back home. It was not safe for a sixteen-year-old girl to be alone.

"I don't even know if my mother is alive," Francisco said as he folded a sheaf of paper ready to post, "and by the time she gets this, I might have died. Of boredom."

Antonio tried to cheer his friend, even though he was feeling equally frustrated. The tedium of the wait was maddening them all.

Even if periods of inactivity have a timelessness about them, they never go on forever and, sure enough, fighting soon resumed. Within a day or so, they were on the front line, where the relentless rat-a-tat-tat of machine guns, the boom of cannon, and the shouts of "*Fuego!*" soon replaced the ennui.

Suddenly they were ordered to try to take command of a nearby ridge. As they dug in at the bottom of the slope, several battalions of Nationalist soldiers swept over the brow of the hill and charged toward them. At the moment when they could almost see the whites of their eyes, the order to fire was given. Some turned and ran for cover; others were mown down. The machine guns went briefly silent as their belts were replaced, but the volleys of gunfire from the Nationalists went on for some minutes. An order was given to several dozen of the Republican soldiers, including Antonio, to advance up the ridge where they could be in a position to fire at the Nationalists, but heavy artillery drove them back. The soldier next to Antonio was blasted open. His blood sprayed everyone within a few meters, and through the smoke Antonio tripped over another body that lay spread-eagled across his path. Uncertain whether he was dead or alive, Antonio carried him back to their base. Only half of the unit survived the day. It was a brutal introduction to the reality of this conflict. The image of the shattered bodies haunted him that night.

The Nationalists, determined to drive the Republicans out, continued their assault on some last key positions. There were huge numbers of casualties, including many among the idealistic bands of International Brigaders, some of whom had not held a rifle before. Theirs were often unreliable weapons, old and defunct, with catches that jammed or useless ammunition. Thousands of them would now never get much practice in using them as they were dead within hours. In one afternoon, Antonio counted dozens who had been killed in an assault not far from their own location. Their sacrifice seemed utterly futile.

The course of the battle changed when Soviet planes went into action and began to prevent the Nationalists from protecting their own forces. Nationalist bombers were now being driven off by Soviet fighters.

At the end of February, the battle was over. Both sides had suffered huge losses, but the Nationalists had advanced only a few kilometers. Every centimeter of dust they had gained had cost them many lives. As a mathematical equation, it made no sense at all, but in terms of morale, the Republican confidence was boosted. It was a stalemate they regarded as a battle won.

Francisco failed to see it as a victory.

"We've lost thousands and so have they. And they've taken some ground," he pointed out.

"But not much, Francisco," signed Salvador.

"It just seems a bloody mess to me, that's all," said Francisco angrily.

No one was going to disagree with him. A "bloody mess" was precisely what it was.

They returned to Madrid for a short while. This was a place where they could still get a haircut, a shave, clean clothes, and even stay in a comfortable bed. Life there was continuing as normal in spite of the threat of air raids. Once or twice they heard that the legendary communist leader Dolores Ibarruri was in their neighborhood and joined a throng already amassing to hear her. The tireless, black-clad figure of Ibarruri, known by everyone as La Pasionaria, "The Passion Flower," was a common sight on the streets of Madrid. She never failed to rally those with flagging spirits.

When Antonio caught sight of the chiseled face for the first time, it was as though he had inhaled pure air. They had all often heard her voice on the radio or when it was broadcast from the traveling loud-hailers that had toured the front line, but the real person had a majesty that the voice alone did not convey. The woman's physical presence was extraordinary, and her immense power and charisma radiated around the square.

In an unconscious gesture that came so naturally to Spanish women, she clasped her hands together. First she addressed the women, reminding them of the sacrifice they must make.

"Prefer to be widows of heroes, rather than wives of cowards!" she exhorted them, the rich timbre of her voice booming above the heads of the quiet crowd.

The solid flesh and blood of the woman inspired them all. They needed, all of them, to be as strong as she.

"*No pasarán!*" she called out. "They shall not pass!"

"*No pasarán!*" the crowd chanted. "*No pasarán! No pasarán!*"

Her pure conviction gave them hope. While they were standing, ready to put up this resistance, the Fascists would never enter their city, and La Pasionaria's clenched fist punching the air reinforced their belief that this could never be. Many of these men and women were exhausted, disillusioned, fearful, but she made them believe that the fight was worth continuing.

Salvador absorbed her magnetism and the warm response of the crowd. Ibarruri had been too far away for him to read her lips, but she had held his attention nevertheless.

"It's better to die on our feet than live on our knees!" she exhorted them.

There was not a man, woman, or child left unmoved.

When her speech came to an end, the people dispersed.

"She's inspiring, isn't she?" said Antonio.

"Yes," replied Francisco, "she's an extraordinary woman. She actually makes you think it's possible."

"Well, she's right," said Antonio. "And you mustn't stop believing that."

# CHAPTER 24

For a few days, Mercedes wandered aimlessly through the streets of Almería. She knew no one in this city now. Occasionally there was a glimpse of a half-familiar face, but it was just someone that she had seen on the road from Málaga. They were not friends, just other people like her, all of them in the wrong place, still on their feet, trudging from one queue to another.

For those with families, staying in Almería was the only choice, since the effort of moving again was beyond the realm of possibility. For Mercedes, remaining here was the option she favored least of all. She stood in a street where many other refugees loitered, all strangers to each other and to this city. She could not imagine staying. It was the one thing she knew.

So she faced a choice. The easiest course of action would have been to return home to Granada. Anxiety for her mother grabbed her hard, and she felt a surge of guilt that she was not there with her. She missed Antonio, too, and knew that he would be doing what he could to comfort their mother. Perhaps her father had been released. If only there was some way of finding out.

She had been away for almost a month now and desperately missed the café and the homely apartment above it, where every dark stair and window-ledge was so familiar. She allowed herself the momentary self-indulgence of remembering some of the things she loved about home: the sweet, indefinable scent of her mother, the dim light that cast a faint yellow glow on the staircase, the muskiness of her own bedroom, the thickly layered brown paint on the doors and window frames, her old wooden bed with its heavy green wool blanket that had kept her warm for longer than she could remember. A wave of intense longing descended. All the small comforting things seemed very far away in this shattered, unfamiliar place. Perhaps these details of life were what mattered most of all.

Then she thought of Javier. She remembered the first time she saw him and how her life had changed in that instant. Her recollection of the moment when he had looked up from his guitar and his dark-lashed, limpid eyes gazed out toward her in the audience was vivid. He had not seen her then, but she remembered the effect of his look. It was as though his eyes transmitted heat, and she had melted in their intensity. After her first dance for Javier, each subsequent encounter had been like a stepping stone across a river, each one taking them closer to the other bank where she had assumed they could never be apart. Their desire to be together had been mutual, passionate, and absolute. Separation from Javier was like a dull, perpetual ache that would never go away. An illness.

One day, about a week after Manuela and Javi had been killed, across the street, the discreet doorway into a church caught Mercedes' eye. Perhaps the Virgin would help her decide which direction to take.

Behind the battered entrance lay an interior of baroque grandeur, but it was not this that surprised her, since many churches had almost unnoticeable side-street doors that belied the immensity of the church hidden within. What really astounded her were the number of people inside. It was not as though they had come here for safety. There had been no divine protection for religious buildings in these times of turmoil. Churches were as vulnerable as anywhere, whether they were destroyed from the air by Nationalists or burned down by supporters of the Republic. Many aisles and naves were now open to the elements, and pulpits and organ lofts had become the nesting places for birds.

In spite of losing their faith, men and women sought safety and warmth in this open church. Some memories of what religion had once meant returned to Mercedes, and yet it seemed a lifetime ago that she had gone each week to confess her sins and decades since she had taken her

First Communion. Candles flickered before an icon of Mary, and the eyes of the Holy Virgin met Mercedes' gaze. The Hail Mary was an incantation that used to flow out of her like water from a tap. Now she resisted the temptation to recite it all. It would be hypocrisy. She did not believe. Those eyes that caught hers were just oil on a canvas, a chemical compound. She turned away, the smell of wax lingering in her nostrils. She almost envied those who could find comfort in such a place as this.

Around the curve of the apse, layers of cherubs reached up to heaven. Some looked out at the congregation with a mischievous grin. Beneath them sat the Virgin, the limp Christ lying in her arms. Mercedes studied her, looking for some message or meaning, but realized that her expression did not begin to capture the pain of the woman she had seen on the road from Málaga a few days earlier: a mother who, like Mary, had been nursing the corpse of her child. It was obvious that the painter of this *Pietà* had never seen the real thing. His depiction of pain was not even an approximation. The image seemed an insult to grief. In every small side chapel, she saw vulgar portrayals of suffering and anguish and from each ceiling corpulent angels looked down, smiling.

Walking away from the main altar, she found herself face to face with an upright, life-size Mary made of plaster. Glass tears glistened on her smooth cheeks; the eyes were strong and blue; the mouth slightly downturned. She gazed out at Mercedes through the bars of the locked chapel, incarcerated along with a small vase of faded paper flowers. While others could project their hopes and dreams on these figures and believe they found comfort, if not always definite answers, Mercedes found their stagy symbolism absurd.

The pious knelt on the steps of every side chapel or sat with their heads bowed in the main body of the church. Everyone seemed at peace, and yet Mercedes was churned up with anger.

"What use has God been?" she wanted to cry out, to break the reverend silence that reigned in this lofty space. "What has he done to protect us?"

In reality, the Church had acted against them. Many of the Nationalists' actions against the Republic had been done in the name of God. In spite of this, she could see that many of the citizens of Almería clearly still held on to their belief that the Virgin Mary would help them. For those whose lips moved in prayers of supplication but who did not really expect answers, this place clearly still provided comfort, but for Mercedes, coming in here to find guidance, it now seemed laughable. The saints and martyrs, with their painted-on blood and theatrical stigmata, had once been part of her life. Now she saw the Church as a sham, a cupboard full of redundant props.

She took a seat for a while, watching people come and go, lighting candles, muttering prayers, gazing at icons, and wondered what it was they felt. Did a voice reply when they prayed? Did it respond immediately, or was it heard the next day when they least expected it? Did these frozen-eyed figures of the saints really become flesh and blood to them? Perhaps they did. Maybe these people, with their tear-filled, pleading eyes, and hands so tightly locked that their fingers whitened, were really engaged with something beyond her understanding, something supernatural. She could neither grasp it with her mind nor feel it with her heart.

There was no divine hand. Of that, she was now certain. For a moment she wondered if she should pray for the souls of Manuela and her little boy. She thought of them, innocent, harmless, and their annihilation only added to her conviction of God's absence.

With the realization that she had neither faith nor belief to help her, she knew that her decision would have to be made alone. At that moment, an image of Javier, more beautiful than any of the handsome saints depicted in oils, came into her mind. Perhaps for the devout, the huge space of the imagination was occupied by God. For Mercedes, it was Javier who filled it. She worshipped him body and soul and believed him worthy of it.

The warmth of the church, the semi-darkness, and the strong, musky scent of candles held her in an embrace; she could imagine this physical comfort being enough to bring people in and keep them there. It would have been easy for her to sit there, too, but the stuffiness had become overwhelming and she had to get out for air.

The street outside was silent. A desperate dog scavenged. Another one chased the pages of a newspaper that flapped like a dirty bird struggling to fly. They eyed Mercedes suspiciously and, for a moment, hungrily. These animals had probably not eaten for days. In former times they had survived on the generous leftovers from restaurant bins, but now there was nothing for them, not even the occasional carcass.

She now knew with blinding certainty what anyone who had ever felt the compelling force of reciprocated love would understand: that she could not go back to Granada. She recalled the way in which her mother had encouraged her to leave and knew she could count her among those who would not condemn her for walking away from her home city rather than toward it. Mercedes believed that Javier was her one unique opportunity for love, and so whatever bitter end or consummation it might lead to, she had to find him. Even the activity of searching and the unerring belief that he could be found would alleviate the pain of separation.

With no idea of where her feet were taking her, she ambled along. It gave her time to reflect. Perhaps she was no different from the people in church. Perhaps this belief, this knowledge, was what they felt too. They "knew" that God existed, and their belief in the miracle of the Resurrection was unshakable. Her faith was this: she knew that Javier was still alive. As she stood on the pavement, the decision made itself for her. She would head north, following her instinct and the only other information she had, which was that his uncle lived in Bilbao. Perhaps her loved one would be there, waiting for her.

Though she had little fear now, it was still undesirable for a woman to travel alone, and she knew she would be safer in the company of others. Almería was bursting with refugees, and there were plenty of them who would be making their way out of the city with whom she could travel. Having decided to make inquiries, she struck up a conversation with two women. Though they were planning to stay for a while themselves, they told her of a couple they knew who were about to set off with their daughter.

"I'm sure I heard that they intended to leave soon," the younger woman said to her sister.

"Yes, that's right. They have family in the north somewhere, and that's where they're aiming to go."

"When we've got our bread, let's go and find them. You can't go on your own, and I'm sure they'll be happy for the company."

In due course, hugging their segments of loaf, they made their way to a school on the edge of Almería where the two women, along with hundreds of others, were camped out. Mercedes found it strange to see classrooms where adults now outnumbered children and where chairs and desks had been piled in the corner and old blankets lay strewn across the floor. The walls still carried cheerful displays of children's drawings. They seemed incongruous now, a reminder of how the old order had been turned upside down.

The sisters found the place where they had left their few belongings, and in the same room sat a middle-aged woman. She appeared to be darning a sock, but on closer inspection Mercedes saw that she was trying to sew up her shoe. The leather was so soft and worn that it could be pierced with an ordinary needle. She was more or less remaking this battered footwear. Without it she could go nowhere.

"Señora Duarte, this is Mercedes. She wants to go north. Can she come with you?"

The woman carried on sewing. She did not glance up.

Mercedes fingered the rounded toes of her dance shoes, one in each pocket of her coat. Sometimes she forgot about them, but the comforting weight of them was always there.

"We aren't going yet," Señora Duarte said, looking up now into Mercedes' face. "But when we do, you can come with us, if you like."

The words were spoken without a trace of warmth, let alone a genuine welcome. Though it was stuffy here, Mercedes felt herself shudder. She understood how people could be stripped of their ability to care about others. Many had seen terrible atrocities, and she could see that in this woman's eyes. Here was someone beyond the stage where she could take an interest in strangers and perhaps even her own family.

Moments later, a young woman of about Mercedes' age appeared.

"Did you get any?" asked her mother, once again speaking without looking up.

"As much as they would give me," replied her daughter. "But it wasn't much. Hardly enough for one really."

"But there are three of us, including your father, and four now if this girl is going to attach herself to us," she said, indicating Mercedes with an upward movement of her head.

Mercedes stepped forward. The woman who had introduced them had gone now.

"Some acquaintances of yours said I might be able to come on the road with you, as we're all planning on going in the same direction. Would that be all right?"

Mercedes spoke with some hesitation, unsure of whether she might get the same cool reception from the daughter.

The girl eyed her up and down, not with suspicion but with interest. "Yes, I'm sure it would." She spoke with unmistakable warmth.

"Come and find somewhere to cook these with me," she said, waving the pathetic package of lentils. "I'm sure we can make them stretch—and I see you've got some bread."

The two women then found themselves in a queue for a small kitchen. They were all used to standing in lines now. This was where acquaintances might become friends.

"I'm sorry my mother doesn't seem very friendly."

"Don't worry. I'm a total stranger. Why should she be?"

"She didn't used to be like that."

Mercedes looked into the girl's face and saw someone like herself. She had a girl's complexion with an old woman's eyes. They were full of grief, as though she had already experienced enough suffering for a lifetime.

"It was my brother. Eduardo. He was walking with three friends. They were ahead of us in a group and we got separated. Mother's shoes had worn down to nothing, and her heels were cracked and bleeding. She couldn't go very fast, and Eduardo had grown impatient. In the air attack we had a lucky escape, but when the planes had gone and we carried on walking, we saw them. All four of them. Dead. Lying in a row. They'd been moved from the middle of the road so that people didn't have to walk around them. The other parents hadn't caught up with them yet, so we were the first to realize who they were."

Mercedes felt she had been there, and indeed it was perfectly possible that she might have passed the very spot a few moments earlier.

"We had missed them, by a moment. You know when you're late to meet someone and when you get there, someone says, 'Oh, they've just gone,' and you have that sense of loss and waste. Well, it was like that, but for good. Eduardo had gone. We had missed him by a moment. He was still warm. It was impossible to take in that he was no longer alive. His body was there, but he just wasn't in it anymore."

Tears coursed down her cheeks. Mercedes could feel the enormity of her loss. She was reminded of when she saw her own brother's lifeless body. Ignacio had been dead for many hours, and she had been shocked by her own reaction. It was not her brother, and she remembered realizing that there was a difference between a body and a corpse. The latter was like an empty shell on the beach.

Mercedes found herself bereft of useful words. There had been hundreds of mortalities on that road from Málaga, but an individual death, even in the overall scale of suffering, would never lose its impact.

"I'm so sorry. How terrible . . . how terrible."

"They'll never recover; I know they won't. My father didn't speak for two days. My mother never stops crying. And I'm meant to be the strong one . . ."

For a few minutes they stood in silence. The girl herself looked as though she had been weeping for days. Eventually she spoke.

"My name's Ana, anyway," she said, wiping her eyes.

"And I'm Mercedes."

No one else in the queue even listened to their conversation. The story Ana had told was nothing out of the ordinary in times like these.

While Ana stirred the mean mixture of lentils and water, the girls continued to talk. Mercedes told her that she needed to get to Bilbao, and Ana explained that her parents were aiming for her uncle's village in the north. Her father's brother, Ernesto, had never supported the Republic and her father did not have firm political views, so he had persuaded her mother that they should set up a new home, closer to his family, where they might be safe. He was convinced that it was only a matter of time before Franco took Madrid, and following that it would only be a few days before the whole country was in Nationalist hands. It was a long distance to travel, but their apartment in Málaga had been destroyed, and it was doubtful they would ever return now. Her father had never held membership in a trade union or any other workers' association, so he reckoned he was free to shift his allegiance at will.

Mercedes' sole aim was to find Javier, whether he was in Nationalist or Republican territory. She knew that he was most likely to be in the latter but decided to keep this to herself. Even now she could see that keeping politics a private matter with this family might stand her in good stead. It was enough for her that they shared the same broad destination.

"I'll be really glad if you come with us. My parents hardly speak, and we've got a long way to go. I could really do with some company."

By the time they had returned to Ana's mother, her father was also there. He had been queuing all afternoon and had an onion and half a cabbage to show for it. Introductions were made, and Mercedes was welcomed politely by Señor Duarte.

Though he had no bandages or visible signs of injury, Duarte was like a wounded man; it was as if he might snap beneath the burden of his grief. He certainly did not want to make conversation. Mercedes realized that these people were much younger than she had at first thought. Señora Duarte could easily have been mistaken for Ana's grandmother, and Mercedes wondered if it was the death of their only son that had aged them so many decades beyond their years.

Señora Duarte was a little friendlier now, perhaps because of the additional loaf that Mercedes offered her, and they formed a tight circle before sharing the soup among four enamel bowls and dividing up the bread. There were other people in the room, and it was considered bad manners to display what you were eating, however little it was.

"So, Mercedes, you want to come up to the north with us?" said Señor Duarte, breaking the silence when they had all finished their meal.

"Yes, I do," she answered. "As long as I'm not going to be in the way."

"You won't be. But you will have to understand something."

Ana looked nervously at her father. She did not want him to scare away her new friend.

"Let me do the talking when we get stopped," he said brusquely to Mercedes, his cold eyes fixed on hers. "As far as anyone is concerned, you two are sisters. You do understand that, don't you?"

"Yes, I think so," she said.

She felt uncomfortable with his manner, but she would have to put this aside; the mother seemed kind enough, and it would make sense to be part of a family. To get to Bilbao, they needed to cross territory occupied by Nationalist troops. That did not seem to concern Ana, so Mercedes told herself she must not worry either.

After their meager supper, the girls intended to go for a stroll in the street to get away from the overcrowded building, but as they were about to leave, they heard the unexpected sound of music coming from a classroom down the corridor. It drew them toward it. For the first time in weeks the sound of something other than conflict reached their ears. Even when the bombs were not falling, or when they were not being strafed or machine-gunned, the noise of it all had left a continual ringing in their ears. The delightful fluid sound of an arpeggio quickened their heartbeats and hastened their steps.

They soon found where the music was coming from. Already encircled by people, the top of his shiny bald pate reflecting the light from a single bulb illuminating the room, they saw the *tocaor*. His whole body was curved as though to protect his guitar.

People streamed from every door in the corridor and gathered in the room, and a crowd of children sat on the floor looking up at him. During the journey from Málaga, they had lost the naïveté of childhood and now seemed to understand the tragic potency of this sound.

No one knew the *flamenco*'s name. He seemed not to have any family with him. By the time Mercedes and Ana arrived, several people were accompanying him with quiet *palmas*. His long, stained fingernails skimmed lightly and airily across the strings. He was playing for himself, but he occasionally looked up and his eyes registered the growing crowd. Mercedes slipped back to her own classroom. There was something she might need.

As she returned, she heard a familiar sequence of notes that sent a shockwave through her. Just four notes played in a unique sequence, and she could tell this *toque* apart from a million others. It was a melody that meant more to her than any other. A *soleá*. It was the first piece she had ever danced with Javier. The melancholy of the tune might have lowered her spirits, but instead she took it as a sign that she would see him again. The thought lifted her heart.

Other people recognized the *compás*, too, and clapped in time with the beat. For a while she held back and then, almost involuntarily, she found herself removing the shoes from her pocket and slipping them on to her feet, buckling them with shaking fingers. The soft leather felt so familiar, so warm. She did not hesitate to step round the children who were sitting just a few feet from the guitarist. Her steel heelcaps click-clacked on the parquet as she approached the *guitarrista*. The children gazed with rapt attention at this girl, who now blocked their view of the musician.

A year ago, it might have seemed audacious to present herself to a stranger, ready to dance, but such rules no longer mattered. What did she have to lose in front of an audience who knew neither her nor her family? They were all strangers to each other here, brought together by bitter circumstances.

The man looked up and gave her a broad, encouraging smile. He could tell from her attitude, her position, and the way she held herself that she had danced many times and would know how to direct him.

She bent to whisper in his ear, "Can we have the same again?"

As he listened to her, his fingers chased a tune up and down the strings, his nails flicking the strings with a virtuoso's dexterity.

The arrival of this girl by his side felt like a glimpse back to an old life where evenings might evolve with delightful spontaneity. He was often hired for *juergas*, and the only guaranteed thing was the uncertainty of how the evening might unfold, who would play well, how the women would dance, whether the gathering would have any spirit, any *duende*.

He smiled up at her. For Mercedes and everyone else who caught a glimpse of his face at that moment, it was as if the sun had burst out on an otherwise dull day. Such glimpses of warmth had become a rare thing of late. Now, from the introductory passage, emerged the *soleá* that she so much wanted him to repeat. Mercedes began to clap her hands, just lightly at first, until she could feel that the audience had the rhythm running right through them and could not tell it from the beating of their own hearts. Some women joined their hands together with her, eyes fixed on this girl who had come from nowhere to take center stage. As their *palmas* strengthened, she began to tap her right heel until she established a stronger and more forceful beat. A moment later she banged her left foot down hard and the dance began, her wrists and arms moving in fluid motion above her head, her long slim fingers so much thinner than they had been a month before.

For the first time in days, the profound sense of defeat that many of these people had carried about with them was lifted.

The *tocaor*'s playing echoed her movements, increasing in passion as the dance went on. It was almost violent now, the way in which his nails ripped through the strings and tapped on the plates on the front of the guitar. Slung across his back, this instrument had been carried for miles, withstanding several falls on the way. Though these accidents had done miraculously little damage, the way he was playing it now made it seem as though he was hell-bent on its destruction.

He had complete confidence in the strength of its pinewood body to withstand this treatment, and now he used his instrument to express not just his own anguish but that of his audience. The music echoed it.

For the duration of the dance, this stranger became someone else for Mercedes. When she had danced for that first time in the *cueva* two years earlier, she and Javier had been equally unknown to each other. Her eyes shut tight with concentration, the music had transported her back to that same evening, and once again she gave every part of herself.

After the *soleá*, with its strong, quiet control and an expression of feeling that ran unfathomably deep, the crowd was almost tense with its agony and pathos. They knew that this was a spontaneous performance. The mutterings of "*Olé*" were hushed. It was as if they did not want to break the spell.

The *tocaor* knew to relieve the atmosphere with the lighter mood of the *alegrías* and found his dancer more relaxed as she picked up the new beat and felt her way into the movements. The stiffness Mercedes had felt from all the weeks without dancing had gone, and now she was able to bend and twist her body with the same suppleness she used to have and to click her fingers with their usual sharp precision.

The joy of this dance took everyone's mind away from shattered lives and burned-out homes, from the images of corpses and the cruel faces of the people who had driven them out of their own city. Many of them joined in, clapping the rhythm more enthusiastically as the minutes went by.

By the end, Mercedes was tired. Sweat ran down her neck and down her back; she could feel it trickle between her buttocks. She had given everything of herself, forgetting both where she was and almost who. Like the audience, she had been transported away from the present. In her mind she had been at a fiesta, surrounded by family and friends. She eased her way through the applauding crowd to the edge of the room where she saw that Ana was standing. Her new friend's face was beaming in admiration at the way Mercedes had danced.

"*Fantástico*," she said simply. "*Fantástico*."

The guitarist had not missed a beat. There was not a breath between the final, closing stamp of Mercedes' *alegrías* and the quiet first chord of his next piece. His audience was entranced, and he wanted to hold them in that state.

It was almost an impossibility that the music he was making came from only one guitar. The volume of sound and the depth and richness of the notes seemed to come from several instruments, and when the warm tone of the guitar's hollow body being tapped was added, it magnified into layers of rich velvet. With the sound of the *palmas* and now one or two people tapping the rhythms on their chairs and on tabletops, music emanated from every corner. Everyone in that room was enraptured now, swept along by a fast-flowing river of notes.

Mercedes tapped her fingertips gently against her palm. She stood leaning against the wall with Ana, their shoulders touching.

A man emerged from the shadows. He was a bulky individual, a head above most of the men there. He had a mass of dense, dark curls that fell well below his collar, and the texture of this hair was coarse. His pitted skin was only half concealed by the patchy stubble of an unshaven face. The audience cleared a path for him since his manner showed that he would not hesitate to push his way through. There was no warmth in his gruff face.

As the guitarist brought his piece toward a conclusion, the new arrival was drawing up a chair. The two men looked easy together, side by side, as though they had met before. For a moment they spoke under their breath, though the *guitarra* never lifted his fingers away from his strings, continuing to pick out a tune while they whispered, not for a second losing the attention of the crowd.

The audience could not locate the source of the first sound they heard. It seemed unconnected to the singer. Everyone who had watched this man take his place to perform had a preconceived idea of how he would sound, but the reality of it defied their expectations. From his lungs came a low, sweet note, quite unlike the gypsy rasp that they had expected. It was the soft sound of someone's soul. After an introductory passage to the song, a *taranta*, the voice began to climb and the gypsy *cantaor*'s fingers and hands started to express the emotions that poured from him. In the low light of the room, his big pale hands stood out against his black jacket and performed like puppets in a mime show. The characters they played were pity, anger, injustice, and grief. It was the story of the gypsy ghettos that he had been telling his whole life, and the tragic essence of his words seemed more appropriate than ever before to the exiled Malagueños.

This audience understood him now. When they looked at themselves, they realized that the roughness of his demeanor only mirrored their own. This was how they all appeared now—coarse, dirty, hunted, sad.

Ana turned to Mercedes at the end of the first *cante*.

"I wonder if he always sings like this," she said.

"Who knows?" responded Mercedes. "But it's the most beautiful sound I've ever heard."

The appreciation for the *gitano* was immense. He described their story and their lives. In his expression their own feelings were miraculously told.

"How does he *know*?" muttered Ana under her breath.

Before the evening ended, many others danced, some with such exuberance that the dark mood that hung over Almería seemed to lift. Another guitarist appeared, followed by an elderly woman with astonishing mastery over the castanets that she had kept in the pocket of her skirt since leaving home. Rather as a pair of shoes had been for Mercedes, these simple pieces of wood had brought great comfort to this old lady every time she felt the reassuring shape of their cool domes beneath her fingertips. For her, they were the only continuity in this strange, awful nightmare of the new life suddenly thrust upon her.

It was a *feria* like no other. By four in the morning, almost every man, woman, and child sheltering in the school had squeezed into the room. It was rarely hotter than this in August. People forgot their situation and smiled. It was only when the *tocaor* finally exhausted himself that the evening came to an end. Everyone had a few hours of the deepest sleep they had enjoyed for many days, and even dawn's gray light did not stir them.

Mercedes and Ana shared a blanket on the same patch of hard floor. Friendships were formed quickly under these circumstances, and when the girls woke, they remained huddled under the blanket, exchanging their stories.

"I am looking for someone," Mercedes explained. "That's my reason for going north."

She could hear her own voice, so resolute and determined, but the look she saw on Ana's face made her realize how ridiculous this might sound.

"And who is it you are looking for?"

"Javier Montero. He has family near Bilbao. I think he might be trying to get there."

"Well, we're all going in the same direction," Ana said. "And we'll do our best to help you. We'll be leaving later today. He'll be ready by then." She nodded in the direction of her father, who still lay sleeping, a motionless shape under a blanket by the wall.

Mercedes already knew that she could not expect any warmth from Ana's father. The night before, when she had returned to the classroom to fetch her dancing shoes, she had overheard a conversation that shocked her. Just before going in, she had heard raised voices and her own name.

"Look, we don't know anything about this Mercedes girl," Señor Duarte was ranting to his wife. The classroom had been vacated by most of its occupants, who had gone to find the music that was drifting so irresistibly toward them. "Suppose she's a communist?"

"Of course she isn't a communist! Why do you say things like that?" Mercedes continued to listen at a crack in the door.

"Because there are communists everywhere. Extremists. People who have caused all of this." With a sweeping arm movement, he indicated the chaos of miscellaneous possessions around them, all such potent symbols of deracination.

"How can you say it's their fault?" Señora Duarte asked. Her voice was raised. "You're beginning to sound like your brothers."

Mercedes was transfixed by the argument. Ana had said that her father was very angry with the Republican government, but she realized herself how careful she would have to be now.

"Without those *rojos*," he spat out the word as though it was phlegm, "none of this would be happening."

"Without Franco, it wouldn't even have begun," she retorted.

Señor Duarte's fury now overcame him, and he lifted his hand to strike his wife. This answering back of hers was intolerable.

She raised her arm to parry the blow. "Pedro!"

He regretted his action immediately, but it could not be undone. He had never been roused to hit his wife before, perhaps because she had never stood up to him in this way.

"I'm sorry, I am sorry," he whispered almost helplessly, full of remorse.

Mercedes was horrified to see a man striking his wife. She knew for certain that her father would never have laid a finger on her mother and wondered for a moment if she should intercede. Señor Duarte was obviously casting about wildly for somewhere to place the blame for his only son's death. In his view, everyone was guilty, not just the bombers, who had mown down his son, and the Nationalist troops, who had seized half the country, but also the Republicans for failing to put up a united front.

Señora Duarte was stirred to continue the argument: "So you're saying that you'll live under the Fascists and just go along with them, rather than stand up for what you voted for?"

"Yes, I'd rather do that than die . . . yes, I would. Because dying is pointless. Think of our boy," Señor Duarte retorted.

"Yes, I do think of our boy," answered Señora Duarte. "He was killed by the side that you now want to support."

Grief and anger clashed within them both. There was no possibility of their discussion taking any rational course.

Señora Duarte tearfully left the room, and Mercedes hid in the shadows as she passed. She had needed her shoes and seized the moment to run in to fetch them. Señor Duarte looked up. He would always wonder if they had been overheard.

That afternoon the four of them would be ready to leave. There was a bus departing for Murcia.

# CHAPTER 25

The Granadinos were leaving Madrid for the second time. La Pasionaria's rousing words would go with them to the front line.

For a while, the Italians had been withdrawing their troops from the Jarama area and now, in early March, they began a new offensive at Guadalajara, thirty miles northeast of Madrid. This was what the trio had been waiting for, and their morale was high as they faced new action. The reality of the conditions they would be fighting in, however, was not what they had envisaged. With a huge armory of tanks, machine guns, planes, and trucks, Mussolini's men were about to commence a massive assault on Republican territory.

By the time Antonio, Francisco, and Salvador arrived at the front, the Italians had already broken through and were in a position of dominance. With the strength of their artillery, it was looking bleak for the Republican forces. Then the weather changed. Sleet began to fall, and from then on the elements played a role almost as significant as the guns.

Shivering in a sparse copse under leafless trees that afforded no protection, everyone began to stiffen with cold. Dampness extinguished their cigarettes.

"Jesus," said Francisco, examining his palm. "I can hardly see my own hand. How are we going to tell our own men from the Fascists?"

"It won't be easy," said Antonio, pulling up his collar and folding his arms tightly to keep warm. "Perhaps it will let up."

He was wrong. During the day, the sleet turned to snow, and then fog descended. As the Republicans began their counterattack on the ground, the Italians, in tropical gear, were suffering even more from the cold than they were. Arctic temperatures became the enemy of both sides, and many died from hypothermia. To his satisfaction, Antonio learned that the Italians had been overambitious about the speed they could move at, and in the chaos of the fog and snow their units were losing communication with each other. Their fuel was beginning to run low, vehicles were getting stranded, and aircraft were struggling to take off.

The Republicans were becoming more dominant by the hour.

"Luck seems to be on the right side for once," Antonio signed to his friends.

"Perhaps it's because we're here," quipped Salvador, with a smile. "Franco's had it now."

If the Italians had little communication with each other, for much of the time Antonio's militia band had an only marginally clearer idea of the whole picture. Action raged all around them, but almost zero visibility allowed them to see little of it. In the cold chaos, Antonio could hear the agonizing cries of dying men, some shot by their own side.

Antonio had kept as close as he could to Salvador when they advanced into battle. He had already proved his courage at Jarama, but nevertheless Antonio felt a great sense of responsibility toward his friend.

Salvador had already found certain advantages to being deaf in battle. He could hear neither the whine of bullets nor the screams of the wounded, but nor could he hear the warning cry of a friend. To the very moment of his death, Salvador experienced no fear. All he saw was a brief glimpse of the grimace that registered on his friend's face. The cry of anguish that then followed was not the victim's but Antonio's as he watched his oldest friend, the beloved El Mudo, fall to the ground.

The blood-soaked shirt was Antonio's. It turned red as he cradled his dying friend. And the earth about them changed to scarlet as it absorbed the rest.

On this battlefield there was no time for the self-indulgence of grief. Salvador had been killed at the end of the day's fighting, so, unlike many whose bodies lay for hours where they had fallen, Francisco and Antonio were soon able to bury him. The frost-hardened soil did not make it an easy task. As they hacked at the solid earth, they were warmer than they had been for days. It takes a sizable space to bury a man's body, and the great mound that lay to the side of the hollow seemed absurd next to Salvador's shrouded corpse.

The next day they were assigned to the task of gathering equipment left behind by the Italians. Others were given the task of guarding prisoners and Antonio was glad that they had been spared this duty. He would not have trusted Francisco to give them humane treatment. Nor himself, for that matter.

Fury fueled them from this moment. There was no need for any further reminder that they were fighting for the right cause. Though everyone knew it already, the abandoned weapons and other material they were gathering proved that Italy was breaching an agreement of non-intervention that was supposedly being observed in Europe. This policy, not to take sides in Spain's internal conflict, was already being flouted by several countries, and the documents the Republican militia seized were useful to the politicians as evidence of this. The equipment itself was a huge boost to the Republican cause, too. They needed every piece of artillery they could get.

When the battle at Guadalajara was over, they returned to Madrid. If their homes were close enough and they still had family to visit, men might go back to their villages on leave. For Antonio and Francisco, there was no question of visiting their home city. Granada was firmly in Nationalist hands, and traveling there would have resulted in certain arrest.

They stayed behind in the capital to help strengthen the barricades. Though it was hard to defend the city from the air, the aim was to build a strong enough defense to turn the capital into a fortress. For many days Antonio and Francisco worked on building walls of rain-sodden sandbags, their bulbous shapes as smooth as huge rounded pebbles. Many of the city's buildings now looked like honeycomb, their windows blasted out with the force of explosives. They were a constant reminder of the need to protect Madrid, even if Franco had now moved the focus of his offensive elsewhere.

Antonio and Francisco missed Salvador sorely. Their friendship had depended on his moderating influence, and his absence left a void at its heart. After caring for him for so many years, their sense of failure at not having protected him from the enemy bullet was immense. Combined now with a period of uncertainty over where the fighting would take them, disillusion began to set in. The left was becoming increasingly fragmented, and Franco would take advantage of its lack of cohesion.

"The problem is that there is still no unity, no solid core," said Antonio anxiously. "So what hope have we got?"

"But if people have strong principles, Marxist or communist, why should they give them up?" asked Francisco. "If they did, would they still fight?"

"There are plenty of people with passion around," answered Antonio. "Even if they aren't extreme in their politics. And lots of us are prepared to fight. But until the leaders agree on a few things . . ."

" . . . We won't get anywhere," finished Francisco. "It's beginning to look as though you're right."

Though the militia brigades were now united into the Popular Army, there were factions growing within factions among those opposed to Franco. The struggle against Franco seemed to be intensifying, but inside the ranks of communists, anarchists, Marxists, and many other smaller groups, there was infighting, backbiting, and disagreement. Antonio longed for the leaders of each group to see that the only way forward was unity, but each day seemed to bring new divisions and arguments.

# CHAPTER 26

Mercedes was nearing the end of her bus journey to Murcia. She gazed out of the window and thought of her parents. Señor and Señora Duarte had not spoken for the entire duration of the six-hour journey, and she reflected that the hostility between them was something that would never have been possible between Concha and Pablo. Even when there might have been disagreements between them, the overriding atmosphere was always warm.

Ana had slept for most of the ride.

In Murcia, as in so many places, people were reduced to begging on the street, but their hands were only held out to others in a similar state of need. As they descended the steps of the old rickety vehicle that had brought them, the girls caught sight of an elderly man playing a trumpet while his dog danced.

"Look, Mercedes!" Ana tugged Mercedes' sleeve with delight. For an instant the spectacle had some charm and brought the first moment of light relief to their day. "It's sweet, but look how scrawny it is . . ."

The dog's eyes were as sad as his master's, and the sight of this duet, initially so charming, now seemed pathetic. It was demeaning both for the animal and his owner. A couple of coins that were tossed into the hat in front of them probably more than made up for the degradation, but few people actually lingered to watch.

"I can't think of anything but my stomach," complained Ana. "It's the only part of my body that I can feel." Her bottom and legs were numb from sitting most of the day. "I wonder where we can eat."

The shops here were not badly stocked, but the Duartes had to make sure that their money lasted a while. Señor Duarte had withdrawn everything they had in the bank some weeks before, and they had no way of telling how long this would have to last them. He was keeping the purse strings tight.

Though they seemed willing to share with Mercedes, her conscience often pricked her. Apart from her company and conversation (and she was aware that Ana depended on her completely for both), she had little to give in return. She had run out of money many days earlier.

Ana and Mercedes wandered off while Señor Duarte looked for somewhere to stay. As they walked along, the image of the dancing dog with its frilled collar remained with Mercedes. It suddenly seemed obvious what she must do, even though the idea of it filled her with trepidation. If she could find someone to play for her, she would dance, and then, if someone paid, she could give something back to this family. In this way she would not be a burden.

They went first into one of the cafés in the square. Like the rest of the town at this hour, it had the air of abandonment. Many of the younger men had gone off to join the militia, so it was as though a whole layer of their society had vanished. The middle-aged man running the bar was jovial enough, though. He would still have plenty of customers that night, and he was getting the place ready. Alcohol was still in reasonable supply and people were drinking plenty. Business was not bad. He smiled at the two girls as they walked in.

"Can I help you?" he asked.

"We would like to ask you something," Ana said boldly. "My friend wants to dance. Could she do that here?"

The barman stopped polishing the glasses. "Dance? In this café?"

He reacted as though it was an extraordinary request, even though these wooden floorboards had taken a hammering from some of the region's greatest dancers. On the wall behind the bar there was even a signed photograph of the celebrated *bailaora*, known as La Argentina.

In former times, dancing had been such a simple act: a natural response to music, enjoyed by everyone from child to adult. Now even such an innocent activity as this had political undertones.

It had not surprised anyone that the sensual, free-spirited art of flamenco that had thrived in so many parts of Spain did not meet with the approval of Franco's strict and sanctimonious regime. What was more alarming was the sense of disapproval in some Republican areas, where posters had begun to appear listing dance as nothing less than a crime. They had been put up by the anarchists and instilled both guilt and fear. When Mercedes spotted one of these on a wall in Murcia, she was chilled by it. How could dancing ever be outlawed?

"*GUERRA A LA INMORALIDAD*," screamed the poster headline. Along with drinking in bars, visiting cinemas and going to the theater, dancing was listed as an obstruction to the fight against Fascism.

"*El baile es la antesala del prostitución*," the poster continued— "Dancing leads to prostitution."

To connect dancers with prostitutes might have had some validity in the cities, but these innocent young women who stood in his bar seemed far too sweet and naïve. The café owner was a Republican and as appalled by the prospect of criminalizing dance as Mercedes.

"And what would you want for it?" he asked, trying to put on a businesslike tone to conceal what was going through his mind.

"Payment of some kind," said Mercedes, putting on her best act of confidence. It would be the first time she had ever specifically danced for money, but life had changed and so had the rules.

"Payment . . . Well, I suppose if it attracted more people into the bar, then I could justify paying you. And if customers wanted to give you something, there'd be nothing wrong with that, I suppose. All right. Why not?"

"Thank you," said Ana. "And is there anyone around here who could play?"

"I should think so," the proprietor said, rather amused now. Every village and hamlet around here had someone that could play well enough to accompany a dancer. He could have someone there at nine, and they could practice a few things out in the courtyard before they performed.

"There's just one other thing," he said. "I think you should wear something more . . . um, suitable."

Mercedes flushed, suddenly embarrassed by her appearance. She had been wearing the same skirt and blouse for several weeks now. There had been few opportunities to wash her clothes, and she had grown used to the grime.

"But I don't have anything else," she confessed. "This is what I left home with. Just shoes, that's all I have."

"María! María!" The man was already shouting up the stairs that led directly from the bar, and a moment later a slight woman, his wife, appeared.

There were no introductions.

"She's going to dance tonight," the man said, pointing at Mercedes, "but she needs a dress. Can you find something for her."

The woman sized Mercedes up and turned her back.

"It won't take her long," said the bar owner. "Our daughter used to dance—she was a bit fatter than you, but something will fit."

Moments later the wife returned. She had two dresses slung over her arm, and Mercedes tried them on in the backroom. It was strange to feel the weight of the ruffles again and the eloquent way in which they moved around her ankles. There was one, red with huge white polka dots, that fitted her better than the other. It gaped around the chest and the arms, but anything would be better for dancing in than her threadbare skirt.

The girls left, promising to return later that evening.

The guitarist was competent enough, a man of about fifty, who had played in many *juergas* but was more contented as a soloist than an accompanist. They worked through a repertoire that pleased and distracted the audience for a few hours and from time to time there were a few mutters of "*Olé.*"

Mercedes was surprised by how mechanical it felt to dance just in order to earn money. It was so unlike the emboldening experience of the night in Almería. But coins were tossed into the cup that Ana took around, and the café owner took a handful of change from his till and handed it to her with a smile. His takings had been improved that night.

"It was so wooden," Mercedes lamented to Ana as they went to sleep.

"Don't worry," consoled Ana. "The crowd didn't notice. They just loved the entertainment. You were better than the dog anyway!"

Mercedes laughed. "They would have been better off at a puppet show," she said.

They repeated the formula in several towns as they journeyed slowly toward Bilbao. Mercedes learned what pleased the audience and what failed to stir them, and discovered a new way of dancing that was competent and functional. Only a few members of the audience noticed how little of herself she gave. She knew that she would never move anyone this way, but it was a way of making a living, and she was happy to share the money with Ana and her parents. Dance was saving her in a different way now.

During the hours when they were traveling by bus or in a farmer's truck, Ana's parents remained mostly silent, and Mercedes often found herself observing Señor Duarte and wondering how hard it was for him to pretend she was his daughter. By the middle of March they had crossed into Nationalist territory. Señor Duarte was even more tense than before. There were informers on every street corner.

"No more dancing now," he said one night to the girls. "We don't know how it will be received here."

"But does it matter, Father?" exclaimed Ana. "Everyone loves Mercedes' dancing, so what's the harm in it?"

"It means that people notice us. And we don't want that. We want to lie as low as possible."

The nights of dancing had added so much color to the journey. Mercedes had begun to enjoy the release of each performance, and her enthusiasm for it had returned. She was sorry to give it up but understood why the Duartes felt the need to restrict it.

Señor Duarte trusted no one, and it was often difficult to tell where people's sympathies truly lay, even though they were now well inside Nationalist-held territory.

There were several episodes when they were challenged by the Civil Guard during their journey. "Where have you come from? Where are you going?" they barked, their polished patent hats perched on top of their heads. These men were experts at detecting the slightest sweat that might break out on an interviewee's brow or the way that eyes did not meet their stern look. A shifty glance or a sense of discomfort immediately aroused suspicion and earned protracted questioning.

Señor Duarte could answer their interrogations honestly enough. He had taken his family out of Republican territory and his destination was his brother's house in San Sebastián. They correctly deduced that he supported Franco, and some of them noticed the woman's expression, the scent of fear, her silence. It was puzzling but did not bother them. In their view, it did no harm for society if women lived in fear of their husbands. What they were looking for were subversive elements, and this woman and her two daughters who feigned disinterest in everything around them seemed harmless enough.

After a month together, they finally reached the junction in the road where Ana and her parents would go toward her uncle's village and Mercedes would continue going north toward Bilbao, crossing once again into territory held by the Republicans. Mercedes and Ana tried not to contemplate the next stages of their journeys, which they would be making without each other.

Señor Duarte's farewell was perfunctory, while the *señora*'s was warm.

Their daughter held on to Mercedes as though she might never let go. "Promise me that we will meet again," Ana urged.

"Of course we will. As soon as I am settled, I shall write to you. I have your uncle's address."

Mercedes was determined to control her emotions. Promises of a reunion relieved them from the unimaginable possibility that they might never see each other again. In those weeks they had not been separated for a moment, day or night. No sisters were ever closer.

# CHAPTER 27

It was mid-March now and, in Granada, Concha continued to run El Barril alone. It kept her occupied while the weeks passed with almost intolerable slowness. The routine provided her with the only structure she had in her life now that she had stopped going to see Pablo in prison. In the first months after his arrest, Concha had visited him as regularly as she could, but as the conflict continued, it had become increasingly hard. The roads were dangerous, she was always afraid of arrest, and the journey was taking its physical toll. Two weeks earlier, Pablo had made her promise not to come.

In the half-light, through a double layer of metal grilling, they had stood and looked at each other in shadowy outline. The distance between them precluded all conversation apart from a few remarks shouted above the din of other couples exchanging information. There could be no sharing of confidences or fears, with the guards standing close by. Each visit Concha had observed how her husband seemed visibly diminished, but through the haze of metal she was unable to see how ill he really looked. It was just as well.

"Someone has to keep their strength, *querida mia*," Pablo had said, almost inaudibly through the mesh.

"But it should be me who is locked up," she replied.

"Don't say that," scolded Pablo. "I would rather be in here than have you in some awful place."

Everyone knew what happened in the women's prisons, and Pablo would have spared his wife at any price. They were shaved and purged with castor oil, often raped and branded. No man would allow his wife to suffer these indignities if there was an option, and Pablo never regretted having made this choice.

"Please don't come," he begged. "It's not doing you any good."

"But what about the food parcels?"

"I'll survive," he said.

Pablo did not like to tell her that very little usually remained in them by the time the light-fingered guards had checked their contents and handed them over. He knew that his wife would have made the most enormous sacrifices to get these packages of food and tobacco to him and it was better that she was not disillusioned.

Concha ceased her visits but was endlessly racked by guilt. It could so easily have been her that was tortured and half-starved in a cell, and she carried this thought around with her every minute of the day. She tried to distract herself from thinking too much about what had happened to Pablo, knowing that anger and despair would do nothing to alleviate her situation.

Another source of anxiety for Concha was the lack of news from her children. Salvador's mother, Josefina, was the only one with any news of the boys. She had returned to Granada a month after they had left for Madrid only to find a letter from the militia informing her of her son's death. There was no other information to be had, but she also received two funny and eloquent letters that he had written before his death, describing in detail what they had done. Salvador had a gift for writing and description. She shared these letters with Concha and María Pérez, and the three women spent hours together poring over them.

Concha knew that Mercedes would never have reached Málaga and hoped that she was now somewhere with Javier but too afraid to return to Granada. She was sure that all this uncertainty would be over soon so that they could all be reunited, and she yearned for a letter from her daughter.

Mercedes realized how independent she had become. She missed her friend Ana, but solitude was something she had grown accustomed to. It seemed a lifetime ago that anyone had looked after her, and the memory of how her brothers had fussed over her was a distant one.

She was now almost in the Basque country, and she calculated that it might be only a few days before she reached Bilbao. Mercedes had her shoes and the dancing dress the café proprietor's wife had given her in a bag, as well as a few other spare items of clothing that she had been able to afford with the money she was earning. She had not planned to dance once she was on her own, but one night, in a small place that only just qualified as a town, the circumstances seemed right.

When the bus reached its final destination late that afternoon, Mercedes soon found somewhere to stay. Her room overlooked a side street leading down to the square, and by leaning as far as she safely could out of her window, she caught a glimpse of the activity going on in there. Something seemed to be happening, so she went down to get a closer look.

It was March 19. Mercedes was oblivious to the significance of the day. In the small square people were congregating. Two small girls ran around, chasing each other, squealing, rattling their castanets, and almost tripping over the flounces of their cheap flamenco skirts. This dusty square, with its gently trickling fountain in the middle, was the center of their universe. It was the only place they had ever known, and Mercedes envied them their oblivion to the events taking place not so far away. Their parents had worked hard to keep them from feeling the effects of the shortages that afflicted the urban areas, and the occasional quiet boom and flash in the night sky from a faraway bombardment seemed a world away to the children of this apparently self-contained community. One or two of them knew the terror of it—their fathers had disappeared in the night—but the community was still functioning as normal.

Mercedes saw girls sitting on a wall chatting, some plaiting each other's hair, others spinning around with their fringed shawls. A group of boys eyed them from a distance and occasionally were rewarded with a surreptitious sideways glance cast in their direction. There was a slightly older boy holding a guitar. He was strumming a few notes with the kind of nonchalance only ever achieved by the self-confidently handsome, and when he looked up, he noticed Mercedes watching him. She smiled. He was probably not much younger than she, but she felt a hundred years older. She was fearless now and had no hesitation in approaching him.

"Will there be dancing later?" she asked.

The disdainful look he gave her provided the answer. With the small wooden stage erected close by, this village was clearly prepared for a fiesta. It would be the first that Mercedes had seen for many months, and even if the religious connotations meant little, the ritual, music, and dancing had their own vibrancy. She would not be able to resist it.

"It's the feast of San José!" he said. "Didn't you know?"

Later on in the evening, she saw the young guitarist again, along with an older man, seated on chairs at the edge of the stage. It was around eight o'clock now, and it was the first evening of the year that the little warmth of the day lingered into the night. At which precise moment the stage of gently tuning up turned into the beginning of the *alegrías*, it was hard to tell, but applause rippled across the crowd.

The rhythms of the music seemed to come from opposing directions, working against each other and merging again like currents at the confluence of two rivers. Father and son made music that intertwined. They crossed over each other, blended, and receded again, pulling back in their original direction. There were supremely pleasing moments when the two instruments made the sound of one and then moved away from each other back to their own melody. Even the discords seemed harmonious, minor and major chords sometimes engaging in polite collision.

Mercedes sat close by, patting her knee as she caught the rhythm, and smiled. This music was something sublime. For a while the strife-ridden outside world ceased to exist.

When this heavenly performance finished, the father looked up to catch Mercedes' eye. It was her turn. When she had spoken to the older guitarist earlier in the evening, she had learned that he and his son were also outsiders. They had left Sevilla a few months earlier and were biding their time until they returned. It seemed too dangerous at present.

"They'll be pleased to see someone dancing true flamenco!" he had said smilingly, showing a huge gap between his front teeth.

On the small wooden stage, where both boys and girls and one or two older women had already performed, Mercedes' dance turned into something much more than the usual display of passion and strength that characterized flamenco. The primitive power of her gestures reached out to the audience. There were mutterings of "*Olé*" from both men and women, who were astonished by this magnificent dancer. The *guitarristas* may have made them forget, but Mercedes reminded them that their country was being torn apart. Her movements embodied the anguish they all felt when they thought of the guns and cannons that were being turned against them. After dancing for twenty minutes, she had no more to give. Her final stamp, planted with a mighty "crack" on the wooden boards, was an unmistakable gesture of defiance. "We will not submit" it seemed to shout, and the audience erupted into applause.

People were curious about her. Some of the people she talked to that night could not understand why she was making for Bilbao, which they imagined was full of danger.

"Why don't you stay here?" inquired the woman whose house she was staying in. "You'd be much safer. You can keep that room for a while if you like."

"You're so kind," answered Mercedes, "but I must keep going. My aunt and uncle have been expecting me for a long time."

It was simpler to lie than to tell the truth. She had not lost faith in finding Javier, even if, in her mind, the image of him was fading. She would wake up in the morning and search her imagination in vain for an image of his face, and sometimes there was nothing at all, hardly an outline. Sometimes she had to take the photograph of him out of her pocket to remind herself of his features, the liquid oval eyes, the aquiline nose, the beautiful mouth. That perfect moment in Málaga when the picture was taken seemed so long ago, in another lifetime. The image of such a dazzling smile seemed something that would exist only in history books.

Being separated from everyone she knew, and everywhere that was familiar, had created a growing sense of emptiness. From the moment when the Duarte family had disappeared from view, she had felt insubstantial and unconnected to the world. Was it for weeks or months that she had been away? She scarcely knew. There was nothing to measure time against. Its solid framework had turned to dust.

Perhaps the only thing she knew for certain now was that having come this far, she had to push on to her destination. She ignored a new but persistent doubt that she would ever find the object of her quest.

She got up in the dark that morning to be sure of catching the bus that she had been told would take her to Bilbao. For a few hours the vehicle rattled along. Eventually it dropped her on the edge of the city, and it was not long before Mercedes began to realize why her plan to go there had been met with such incredulous looks the previous night.

She was given a lift from the outskirts by a doctor, who left her in one of the city's main squares.

"I don't want to put you off," he said politely, "but you won't find things easy in Bilbao. Most people are trying to get out of here."

"I know," answered Mercedes, "but here's where I need to be."

The doctor could see that she would not be deterred, and he did not ask questions. At least he had done what he could. Like this young woman, he would not be going to Bilbao unless he was compelled, and for him it was a hospital full of wounded that drew him.

"I honestly don't think it'll be long before this place falls, so take care of yourself."

"I'll try," she said, doing her best to raise a smile. "Thanks for bringing me here."

The city was in chaos. There were frequent air raids and a sense of fear and desperation and panic. None of these were things that she had seen in Granada the previous summer, or even in Almería among the traumatized refugees from Málaga.

Bilbao seemed a world away from some of the small towns where she had stayed, which were physically if not mentally untouched by the conflict. This city was receiving a continual battering. Day and night it was bombarded from the sea and from the air. The port was blockaded, and food shortages were at critical level. The diet was rice and cabbage, and unless you were prepared to eat donkey, there was no meat. The sight of dead bodies was common. They lay in the streets, lined up like sandbags, and early each morning were ferried to the morgue in carts.

There was only one reason that she would have come to this hell and that was to follow up the final clue she had for finding Javier. On a small scrap of paper folded inside her purse was an address. It was where she might find him. Even the slimmest possibility filled her with a sense of excitement, and she was now impatient to get there.

The first few people she asked were strangers to the city, just as she was. A shopkeeper would be more likely to give her directions, and she pushed open the first door she came to. It was a hardware shop, but it displayed about as much stock as the average kitchen. Customers were non-existent, but the old shopkeeper still sat in a dark corner by his till, carrying on the pretense that business was as normal. When he heard the chime of the bell, he peered over the top of his newspaper.

"Can I help you?"

Mercedes' eyes needed to get accustomed to the gloom, but she followed the source of the voice, bumping into a table loaded with dusty pans as she did so.

"I need to find this street," she said, unfolding the paper. "Do you know where it is?"

The old man removed his glasses from his top pocket and carefully put them on. He ran a stubby finger across the address.

"Yes, I know it," he said. "It's in the north of the city."

On the reverse side of the paper, using a blunt pencil, he drew a map. Then he opened the door of his shop and took Mercedes out onto the pavement, instructing her to follow the road they stood on as far as it went and then to take a series of turns before she met another main road that would lead her eventually to her destination.

"Ask again when you get closer," he advised. "It will probably take you half an hour."

For the first time in weeks, Mercedes felt a surge of optimism, and the smile she gave the old man was the first he had seen for a long time.

It seemed strange to him that this young woman was apparently so excited about visiting the most bomb-ravaged area of his city. He did not have the heart to warn her.

As Mercedes worked her way toward her destination, meticulously following directions, her smile gradually faded. In each street, the extent of destruction seemed greater than it had been in the previous one. At first, she noticed a few shattered windows, most of them boarded up, but within half an hour of setting out walking, the condition of the buildings was noticeably worsening. By the time she caught a glimpse of the sea and knew she must be close to her destination, many of these apartment blocks were just shells. At best, they composed the four outside walls, with gaping cavities at the center, like boxes without lids. At worst, they had been razed to the ground. Miscellaneous possessions lay scattered among their ruins: broken furniture and a thousand personal effects left behind in the scramble to evacuate.

Mercedes had to ask a dozen times if she was going in the right direction. Eventually she found the street name, attached to the first block on the corner. Only this end-building was still standing; the rest of the street was badly damaged. It looked as though a bomb had landed right in the center of the road and blasted everything within a fifty-meter radius. It was obvious even from where she stood that all the apartments must be empty. Their windows were black and dark, like eyesockets in a skull. She worked out in which block Javier's aunt and uncle had lived, and it was clear that they could no longer be there.

The street was deserted, like every single one of these buildings, and she assumed that anyone who had been at home when the bomb landed must be either injured or dead. The last shreds of hope that she had clung to for all those weeks were gradually disappearing. She had wanted so much to find Javier in this city, and the irony now was that she hoped he had never reached Bilbao at all. Mercedes felt herself trembling. She was ice-cold, numb with shock.

Her fist closed around the scrap of paper with Javier's address, molding it into a hard ball. Later that day she would notice its loss without concern. She was now truly without direction.

The next few hours of Mercedes' stay in Bilbao were spent in a queue for bread. The length of this straggling line far exceeded any she had seen in Almería or any of the other towns in Republican territory. It snaked down one street and around the corner into another. Mothers with small children tried to deal with the whining of their offspring as best they could, but if they were hungry when they joined the queue, three hours of waiting only worsened the hunger pangs. Patience began to run out, as did the certainty that there would be anything for them at the end.

"There were nearly a hundred people in front of me yesterday," moaned the woman in front of Mercedes, "and then the shutters came down. Bang. Nothing."

"So what did you do?" she inquired.

"What do you think we did?"

The woman's manner was aggressive and her speech coarse. Mercedes felt obliged to engage in conversation, though she could happily have stood in silence. She was totally preoccupied with thoughts of Javier and merely shrugged in reply.

"We waited, didn't we? There was no way we were going to lose our places, so we slept on the pavement."

The woman was determined to continue, in spite of the fact that Mercedes did nothing to encourage her.

"And you know what happened then? When we woke up, these other people had moved in front of us. Taken our places."

As she spoke these last words, she punched the clenched fist of one hand into the flattened palm of the other. Reliving the moment of finding herself usurped in the queue, she felt her anger returning.

"So you see, I have to get some of that bread. There's no choice."

Mercedes had no doubt that this woman would stop at nothing to feed her family, and her threatening manner suggested that she would resort to violence to do so.

Mercedes was in luck herself that morning. Supplies did not run out before she reached the front of the queue, but she knew nevertheless that the woman resented her because of her admission that she had no dependents. Since strict rationing was not in force, those with children often felt they were inadequately supplied. This woman clearly felt that the world was against her and, worst of all, it was cheating her family. Mercedes could feel the woman's eyes boring into her as she picked up her loaf from the counter. Such sparks of hostility between people even on the same side was one of the worst aspects of this war.

Despite the feeling of growing desperation there, Mercedes decided not to leave Bilbao immediately. She had done enough traveling and felt there was nowhere else to go. In the days after she had seen the derelict wreck of Javier's uncle's home, she allowed herself to hope that he might be elsewhere in the city. It was pointless being in a rush to leave now, and each day she made new inquiries.

One of Mercedes' immediate needs was for a roof over her head, and she soon found herself in conversation with a mother she met in one of the food queues. María Sánchez was so beset with the grief of losing her husband that she was only too happy to accept the offer of help with her four children in return for accommodation. Mercedes shared a room with the two daughters, and soon they were calling her *Tía*, Aunt.

# CHAPTER 28

The end of the Battle of Guadalajara in March had marked a break in Franco's attempts to take the capital and the turning of his attention to the industrial north: the Basque area was still stubbornly resisting. Meanwhile, Antonio and Francisco were back in Madrid, which, though not the focus of Franco's campaign, still continued to need defense.

They had weeks of relative inactivity, during which they wrote letters, played cards, and occasionally engaged in a skirmish. Francisco, as ever, was desperate to be at the center of the action again, while Antonio tried to be more patient. He was always hungry, not just for bread but also for news of events in other parts of the country. He devoured the daily papers as soon as they appeared on the newsstands.

At the end of March, they heard of the bombing of the defenseless town of Durango. A church had been targeted during Mass, and most of the congregation had been killed, along with some nuns and a priest. Worse still, German fighters had strafed fleeing civilians, and about two hundred and fifty people were killed. There was another event, however, the destruction of the ancient Basque town of Guernica, that had greater implications for both Antonio and Mercedes, even though they were separated from each other by hundreds of kilometers, and both far from home.

The late April day when the news was broadcast that Guernica had been reduced to a blackened shell was one of the darkest moments in this conflict. Sitting in Madrid's spring sunshine, Antonio found his hands shaking so violently that he could hardly hold his newspaper. It was a place neither he nor Francisco had ever been to, but the description of its horrific destruction marked a turning point.

"Look at these pictures," he said. There was a catch in his throat as he passed the paper across to Francisco. "Look . . ."

The two men surveyed them with disbelief. Several photographs showed the twisted wreckage of buildings, and human and animal corpses strewn across the street; it had been market day. The most shocking image of all was the body of a lifeless child, a small girl. There was a label around her wrist, like a price tag on a doll. It recorded where she had been found, should her parents ever turn up to find her in the morgue. It was the most appalling image they had seen, either with their own eyes or reproduced in newsprint.

The town had been systematically attacked by wave upon wave of mostly German and some Italian bombers, which over several hours dropped thousands of bombs and machine-gunned civilians as they fled for their lives. An entire community had been wiped out, with whole families perishing in their flaming homes. There were reports of victims staggering through the smoke and dust to try to dig out their friends and relatives, only to be killed as another wave of bombers passed over. More than fifteen hundred people died in that single afternoon.

The massacre of innocents disgusted them more than the death of comrades whose lives had been lost in some kind of equal if unjust combat.

"If Franco thinks he'll win by destroying all these towns," said Francisco, his hatred all the more intense with every Republican defeat, "then he's wrong. Until he walks into Madrid, he has nothing . . ."

The obliteration of Guernica was keenly felt by Antonio and Francisco, and everyone else who supported the Republic, and reinforced the determination of the militia to stand against Franco.

If the massacre in Guernica strengthened resolve in Madrid, in Bilbao it instilled terror. The effect on the residents of this northern city, and on those who had gone there for refuge, was measured panic. If Franco could wipe out one town in this manner, then he would presumably not hesitate to do the same with another. The thoroughness of the bombing shocked even those who had been exposed to the relentless daily attacks in Bilbao, and in the streets and the queues they talked of little else.

"Did you hear what they did? They waited until it was four o'clock in the afternoon. Everyone was coming out of their houses to go to market, and they chose that moment to drop their bombs."

"And they came again and again and again. For three hours . . . until everything was flattened and almost everyone was killed."

"They say that there were fifty planes and that the bombs came down like rain."

"There's nothing left of the place . . ."

"We have to try and get the children out," said Mercedes, to Señora Sánchez.

"There isn't anywhere safe for them to go," she responded. "If there was, I would have sent them there a long time ago."

Señora Sánchez had become so resigned to the state of affairs in Bilbao that her imagination could not look beyond the present. Survival, for her, was not a question of planning an escape route but of living day to day and praying for deliverance.

"I've heard there are some boats going and that they'll be taking people to safety."

"Where will they take them?"

"Mexico, Russia . . ."

There was a look of sheer horror on Señora Sánchez's face. She had seen a photograph of children arriving in Moscow by train. It looked so unfamiliar: banners in an alphabet she could not decipher, little communist children meeting them with flowers, the faces of the people waiting for them, so different, so foreign . . .

"How can I even think of letting my children go to any of those places? How could you even suggest it?"

She wept from outrage and fear. She could not even contemplate the distances that they would have to travel and could not picture what was at the end of such a journey. Her instincts told her to keep her children close.

"It would only be for a while," Mercedes assured her. "It would keep them out of harm's way while all this is going on, and they wouldn't be starving."

People were now lining up to apply for places on these boats for their children, and the queues were even longer than those for bread. The horrors of Guernica, the bombing of innocent people, and the methodical destruction of an entire town had made everyone in Bilbao face the brutal truth: the same could happen to their own city.

Such complete annihilation could be perpetrated by land, sea, or air, and there was no safe haven for them—not in Spain at least. Like so many other parents in Bilbao, in the past few days Señora Sánchez had faced the fact that the best thing for her offspring would be for them to leave for a safer place. After all, people were saying that it would only be for three months.

For more than eighteen hours, Mercedes waited with Señora Sánchez and her four children to be seen about their application for evacuation abroad. Everyone was nervous, occasionally glancing up at a bright, empty sky, and wondering how many minutes' grace they might have between the first glimpse of a bomber and the earthquake rumble of an explosion. They were queuing up for places on the boat that was to go to England, the *Habana*. Though Señora Sánchez had no image of it in her mind, she knew that Great Britain was closer than some of the other places on offer, and for that reason she would see her children again much sooner.

After all these hours of patience, it was finally María Sánchez's turn to make the case for her precious sons and daughters.

"Tell me the ages of your children, please," demanded the official.

"They are three, four, nine, and twelve," she answered, indicating each one in turn.

The official scrutinized them.

"And what about you?" he asked, addressing Mercedes.

"Oh, I'm not one of her children," she replied. "I've just been helping look after them. My name isn't on the application."

The man grunted, marking something on the form in front of him.

"Your two youngest are below the age requirement," he said, addressing Señora Sánchez. "We're only taking them between the ages of five and fifteen. Your older two might qualify, but first I need you to answer a few questions."

After that, he barked out a list that demanded instant, accurate answers: father's occupation, his religion, and the party he had belonged to. María answered them truthfully. There seemed no point in lying now. Her husband had been a trade union member and a member of the socialist party.

The official put down his pen and picked up a file that lay on his desk, opened it, and ran his finger down a column, counting silently. For a few minutes, he continued to make notes. There had to be an allocation of children from parents of all the various political parties in proportion to the voting patterns in the most recent election. The children were signed up for one of three groups: the Republicans and Socialists, the Communists and Anarchists, and the Nationalists. It seemed that the boat was not quite full and that there was space for some more from the Socialist party.

"And you," said the official, looking at Mercedes, "would you like to join the boat as well?"

Mercedes was completely taken aback. It had not occurred to her that she would be given a place. She was too old to qualify for one of the children's places and had resigned herself to staying in Bilbao. She had had no ambition to get herself onto one of the boats that took adults to faraway places. In her mind, such journeys would have been an admission to herself that she would never find Javier.

But she had to cling to the ever-shrinking hope of finding him, given that the other option, to retrace her steps, was now ruled out.

"We need a certain number of young women to look after the younger ones and there is a space. If you have been taking care of children for a while, you might be just the sort of person we need," said the official.

Mercedes could only dimly hear his voice, so filled was her mind with this new dilemma.

"Mercedes!" exclaimed María. "You must go! What a chance!"

For the first time since she had known her, Mercedes saw the colorless expression of resignation melt away from the woman's face.

Mercedes felt as though a hand was being held out to her and it would be ungrateful of her not to take it. People were clamoring for spaces on these boats. She told herself she could be back in a few months' time, reunited with her family. But to abandon the search for Javier was unthinkable.

The two older children, Enrique and Paloma, whose fates had already been decided, stood looking at her, with pleading expressions. They badly wanted her to come with them to this unfamiliar destination and instinctively knew that their mother would be happier if she was on the boat with them. Mercedes looked at their wide, hopeful eyes. Perhaps for the first time she would do something really useful and take responsibility for someone other than herself.

"Very well," she heard herself say. "I'll go."

There were a few formalities. First a medical. Mercedes took her two charges to the office of the *Asistencia Social*, and they waited in line until the English doctor was ready to see them. There was not much conversation since neither spoke the other's language.

Paloma and Enrique were each given a clean bill of health. A hexagonal card with the words *"Expedición a Inglaterra"* and their own personal number was pinned to their clothing, and they were instructed to wear it at all times.

"What are you going to take?" Paloma asked Enrique excitedly, as though they were going on a pleasure trip.

"Don't know," he said miserably. "Chess set? Not sure. Don't know if there'll be anybody to play with."

They were allowed only one small bag each, with a change of clothing and a limited number of possessions, the choice of which would have to be very carefully thought out.

"I'm going to take Rosa," said Paloma decisively.

Rosa was her favorite doll and her imaginary friend. If Rosa came on this journey, Paloma knew everything would be fine. Her older brother was not so confident. He was anxious about where they were going, but his seniority in the family obliged him to put on a brave front.

Mercedes' only possessions already fitted into a small bag, so she had no decisions to make. The boat was leaving in two days' time, and in every one of those forty-eight hours there was always a chance that she might find Javier. In those two last days in Bilbao she scanned every crowd and every queue in case she caught a glimpse of his face.

At six o'clock on the evening of May 20, thousands of people thronged the railway station of Portugalete. Six hundred at a time, the children were taken on special trains to Santurce, Bilbao's main dock, where the *Habana* was waiting. Some of the parents had traveled no farther than Pamplona in their entire lives, so seeing their children leaving for the unknown was almost unbearable. A few children clung to their mother's skirts, but often the distress was more on the mother's side than on the child's. Some children were cheerful, happy and smiling and anticipating seeing their parents again soon; they viewed this as a boat trip with a picnic, a short holiday, an adventure, and for them the atmosphere seemed exciting and festive. The president had even come to wave them off.

Enrique remained glum right until the moment of departure, unable even to raise a smile for his mother, who struggled to hold back her tears. Señora Sánchez was not going to accompany them on the train to the dock. Her farewell would be on the station platform.

By contrast with her brother, Paloma was full of excitement. She was sick of the sirens and the aching hunger. "It's only going to be for a few weeks," she kept saying to him. "It's an adventure. It might be fun."

As far as all the children were concerned, they were going on a journey to keep them safe. Many of them were smartly dressed: little girls wore ribbons in their hair, their best floral frocks, and white ankle socks, and the boys looked neat in crisp shirts and knee-length shorts.

The *Habana* seemed huge to the children, looming darkly over their heads, ready to swallow them up like a whale. Some of the smallest of them could not even reach up to catch the rope that ran the length of the gangplank. Sailors took tiny hands in their own and, squeezing them tight, escorted the smallest children along the narrow strip of wood to stop them plunging into the canal of dark water between the dock and the ship.

The ship was big enough to take eight hundred passengers, but they had made provision for nearly four thousand children and almost two hundred adults (twenty teachers, one hundred and twenty auxiliaries, of which Mercedes was one, fifteen Catholic priests, and two doctors). They were all on board by nightfall and, after a bigger meal than they had eaten in weeks, slept on board.

At dawn on May 21, the moorings were loosened. There was the clanking of heavy chains, and the passengers felt the first, slow movements of the ship as she began to slide away and move out of the port.

Mercedes felt her stomach lurch. She was immediately unsettled by the unfamiliar rocking (she had never before been on the water), but it was mostly her emotions that induced this nausea. She was leaving Spain. All around her small children were wailing, while the older ones stood by them, bravely holding their hands. Mercedes bit her lip, suppressing an almost overpowering need to howl with grief and loss. After days of anticipation and preparation, everything was happening too quickly. With every second, the distance between herself and Javier increased.

A spray of salt water mingled with the tears that ran down her face. The knowledge that she was leaving behind every single person she loved and knew was unbearable, and the temptation to run to the bow of the boat and fling herself into the wash almost overwhelmed her. Only the fact that she had to keep a brave face for the children stopped her.

Enveloped by a feeling of utter bleakness, she watched first the figures at the dockside and then the buildings themselves diminish to pinpricks and disappear from sight. Her hopes of seeing Javier seemed to vanish with them.

"And that," said Miguel, "was the last Mercedes ever saw of Spain."

"What?" Sonia could not conceal her shock. *"Ever?"*

"That's right. And she still couldn't write to her mother to explain where she was because it might be incriminating."

"How awful," Sonia said. "So Concha probably didn't even know she had left the country."

"No, she didn't," affirmed Miguel. "Not until a long time later."

They had finished their lunch in a restaurant near the cathedral and were now strolling slowly back to El Barril. Sonia suddenly felt rather afraid. If Mercedes had left Spain once and for all, perhaps Miguel would have no more information on her. She was about to inquire further when the old man picked up the story again.

"I want to tell you more about Antonio," he said determinedly, increasing his stride as they crossed the square toward his café. "We haven't yet reached the end of the Civil War."

# CHAPTER 29

Throughout the spring and early summer of 1937, Antonio and Francisco were kept in Madrid. The transition between the seasons that year was sudden, with the kind enveloping warmth of May suddenly swept rudely aside by the searing temperatures of summer. The air in the capital was almost unbreathable, and a deep torpor lay heavily over them.

They were both pleased when, at the beginning of July, there was renewed action and they were sent toward Brunete, twenty or so kilometers west of Madrid. The Republican army was aiming to drive a wedge into Nationalist-held territory. If they managed to break the line of communication linking the Fascists to their troops in the villages near Madrid and on the edge of the capital itself, it would end the encirclement of the city. Antonio and Francisco were among eighty thousand Republican troops being mobilized for this campaign, which was also drawing in tens of thousands of International Brigaders.

At first things seemed to go well for them. By nightfall on the first day they had penetrated Fascist territory, Brunete was captured and the village of Villanueva de la Cañada followed. Republican troops now moved on toward Villafranca del Castillo.

Some of the time, Antonio and Francisco were fighting the few small fascist forces that still remained, or collecting munitions and food supplies the Nationalists abandoned in their retreat. Once, their battalion found itself caught in a bombardment, and for four hours shells rained down on them as they sought cover in the ditches on either side of a road. Nationalist planes were now coming over and bombing them too. Dust, heat, thirst, and aching exhaustion affected them all, but none of these things mattered when the scent of victory hung in the air. It had a sweetness that overpowered the pungent odors of blood, sweat, and excrement.

Francisco was euphoric.

"This is it, I think," he said to Antonio, with boyish enthusiasm. "This is it." He was shouting above the sound of artillery fire.

"Well, I hope you're right," answered his friend, who was glad to see something other than anger and frustration pouring out of his companion.

During the first few days, the Republicans felt a strong sense of momentum with this battle. They knew that the Nationalists were aware of it, too, and would be preparing themselves for effective retaliation. This was crucial territory, and if the Republicans achieved their next aim and took the hills above Madrid, their objective would be won.

But having been initially unprepared for this offensive, the Nationalists now moved vast troop numbers into play and began a vicious counterattack. The Republican air force had achieved supremacy in the air at the beginning of the battle, but within a few days the Nationalists were superior in the sky and now repeatedly bombed Republican lines.

Sitting in shallow trenches, the earth too hard and dry to allow them to be dug any deeper, Antonio and Francisco knew they were in trouble. After the initial wave of optimism, they could see that victory was going to take longer to grasp than they had thought.

One after another the Nationalist aircraft came, bombing them with almost tedious regularity. The artillery fire was relentless, and the noise of it crushed their morale. The heat began to intensify. Rifles' catches that had frozen up the previous winter were now too hot to touch, and the battlefield turned into a living hell.

There was little talking in the trenches, but occasionally some seemingly senseless instruction was barked out and passed between them.

"They want us over there," said Antonio one day, indicating an area thinly planted with trees.

"What? Where there's no cover at all?" shouted Francisco above the noise of an exploding shell.

In the brief respite from aerial bombardment, a group including Antonio and Francisco clambered out of the trench and ran for cover in the copse. They heard the crackle of sniper fire, but no one was hit. Most of Antonio's unit had been lucky so far during this conflict. Though they achieved little, they did not lose their lives.

Blackened corpses of Republican militiamen littered the landscape. Occasionally they were retrieved, but often they just lay there, cooking in the heat, food for the flies. It was a desolate area. The landscape of pale earth was becoming more bleached by the day. Stray wisps of grass caught in the firing line would ignite and go up in brief, bright flames, only adding to the heat for anyone standing close by.

The appalling inadequacy of the supply lines soon became a problem. It was not just ammunition the Republicans lacked but food and water.

"We have a choice: drink this filthy muck that could give us typhoid or die of thirst," said Francisco, holding up a battered enamel mug. The water situation was critical. He took a swig of brandy from a flask, wishing more than anything that he could swap it for a mouthful of pure, clean water. "You know there are dead animals lying upstream," he added.

Some of the men around him tossed their water ration onto the earth and watched it disappear into the ground. They knew Francisco was right. They had watched one of their fellow soldiers die of typhoid in front of them the previous day.

Aerial bombardment increased, and in this exposed landscape it was often mere good fortune to survive. When a bomb fell, dried earth flew into the sky. Huge stony clods landed on the soldiers' heads, sprayed into their faces, and filled their ears. Neither skill with a rifle nor accuracy with the throwing of a grenade played a part. Bravery did not increase anyone's chances, but nor did cowardice.

"You know what we are," said Francisco one night, when calm had descended and there was a moment of peace to allow them to talk. "Target practice for German planes."

"You're probably right," muttered Antonio. In spite of his habitually positive stance, he was feeling increasingly disheartened.

It appeared that the Republican leaders did not communicate with each other and were uncertain about basic directions and even less sure about their position. The initially firm and well-thought-out strategy was now obscured by dust and chaos.

In spite of huge numbers of Franco's infantry dying when their lines were bombarded, the Nationalists had continued to bomb Republican airfields and considerably weakened their capacity in the air. The Republicans found that they were now struggling to defend the territory that they had gained at the beginning of the campaign.

By the last week of July, with temperatures still unbearable, the air power of the Nationalists had become the dominant factor, and many Republicans tried to flee. Some were shot by their own side as they ran away. Eventually firing ceased. Ammunition was all but spent and burned-out tanks dotted the landscape.

It seemed that, because of bad communications, poor leadership, confusion about the geography of the area, a poor supply system, and Nationalist air superiority, the initial Republican gains ultimately meant little. This victory did not have the sharp lines of certainty, and the mess of war allowed both sides to feel that they had won. Leaders on the left claimed Brunete a masterpiece of cunning, but with the gain of a mere fifty square kilometers at the expense of twenty thousand lives and at least as many wounded, it was a small advance won at a very high price.

"So this is winning," said Francisco, stabbing his heel into the ground. "And this is what it feels like to be the victors."

His bitter words reflected the discontent among his fellow troops and the anger over the pointless losses of this battle.

Where was La Pasionaria now to rouse them and to remind them that they must not give up? With communist leaders telling them that this was a triumph, they knew they would be called on to continue the fight, but for now they were glad to return to Madrid for some rest. There would be other fronts to fight later.

For a few months, Antonio and Francisco were back in the capital, where everyday life would still carry on a masquerade of normality that could suddenly be shattered. Even when they were enjoying a cool drink in the sunshine, an air-raid siren would send them running for shelter, reminding them of the threat that continually lurked in this city. Antonio's thoughts often strayed toward Granada, and he wondered what life was like in a city where the Fascists had taken over. There would be no bombs dropping, but he doubted whether his beloved mother would be sitting in the Plaza Nueva eating an ice cream.

A new offensive took place on the Aragón front that autumn, but Antonio and Francisco discovered that their unit would not be among those heading into battle.

"Why aren't we going?" moaned Francisco. "We can't sit around here for the rest of our days."

"Someone has to stay and defend Madrid," said Antonio. "And that campaign looks like complete chaos. Why do you want to be cannon fodder?"

Antonio believed in what they were doing, but lives were being wasted now and it angered him. He did not want to be an unnecessary sacrifice. The papers they read in Madrid carried the detail of internal divisions on the Republican side that were doing nothing to help them. The Marxist militia and the trade union groups were being deprived of weaponry by the communists, who were now determined to take charge, and disputes were breaking out in their own ranks that would only hinder their cause.

Antonio could never understand why his friend desired action for its own sake, and just as he expected, news of huge loss of life on the Aragón front began to filter through.

In December, though, they were on the move. Loaded into a lorry, at the beginning of the bitterest winter anyone could recall, Antonio and Francisco were taken toward the town of Teruel, east of Madrid. Teruel was held by the Nationalists, and the Republicans hoped that Franco would divert troops from Madrid if they made it their target. There were fears that Franco was planning a renewed assault on the capital, and the Republican leaders knew that something had to be done in order to draw their forces away.

The attack on Teruel took the Nationalists by surprise, and for a while the Republicans enjoyed the advantage, eventually capturing the garrison. Grounded by severe weather, German and Italian planes were initially unable to join the conflict, but even without them, the Nationalists had the advantage of more weaponry and more manpower. They proceeded to use both to the full and subjected Teruel to a relentless battering.

The landscape itself was cruel: flat and barren, with bare, chiseled hillsides. Antonio and Francisco, who were positioned inside the town and almost dead with cold, watched as dozens of their comrades died on this wasteland. They were both so hardened to discomfort now that Antonio wondered if they would one day cease to feel pain. The only time that Francisco did not complain about the general state of this war and the inadequacies of Republican leadership, was when he was immersed in danger and death. Even a hacking cough did not appear to bother him, and often he seemed at his most contented when he was in the midst of machine-gun fire.

On Christmas Day, they were camped out on the outside of town. Snow had been falling for days and the soldiers' clothes were sodden. There was no hope of drying anything out. With saturated boots more than double their usual weight, walking was more arduous than ever.

Francisco was wheezing badly now. He was holding a cigarette, but it fell to the ground as he doubled up, his whole body racked by a fit of coughing.

"Look, why don't you sit down for a while or even come in here?" suggested Antonio. He put his arm around his friend and guided him toward a makeshift tent that was being used for medical supplies.

"It's nothing," protested Francisco. "Just flu or something. I'm all right." He brusquely shrugged off Antonio's guiding hand.

"Look, Francisco, you need some rest."

"I don't," came his voice in a rattling whisper, his throat full of phlegm.

Antonio looked Francisco in the eyes and saw they were full of tears. It could have been the cold that made them water in this way, but Antonio could see a man at breaking point. His friend's heaving chest and the exhaustion from fourteen sleepless nights in the damp had pushed even this tough individual beyond endurance. Pain or injury he might have borne with some fortitude, but this was sickness and his body was failing him.

"I have to be strong," he sobbed in desperation. To find his body placing such limitations on his desires and to encounter his own frailty were harder to endure than sickness itself. He felt so ashamed.

Antonio put his arm around Francisco and found himself supporting his entire weight. Through the thick cloth of his uniform he could feel his friend's raging fever. Francisco was steaming.

"I don't . . . I don't . . . I want to . . . Don't . . ." As he slid into a state of shivering delirium, his sentences became rambling. Within the hour, he had slipped into unconsciousness and that night was taken away from the battlefield to a military hospital.

The enemy in this battle was as much the horizontal sleet that sliced into their faces as the strafing bullets. The dampness sat in their lungs. Many men died of the cold. They simply did not wake up in the morning. Some of them had used alcohol to anesthetize themselves, and it had relaxed them into such deep slumber that their hearts forgot to beat. At least in the snow their bodies would not immediately putrefy.

The campaign continued for another month into the New Year. With Francisco on sick leave back in Madrid, Antonio found he was able to detach himself from the horrors around him. Francisco was always angry with his own side as well as with the enemy, and his continual protests had merely exacerbated their disgruntlement.

Antonio survived these weeks on the Aragón front but always felt less than heroic. Before the battle was over, along with many others, he fought in the streets of Teruel, engaged in hand-to-hand combat. Until now he had always fired abstractly into the distance, but one day he saw his enemy face-to-face and knew the color of his eyes.

In that fraction of a second, before the moment of no return, Antonio hesitated. There was a man in front of him, younger than himself, crinkly haired, sharp-boned; they could have been mistaken for cousins. The color of his shirt was the only clue that told Antonio this man was on the Nationalist side. It was purely a matter of pigment in the dye that instructed him to end this man's life, and if he refrained now, he would probably lose his own.

Antonio discovered that there was nothing more brutalizing than to drive a bayonet into another human being, and in this killing he felt part of himself die too. He would never forget the way in which this boy's look of fear contorted into an expression of pain before petrifying into the gargoyle features of death. It took less than thirty seconds for Antonio to see his victim pass through these stages and to hear the thud of a body landing heavily on the ground in front of him. It was horrifying.

Returning to base that evening, a few men short, Antonio reflected on how arbitrary it all was. For the first time since he had become a fighting man he felt like a pawn on a chessboard. There were lives being sacrificed on the whim of someone most of them would never meet.

The tug of war over Teruel continued until February when the Nationalists took the town back from the Republicans. It had been another campaign with massive waste of life on both sides and little gain. Antonio tried not to see this as a turning point in the conflict, but the one chilling thing it seemed to prove was that Franco's resources were apparently limitless.

CHAPTER 30

Antonio, now feeling very pessimistic, had a few months back in Madrid and was no longer so desperate to join the latest battle against Franco. The Fascists launched a new offensive in Aragón with the aim of slicing in half the broad north-south strip of Republican territory on the country's Mediterranean coast, and by the middle of April 1938, they had successfully made a passageway to the sea, splitting Republican territory into two. Catalonia in the north was now separated from the center and south.

By mid-summer Francisco had recovered. The unit in which he and Antonio served was once more part of the defense of the city. Until Franco took the capital, the Republicans were determined to fight on.

Everyone now expected Nationalist troops to march north and take Barcelona, where the Republican government had moved in the previous October, but instead of this they turned south toward Valencia.

There were acute shortages of everything for soldiers and civilians alike in both sections of the Republic's divided territory: not just food and medical supplies but morale too. There was also a growing sense of panic and fear at the isolation in the separate parts of their territory, and communication between the two areas could only be carried out with difficulty. In the cities, there were still people who had secretly supported the Nationalists since the beginning of the conflict, and these networks of informers added to the unease.

Antonio and Francisco were about to join another battle. It was almost an act of desperation on the part of the Republicans. Their objective was to reunite the two parts of their territory.

"How do you rate our chances?" asked Francisco, as he laced up his boots before they went off to this new front on the River Ebro.

"Why bother to speculate?" answered Antonio. "We've got fewer guns and fewer planes, so I'd prefer not to think about it."

Though he felt pessimistic, they were strong in numbers if not in weapons. A huge Republican army of eighty thousand men had been deployed. Conscription had brought in thousands of boys aged only sixteen as well as middle-aged men. On the night of July 24, thousands of them crossed the River Ebro from north to south and attacked Nationalist lines.

The surprise nature of the attack gave an initial advantage, but Franco coolly ordered reinforcements. He saw this as his opportunity to annihilate the Republican army.

One of his first actions was to open the dams in the upper reaches of the river in the Pyrenees. This raised the water enough to sweep away the bridges on which the Republican troops were relying in order to receive supplies, and thereafter Franco continued to bomb the bridges, destroying them as regularly as they could be repaired. As well as moving thousands of additional troops into the area, the Nationalists also brought in huge amounts of their air force and for the first few days, the complete absence of defending Republican aircraft allowed German and Italian planes to attack the Republican army.

Temperatures soared to extreme heights in the first month of this engagement, creating an inferno reminiscent of Brunete. The lack of cover was similar, too, but the violence was even more intense. For weeks, the Republicans, increasingly dehydrated and starving, were relentlessly bombarded on the ground and from the air. German equipment, particularly aircraft, was limitless, and Franco was happy to sacrifice as many of the hundreds of thousands of troops under arms as it took, in order to wipe the Republicans off the face of the earth.

On a blazing afternoon, attempting to find cover in a valley, with the Fascists occupying a ridge above them, Francisco successfully fired on several of the enemy who had proved to be sitting targets.

"We need to get a lot more of them than that," shouted Antonio.

After weeks of anticipating a bullet at any moment, the expectation of it can diminish when it does not come. During those months on the Ebro, Francisco's sense of immortality grew. Antonio thought it was typically perverse of his friend that, as conditions and prospects had deteriorated, Francisco had become increasingly positive.

"We've come this far," he said optimistically. "I don't think anything will get us now." Having survived near fatal illness, he was not going to be beaten by anything else.

It had not been possible to dig trenches in the solid ground, and their unit had built up a small makeshift fortress from rocks and boulders. They were having an hour of rare respite from enemy shelling, and there was welcome shade behind the wall that they had made for themselves. Five of them, leaning almost comfortably, sat smoking.

"Think of it this way, Antonio. Franco has to get the help of the Germans and Italians," Francisco quipped. "We're fighting them alone. A bit of Russian support maybe . . ."

"But look at what's happening to our numbers, Francisco . . . We're being systematically wiped out. Swatted like flies."

"How do we know for sure?"

"Maybe you should believe some things you're told," said Antonio wearily.

That afternoon, the Granadinos were separated when they suddenly found themselves under attack. From a hill above, the enemy pounded them, and for an hour or so shells poured down in a relentless storm. There was nowhere to take cover, and the shriek of bullets drowned out any instructions they were given. In occasional moments of silence, cries of agony could be heard.

When Francisco's end came, he felt no pain. He was quite literally swept away by the force of the shell that landed beside him and there was little left to recognize. Antonio, who was fifty or so meters away at the time, identified what remained of the body. A distinctive gold ring worn on the middle finger of his right hand put any doubt aside. It sickened him to do so, but Antonio carefully removed the ring from the incongruously icy severed hand and replaced the hand by the rest of the body. As he drew a blanket over Francisco, he realized that his eyes were dry. Sometimes grief is too great for tears.

A fortnight, in early October, the battle would be over for Antonio too. It was getting dark and fighting was almost finished for the day.

"It's very quiet out there," said a fellow militia. "Maybe they're retreating."

"Some chance," replied Antonio, reloading his rifle.

He spotted some movement in a copse above them and raised his weapon. Before he had the chance to fire, he felt a sudden, shocking pain in his side. He sank to the ground, slowly, unable to cry out or shout for help, and his comrade thought he had tripped over one of the rocks that littered the hard, treeless terrain they were crossing. Antonio felt light-headed, detached. Was he dead? Why was someone leaning over him, a kindly, muffled voice asking him something he could not understand . . . ?

When he came round, the excruciating agony of it all was more than Antonio could bear. He was delirious with the pain and bit down, hard, on his own arm to suppress the need to scream aloud. Supplies of chloroform were running out in the medical tent, and the air was thick with screams. There was little more than brandy to anesthetize these men, whether it was from shrapnel wounds or amputation that they so desperately needed relief. Days or perhaps weeks later, detached from both time and place, he watched himself being eased onto a stretcher and slotted into a compartment of a train specially adapted for the wounded.

A while later, emerging slowly from this dream state, he found himself in Barcelona which, though under attack, had still not fallen to Franco. The train had trundled north from the Ebro to take the wounded to safety, the red cross on its roof a plea for clemency to the Fascist pilots that prowled the skies.

The process of recovery for Antonio was like the transition from darkness to light. As the weeks went by, the pain gradually decreased, his breathing became deeper, and his strength returned; it was like a slow but magnificent dawn. When his eyes remained open for more than a few minutes at a time, he realized that the figures that constantly moved around him were women, not angels.

"So you're real," he said to the girl who held his wrist to take a pulse. For the first time he could feel the cool pressure of her fingers.

"Yes, I'm real," she replied, smiling down at him. "And so are you."

She had watched the life in this skeletal figure ebb and flow in the past few weeks. It was the same for most of the patients here. It was a matter of luck and the efforts of the nurses, who did their very best, as each day more of the dying had arrived to fill the already overflowing wards. The lack of medicine meant that many died unnecessarily. Their malnourished state gave them little resistance to any infection and there were men who had lived through the onslaught of the Ebro, only to be wiped out by gangrene or even typhoid in their hospital beds.

Antonio knew nothing of the previous few months' events, but as he emerged once more into the world, he learned of them. The Battle of the Ebro was over. At the end of November, three months after they should have admitted the complete failure of the entire initiative and retreated, the Republican leadership had finally withdrawn what remained of their army. Massively outnumbered and outmaneuvered at every stage, they had been too stubborn to admit defeat until thirty thousand of their own men lay dead and more than the same number again had been wounded.

It was rarely quiet in the ward. Apart from the sheer volume of patients, the sound of conflict infiltrated almost continually. It was quieter than the battlefield, but the bombardment was continual and the thundering cracks of anti-aircraft fire punctuated the occasional moment of peace. As Antonio became more conscious of these sounds, he pondered what was to come next. He was walking a little each day now and gaining strength by the hour, and it was nearly time to leave the confines of this ward, which had become his home. If only he could go to his real home to see his mother. He yearned for sight of her, and his father too, but of this there was no question. Nor was there any possibility of rejoining what remained of his militia. He did not have the strength yet.

When the Fascists' assault on Barcelona intensified, Antonio moved into a hostel. He was with many others just like himself who had been displaced and weakened but who hoped to take up arms again in the future. They were still soldiers.

The New Year crept in: 1939. There was no cause for celebration. A sense of the inevitable permeated the streets. The shops had been stripped of food, fuel had run out, and the last desperate calls for resistance echoed around the empty streets. Barcelona was fatally wounded and nothing could save her now. On January 26 Fascist troops marched in and occupied an almost deserted city.

# CHAPTER 31

When Barcelona fell, half a million began their journey into exile, all of them weak from months of undernourishment and many recovering from injury.

Antonio found himself in the company of another member of the militia, Victor Alves, a young Basque, who had been conscripted at the age of seventeen. Untrained in the use of a rifle, he had been wounded on his first day on the Ebro; his family had left a few weeks earlier for France, and he hoped to reunite with them.

There were two possible routes into France that had to be weighed up. The first was over the Pyrenees. For Antonio and Victor, recovering from wounds, the craggy terrain would not be the only problem. Snow would impede them every step of the way. Antonio had heard that children were almost waist-deep in it in some places, and the elderly and infirm regularly lost their sticks in the deep drifts. Many slipped and stumbled on the ice, and the going was painfully slow.

In addition to this, though Antonio and Victor might have had very little to take with them, there were few who had resisted the urge to take some possessions, and their discarded chattel buried in the snow created further invisible hazards for those behind them. In the springtime, when the mountain's white blanket had melted away, there would be a curious trail of bric-a-brac uncovered in the thaw. Useless but sentimental items—a precious perfume bottle or a religious icon—and useful but unsentimental things—a metal cooking pot or a small chair—were scattered along the way.

The alternative to the treacherous mountain route was the coast road, though the danger there was the border control. They agreed that they had no alternative but the latter and set off, part of a huge column of people making their way north.

Everyone struggled with household items, blankets, bundles of clothes, and anything else they had considered essential for their journey to another life. Women on their own with several children had the most difficulties. Antonio often tried to help. He had brought nothing with him but his rifle. He had no other possessions and was used to living in the same clothes for weeks on end. There were many others, though, who had packed as much into a bag as they could fit and now struggled.

"Let me help you," he insisted to one woman, whose own child carried a baby while she fought tearfully with a bag whose handles had snapped under the strain. A third child tripped along next to them, snugly shrouded in several blankets. Between them, Antonio and Victor carried both baby and baggage, and soon they were distracting the little boy with a marching song. Antonio thought back to his journey out of Granada with the band of militia when they had sung to boost morale. It had worked then and it worked now.

Even Antonio, who had seen the most appalling sights on the battlefield, was still occasionally shocked by what he saw on the way. Women gave birth while female relatives gathered around them to shield with their skirts the mystical moment of entry into the world.

"What a dangerous time to be born," muttered Antonio as he heard the plaintive cry of a newborn.

It was a two-hundred-kilometer trek, and after a week of walking, Antonio finally reached the border at Cerbère. He looked across toward the sea and for a moment felt a flicker of optimism pass through him. The Mediterranean caught the shafts of sunlight that penetrated the heavy February clouds, and in the patches of leaden gray water there were expanses of silvery light. There before them was France, another country. Perhaps they would find a fresh beginning there. In this great exodus, the trail of the ragged and forlorn had to believe in a new start, a promised land. There were some who were indifferent now to their own country, a place where they had neither family nor home nor hope.

Though most in this queue had given up their burdens, soldiers clung to their rifles. There was nothing else they required. Working on the stiff catches through long nights of boredom, they were now confident that these battered Russian weapons would keep them safe.

"What's happening up ahead?" asked Victor.

"I don't know," answered Antonio, craning to see over the forest of a thousand mostly behatted heads. "Maybe they've closed it again."

It had been rumored that the French had shut the border for a while. They had been overwhelmed by the numbers. The crush of people was now building up behind, but everyone seemed subdued; no one was impatient. They had come this far and just a few meters in front of them was their destination.

After an hour or so they began to move forward. Antonio could see the border control and heard the unfamiliar sound of French voices. The harsh tone was not what they had expected.

*"Mettez-les ici!"*

The words may have meant nothing, but the gesticulation and the pile of guns and possessions to one side of the road said everything. The French were making their message clear. Before they left Spain, the weary exiles were expected to leave their arms behind, and many were being forced to dump their possessions too. A few meters ahead of them, Antonio noticed an old man engaged in a furious altercation. That would be a mistake, he thought to himself, to start a fight with the border guard, especially when you were as frail as this old warrior. What ensued was worse.

They made him empty his pockets in front of them, and when they noticed his fingers folded into a fist, one of the guards shoved him in the shoulder with his bayonet.

*"Qu'est-ce que vouz faites? Cochon!"*

Another grabbed the old man from behind, while a third, realizing that the fist contained something other than an intention to lash out, prized the bony fingers open one by one until the palm was exposed. What did they expect to find? A handful of gold, a secreted pistol?

On his outstretched hand lay nothing more than a small mound of dirt, a pathetic sample of Spain's soil that he had brought with him over the mountains.

"*Por favor,*" he pleaded.

Before he uttered even the last syllable of his entreaty, the guard had brushed the grit from his hand, sweeping it away in one stroke. The man looked down at the specks of earth, the remnants of his *patria* that traced the veins of his palm.

"*Hijo de puta!* You bastard!" he cried out, choked, his passion spilling over. "Why did you . . . ?"

The guards laughed in his face, and Antonio stepped forward to hold the man gently by the arm. Tears coursed down his face, but he was still full of fury and poised to lash out. This anger would only provoke these French to further insult, and there was nothing to be gained from that now. The precious Spanish soil had already been trampled beneath their boots. The old man was given another shove in the back. If he did not make any further fuss, he would soon be in France.

Now the guards turned their attention to Antonio. One of them grabbed the end of his rifle. It was a provocative gesture, and totally gratuitous, given that the pile of abandoned weapons by the side of the road was a clear indication that they had to enter France unarmed. It hardly needed reiteration. Antonio handed his over without a word.

"Why should we give them up?" Victor spat under his breath.

"Because we have no choice," answered Antonio.

"But why are they making us?"

"Because they're afraid," said Antonio.

"Of what?" exclaimed Victor incredulously, surveying the emaciated men, women, and children around him, some bent double like large snails under the remaining burdens they carried, all of them bowed over with exhaustion.

"How can they be afraid of us?"

"They're worried that they might be letting in a bunch of armed communists who are going to overrun their country."

"That's mad . . ."

To some extent it was, and yet they both knew that in among the disorganized ranks of broken militia, there were extremists and that in France rumors of *rojo* behavior had been wildly exaggerated for the duration of this conflict. For those who had expected a welcome, there was to be only disappointment. The presence of the International Brigades in Spain had given them the idea that support and solidarity from other nations was something they could expect anywhere and everywhere, but it was a false one. The cool brutality of the border guards wiped out the remaining hope they might have had.

Once beyond the border post, the road wound down toward the sea. The coast was wild and rocky, the air sharper than in their own country. But the walk was downhill for a while, and that in itself was a relief. The movement of the crowd seemed mechanical now. They were chaperoned by French police who were impatient to move them along.

"I wonder where they're taking us."

Antonio was thinking aloud. There had been rumors that the French, though unwilling to let them inside their country, had prepared somewhere for them to stay. Anywhere to rest their heads would be a relief after these days of shuffling along in freezing temperatures.

As they came down toward the sea, the dampness penetrated their bones. Victor did not respond to his companion, and the two men walked along in silence. They were almost paralyzed with cold, and perhaps this numbed their reaction to what they now faced.

Antonio had assumed that they would turn inland, away from the cruel space of the sea, but soon they were approaching the vast expanse of beach whose sands stretched farther than the eye could see. They saw huge enclosures marked out with barbed wire and did not immediately realize that these areas were their destination. Surely these were pens for animals, not human beings? In some places the fencing stretched out into the sea itself.

"This can't be where they're going to keep us . . ." Victor allowed himself to say the unsayable. He looked across to the line of black guards who were now guiding people with the blunt ends of their rifles into the enclosures.

"We've swapped the Moors for these bastards? Holy Mary . . ."

Antonio could sense his friend's rage building. He shared his disgust that the French were using their Senegalese troops to keep the Spanish exiles in order. Many of them had experienced the brutality of Franco's Moorish soldiers, the cruelest of all the Fascist forces, and they thought they recognized the same heartless expression on these black faces.

They did not listen to the appeals of families who were keen to stay together, separating them according to the rules of arithmetic rather than kindness. All they cared about was the efficient subdivision of this massive horde of people, and to divide strictly according to numbers was the only way they knew to keep control. The French feared refugees would swamp their small border towns, and their concern was not without foundation. The town of St. Cyprien, which had a population of little over one thousand, would soon find itself home to more than seventy-five thousand strangers, and the only place this town had for them was the huge expanse of unusable land right by the sea: the beach. It was the same for the other towns farther along the Côte Vermeille at Argelès, Barcarès, and Septfonds too. The only place they could find for the refugees was on the sand.

Living conditions were appalling. To begin with, the refugees were housed in improvised tents made out of wooden stakes and blankets, with no protection from the elements. In the first weeks, the beaches were battered by rain and gales. Antonio would volunteer each night to keep watch for an hour; otherwise people would get buried alive in the sand, the loose particles whipped up by the wind to form mounds over the weak and vulnerable. On these desolate wastelands, sand filled eyes, nostrils, mouths, and ears. People ate sand, breathed it, and were blinded by it, and the relentless exposure drove some men mad.

There was very little food and one small spring to serve the first twenty thousand who arrived. There was no proper treatment for the sick. Thousands of severely wounded had been evacuated from the hospitals of Barcelona, and in many of them gangrene had taken hold. The guards separated out those who showed symptoms of dysentery; the repellent stench was usually enough to identify them, and they were left to rot in a makeshift quarantine. Other diseases were rife too. Tuberculosis and pneumonia were both common, and each day the dead were entombed deep in the sand.

Perhaps the thing Antonio hated most of all was the way in which they were led en masse to defecate. Certain areas by the sea had been designated for the purpose, and he dreaded the moment when his turn came to strain into the sea under the contemptuous glare of the guards. To be taken to this foul area of the beach where the wind sent soiled scraps of paper and sand flying into the air was the most degrading thing of all.

Apart from certain daily routines such as this, there was a sense of utter timelessness on the beaches. The continual washing in and out of the waves and their relentless pounding rhythm echoed nature's disregard for the human tragedy being played out on these sands. The days turned into weeks. For most people time passed unmeasured, but Antonio kept tally by cutting notches on a stick. For him it alleviated the agonizingly slow passage of time. Some, fearing they might go mad with boredom, devised ways of combating it—games of cards, dominoes, and wood carving all helped. A few even made sculptures out of the scraps of barbed wire they found sticking out of the sand. Occasionally in the evenings there would be poetry readings, and from time to time, at the dead of night, the dark, piercing sound of *cante jondo* could be heard coming from one of the tents. This was the most primitive form of flamenco song, and its pathos made Antonio's hairs stand on end.

Then one night, there was a dance performance. The guards looked on, bemused at first and then mesmerized by the spectacle. It was dusk. A small area of solid dance floor had been constructed from old crates that someone had found by a food tent, and a young woman had begun to dance. There was no music to accompany her, just the sound of rhythmic clapping, which grew and swelled and became an orchestra of palms, some soft, some sharp, rising in a crescendo and fading away as the strikes of the woman's feet on the boards guided them.

The dancer was scrawny, once more buxom perhaps, but months of near starvation had melted away her curves. The sense of rhythm, which lived in the untouchable part of her, remained, and the sinuous movements of her arms and fingers were accentuated by their painful thinness. Strands of her dark hair, matted with salty spray, adhered to her face like snakes and she made no attempt to brush them away.

She may not have had the heavy tiers of a flamenco skirt swirling about her ankles or the accompaniment of a guitar, but in her mind she had both of these and the audience felt and heard them too. Her best fine-fringed silk shawl had been incinerated, along with everything else she owned, when her house had been struck in an air raid. What she twirled around her now were the tattered remains of a headscarf, its fraying hem a distant echo of an expensively tasseled edge. The audience gathered quickly, and men, women, and children witnessed an incongruous display of sensuality and passion in these heartless surroundings. The dance made them forget and for its duration drowned out the sound of the waves. She danced on and on in the cool of the night, hardly perspiring. When she seemed to have no more to offer the audience, she would begin again with the gentle tapping of a heel. The spectacle summoned memories in every spectator, of the *ferias* and other happy times that had constituted the now annihilated normality of their lives. In their own minds, every member of the audience was somewhere far away, over the mountains, in a home village or town, with friends or family.

Antonio thought of his sister. Where was Mercedes now? he wondered. There was no means of getting news. He still occasionally sent heavily coded letters to his aunt Rosita in case there was a possibility that she could pass them on to his mother. For all he knew, Mercedes could be somewhere on these beaches. He wondered if she had found Javier and if she was still dancing. For a moment Mercedes seemed more real to him than the woman who danced before him. The furrowed brow that scored a deep trench in this woman's face reminded him of how his sister used to concentrate while she danced. There the similarity ended, though, unless the picture of Mercedes that he carried in his mind was out of date. Perhaps she had lost the childlike roundness of her features and now looked as birdlike as this gaunt creature in front of him. He wished he knew.

At the end of a *bulería*, the joyful dance that seemed so out of place here, a small child, his face plastered with dirt and snot, had pushed his way to the front of the crowd.

"*Mamá! Mamá!*" he sniveled, before the *bailaora* swept him up into her arms and disappeared again into one of the far huts, mindful once again of where she was.

After a few weeks went by, the French announced a rebuilding program. There was a surge of new purpose. Able-bodied men such as Antonio and Victor were instructed to begin dismantling the shantytown of ragged tents and to start constructing wooden huts in ordered rows. Being occupied with manual work engaged both their minds and bodies, but it disturbed them too. Even the burning of the old rugs, some of which had been dragged across the mountains by those who sheltered beneath them, was a painful separation from the past. The new *barracas* might give them better protection, but there was a depressing sense of permanence about them.

"So this is home now, is it?" many of them mumbled.

They had perceived this camp as somewhere temporary, a place to pass through before finding somewhere else more amenable to live. Suddenly it seemed as though it might be forever.

"We're not exiles; we're prisoners," Victor said with determination. "We have to get out."

"I'm sure they'll work out what to do with us soon," Antonio reassured him, even though he agreed with him entirely.

"But we can't go on pretending that this is some kind of safe haven!"

continued Victor, his youthful fighting spirit refusing to wane. "Shouldn't we be trying to get back to Spain? We're just sitting here playing cards, listening to people reading Machado's poetry, for God's sake!"

He was right. They were captives in this outdoor prison. Currently the only way of getting out was to volunteer to become part of a working party. Having been loaded onto a cattle truck and driven to an unknown destination many miles away, men were then inspected for strength like livestock and hired out for heavy-duty manual tasks such as repairing roads and railways, and farming. It hardly constituted liberation. It was more like slavery.

Like many fighting men, Antonio calculated that staying in the camp might put them in a better position to escape back over the mountains and resume the struggle against Franco. He also felt committed to teaching a small group of children who gathered each day to watch him draw letters in the sand. At all costs he wanted to avoid the possibility of finding himself hundreds of kilometers away in an unknown French village, the unpaid laborer of a hostile nation which just about tolerated his presence but no more.

He had enough regrets over being out of Spain as it was. When he had fled Barcelona all those weeks earlier, he had followed the northward-fleeing crowd. Since then, he had agonized. Perhaps he should have headed south to Madrid. What had seemed like a safety net had become a noose that had closed in tightly around him.

In many of the militia, there was a residual belief that while Madrid still stood, everything was not quite lost and they should be there to protect what remained. For some, survival was about resignation. They began to watch the sunrise and to appreciate the brief but intense moment of beauty when they could look across the landscape and see their own country emerge through the mist. It seemed close enough to touch.

For a few months they retreated into the safety of routine and a pattern of rituals that helped them map out their days. They gave street names to the rows of *barracas*, and even hotel names to the huts themselves. In ways such as this, they tried to make their lives worth living.

For some it was about small acts of rebellion and subversion, such as the carving of a sand bust of Franco that was coated in syrup to attract the flies. Victor had been one of the instigators of this and his confrontational attitude had already been noticed. The guards knew he was one of the troublemakers, and they were waiting for him to step out of line again. His slowness to join the queue for dinner one day was all it took. He was buried that night, right up to his neck, in the sand. It filled his eyes, ears, and nostrils, and almost choked him to death. Even the guard took pity, and at three in the morning gracelessly held a cup of water to his lips.

Antonio nursed Victor when he staggered back to the hut that night. The boy was half demented, crazy with thirst and rage. His body could scarcely accommodate the hatred he felt for these guards, and his anger was murderous.

"Try to think of something else," said Antonio calmly, sitting at the end of his bed. "Don't let them have the satisfaction of your anger. Keep it stored up for later."

This was easy to say, but an act of such sadism had provoked deep hatred in this fiery youth.

In the spring, the skies became bluer, and when the sun emerged fully, the gray sands turned gold and the sea reflected the bright sky. It was only then that they remembered how they used to love beaches. Once places of recreation where the children had splashed in the surf, this coastline now mocked all those happy memories.

But the spring brought with it the worst day of all. News reached them that the Nationalists had entered Madrid. What had been inevitable for many months had become a reality. On April 1, 1939, Franco announced his victory. He received a congratulatory telegram from the Pope.

In Granada there was great celebration and flag waving among Franco's supporters. Concha lowered the shutters, locked the door of the café, and retired into the apartment above. It would have been insupportable to see the glee and triumphalism on the faces of all the right-wing citizens of Granada who were such an overwhelming majority of its population.

She emerged two days later and looked out of her windows at a new and hostile country. It was one she had no wish to see.

Many refugees had to face the reality that returning to Spain would be dangerous. What had been a temporary escape would now be longer term. There was no amnesty for those who had fought against Franco, and returning militia knew they could be arrested the minute they set foot back in Spain. There were reports of mass executions of Franco's enemies. The safest option was emigration.

"Why don't you apply too?" suggested Victor, who had just discovered his family had already set sail for Mexico.

"I couldn't give up on my country," said Antonio. "My family might not even know I'm alive, but if they do, they'll be expecting me to find my way back."

"We probably wouldn't stand a chance of getting a place anyway," said Victor. "I've heard the evacuation committee has been swamped with applications."

He was right, the *Servicio de Evacuación de Republicanos Españoles* received two hundred and fifty thousand requests, and only a small number of these could be granted places on the boats that were leaving. Victor was lucky, though. He got a place to go to South America and was soon to embark. His father's name was recognized by the *Servicio* and was influential enough to get him passage.

The French were keen to repatriate all these refugees to whom they had reluctantly given a temporary home, and Franco wanted them back too. Loud-hailers sent out messages urging people to cross back over the mountains into a new Spain.

It was a dilemma for them all. France was threatened by invasion from Germany and, for anyone who stayed, there would be new dangers.

"The one thing I won't be is a slave for Hitler," declared Antonio.

He decided to take his chances and return to Spain. He would make his way back to Granada. Surely the new regime needed teachers as much as the old? Every day since he had been away he had thought of his parents and wondered what their lives were like. Even though he had continued to send them letters, he had received nothing for over a year, but he hoped his father might have been released by now, given that he had committed no crime. Without a photograph of them, their image in his mind had faded. He could recall his mother's black hair and upright bearing, his father's rotund stomach and crinkly gray hair, but if he saw them at this moment, he feared he would fail to recognize them.

Many others felt the same urge to go home and, like Antonio, chose to ignore the terrifying reports of executions and arrests. He set out with some other militia who had also fought on the Ebro and who, like him, were eager to leave France, where they had encountered little other than hostility. Their route took them over the Pyrenees, and as they climbed, Antonio took a last look back at the hated beaches. He wondered if he would ever rid himself of the filthy taste of grit or the memories of the gratuitous cruelty he had seen on that sandy wasteland.

# CHAPTER 32

As he came over the mountains and saw the plains stretching toward Figueres, Antonio had expected to feel a surge of pleasure at the sight of his own beloved *patria*. No such thing happened. It looked different to him now. Spain was his own country, and yet it was a foreign place, somewhere now ruled by a Fascist. He hoped his love for it might be rekindled when he got back to his own city.

He stood on this mountain ridge, watching an eagle soaring high into the sky, and looked south. More than nine hundred kilometers southwest of where he stood was Granada. How he envied the bird's power of flight.

Once they were down the mountain, the men went their separate ways. It was safer that way. Antonio's plan was to take a route through the bigger towns. It would be more anonymous, and it would give him a greater chance of avoiding curious eyes. There were so many people returning to their homes that he was sure he could slip through incognito. He had not allowed for the watchfulness of either the Civil Guard themselves or for the informers who reported their slightest suspicions about any newcomers.

It was around eight in the evening when he approached the outskirts of Girona. Night was falling so this seemed a safe enough time, and he had chosen a quiet street to walk down. Seemingly from nowhere, two uniformed men stepped into his path and demanded his name.

He had no satisfactory papers, and his appearance left no room for doubt about which side he had fought on in the recent conflict. It was nothing to do with a uniform or a telltale red star badge. These Civil Guards could simply sniff out a supporter of the Republic and former member of their militia, and this was enough to warrant arrest.

He was incarcerated close to the town of Figueres where conditions were predictably primitive. As he entered prison, Antonio was tossed a rough blanket and cigarettes. He now understood why the latter were considered more important than food. The straw mattress he slept on was infested with lice, and the only way of keeping them away from his face at night was to smoke.

A week later, Antonio was summarily tried and sentenced to thirty years' imprisonment. For the first time in more than two years he addressed a letter directly to his mother in Granada. The Fascists were happy to guarantee the delivery of missives that further demoralized the families of such subversives as Antonio Ramírez.

The hardship in prison was no revelation to Antonio. He did sometimes wonder how resistant to physical suffering a man could become without losing his humanity. The sheer discomfort of camping out on stony ground in the freezing temperatures of Teruel, the blazing heat of Brunete, the searing agony of his injury, which had made death look like a welcome escape, and the abject squalor of the early days in the sand camps of France: all of these had left their mark. The scar tissue that formed around these wounds, both physical and mental, was tough, and pain had become an ever-diminishing sensation. Antonio was anesthetized.

The prisoners' food was minimal and monotonous. Breakfast was a bowl of gruel, lunch was beans, and supper the same, sometimes with a fish head or tail. Occasionally there were tinned sardines.

The months passed. Antonio and most of his fellow prisoners were stubbornly resistant to the cruelty of the guards, but a few of them literally pined away, as men do when there is nothing to live for and no hope of this changing.

They kept themselves occupied with talk of escape, but the only attempt made had been so cruelly punished, and in view of them all, that they did not have the stomach to repeat it. The screams of those involved seemed still to echo around the yard.

For a while the most subversive activity they could engage in was a refusal to sing the new regime's patriotic songs, or to talk during the sermons which they were obliged to listen to in the courtyard. Even for that, they could be punished. No excuse was too flimsy for the guards to beat them with loaded riding crops.

The most terrifying moment of each day was the reading of the *saca*, when the names of the men who were to be executed the following day were called out. One morning at daybreak, a longer list was called out. This was not the usual dozen or so; this time the names went on and on. There were hundreds. As he stood there in the aching early morning chill, Antonio felt his blood freeze.

Just as the human brain will pick out the one face it recognizes in a crowd, Antonio heard his own name in the almost indistinguishable hum of all the others. Among the monotonous list of Juans and Josés, the words "Antonio Ramírez" jumped out at him.

There was silence as the list finished.

"All those named—in line!" the order was barked.

It took several minutes for the men who had been named to move out and form a queue. Without any further explanation, they were herded out of the prison gate. The air reeked of the sour odor of men sweating beneath filthy shirts. It was the smell of fear. Are they really going to kill all of us? Antonio wondered, his legs shaking with such terror that he struggled to control them. There was no time for goodbyes. Instead, furtive glances were exchanged between a few of them who had formed a bond during their long period of incarceration together. Those staying looked at those leaving with pity, but all were united in the common determination that the Fascists should not see fear on their faces. It would give them too much satisfaction.

Antonio found himself being marched out of the prison and toward the town. It was not uncommon for prisoners to be moved from one jail to another, but in these numbers he knew it was unusual. As they approached the railway station, the great crowd of them was ordered to a halt. He realized that they were going on a journey.

For many hours, the train rattled along.

"It's like being in a crate," Antonio heard one man murmur.

"Nice of them to leave the lid off," responded another.

"Unlike them really," said another sarcastically.

Even though they were being taken to a new place, the way they were treated was just the same. More than one hundred of them stood in each cage trundling south. Some clung to the bars, peering through the slats at the changing landscape, which was gradually flattening out as the day went on. Others, stuck in the middle, could see only the sky.

For a few hours they were lashed by rain, but eventually the clouds passed away and Antonio judged from the sun that they were heading roughly southwest. After many hours, the train rattled to a halt and the gates of their cages opened. They tumbled onto the hard, dusty ground, many of them relieved to rest their exhausted legs.

A group of armed soldiers stood guard over them, weapons cocked, looking for an opportunity to use them. Even if they had wanted to escape, the landscape provided no opportunities. In one direction there were a few outcrops of rock, in the other, nothing at all. There was nowhere to run. A bullet in the back would have been the reward for anyone trying it.

With unconcealed contempt, a few lumps of bread were thrown into the middle of them and the prisoners swarmed around it like a shoal of fish, grabbing, snatching, desperate, all remaining dignity gone.

Antonio watched a dozen men reaching toward the same piece of bread and was sickened by the sight of his own wasted, filthy-nailed hand trying to grab a crust from another man's fingers. They had been reduced to animals, turning on each other in this way.

Then they were loaded back into the train, and for many hours more, they trundled on until the train juddered to a halt. There was a momentary stirring among them.

"Where are we?" shouted someone in the center.

"What can you see?" called out another. "What's happening?"

It was not the end of the journey. Antonio fell out of his cattle cage once again and saw a dozen trucks waiting for them. They were ordered to climb aboard.

The men were more tightly crammed in than ever, moving in one united motion as the trucks swayed this way and that over bumpy ground. After an hour or so, there was a crunching of gears and the sudden application of brakes. They were all catapulted forward in one jolt. Doors opened and then slammed shut; bolts were drawn across; there was the sound of shouting, orders, an altercation somewhere. Once again, bowels stirred with fear. They seemed to be in the middle of nowhere, though in the far distance Antonio thought he could see the outskirts of a city.

There was a general murmuring among the men.

"Seems odd to have brought us all this way just to kill us," pondered the man against whom Antonio had been jammed face-to-face for the past four hours. The foul stench of his breath had almost asphyxiated him. He knew that his own could not be sweet, but this old soldier's toothless mouth and rotting gums had literally made him retch.

Antonio was about to respond when someone cut across him: "I think they would have done away with us by now if that's what they planned."

"Don't be so sure," said another pessimistically.

The debate continued until they were interrupted by an order barked out by one of the soldiers. They were instructed to walk along a track that led from the road, and soon they saw their destination. A row of huts now came into view. For many the relief was too much. They wept, certain now that they were going to live another day.

They were marshaled into rows on a piece of ground in front of the huts and addressed by an army captain, his mean mouth and sharp cheekbones all that they could see of his face. It angered Antonio that his eyes were obscured by the peak of his cap. The crowd was silent, expectant, for the first time optimistic, as they watched his thin lips move.

"Owing to the generosity of our great General Franco, you have undeserved good fortune," he said. "On this day, you have been given another chance."

There was a murmur of relief among the crowd. The tone of this speech disgusted Antonio, but the content of it excited him. The captain continued. He had a message to deliver, and he was not going to be deterred.

"You will no doubt have heard that a law has been passed to allow the Redemption of Penalties through labor. For every two days worked, your sentence will be reduced by one day. For scum like some of you, this is more than you deserve, but the Generalissimo has decreed it."

He sounded like someone swallowing a bitter pill. Clearly he did not approve of this leniency and would have preferred to see these men suffer the maximum punishment, but Franco's word was supreme and he was obliged to carry out orders.

He continued: "More important, you have been selected for the most glorious of all tasks."

Antonio began to feel apprehensive. He had heard of prisoners being used as forced labor on building projects, such as the reconstruction of towns like Belchite and Brunete, which had been devastated during the conflict. Perhaps this was his fate.

"This is what El Caudillo said when he announced his plans for this project. I quote . . ."

The captain drew himself up to his full height and adopted an ever more pompous tone. The irony was that his voice was considerably deeper and more masculine than that of Franco, with whose reedy, strangulated tones they were all familiar. "'I want this place to have the grandness of the shrines of old . . . to be a restful place of meditation where future generations can pay homage to those who made Spain a better place . . .'" His singsong delivery of Franco's words was almost worshipful, but his voice soon reverted to a harsher tone.

"The place that you have been chosen to construct is The Valley of the Fallen. This monument will commemorate the thousands who died in this fight to save our country from the filthy Reds—the communists, the anarchists, the trade unionists . . ."

The captain's voice had gradually risen. He had worked himself up into such a fury of revulsion that his cap shook and the veins stood out on his neck. His hysteria was barely repressed. Those closest to him felt the spray of furious spittle that flew from his lips on the utterance of those last words. He was almost screaming now, though there was little need, given the total silence of his audience.

Everyone had heard rumors of this plan. What it confirmed to them was that they were in Cuelgamuros, not far from Madrid and close to El Escorial, the burial place of the kings. Franco had one clear purpose in this project. Although this place would commemorate the soldiers who had died for his cause, it would principally be a mausoleum for himself. The fanatical, power-intoxicated captain had finished speaking now. He left it to his inferiors to marshal the prisoners into the huts.

"So now we know why they have brought us all this way . . ." said the old man who had been by Antonio's side all through the journey. "I suppose it makes a change from being locked up."

To some people, this old man's resilience had been a tonic, while for others his relentlessly cheerful voice had begun to grate. After all these months, years even, of hardship, it seemed extraordinary that anyone's voice could be so completely free of bitterness.

"Yes, it looks as though we'll see a bit more of the sky," Antonio responded, trying to sound positive.

The hut that was to be their new home was very different from the last prison they had been in, where for days on end they were shut away in a windowless cell, the only light source an electric bulb, which had illuminated them twenty-four hours a day. It was squalid here, but at least there were windows all down one side and two rows of around twenty beds with a decent space between each one.

"This doesn't look so bad, does it?"

Above the cacophony of a thousand other men gathering on the scrubby ground outside the huts, all waiting to receive their next instructions, the old man's cheerful voice challenged Antonio. He wondered why some people were so richly endowed with a cheerful disposition when all around them the world seemed to be disintegrating.

Laid out on the straw mattresses were brown uniforms, and orders were given to put these on.

"You could get two of me in here," said the septuagenarian, rolling up the sleeves and trouser legs. He looked absurd. "Lucky there isn't a mirror."

The old man was right. He did look ridiculous, like a child in his father's clothes. For the first time in perhaps months, Antonio smiled. It was an unfamiliar feeling. His laughter reflex had atrophied many months before.

"How do you manage to be so cheerful all the time," he asked, struggling to do up his buttons. His fingers were stiff with cold.

"What," said the old man, "is the point of being any other way?" Arthritic hands were not making it easy for the older man to fasten his jacket either. "What can we do? Nothing. We're powerless."

Antonio thought for a moment before responding. "Resist? Escape?" he suggested.

"You know as well as I do what happens to anyone who does. They are destroyed. *Completely.*" He spoke the last word emphatically. His tone had changed altogether. "For me, it's about protecting the human spirit," he continued. "For others, it will be about fighting until their dying breath. My resistance to these Fascists is to go along with them, to smile, to show them that they can't crush my soul, the very core of me."

Antonio was surprised by the answer. He had not expected it. Like everyone who had been in that cattle cage, this man had looked like a destitute laborer. Materially, he had even less. He did not even own the clothes he stood up in. His accent and the way he phrased his words suggested something else, though.

"Has it worked," inquired Antonio, "this approach of yours?"

"So far, yes," the old man said. "I have no religious faith. You could say that I am an atheist and have been for many years. But a belief in protecting your own essence, believe me, gives you such strength to survive."

Antonio looked over the man's shoulder at the sea of two hundred other men now reduced to a shapeless blur of humanity by the dung-colored uniform. It was an amorphous mass, where individuality had finally been annihilated, but in its midst were doctors, lawyers, university professors, and writers. Perhaps this man was one of these.

"So what did you do before . . . this?" asked Antonio.

"I am a professor of philosophy at the University of Madrid," he answered unhesitatingly, with a deliberate use of the present tense.

He continued now, happy to have Antonio's attention, "Look at how many people have been driven to suicide. Probably thousands of them. That's the greatest victory for the Fascists, isn't it? One more prisoner condemned to the fires of hell—and one less mouth to feed."

The man was so pragmatic, so realistic about their situation that Antonio was almost convinced. He had seen several suicides himself. The worst of these had been only a few days ago in Figueres before they were moved here. A man jumped up to grab the lightbulb that hung by a wire from the ceiling, and in a swift movement, before he could be stopped by either friend or Fascist, he had struck the bulb on the edge of a chair and plunged the jagged shard into his vein.

Guards had eventually arrived to drag away his body. They had seen it all before. It was too much bother to shorten the cord.

"Well," said the university professor, jamming on the round hat that had sat on top of the uniform. "I think we're meant to get started."

His cheerful enthusiasm was, for a moment, infectious.

"You see this?" he said, pointing up at his hat. The "T" with which it was emblazoned stood for *Trabajos Forzados*—Forced Labor. It marked him out as a slave.

"Yes," responded Antonio. "I see it."

"They can enslave my body," the professor said, "but my mind is my own."

For every individual there had to be a reason to survive, and this man seemed to have found his.

By now the rest of the room had cleared. In spite of their empty stomachs, they were expected to work today. There were two hours until darkness, and their enslavers were not going to allow them to be wasted.

Marching in single file through an area of dense forest, the new arrivals eventually reached the edge of the site. As they came into the immense clearing, the very scale of what they saw shocked them.

Thousands upon thousands of men worked in gangs. The motion was continuous, streamlined, ordered, and it was clear that they were engaged upon some relentless, gargantuan, never-ending task. As they moved in one direction, they bore a load and then returned empty-handed for another, like ants moving to and from their anthill.

Antonio's group was taken toward the vast exposed face of the hillside. At first glance, it looked as though they had been assigned to literally move a mountain. The noise was deafening. Occasionally from within they heard a rumble. It was obvious what they were expected to do. A gigantic hole was being made in this towering rock. Any orders would have been inaudible in the cacophony that greeted them. There were piles of stone in front of them. Some men worked at breaking them down with pickaxes. Shards flew everywhere. The rest picked up the fragments in their bare hands and began to carry them away. Frequently, there was the shout of an order, a castigation, a raised stick. It was a vision of hell.

Antonio's hope that working in the open was going to give them a glimpse of the sky was soon dashed. The air was opaque with dust. Even the illusion of freedom that had been dangled in front of them that afternoon had evaporated. With one hand the Fascists had given, and with the other they had taken away.

# CHAPTER 33

While Antonio was building Franco's tomb, Concha Ramírez was still running El Barril, determined to keep the family business going. Like anyone who had been on the wrong side during the conflict, she suffered from the stigma of having a husband and son in prison. Concha was continually harassed by the Civil Guard and her premises often subject to search and scrutiny. These were purely tactics of intimidation, but there was nothing she could do to prevent them. Many of those in her position found that their children could get nothing but menial work, and some, whose children tried to return home after fighting for the Republic, were immediately incarcerated. One of Paquita's brothers had been executed that month.

One Thursday afternoon, a few months after Franco declared his victory, Concha was in the kitchen and heard the sound of the café door being pushed open. It had been a busy lunchtime.

A late customer, she thought with irritation. Hope they aren't expecting anything to eat.

She bustled into the bar to tell the latecomer that she had finished serving food and stopped in her tracks. She tried to speak, to say a name, but nothing came out. Her mouth was dry.

In spite of his hollow eyes and the unfamiliar stoop of his body, she would have immediately recognized this man in a crowd of a hundred thousand others.

"Pablo," she whispered inaudibly.

He stood there, one hand gripping the back of a chair. He could no more speak than move. Every last shred of energy and willpower had been spent on reaching home. Concha crossed the room and held him in her arms.

"Pablo," she whispered. "It's you. I can't believe it's you."

And that was the truth. Suddenly Concha Ramírez did not trust her own senses. Was this pale shadow her husband? For a moment, she wondered whether the frail, insubstantial being that she held in her arms was even real or just a figment of her imagination. Perhaps Pablo's death sentence had finally been carried out, and this was just a spectre that appeared to her. Nothing was beyond the realms of possibility in her imagination.

His silence did not reassure her.

"Tell me if it's you," she persisted.

By now, the old man had taken a seat. He was so weak with hunger and exhaustion that his legs could no longer hold him.

Looking into hers with his own watery eyes, he spoke for the first time. "Yes, Concha, it's me. It's Pablo."

Now, holding both his hands in hers, she wept. Her head shook from side to side with pure disbelief.

For an hour they sat like this. No one came into the café. It was the dead hour.

Eventually they rose and Concha led her husband up to their bedroom. Pablo lowered himself unsteadily onto the edge of the bed, the left side. It had been empty for so long. His wife helped him undress, removing the ragged clothes that hung off him, and tried to conceal her shock at his emaciated body. His was an unrecognizable torso. She turned back the covers and helped him climb in. The unfamiliar coolness of the sheets chilled him to the bone. Concha followed him into the bed and held him in her arms, transferring the warmth of her body to him until he almost burned. For hours they slept, two slim bodies entwined like stems of a vine. People came and went from the café downstairs, puzzled and mildly concerned by Concha's absence.

It was not until he woke that Pablo asked after Antonio and Mercedes. Concha had dreaded this moment and had to tell him what she knew: that Antonio was now in prison and that she had heard nothing from Mercedes.

That same day, they puzzled over the reasons for Pablo's release. It had come out of the blue. One night, following the daily reading of the death list, he had been taken to one side and told that he would be leaving the prison as well. What awful trick was this? he had wondered, his heart beating with sheer terror. He had not been able to ask questions, fearing that any response on his part might jeopardize this reprieve.

With the necessary papers to validate his release, he had worked his way back to Granada, by truck and by foot. It had taken him three days. And all the while he had puzzled, Why him?

"Elvira," said Concha. "I think it was something to do with her."

"Elvira?"

"Elvira Delgado. You must remember. The wife of the matador?" Concha hesitated.

Pablo seemed to have forgotten so much, so many details from his life before imprisonment. In the past twenty-four hours, she had sometimes noticed a blankness in her husband's expression and it alarmed her. It was as though some part of him had been left behind in his prison cell and had not returned to Granada.

She continued, undeterred. "She was Ignacio's mistress. I believe she used her influence and got her husband to intervene for you. I can't think of any other explanation."

Pablo looked thoughtful. He had no recollection of the woman Concha referred to.

"Well," he reflected finally, "I suppose it doesn't matter why or how it happened."

Concha was right. It was Elvira Delgado's doing, but there was no question of finding her to say thank you. Any acknowledgment of her involvement would compromise both parties. Many months later, Concha passed Elvira in the Plaza de la Trinidad. Concha recognized her from her regular appearances in *El Ideal*, but even if the familiar face had not caught her eye, the vision of glamour in a red, tailored coat extravagantly trimmed with fur would have made her look twice. Others turned to stare. The woman's full lips were painted to match her crimson outfit, and the black hair, piled high on her head, was as glossy as the dark mink that edged her collar.

Concha's pulse quickened as Elvira approached. It was strange for a mother to come face to face with the sensuality that had so seduced her own son and to acknowledge its power. No wonder he had taken risks to be with her, thought Concha, as she drew close enough to notice the smooth perfection of her skin and to catch a whiff of her scent. It was tempting to speak to her, but the younger woman's purposeful stride was so very sure. Elvira's eyes were fixed determinedly ahead of her. She did not look like someone who would take kindly to being accosted in the street. A huge lump had risen in Concha's throat as she thought of her beautiful son.

Pablo told Concha little about his time in prison. He did not need to. She could imagine it all through the lines on his face and the scars on his back. His entire story, with all its physical and mental torture, was etched on him.

It was not only because he wanted to put those four awful years behind him that made him stay as silent as possible about his time in prison. Pablo also believed that the less he described to his wife, the less she would dwell on what Emilio might have suffered before he died. The prison guards were imaginative in their cruelty, and he knew they kept their worst for homosexuals. It was better to keep her mind off the whole subject.

What he hated more than anything now was the sound of tolling bells.

"That noise," he moaned with his head in his hands, "I wish someone would just take them away."

"But they're church bells, Pablo. They've been there for years, and they're probably going to be there for another few."

"Yes, but a few other churches have been burned down, haven't they? Why couldn't that one have been?"

The nearby church of Santa Ana was where they had been married and their eldest two children had taken their First Communion. It had been a place of such happy and significant memories, but now it was somewhere he could no longer abide. In prison, the collusion of the priest with the torture of its inmates made him as guilty as the guards themselves. His spiteful and cynical offer of last rites to those condemned had made him the most despised individual in the entire institution. Pablo now hated everything to do with the Catholic Church.

In the last prison, where he had spent a whole year, his cell had been in the shadow of a bell tower. Night after night the bells tolled on the hour, wrecking the precious little sleep he had to remind him of the relentless passage of time.

Each morning when she woke and found Pablo beside her, Concha rejoiced. His presence constantly surprised and thrilled her, and over the following months she watched him gaining strength and vigor.

A month or so after Pablo's return, a letter was delivered. It was concise and carefully worded.

> *Dear Mother,*
>
> *I have moved to another part of Spain, my glorious patria. I shall not be able to come to see you for a while as I am working on a special project for El Caudillo to help rebuild our country. I am at Cuelgamuros. As soon as I have permission, I shall invite you to visit.*
>
> > *From your loving son,*
> > *Antonio*

"What does it mean?" asked Concha. "What does it really mean?"

The terse words and the formality of tone made it obvious that Antonio was hiding something. His reference to Franco as El Caudillo, "the great leader," had to be ironic. Antonio would never use words that implied such acceptance of the dictator except under duress. The letter bore all the evidence that the writer knew it would be censored.

Pablo read it for himself. It was so strange that his son made no reference to him. He felt he no longer existed.

"He doesn't mention you because he assumes you are still imprisoned," said Concha. "It's safer that way. Better not to draw attention to the fact that you have family in prison . . ."

"I know, you're right. They'd just use it as an excuse to victimize him."

They puzzled a little more over what if anything lay between the lines and wondered what the special project might be. All they deduced was that their son was in a work camp and that he had become one of the hundreds of thousands of men being forced to labor for Spain's tyrannical new regime.

"If he's working, at least they'll want to keep him alive," said Concha, trying to sound optimistic for her husband's sake.

"Well, I suppose we'll just have to wait and see. Perhaps he'll write again soon and tell us a bit more."

Neither of them admitted that their stomachs churned with anxiety, and they sat down to reply to the letter together.

Antonio was overwhelmed with pleasure when he received the envelope with a Granada postmark. Tears pricked the back of his eyes as he read that his father had been released from prison, and when he reached the sentence where his mother promised to come and visit, he thought his heart would burst. Laborers at Cuelgamuros were allowed visitors, and some families even set up home to be close by. It might take Concha a few months to plan, but the idea of the visit sustained them all.

# CHAPTER 34

Antonio wrote back. His second letter gave them more detail of what he was actually constructing, and he even sent them some money. To give the project legitimacy, laborers were paid a salary, albeit a pittance.

"There's something particularly cruel about having to construct a memorial for your enemies," said Pablo. "It's a sick joke, really."

By now Antonio was almost accustomed to the new routine of his life. He was strong and capable of carrying sizable loads, but there was little to alleviate the tedium. Death and injury were common inside the mountain, and new workers were continually sent in to replace the killed and maimed.

One day Antonio found that he had a new job. It had been his greatest fear. He had tolerated the worst imaginable conditions and pain that will push a man to breaking point, but the irrational fear of being trapped inside a mountain was greater than all of these. Claustrophobia was something he could not control.

Those assigned to the rock face walked in darkness toward their work. The further they went in, the lower Antonio's temperature dropped. His sweat was cold, all encompassing, dominating his whole body. For the first time in these years of extreme suffering, he had to restrain himself from weeping. It was irrational. It was not the darkness but the oppressive sense of the mountain above him that terrified him witless. So many times before the explosions began, he would have to suppress his desire to scream, but occasionally, when they stopped for the stones to fall in front of them, he would allow himself to roar with fear and with the hopelessness of it all, his tears mingling with the filthy sweat that ran down his body and soaked him right down to his boots.

The granite was resistant, but each day they went a little deeper into the darkness. Only a megalomaniac would conceive of such an immense cave of this kind, thought Antonio. It was no less than an underground, man-made cathedral. Sometimes, first thing in the morning, there would be a quiet mystery about it. Before the drilling and the hammering began, he tried to make himself imagine he was going somewhere peaceful, church-like, but soon the terror of claustrophobia overwhelmed him again and he saw himself walking into the center of the earth, perhaps never again to return.

He endlessly repeated to himself that he would soon be out, but with no light and without a wristwatch, there was no means of knowing when. Eventually he retraced his steps, but each day seemed an eternity.

Weeks turned into months. Progress was slow. In the overall scale they scarcely seemed to have scratched the mountainside. The workers began to learn more about this grand scheme. It was supposed to be finished in one year.

"That's about as likely as Franco sending us home for Christmas," said Antonio. "We've already been here for a year, haven't we? And it looks the same as when we arrived!"

He was right. It would be twenty years before The Valley of the Fallen was completed, and it would take twenty thousand men to finish it.

Each week dozens of workers were dying, killed in explosions, crushed by landslides of rocks, or electrocuted. Many of those who labored at the rock face itself contracted a sinister disease. As they drilled and hacked at the rock face, the air became filled with dust, and though they held sponges to their faces, microscopic particles of silica found their way through and filled their lungs with crystals.

The work was exhausting, and the teams of workers were in a constant state of flux. Friendships were hard to form. On rare occasions someone would be granted their freedom, but others were less lucky. The professor had been taken away only a few weeks after their arrival at Cuelgamuros.

It appeared that he had been guilty of committing many, albeit bogus, crimes against the state, the most offensive of them being that he was an intellectual and a Jew. Even as he had been taken from the hut at the crack of dawn one day, he had smiled at Antonio.

"Don't worry," he had said. "At least I won't be going to Mauthausen."

Professor Díaz had spent a year in France under German occupation. Many of his fellow Jews had been rounded up and removed to the notorious concentration camp. Antonio had admired Díaz enormously. He was the only person he could have called a friend in this godforsaken place, and even if the man himself faced his execution with stoicism, Antonio was horrified by the prospect of it.

After this, Antonio made no new friends. At the end of each day, lying exhausted on his straw mattress, he would close his eyes. Only his imagination saved him from insanity. He practiced hard to free his mind from this place, and they were simple, familiar images he needed. Never of women—such urges had become distant memories now. Usually he was sitting at a table with Francisco and Salvador; there was the alluring fragrance of brandy, the sound of conversation, the sensation of a fresh *polvorón* crumbling to sweet powder on his tongue. No one could reach him here and eventually he slept.

It was the man who slept on the mattress next to him that first noticed there was something wrong with Antonio.

"I don't know whether you cough all day—it's too noisy to notice—but you're doing it all night long. Every night."

Antonio could detect a note of irritation.

"It's keeping me awake," his neighbor complained.

"I'm sorry. I'll try to stop, but I must be doing it in my sleep . . ."

The close, smoke-filled atmosphere of the huts encouraged the spread of germs, as did the dampness in the Guadarrama air, and Antonio was not the only worker who tossed and turned throughout the hours of darkness.

Within a few weeks, Antonio himself ceased to sleep. All night he sweated, and now when he coughed, he saw his palm was stained crimson with blood. He was racked with chest pains.

Antonio was one of many who contracted silicosis. The hated mountain had buried a part of itself within him.

The sick were not kindly treated, and many worked until they collapsed. Antonio intended to do the same, but one day his body would no longer obey him. He could not even lift himself off his sweat-soaked bed. He experienced none of the peace that is meant to descend before you meet your maker, and through a haze of delirium, all he felt was anger and frustration.

One night there was a passing glimpse of his mother. Antonio had some distant recollection of receiving a letter from her to say that she was planning to visit, and he wondered if this was her standing over him with her dark hair and tender smile. He experienced a fleeting moment of peace, but no other angels came for him, and even in a state of semi-consciousness he knew that he was losing hold. The priest that sometimes exploited such men for a last-minute conversion did not bother to visit. Antonio was regarded as beyond spiritual reach by the authorities.

Finally, after some hours of fever, he was aware of the most terrible, burdensome sadness. He was saturated with tears, sweat, and grief, and everything was sliding away from him. Death now rolled in like a high tide and nothing could hold it back.

Throughout the past year, though they had both been entirely unaware of it, Javier Montero had been living only meters away. Along with his father, he had been rounded up in Málaga when the city was overrun in February 1937 and he had spent the entire duration of the war in prison. His only crime was to be a gypsy and by definition, therefore, a subversive. His path and Antonio's had almost crossed a hundred times, but both had become so stooped that they rarely looked up. The intervening years had ravaged them both.

Javier was in a group whose grim task that day was the burial of any dead. Occasionally he caught sight of his once beautiful hands now folded over the handle of a spade, bleeding, calloused, crisscrossed with granite cuts. It had been four years since his slender fingers had wrapped themselves over the fingerboard of his guitar and almost as long since he had heard the sound of music.

"You know, we're probably the lucky ones," said his fellow grave-digger as they swung their pickaxes at the hard earth. "I reckon this is softer than that granite."

"I suppose you might be right," answered Javier, trying to appreciate the levity in his tone.

They moved the body into position and lowered it into the grave. There was no shroud and the earth from Javier's spade fell directly onto the man's face. These were Antonio's last rites. There were no rituals on this hillside.

Neither gravedigger looked, but for a few minutes they kept silent. It was the most and the least they could do.

A few days earlier, Concha had set out from Granada to make the long-promised visit to Cuelgamuros. At the entrance, she was obliged to register herself and then, having stated her business, was directed to a small building, situated slightly apart from the long rows of dormitory huts, which stretched away into the distance.

She gave Antonio's full name, and then the sergeant ran his finger down the lists of workers' names. There were dozens of entries and she stood patiently while he turned page after page. He sighed, apparently bored. Though she could not read any of the names upside down, Concha could see that some of them had lines through them.

Then his finger came to a stop, halfway down a page.

"Dead," he said dispassionately. "Last week. Silicosis."

Concha's heart almost stopped beating. His words came like stab wounds.

"Thank you," she said politely. She was determined not to show any weakness in front of this man and wandered out blindly, not really know-ing where she was going now.

It was five o'clock in the afternoon and some of the workers had returned to their huts after a twelve-hour shift. Javier glanced out of his window. He noticed a woman. Apart from the wives of laborers who had come to live nearby, it was rare to see anyone female, but what made him look twice was that it was a face he thought he recognized. He slipped out of the hut and hastened after her.

The woman was wandering slowly now, and it took only a moment for him to catch her up.

"Excuse me," he said, touching her lightly on the arm.

Concha assumed it was one of the guards about to reprimand her for wandering into a forbidden area. She stopped. She could feel nothing now, certainly not fear.

Javier had not been mistaken. Though her hair was now streaked with gray, she was unchanged.

"Señora Ramírez," he said.

It took Concha a few moments to realize who this skeletal creature actually was. He had changed considerably, but the huge distinctive eyes remained the same.

"It's me. Javier Montero."

"Yes, yes," answered Concha, so quietly that birdsong would have drowned out her voice. "I know . . ."

"But what are you doing here?" he asked her.

The first thing that went through his mind was that Señora Ramírez had learned that he was here and had come with news of Mercedes.

"I came to see Antonio," she replied.

"Antonio! He's here?"

Concha's head dropped. She could not answer, but the tears that ran down her face told him enough.

They stood for a while. Javier felt awkward. He wanted to embrace Señora Ramírez as he would his own mother, but it did not seem appropriate. If only he could comfort her in some way.

It was getting dark now, and Concha knew that she would have to leave soon. She must be out of here by nightfall. When her tears had subsided, she finally spoke. There was one thing she must do before she left.

"I don't suppose you would know where he was buried. I would just like to go there before I leave," she said with all the self-control she could muster.

Javier took her arm. He led her gently toward the burial ground, which was situated a few hundred meters beyond the huts. In the clearing among the trees she could make out the section of ground where the earth had recently been disturbed: it was ridged like a plowed field. They approached the spot and Concha stood for a few moments, her eyes shut, her lips moving in prayer. Javier remained silent as the realization dawned that Antonio's burial must have been on his shift. Even the sound of his breathing seemed intrusive.

Eventually Concha looked up. "I must go now," she said decisively.

Javier took her arm again. They passed a number of workers on their way to the gates, who gave him quizzical looks. There was something he was desperate to know, and he could not let Señora Ramírez leave without asking her.

"Mercedes . . ."

Concha had almost forgotten about her daughter in the past hour, but she had known that the moment would come when she had to tell Javier that Mercedes had gone to look for him and never came back.

"I can't lie to you," she said, taking his hand. "But if we hear from her, I'll write to you straightaway."

It was Javier's turn to be lost for words.

As the gate clanged shut behind Concha, she shuddered. Drawing her coat tightly around her, she hastened away. In spite of the fact that her son was buried there, she could not get away fast enough.

One day, an immense cross would soar one hundred and fifty meters into the sky on the mountaintop, majestic, arrogant, and victorious. With the figures of the holy saints kneeling at its base, it would be positioned above Franco's tomb, and on some days its long shadow would touch the wooded place where Antonio's body lay in an unmarked grave.

PART III

# CHAPTER 35

*Granada, 2001*

The shadows were lengthening over the square outside El Barril as Miguel's words died away. Sonia had almost forgotten where she was. She was astonished by what he had told her.

"But how could all this have happened to one family?" she asked.

"It wasn't just the Ramírez family that these things happened to," replied Miguel. "They weren't unusual. Not at all. Every Republican family suffered."

Miguel's energy seemed to be flagging, but he had been tireless in the telling of this story. Sonia viewed the café with different eyes now. The sadness of what had happened to these people seemed to linger there.

The old man had talked for several hours, but there was still a part of the story missing. It was the part that she was most curious to know.

"So what did happen to Mercedes?" she asked. The pictures of the dancer on the wall above them were a constant reminder of why she was really here.

"Mercedes?" He sounded vague. And Sonia worried for a moment. Perhaps this obliging old man had forgotten of her existence. "Mercedes . . . yes. Of course. Mercedes . . . Well, for a long time there was no contact at all because letters could be so incriminating and she felt her mother was probably under enough suspicion without being accused of having a *roja* for a daughter."

"So she was still alive then?" Sonia's hopes were raised again.

"Oh yes," said Miguel brightly. "Eventually, when it was safer, she began to write letters to Concha here at El Barril."

Miguel was rummaging around in a chest next to the till.

Sonia's heart beat furiously.

"They're here somewhere," he said.

Sonia was trembling now. She saw in his hand a neatly tied bundle of letters written by the girl whose photograph had come to obsess her.

"Would you like me to read some of them to you? They're in Spanish." He came to sit down on the chair next to hers.

"Yes, please," she said quietly, staring at the yellowing dog-eared envelopes he held in his hand.

He carefully removed a dozen fine airmail sheets from the envelope at the top of the chronologically ordered pile and unfolded them. The letter was dated 1941.

The script was unfamiliar. Sonia had never seen her mother write by hand. Her illness had made it difficult, and in her memory Mary had always used a typewriter.

The letters from one side of the paper showed through to the other, making the task of reading a challenge. The old man did his best, reciting each sentence in Spanish before translating into rather old-fashioned English.

> *Dear Mother,*
>
> *I know you will understand why I have not written for so long. It was because I was anxious not to incriminate you. I know I am regarded as a traitor for staying out of Spain, and I hope you will forgive me for this. It seemed the safest way for all concerned.*
>
> *I want to tell you what happened after I left for England on the* Habana *four years ago. . .*

With every minute that passed, the expanse of water between Mercedes and her homeland widened. The wind got up not long after they set sail, and as they sailed out into the Bay of Biscay, the waves began to roll. The roughness took everyone by surprise. Many of these children had never been on a boat before, and the violence of the rocking motion terrified them. Many had begun to cry as they sensed their disorientation and were gripped by the first gagging moments of nausea.

Even the color of the sea seemed alien. No longer blue, it was now the color of churned-up mud. Some of the children were immediately sick, and as the journey continued, even the adults were retching. Soon the decks were slippery with vomit.

In spite of Mercedes' protest, Enrique was separated from her and put on an upper deck. For many hours she lost sight of him and felt that she had already failed his mother.

"You aren't here only to look after those children," scolded one of the older assistants.

She was right. Mercedes' role on this journey and beyond it was to take care of a bigger group, and her concern for just two of the children was frowned upon by several of the teachers and priests.

That night, the children slept where they could as the boat rolled up and down. Some of them nestled into the bottom of a lifeboat; others curled up on huge coils of rope. Soon Mercedes was incapable of offering them comfort. Queasiness overcame her. When the rough seas became calm again the next day, the relief was immense. The coast of England had been in sight for some time, but only when the sea ceased to hurl them around did they notice the thin dark line on the horizon that was Hampshire's coastline. By six thirty on that second day they were docking at Southampton.

The dead flat calm of the harbor was complete sanctuary, and as quickly as it had arrived, the awful seasickness disappeared. On the deck of the ship, small hands held on to the railings and peered over to look at this new country. All they could see were the dark harbor walls that loomed over them.

There was the noisy business of docking the ship to be completed, and they heard the alarming clank of the anchor chain, and huge ropes as thick as arms were thrown down on to the quayside. Grizzled men looked up at them with a mixture of pity and curiosity. They meant no harm. There were shouts in a language they did not recognize, gruff aggressive voices, and the bellowing holler of the docker who had to make himself heard above the general cacophony.

The sun came out through the clouds, but the novelty and excitement of this adventure had worn off. These children wanted to be at home with their mothers. Many had become separated from siblings during the journey and it took time to sort them into groups, but the hexagonal badges helped, and each one of them was soon allocated to a helper. Mercedes had hoped for the opportunity to get to know her charges on the journey, but the storm had stolen the moment.

Before disembarkation the children underwent another medical examination, and colored ribbons were tied to their wrists to indicate if treatment was required: a red ribbon meant a journey to the corporation baths for delousing, a blue ribbon meant that infectious disease had been diagnosed and a visit to the isolation hospital was required, and a white ribbon showed a clean bill of health.

All the poor mites looked bedraggled. Hair, so beautifully brushed, ribboned, and carefully plaited almost two days earlier, was now matted into hard clumps. Smart knitted jumpers were stained by vomit. The *señoritas* did their best to make them presentable.

Finally, the children had to be reunited with their possessions and given back the very little they had brought with them. Small girls now clutched a favorite doll and boys stood bravely, like little men. By the time they were all assembled and ready to leave the ship, they had been docked for some time.

The curiosity was mutual. Everyone stared, wide-eyed. The Spaniards looked at the English, and the English gazed at the foreign children edging their way along the deck. Britain had heard so much about the barbaric behavior of the *rojos* in Spain, how they had burned down churches and tortured innocent nuns, that they expected to see little savages. When these wide-eyed children, some of them still managing to look smartly dressed, came into view, they were amazed.

Among the first English people the Spanish children saw were members of a Salvation Army band. Mercedes did not quite know what to make of them, in their dark uniforms, blasting their bright tunes from gleaming trumpets and trombones. They seemed rather military to her, but she soon learned that they meant well.

Southampton looked like a town in fiesta. Its streets were bedecked with bunting, and the Spanish children smiled, imagining this was put up to welcome them. They would discover only later that it was left over from the celebration of the recent coronation.

Those who had been given a clean bill of health were driven in double-decker buses from Southampton for a few miles to North Stoneham, the place that was to be their temporary home. It was a huge encampment spread over three fields, with five hundred white, bell-shaped tents in neat rows. Each tent would accommodate eight to ten children, with boys and girls separated. "*Indios!*" exclaimed some of the children with excitement when they saw them.

"They think it's all a big game of cowboys and Indians," said Enrique scornfully to his sister, who stood next to him clutching her doll.

For Mercedes, it immediately invited comparison with the makeshift tents that people had improvised on the road from Málaga to Almería. But here there was order, safety, and, most touching of all, kindness. In these green meadows they had found sanctuary.

The organization was impressive. As well as the divisions between girls and boys, there were separate areas for the three groups of children, divided according to the politics of their parents. The organizers wanted to minimize the aggression between rival groups.

The camp was its own self-contained world with its own rules and routines. Queues for food were orderly, though it did take four hours to serve the first meal. Much of what they were given tasted strange to the evacuees, but they were grateful for it and acquainted themselves with new flavors and tastes like Horlicks and tea. Mercedes found some of the children in her care were hoarding food; for so long they had worried about where the next meal was coming from.

They picnicked in the sunshine, but for many days they were anxious whenever they heard the sound of airplanes passing over toward the nearby airfield in Eastleigh. They associated the sound so strongly with the threat of air raids. After a while they began to lie back on the soft English grass and watch the pale puffy clouds, safe in the knowledge that bombers were not going to blot out the sun.

The caretakers kept the children busy with lessons, chores, and gymnastics, but the discipline was kind, and every effort was made to ensure that this place did not feel like a prison. Each day there was a prize for the tidiest tent, and Mercedes made sure that her little charges often won the competition. All of them suffered in some way from aching homesickness, but even the youngest managed to keep their tears until nighttime.

The refugees were much greater in number than originally expected, but the pressure was soon lifted when, in the first week, four hundred were taken to a Salvation Army hostel, and within a month one thousand more had gone to Catholic homes. There were some food shortages but not of the same scale that many of them had experienced in Bilbao. One mealtime, Mercedes examined the old and battered knife and fork she was using and remembered that every single item in the camp was from a voluntary donation. Though they were reasonably well protected from the attitudes of the outside world, she knew that the British government had refused to fund their stay in England. Furious efforts were going on to raise money to feed and clothe them, and they relied entirely on the kindness of strangers.

Though the language barrier protected them from articles in the newspapers that were hostile to their arrival, one piece of news that was not kept from the Spanish refugees was the fall of Bilbao to the Nationalists. In May 1937, only a month after they had sailed away from it, the city had fallen. It was a very black day at Stoneham. Many of the children ran amok, crying and screaming, panic-stricken at the thought that their parents could now be dead. Enrique, along with some other boys, ran out of the camp, determined to find a boat so that they could return to Spain and fight. They were soon found and brought back to camp. Mercedes spent the night comforting Enrique, assuring him that his mother would be all right. As she sat with him, she thought of Javier, too, and once again hoped that he had got out of the city long ago.

News of Bilbao's capture created a dilemma for everyone.

"Surely we can't go back now?" said Mercedes to one of the other assistants.

"No, I don't think we can. I think the children would be in even more danger than they were before," replied Carmen.

"So what's going to happen to us all?" asked Mercedes.

"Your guess is as good as mine, but I don't think we can camp out forever in this climate!"

At some point soon, everyone at the camp in North Stoneham would have to be moved somewhere more permanent. The Basque Children's Committee was already working hard to find a solution. Up and down the country, they were establishing "colonies" in which to house the children, and the destination for each *niño* could be arbitrary. For some it could be another tent, an empty hotel, or a castle. For Mercedes, it was a country mansion.

At the end of July she accompanied a group of twenty-five children, including Enrique and Paloma, to Sussex. They took the train to Haywards Heath, and at the railway station they were welcomed by the town band and local children who had brought gifts of sweets. It was a warm and happy day. From there a bus dropped them in a village fifteen kilometers away, and after that it was a short walk from the village to the gateposts of Winton Hall.

The eagle-topped pillars were imposing if dilapidated. Some of the bricks were dislodged, and one of the moss-covered eagles had lost a wing. Nevertheless, they created an intimidating impression of what was to come. The children joined hands and marched in pairs along the kilometer of rutted driveway. Mercedes walked with Carmen, the teacher in charge of the group. In the past two months the two women had become close friends.

It was hot. The temperature made them feel as though they were back at home. The as yet unharvested fields around them were pale and parched, and the sky was a clear, bright blue. Butterflies basked on the buddleia bushes that grew in profusion along the way, and the younger children squealed with delight at the red admirals that fluttered around their heads. They picked buttercups and daisies from the verge and made up a song. Their walk seemed to pass in no time and they even forgot the weight of their bags.

Mercedes was the first to reach a bend in the driveway where the house came into view. She had seen pictures of English stately homes in books, so she had some idea of what they looked like, but she would never have imagined that one would become her home. Winton Hall was built of a sandy-colored stone and had more chimneys and turrets than some of the younger children could count.

"It's a fairy castle!" exclaimed Paloma.

"Are we coming to live with the new king?" asked her friend.

The owners had been watching their progress along the driveway from an upstairs room and were now at the top of the steps to the entrance. Two spaniels sat at their feet.

Sir John and Lady Greenham had all the trappings of the English landed gentry without any of the wealth. Winton Hall had been built by Sir John's grandfather, who had been a wealthy industrialist, but over the years its fabric had begun to disintegrate around the subsequent generations who lived there.

"Welcome to Winton Hall," said the master of the house, coming down to meet the arrivals.

Carmen was the only one of the group who spoke any English. The children had learned a few words since they arrived, but could not make conversation.

Mercedes knew only "Hello" and "Thank you." Both of these were useful in this situation and she managed to splutter them out.

Lady Greenham remained at the top of the steps, eyeing them all coolly. It had not been her idea to invite the refugees here. It was her husband's whimsical notion. He was a distant relative of the redoubtable Duchess of Atholl, who had established the Basque Children's Committee; now that the children had been dispersed from the camp, she helped them to find homes around the country. Lady Greenham remembered clearly the first time she had heard of her husband's plan to open up their home. "Oh, do let's help these poor dears!" he had exhorted. "It won't be for long." He had just returned from a meeting in London where the Red Duchess, as she was known, had canvassed for support.

Sir John was a kindhearted man and could think of no reason why they should not invite a group of harmless young Spaniards to fill some of their dusty rooms. They had never had children of their own, and it was a long time since the corridors of the house had been filled with any kind of life, apart from the occasional mouse.

"Very well, then," his wife had reluctantly agreed. "But I'm not having boys. Only girls. And not too many of them."

"I'm afraid we can't do that," he answered firmly. "If there are siblings, they have to stay together."

Lady Greenham was full of resentment right from the beginning. Though it was in a state of dusty decay, she retained a strong pride in their home. They had long since dispensed with the servants, who had kept the place immaculate, and now only had a shortsighted housekeeper who occasionally flicked a duster at the cobwebs. Even so, Lady Greenham had a strong awareness of the house's past grandeur and her social standing as its chatelaine.

The children filed up the steps and into the hallway, their eyes as wide as saucers. Dark portraits looked down at them. Paloma giggled.

"Look at him," she whispered to Enrique, pointing at one of the ancestral paintings. "He's so fat!"

She won herself a disapproving look from Carmen. Even though she was sure that their hosts did not understand what she had said, it was obvious what had amused her.

Lady Greenham's rather fixed smile faded. "Now, children," she said, not the slightest bit perturbed that they did not have any idea what she was saying, but raising her voice in case it helped their comprehension. "Shall we just establish a few rules?"

They gathered in a circle around her. For the first time Mercedes took a closer look at the Englishwoman. She seemed about the same age as her mother, perhaps forty-five. Her husband, who had strands of reddish hair brushed ineffectually across his bald head, was probably a few years older than she. His complexion was densely freckled and Mercedes tried not to stare.

Carmen translated as Lady Greenham spoke.

"There is to be no running up and down the corridors . . . Shoes will be taken off before you come in from the garden . . . The drawing room and the library are out of bounds to you . . . You must not overexcite the dogs."

They listened in silence.

"Boys and girls, do you understand all these rules?" said Carmen, to try to break the tension.

"*Sí! Sí! Sí!*" they all agreed.

"Now I shall show you where you're going to sleep," said Sir John.

The children's feet clattered up the bare broad staircase after their hosts.

Lady Greenham stopped and turned around. The children halted too.

"I think we have already broken a rule, haven't we?"

Carmen flushed. "Yes, they have. I'm so sorry," she said apologetically. "Now, children, go back down the stairs and remove your shoes, please."

They all did as they were told, and their dusty shoes now formed an untidy pile at the foot of the stairs.

"I'll show you where to put them later," said Lady Greenham. Her own court shoes hammered along the corridor now as the walk to their bedrooms continued.

One thing Mercedes had observed was that, in spite of the temperature they had been enjoying earlier, as soon as they had stepped over the threshold of this house, all the warmth of the day was left outside.

The boys were to be accommodated in a first-floor room, which had high ceilings, huge sash windows, and a large faded Persian rug, and the girls were to be divided into two separate musty-smelling rooms in the attic, which had once been servants' quarters. There were several beds in each, and they were expected to share in whatever way they could. Carmen and Mercedes would sleep top to tail with the girls.

It was suppertime. Initially the housekeeper, Mrs. Williams, was as unwelcoming as her mistress. In the kitchen she gave them a series of "don'ts."

"Don't leave your plate on the table. Don't bang your cutlery. Don't waste food. Don't let the dogs eat any scraps. Don't let any peelings go down the sink. Don't forget to wash your hands before meals."

Each one was delivered with a mimed demonstration of what they "Must Not Do." Then she smiled—a broad smile that involved every muscle in her face, including her eyes, her mouth, and the dimples in her cheeks. The children could see that this woman had warmth in her heart.

In the grand dining room, where grimy crystal chandeliers hung down from the ceiling, the long table was incongruously laid with green china from Woolworth's and tin mugs. Lady Greenham was hardly going to use her finest porcelain for these little foreigners.

Their first meal was a dish made from mince, followed by tapioca pudding. Most of the children managed to force down the fatty first course, but the tapioca was more of a struggle. Several of them gagged violently, and Paloma was profusely sick on the floor. Carmen and Mercedes rushed to clean up the vomit. It was imperative that Lady Greenham did not hear of it, since this was the sort of calamity that might prove her husband's folly in inviting these children here.

The housekeeper, loyal as she was to her employers, did not want the new arrivals to get into trouble, so she helped clean up and promised not to mention what had happened. She would serve something called semolina from now on, rather than tapioca.

The following day, after a breakfast of bread and margarine, the children were allowed to explore outside. They were baffled as to where its limits lay. There was a formal garden with overgrown lawns and brick-edged parterres, where weeds seemed to grow in greater profusion than the roses, against which they waged an impressive battle. Rather mystifyingly there was a huge sunken space; they deduced from the presence of a now-bottomless rowing boat that was stranded in the middle, its oars sticking out of the mud like flagpoles, that it had once been an artificial lake. Some of them walked around it but found the pathway overgrown and impossible to negotiate. Beyond the lake in one direction was woodland, and in the other there were fields, some of them grazed by cows.

There was a little folly in the garden, which had obviously been a retreat for someone who enjoyed painting. It was circular, so that the light could come in from all sides. An easel leaned against the wall, and the old table was covered with daubs of oil paints, tubes of which still lay on the surface. Paintbrushes stood, tips down, in a cup. No one had been in here for years. Two of the older girls, Pilar and Esperanza, were entranced by this secret hideaway and found some paper and scraps of charcoal. The paper was damp but usable, and they began to draw. Hours later they were still there, utterly absorbed.

Mercedes was drawn to a wooden summerhouse by the lake and pushed open the door. It was full of old deck chairs.

"Let's put some of them out," said Paloma, who was exploring the estate with Mercedes. She dragged one of them into the sunshine, only to discover that the canvas had rotted. "Never mind," she said cheerfully. "Perhaps we could mend some of them."

Later that week, that was exactly what they would begin to do.

Some of the children found the walled area where a few vegetables were still growing. In the past they had been cultivated in industrial quantities, but now only a few onions and potatoes grew. One of the girls went into the greenhouse and found some strawberries growing in a trough. She could not resist eating one and was in a state of anxiety for the rest of the day over whether Lady Greenham had counted them and would notice the missing fruit.

Other children had discovered a disused tennis court and, in a nearby pavilion, the old, rolled-up net. Carmen, with some of the older boys, was now attempting to erect it. The lines were still just about visible, and once they had rooted out some old rackets, all with a string or two broken, a few had begun to pat a ball back and forth across the net. It had been many, many months since they had had fun like this.

At lunchtime, Sir John came to find them. He could hear their laughter and found a group of the children trying to keep a ball in play.

"What's this?" asked Carmen, holding out a giant wooden hammer for him to identify. "There are several of them in a box."

"Ah," he said, smiling. "That's a croquet mallet."

"A croquet mallet . . ." repeated Carmen, none the wiser.

"Shall I show you how to play after lunch?"

"It's a game, then?"

"Yes," he replied, "and we used to play it on that lawn." He pointed to a huge flat sweep of grass that was now covered in patches of moss. "It's a bit bumpy now, but no reason why we shouldn't have a go."

After a lunch of potato soup, some bread, and a lump of cheese that the children thought rubbery but quite enjoyed, they were back in the garden. There was a croquet lesson. Sir John had set up the hoops and now taught a group of them the strange and quirky rules of the game. Even the boys were dismissive of the option to drive another player off the lawn, and adopted a more gentle strategy. They had witnessed enough aggression in their short lives.

The delightful romance of all the garden's different spaces captivated everyone, and on this perfect English summer's afternoon, they all temporarily forgot about the past and enjoyed the present. There was the freedom to run around and the opportunity to sit quietly too. A few of the younger ones had found a bench in the sunshine and started to draw.

Carmen had kept in touch with a few of the other teachers, and conditions in some of their colonies made her appreciate more than ever their good fortune in being at Winton Hall. At one place, the children found themselves being used as free labor in a laundry, and at some of the

Catholic-run homes, the nuns did not hesitate to punish misdemeanors with beatings.

Those who were in Salvation Army camps seemed to have the most complaints: "The stern faces of women in bonnets who make us sing English hymns only remind me of why we had to leave Spain," wrote Carmen's friend. "People in uniform forcing us to conform to their religion! Doesn't that sound familiar?"

It seemed to Mercedes that though their actions were often well meant, some of those who ran the colonies failed to appreciate what these children had suffered.

# CHAPTER 36

One warm summer's day passed after another, and the mood at Winton Hall was generally one of content. Many of the children had recently received letters from their families in Bilbao. Enrique and Paloma were among the lucky ones and now knew that their mother and little brother and sister were all safe.

In the mornings, the children had a few hours of lessons, but afternoons were for recreation. One day a group of them were trying to recall the words of their favorite songs and the steps of some traditional Basque dances. It mattered so much to them that they should not forget the good things about home. Over the coming days they rehearsed until they were word- and step-perfect. They would perform them for Sir John and Lady Greenham and Mrs. Williams, if they were interested.

That night, after supper, they put on a performance. Even Lady Greenham managed to applaud. Sir John's enthusiasm bubbled out of him.

"That was marvelous," he said to Carmen. "Really marvelous."

"Thank you," she said, beaming.

"And I've got an idea! I think you should put on a show in the village!"

"Oh, surely not," Carmen replied. "I think the children would be much too shy."

"Shy?" exclaimed Sir John. "They seem anything but shy!"

"Well, I'll talk to them about it later," said Carmen, not wanting to dismiss his idea. "Do you think that people would pay?"

Over the past few weeks she had become aware that money for their keep was in extremely short supply. Although the Basque Children's Committee waged an enthusiastic campaign for donations, the British public were not always prepared to dig deeply into their pockets for children whom they regarded as communists. In every colony, the exiles were coming up with ways of earning money.

Sir John was right. That night the children all voted unanimously to perform for the public if it could be arranged.

"But it's only three dances and five songs," one of the older girls put forward. "Do you think that's enough if we're charging for tickets?"

There was a general murmur of agreement that this might not be enough. Mercedes did not hesitate to put forward another idea.

"I could dance," she said. "They might not have seen flamenco before either."

"It would certainly make a more varied program," agreed Carmen, who knew of Mercedes' past. "But who is going to accompany you?"

"Well, there isn't a guitarist here," Mercedes said, trying to make light of it, "but I could teach you some clapping rhythms."

Several hands shot up in the half-light. There was certainly no shortage of enthusiasm.

"And I have these," came a voice from the bed at the far end of the room. It was Pilar. They all turned around when they heard the purring sound of castanets. It was like the sound of a cicada, and on this hot night, they almost imagined they were at home. Pilar had been playing with the castanets since she was three or four, and the fourteen-year-old now had extraordinary mastery over them.

"Perfect," said Mercedes. "We have our performance."

The dancing troupe grew now to twenty, and everyone rehearsed frantically for three days. The ones who were not dancing made posters, and Sir John had them put up in the village.

To Lady Greenham's chagrin, Mercedes practiced in the hallway, where the flooring was solid enough to take the force of her steps. The girls sat on the stairs to watch her and peeped through the banister. They had never seen anyone quite like her and were completely mesmerized, clapping and stamping their feet with appreciation whenever she rested.

Pilar sat at the back of the hall. She quietly tapped the beat with her hands first of all, working out the rhythms and then, inaudibly to anyone but herself, she worked out the patterns for the castanets. Only when she was completely sure of them did she move forward and begin to play for Mercedes. She exploited every complex variation of castanet sound, making them trill and sing and snap and clack.

"That's wonderful, Pilar," said Mercedes. She had never heard castanets played more eloquently.

On the night of the performance, every seat in the village hall was filled. Some had come out of pure curiosity to see these "small, dark little people" as they were described by the Basque Children's Committee. For them it was rather like going to the zoo. Others came simply out of boredom. There was little other entertainment in an English village.

The Basque dances charmed the audience. Mrs. Williams had managed to find them suitable material, and the girls had made their own costumes: red skirts, green waistcoats, black aprons, and simple white blouses. They danced with vigor and enthusiasm. Everyone clapped and called for an encore.

The songs enchanted the audience too. Sweet voices in perfect unison sang out "*Anda diciendo tu madre*" and even the most hard-hearted people in the audience melted. Mercedes, standing in the wings, felt a lump rise to her throat as she heard them sing that last word, *madre*. They were so far away from their mothers, and most of them had been so extraordinarily brave.

Mercedes was the last item on the program. The contrast between her and the innocent naïveté of the Basque dances could not have been greater. It was nothing like those mechanical performances she had given on the journey toward Bilbao. Here, into this hall, with its leaking roof and an audience of stony-faced Englishmen and -women, she brought all of her pain and longing. She was wearing the red polka-dotted dress that she had been given all those months ago by the bar owner, and now that she had put on plenty of weight, it was perfectly molded around her reemerging curves.

If the audience had evaporated into the air on this warm night, it would not have mattered to her. Tonight, she danced for herself. Some of them understood it and were drawn in. They eagerly followed every expressive movement with their eyes and appreciated the emotion she was laying bare. When the castanets crackled in the air and matched the rhythm of her feet, they found the hairs on their necks standing on end.

Others found her performance baffling. It was strange, incomprehensible and alien, and it made them feel distinctly uncomfortable. At the end of the performance, there was a moment of silence. None of them had ever seen anything like it. Some then clapped politely. Others burst into rapturous applause. Several people rose to their feet. Mercedes had divided them.

The reputation of the Basque singing and dancing, and the flamenco soon spread. It was even reported in the local paper. Letters came from other villages and towns in the south of England asking the refugees to perform, and all invitations were accepted, as the payments contributed to their upkeep. Once a week they packed their costumes and traveled to another destination. The contrast between the innocence of the traditional Basque dances and the flamboyant style of flamenco astonished audiences wherever they took it. Not a day passed when Mercedes did not think of Javier, and when she danced, it was as though she revived him freshly in her mind and conjured him up again. She needed to keep in practice for when they met again, she told herself.

A few months of relative happiness went by, and the only person who did not seem to be enjoying the holiday camp atmosphere of Winton Hall was Lady Greenham.

"Why does she look like she's sucking a lemon?" Mercedes commented to Carmen one evening.

"I don't think she's that keen on having us here," answered Carmen, stating the obvious.

"So why did she invite us?"

"I don't think she did. It was all Sir John's doing," replied Carmen.

"But actually I think she's just one of those people. You know—never really happy."

Lady Greenham's lips were even more pursed than usual when she strode into the dining room at breakfast time. Sir John was sitting having a cup of tea at one end of the table. He enjoyed the formless hum of a language he could not understand.

"Look!" said his wife, slamming down a copy of the *Daily Mail* on the table in front of him. "Look!"

All the girls had stopped talking. They were alarmed by her apparent anger.

BASQUE CHILDREN ATTACK POLICE shouted the headline.

Her husband turned the newspaper over so that no one else could read it. "That may be the case, which I doubt, but it hasn't happened here, has it? And you should *never* believe what you read in that newspaper."

"But they're clearly not to be trusted!" Lady Greenham said in a loud whisper.

"I think we should go outside to discuss this," Sir John hissed angrily.

They both left the room, and the sound of raised voices could clearly be heard. Some of the children listened at the door, though they understood almost nothing. Carmen pushed them out of the way to hear.

Sir John admitted that he had heard of minor incidents in the villages close to some of the colonies—scrumping of apples, for example, and the occasional scuffle with local boys, and perhaps a broken window or two—but he was absolutely certain that nothing of the sort could happen at Winton Hall.

Lady Greenham's ambivalence about their presence had always been obvious, but now Carmen saw the whole picture. This frosty English-woman was happy to do good works for charity as long as it did not intrude too much on her life. Her husband's "project" had taken it over completely, and she would never feel comfortable with these outsiders. They were foreign and therefore, in her eyes, potentially feral.

Carmen said nothing to the girls but confided to Mercedes.

"I don't think we should do anything about it," said Mercedes.

"We must simply prove her wrong," agreed Carmen. "The children's behavior must be exemplary."

For the next few months, this was how it was. They gave Lady Greenham no cause for complaint.

From November 1937, parents began to write to the Committee. They wanted their children home. Bilbao was no longer being either blockaded or bombarded. In April 1938, Señora Sánchez, whose apartment block had been struck during an air raid, had found new accommodation. She was now ready to reunite her family, and Enrique and Paloma packed their things to return.

Mercedes traveled with the children by train to Dover, from where they were to catch a boat to France before making the onward journey down through Spain. As she sat in the railway carriage with the oranges and golds of the autumnal landscape floating past, she studied her two charges. In the past year, Paloma had remained a little girl. Her doll, Rosa, sat on her lap, just as she had done on the train journey from Santurce to the dock the previous May. By contrast, Enrique had changed substantially. He still had the same worried look, but he had turned into a young man. She allowed herself to imagine the reunion with their mother and felt a stabbing at her heart.

"I'm not sure about going back," Enrique said to Mercedes when he saw that his little sister had dozed off with the motion of the train. "Some of the boys are refusing to go. They don't believe it's safe."

"But your mother has written to you. She wouldn't be suggesting it if she thought it might be dangerous, would she?" Mercedes said to reassure him.

"Supposing it's not her suggesting it, though? Supposing she was forced to write the letter?"

"That's very suspicious of you," Mercedes said. "I'm sure the Committee wouldn't be letting you go if they thought there was any chance of that."

It had not occurred to Mercedes that there was anything untoward about these letters that regularly arrived to summon children home. It seemed the most natural thing that they should be going back to Spain, and it was what had always been planned. Many parents would rather have their children standing beside them raising the Fascist salute than thousands of kilometers away in a foreign land. The rumblings of war were now happening across the whole of northern Europe, so "home" had to be the safest place for anyone.

Mercedes hugged the two children close before handing them over to the person who was chaperoning a whole group back to Spain. Enrique held back his tears, but neither Mercedes nor Paloma could manage to restrain theirs and their farewells were tearful. Promises to meet again were heartfelt.

As she watched the boat leave, Mercedes fought against her desire to return to Spain. With no idea where Javier could be, and real fear of what might happen to her if she returned to Granada, she knew she was better off staying in England. She still had plenty to occupy her here with the children who had not received summonses from their parents. Some of her charges knew these letters would never come, if both their parents had been killed. Mercedes took the train back to Haywards Heath and returned to Winton Hall, where some new children were due to arrive from another colony, which had been shut down. The initial ninety colonies were gradually reduced in number as more evacuees returned home.

A diminishing group of them continued to put on their dance performances, but there was anticipation at every venue now as their reputation grew and the attitudes of local people toward them softened. Occasionally another flamenco dancer would join Mercedes, and two brothers from another colony in Sussex, who were accomplished guitarists, sometimes came too.

When Madrid fell in the spring of 1939, Franco wanted every evacuee and exile still in England to return. Many were warned against it. Destitution, persecution, and arrest were all distinct possibilities.

Mercedes realized she now must take a risk. She wrote a short, careful letter to her mother to tell her where she was, hoping for a response that would give her guidance on what she should do.

In Granada, Pablo and Concha wept with joy when they received the letter and knew that their daughter was alive and safe.

"She's been looking after children all this time!" exclaimed her father, studying his daughter's neat handwriting. "She was only a child herself the last time we saw her!"

"And she's still dancing . . ." said Concha. "It's so wonderful that she's still dancing."

They endlessly pored over the letter, and then they discussed how to reply.

"It will be so lovely to see her again. I wonder when she's coming," enthused the old man for his only daughter.

Concha came straight to the point. She tended to lead discussions and decisions these days. Pablo had been slow since his time in prison.

"I think she should stay in England," she said bluntly. "We can't let her come back here."

"Why not?" asked Pablo. "The war is over."

"It's still not safe, Pablo," Concha said dogmatically. "It's not the best thing for Merche. However much we want to see her."

"I don't understand," he said, slamming his glass down on the table. "She's just an innocent young woman!"

"Well, the authorities wouldn't see her that way," Concha insisted. "She left the country. That's seen as a hostile act, and she has delayed returning. Believe me, Pablo, she's likely to be arrested. I have to know she's safe."

"But what about Javier?" appealed Pablo. "She'll want to come back to visit him."

This was what Concha feared more than anything. If Mercedes knew that Javier was alive and at Cuelgamuros, she would almost certainly return. For her daughter's own sake, she chose to keep this information from her.

At Winton Hall, Mercedes eagerly awaited the response. Eventually, with other letters that came from Spain with stamps showing the new dictator, an envelope arrived from Granada. Even her mother's handwriting made Mercedes tremble. Its familiarity made her seem so unbearably close. She tore it open, hoping for news of everyone, only to be disappointed. There was a single sheet and two stark sentences.

"Father and I look forward to having you at home again soon. Your sister sends her love."

There was so much to read between the lines. Mercedes was thrilled by the news that her father was at home again, but she was puzzled and disappointed by the lack of mention of Antonio. She feared the worst. The second sentence was blatantly clear, though. Her mother's nonsensical reference to a sister gave out a clear message: "I don't mean what I say." Even if Concha Ramírez could not say it in so many words, for fear of the censor's eye, Mercedes knew she was being told not to come home. The rebellious child had long since gone. The mature young woman now heeded her mother's advice.

# CHAPTER 37

In May 1939, as Winton Hall finally said goodbye to the last of its *niños* from Bilbao, Mercedes knew it was time for her to go too. The house had provided her with security and a roof for two years, and she knew she would look back on its grand spaces and romantic gardens with fondness.

Many of the *señoritas* were taking up domestic positions, and others trained as secretaries. All of them now began English lessons. In the past two years in England very few of them had learned more than a handful of words. Living and socializing only with fellow Spaniards, their main concern had been to preserve their own language and culture. Staying in the United Kingdom had been the last thing on their minds.

Like Mercedes, Carmen could not return home. Her father and brother had both been arrested during the early months of Franco's regime. They had joined the resistance, and when the authorities caught up with them, they had just destroyed a bridge outside Barcelona. Both were now sentenced to death. Carmen's mother had also been imprisoned.

When the time came to say farewell, Lady Greenham was almost warm. They suspected this was because she was happy to see them go, but her thin-lipped smile gave nothing away. By contrast, Sir John's eyes were brimful of tears. He did not shed them, but they could see he was awash with emotion. They promised to come and visit, and he nodded silently before turning away.

Mercedes looked forward with both excitement and trepidation to the next few months. Just as she had done when she got on the boat in Bilbao, she hoped that her time of exile would not continue forever.

The obvious place to go was London. There was a sizable Spanish community there now, and job opportunities, too, once she had learned the language.

"It's strange being back in a city," said Mercedes to Carmen, as they walked out of Victoria Station onto a busy street.

"A bit of a relief really," replied Carmen. "I'd had enough of the countryside."

"I'd had enough of Bilbao by the time we left, though," commented Mercedes.

"Well, London isn't Bilbao. We're going to enjoy ourselves here! I'm certain of it."

The London street was packed with people. They all looked smart and purposeful to the two Spanish women.

A Spanish couple had already offered them a room to share in Finsbury Park, and they took a bus to their destination. Sitting on the top deck, in the front row, they enjoyed their journey through the city and could hardly believe their luck in being there. Hyde Park Corner, Oxford Street, Regent's Park, all these places they had heard of, but the reality of them exceeded expectations. The sights were full of color and glamour and vitality. Eventually the conductor called out their stop, and they got off. It was only a five-minute walk to their new home: a Victorian terraced house on a pretty street where cherry blossom was in full, glorious bloom.

Their landlords had come to England before the conflict and had eagerly supported the efforts of the Basque Children's Committee. Mercedes and Carmen were made to feel very welcome. Even the pretty painted ceramic tiles they had stuck on the walls and some framed scenes of the Sierra Nevada made them feel at home.

But the threat from Fascism grew, just as those who had supported the Republic in Spain had feared, and war broke out across Europe. In September 1940, London was blitzed, and for eight months afterward was under constant attack.

"So now our own country is at peace and we're being bombed . . ."

said Mercedes one night as she and Carmen cowered, terrified, in the Anderson shelter at the bottom of the garden.

"There is something ironic about us sitting here in a foreign country, *still* being targeted by Germans," Carmen mused. "But anyway, you're wrong. Spain isn't at peace. How can it be when there are hundreds of thousands of political prisoners?"

This war against Hitler was a terrible one, but when it came to the point where children were being evacuated out of London, there was no comparison between the atmosphere there and that in Bilbao when people had decided to leave. In Spain, the country had turned against itself. There was nothing so poisonous happening in England. There was fear but no terror.

The residents of the terrace often spent the whole night in the shelter. It was the safest place. Mercedes and Carmen would talk for hours about their pasts and what might happen in the future. The latter could take almost any course, so there were no boundaries or limits to their dreams. The territory was unmapped.

English lessons and domestic work kept Mercedes busy. From autumn 1941, what kept her happy was *El Hogar Español*. The exiled prime minister of the Republic, Negrín, had signed a lease on a building in Inverness Terrace, which became the focal point for Spanish exiles who could not return to their own country.

It was the heart of their social and cultural life, and everyone mixed in to socialize and sometimes to sing, from those like Mercedes who were polishing English mantelpieces, to intellectuals and exiled politicians. They even held fiesta weekends. For these events, Mercedes put aside her feather duster and danced. The whirl of her tiered skirt and the sound of her metal-tipped shoes made her feel whole each time. This was who she was, and in her mind she was transported home. There were others who could sing, dance, and play the guitar or the castanets, and on a warm night when the windows were open, people would gather in the street below and listen to the gunshot cracks of the stamping feet and the soulful tunes of the flamenco guitar. From time to time a few of them, including Mercedes, would even perform for the public.

She had begun to receive regular letters and some favorite photographs from her mother now and, in return, finally wrote to tell her story. She deduced from the way Concha described her father that he was not the man he had been. This saddened her and made her yearn to be at home to help. Subsequent letters told her a little more about what had happened to Antonio and also relayed general news of Spain. She concluded that Carmen was right. While men were being wrongly imprisoned and treated as slaves, theirs was not a country at peace. Every time she received a letter with a Spanish postmark, she hoped for a moment it might be from Javier. She knew her mother would forward anything he sent. Not even for an hour did Mercedes give up hope.

As the years went by, Mercedes' English improved. In 1943 it was good enough for her to train as a secretary. Shortly afterward she applied for a job on the southern edge of London, which she was lucky enough to get, but realized that the journey to the offices would be too long. Carmen was happy to move as well, and they found a flat of their own in south London.

Life was as good as it could be, given their sense of displacement. They did not manage to get to *El Hogar Español* as often now, though Mercedes was invited to dance at least once a month there, and her vibrant performances always drew an appreciative crowd.

Mercedes tried not to think too much about the strain her parents were living under. They were running the café reasonably successfully under the new regime, but the continuing grief over the deaths of their three sons never lessened. Concha sometimes thought there could be no more tears left to fall, but that was the great deception of a sadness that lasts a lifetime. It is constantly renewed. Each day meant another walk across freshly broken glass. Each step had to be so careful and tentative, simply to allow them to negotiate the pain of getting from morning to night. The quiet ticking of the clock was about as much noise as they could bear once their customers had left for the evening.

Letters got to England, if slowly. Concha always tried to sound cheerful, but she was keen to discourage her daughter from returning. "You must be having a lovely life there," she wrote, "and if you come home, you will find it so different." It was her way of keeping Mercedes away from a country that would be full of memories and empty spaces.

Mercedes' letters to her parents gave the impression that she was settled in her new life. Though their daughter always read between the lines of their correspondence to her, her parents never thought to look beyond the surface of hers or to question the impression of contentment that she spent so much time creating.

The lack of truth in their correspondence did not mean there was no love between them. It merely meant that they loved each other enough to want to protect the other party.

There was one event that Concha could not conceal. In 1945, Pablo died. It had been one of those severe Granada winters when the raw air reaches into the chest and curls around the lungs, and he had not been strong enough to survive it. It was the hardest moment for Mercedes to bear since she had sailed away from Bilbao. She yearned to return home for her father's funeral but knew she would risking her freedom in doing so. Her mother urged her not to return.

When the war in Europe ended and men returned from the front, the Spanish girls' social life became focused around the local dance hall, the Locarno. After six years of conflict and anxiety, dancing was the perfect antidote. It was a way of sharing what it was to be alive, and it did not require any coupons. Everyone of their age danced the waltz and the quickstep, and as the craze for Latin American dancing swept in, Mercedes and Carmen easily picked it up.

Dance halls were where young men and women conducted their courtships, and most had one clear objective: to find a spouse. Mercedes was an exception. The last thing on her mind was to find a soulmate. She already had one, and when she went out on a Friday and a Saturday night, she had no desire for anything beyond the life-enhancing thrill of the dance.

The men danced with different girls each night, some of them that they had known for their whole lives and others they got to know, but all the while they had in the back of their minds the question of whether they might marry one of them.

The first time Carmen and Mercedes had appeared at the Locarno, they caused a stir. With their sultry looks and thick accents, they seemed really foreign and exotic. Although they wore the same kind of dresses as the local girls, that was where the similarity ended. "They're as dark as gypsies," people muttered.

They had been going to the Locarno every Friday and Saturday for more than a year when Mercedes was asked to dance by a young Englishman she had not noticed before.

"May I?" he asked simply, holding out his hand.

It was a tango. She must have danced with a hundred men before, but he was a cut above the rest. Later that night, she went over the dance again in her mind, and every note of the music came back to her.

For this young man the experience of dancing with Mercedes had held its magic too. The feeling of her light, slight body responding to the merest touch of his palm was very different from the measured clumsiness of most English girls. At the end of the dance, when he was once more sipping a pint with his friends and she was back with her friend, he was not sure that he had really danced with her at all. It was just a memory, something insubstantial.

The following week, Mercedes hoped that the slim, fair Englishman would ask her to dance again. She was not disappointed and smiled her acceptance when he approached. This time it was a quickstep.

He felt something keen and urgent in the way she danced. Without comparison, she was better than anyone he had ever danced with before, and he realized that her movements were not just a sequence of responses to him. Occasionally he felt her giving him direction. This dark Spanish girl was much more powerful than she looked.

"I've met someone who is a wonderful dancer," Mercedes wrote to her mother. "Even when they are trying their best, most Englishmen are so clumsy."

Mercedes' letters to her mother always talked about dancing. It was a cheerful subject unlike any other, and Concha was delighted when Mercedes wrote one day to say that she had won a competition.

"I'm partnering with that very good dancer I told you about, and we have done really well. We have the County finals next weekend, and if we get through, we'll be in the Regionals," she wrote excitedly.

For several years this partnership continued, and they never met anywhere but on the dance floor and occasionally for a cup of tea beforehand. They won every competition they entered, and their style and grace as a partnership dazzled everyone. No other dancers had a chance against them. Watching them was sheer exhilaration, and the judges always spotted the joy on Mercedes' face as she whirled past them.

It was not until 1955 that he proposed, nearly a decade after their first dance. Mercedes was taken aback. In all that time it had not occurred to her that her partner was in love with her. She was completely devastated by the proposal. As far as she could see, it had come out of the blue. She loved Javier and only him and was full of irrational guilt.

Carmen was tough with her. She had found a husband for herself three years earlier and already had her second child on the way.

"You need to face something, Mercedes," she said. "Are you ever going to see Javier again?"

It was a question Mercedes had not dared to ask herself for more than five years now.

"Don't you think that if he was still alive, you would have heard from him?"

She knew Carmen was probably right. Javier knew her mother's address, and if he was alive, he would have written and Concha would have forwarded the correspondence. All the time, though, there was the nagging doubt that letters could go astray and that somewhere, somehow, the man she loved so much was still alive.

"I don't know. But I can't give up on him."

"Well, you mustn't give up on this one either. He is here *now*, Mercedes. You would be mad to let him go."

The next time they danced, Mercedes tried to see her partner in a different light. She had always regarded him more like a brother than a lover. Could that ever change?

After the session, they had a cup of tea. Mercedes felt it was appropriate. They needed to talk.

"All I wanted to say was that you can take as long as you like to think about it. I shall wait. Twenty-five years, if necessary," said her dance partner.

Mercedes studied his face as he spoke. She saw such warmth and kindness that she wondered if she might melt. The pale blue eyes looked into hers, and she could see that his words were completely sincere. There was no mistaking his love.

It took her much less than twenty-five years to make her decision. Within a few months she realized that she would be a fool to let this sweet man go.

"You can't be doing the wrong thing by marrying him," teased Carmen. "If you're as compatible as that on the dance floor, imagine . . ."

"Carmen!" exclaimed Mercedes, blushing. "What a thing to say!"

She wrote to her mother to tell her of her engagement. Mercedes was keen for Concha to travel to the wedding, but she was an old lady now and had too many anxieties about the journey, not least whether she would be allowed back into Spain afterward. Mercedes understood completely. A month before the wedding, a package came from Granada. Mercedes was intrigued when she recognized her mother's shaky handwriting on the brown paper and saw the rows of stamps with Franco's head blackened by the franking machine. Her hands trembled as she struggled to cut through the string with a pair of blunt kitchen scissors.

It was the white lace *mantilla* that Concha had worn for her own wedding. For forty-five years it had been kept in waxed tissue paper and had survived when so much else had been lost. It was intact, if a shade darker perhaps, and unmarked. Its safe arrival seemed little short of a miracle. Beneath the layers of brown paper, her mother had padded the package out with a copy of the Granada newspaper, *El Ideal*. Mercedes put it to one side to cushion the contents. It was a month or two out of date now, but she would look through it later. Even the sight of the masthead made her stomach somersault.

Inside was also a letter from her mother and, in the envelope, a simple, unadorned gold chain.

"I wore this on my wedding day too," she wrote. "My mother gave it to me, and now I am giving it to you. It had a crucifix once, but I took that off some time ago, and now I seem to have lost it. I think you know about my feelings for the Church."

For Mercedes, the only slightly sour note, aside from the fact that Concha would not be there on her wedding day, was the disapproval of her fiancé's parents. Mercedes was foreign and some people were afraid of foreigners in those days. As far as they were concerned, she had come from another planet. They were not that happy either that she was a few years older than their son, but by the time the wedding took place, they had come round a little.

They were married in the registry office in Beckenham. The bride wore a simple knee-length, fitted cotton gown with three-quarter-length sleeves, which she had made herself and her hair was "up" in the Spanish style, with the extravagant lace mantilla cascading over her shoulders. Carmen was a witness and the guests were mostly Spanish exiles who, like her, had remained in the United Kingdom.

Victor Silvester, the great band leader who had seen them dance many times, sent them a telegram that was read out loud at their small reception in a local hotel: "To the happy couple. May your marriage be as perfect as your dancing."

# CHAPTER 38

Miguel had almost got to the end of the pile of letters. Sonia could see that only one sheet remained in his hand. It was past midnight now, and she was worried that he might be getting too tired to go on. Mercedes' story, if it ended here, had a happy ending and perhaps she should be content with that.

"Are you sure you aren't too tired to keep going?" she asked with concern.

"No, no," he replied. "I must read you this one. It's the last she wrote, not long after her wedding."

*England has provided the safe haven I longed for. I still feel an alien in some ways, but there are plenty of kind people here.*

*Of course, what has kept my spirit alive, and has done so ever since I got here, is dancing. It is the one thing that English people seemed to know about Spain: that there are people who dance in big flounced dresses and clack on castanets. Performing reminds me of who I am, and yet sometimes it's better not to dwell too much on that.*

*And, of course, what has made me happiest of all is the wonderful man I have just married. I could tell straightaway when we met that he was younger than me, but he has a kind face and he can dance, as the English always say, "like Fred Astaire." Even though he is fair-haired and pale-skinned and not at all like a Granadino, I am sure you would love. . .*

Sonia held her breath. She hardly dared hear the name.

*. . . Jack.*

Sonia had bitten her lip so hard that it bled. Her neck and chest throbbed with the pain of unshed tears. She was determined not to let Miguel see what impact the letter was having on her. She was not sure it was the right time to explain. He still had a little more to read:

> *No one here really knows anything about Spain, and I have told my new husband very little about Granada and certainly nothing of the horrors of our war.*
> *I still wonder what became of Javier and think of him often.*
> *I know you understand why I haven't returned, given all that's happened to our family and probably the man I loved too.*
>
> *Mercedes*

For the first time, Sonia noticed that she was not alone in fighting back the tears. Miguel's cheeks were damp with them. She was puzzled that he should be so upset when the story was not new to him, and she put her arm around him, handing him one of his own paper serviettes to mop his face.

"I can see you were fond of them, the Ramírez family," she said gently.

They sat for a few minutes in silence. Sonia needed some time to reflect. There was no doubt now. This was her mother's story, and until today she had never known a word of it. She was shaken to the core of her being, and clearly her father would be too if he learned the details of his wife's history. She would have to consider carefully whether such knowledge was really of use to someone in the last years of his life.

Mercedes' tale lay on the table in front of them, and Miguel's misshapen old fingers picked up the pages, carefully folded them along their usual creases, and returned them to the envelope. Sonia registered that these letters had been read and reread many times. It was strange. Why should these letters from her mother to her grandmother mean so much to Miguel? Her heart quickened, and she could not quite tell why. Nor could she bring herself to ask this question.

Miguel was looking at Sonia now. She could see that he wanted to say something.

"Thank you for listening to all of that," he said.

"You mustn't thank me!" replied Sonia, trying to contain her emotion. "It's me who should be thanking you. I did ask you to tell me."

"Yes, but you have been such a good listener."

Now was her moment. She yearned to show Miguel the photographs she carried with her, and now that she knew for certain that Mercedes Ramírez and her mother were one and the same, it did not seem ridiculous anymore.

"There is a reason for that, you know," she said, digging into her handbag for her wallet.

She found the two photographs, one of her mother as a teenage girl in flamenco costume and the other of the group of children sitting on the barrel.

Miguel picked up the former.

"That's Mercedes!" he said excitedly. "Where on earth did you get that?"

She paused. "From my father," she answered.

"Your father?" exclaimed Miguel incredulously. "I don't think I understand . . ."

A moment or two passed before she could actually make herself say the words.

"Mercedes was my mother."

The old man could not speak. Sonia was worried, but within moments he had recovered. He was shaking his head from side to side in pure disbelief.

"Mercedes was your mother . . ."

He was silent for a moment, and Sonia was almost unnerved by the intensity of his gaze.

"And look," he said, pointing to the children in the second photograph. "You realize who these children are, don't you? That's Antonio, Ignacio, Emilio . . . And your mother."

"It's extraordinary," responded Sonia quietly. "It's really them."

Miguel got up slowly. "I think you need a drink," he said.

Sonia watched him cross the room, and a wave of affection for him swept over her. He returned with two glasses of brandy, and they sat for a while longer. There seemed so much more to say.

Sonia explained why she had been drawn to Miguel's café rather than any other.

"It's the prettiest one in the square," she said. "But perhaps it was something familiar about the barrel. I think that picture of them all as children must have been in my mind."

"It was almost as though you recognized it," mused Miguel.

"Well, it is a distinctive feature, isn't it? And I have only just realized what the name of the café means . . . El Barril. I really must improve my Spanish!"

Sonia noticed the clock. It was one thirty. She really had to go. For several minutes, she and Miguel embraced each other in a strong hug. He appeared reluctant to let her go.

"Miguel, thank you so much for everything," she said.

How inadequate these words sounded, but there were none that would have been enough. There were tears in his eyes as she kissed him firmly on both cheeks.

"Will I see you before you leave?" he asked.

"My plane isn't until the afternoon, so I have a few hours in the morning," she said. "I'll come back for breakfast."

"Come as early as you can. There's somewhere I want to take you before you go."

"All right," said Sonia, squeezing his arm. "I'll see you in the morning. Eight thirty?"

The old man nodded.


Just as Sonia was putting a key in Maggie's lock, her friend came up behind her.

"*Hola!*" she said cheerfully. "Have you been out for a secret salsa?"

"Not exactly," Sonia replied. "I've had a really extraordinary day."

Maggie was too excited about her own evening to ask any questions. Though she was tired, Sonia sat up with her and heard all about the new man in her life. This one really was going to be special. Maggie could feel it in her bones.

Before they went to bed, Sonia told Maggie that she might need to come and stay again for a few days quite soon.

"You're welcome any time," said Maggie. "You know that. Just let me know when and I'll make sure I'm here."

After a few hours of sleep, Sonia took the now-familiar route back to El Barril. Miguel knew she would be punctual and already had a *café con leche* waiting for her on the bar. Soon they were leaving the café and going around the corner to where Miguel's battered Seat car was parked.

"The place I want to take you is just a little way out of the city, so we need to drive," he said.

They drove for twenty minutes, negotiating Granada's complex one-way system, passing along wide tree-lined boulevards and winding their way through cobbled streets scarcely wide enough for a single car. They skirted the edge of the oldest *barrio*, and then the road began to climb.

They did not talk much on the way, but even their silences were comfortable. Sonia was busy enjoying the spectacular views of the landscape that surrounded Granada: the flat fertile plains and the dramatic Sierra Nevada. No wonder this place had been such a prize for both Moors and Christians, she thought.

Eventually they reached their destination. Outside a massive ornamental gateway, several dozen cars were parked. It looked like the entrance to a French chateau.

"Where are we?" she asked Miguel.

"This is the municipal cemetery."

"Oh," she said quietly, remembering that he had encouraged her to visit this place once before.

As he was parking the car, a funeral cortège arrived. In addition to the hearse, there were eight gleaming limousines from which a large party of well-dressed mourners emerged. The women all wore black lace mantillas, behind which their faces were hidden. The men's dark suits were well fitting, made-to-measure, elegant. The whole group walked slowly, somberly, behind the coffin and disappeared through the gates, leaving the chauffeurs to lean against their polished hoods and enjoy a smoke.

Miguel looked across at them, and Sonia could feel that he had something to say. His voice had an edge. She recalled the hint of bitterness that she had noticed in her very first encounter with him. It had surprised her then and did so again now.

"There were many people killed in the Civil War who were deprived of a burial like that," he said. "Thousands of them were just thrown into mass graves."

"That's awful," said Sonia in a hushed voice. "Don't their families want to find out where they are?"

"Some of them do," he said. "But not all of them."

They got out of the car and wandered in. Sonia was astonished by the volume and scale of the burial places. Graveyards in England were very different from this. She thought of the South London cemetery, where her mother had been buried, and shuddered. It was a huge acreage of grass with row upon row of small headstones, each space a coffin's width and length. She only stopped to visit once a year but always drove past it on her way to visit her father, and through the railings it was easy to spot the most recent graves. They still had fresh flowers, wreaths of gaudy yellow and orange, DAD in red carnations or MUM in white chrysanthemums, or the occasional heart-stopping teddy bear. With few exceptions, the older ones had nothing or a few dead blooms in a jam jar. Artificial flora were ubiquitous; those who brought them chose to ignore the notion of *memento mori*.

This Granadino graveyard was a very different place. Some of the departed here had tombs the size of small houses. It was like a village made of white marble, with streets and small gardens.

It was a place that invited contemplation, and there were few other people here on this Wednesday morning. Neither Sonia nor Miguel felt obliged to make conversation.

The space was divided into several dozen separate spaces, *patios*, in each of which there were numerous large tombs, crosses, and memorial stones recording the names of the dead. What struck Sonia most forcibly, apart from the huge dimensions of this place, was that no grave seemed to have been abandoned.

There were flowers on them all, which made absolute sense when she read the most commonly inscribed words: "*Tu familia no te olvida.*" "Your family will not forget you."

Most had been true to their promise.

"Can I wander up there?" asked Sonia, impelled to explore.

Miguel had stopped to buy a small plant at the entrance, and she imagined he might not mind being alone for a few moments. She walked purposefully up the pathway that seemed to lead to the boundary of the cemetery, only to find, when she reached it, that there was another area beyond the wall. It almost seemed limitless this place, in both directions. She had no idea how long she walked. She was fascinated by the grandeur of many of these tombs. Some had angels that guarded the entrances to family tombs, fluted pillars, and elaborate stone wreaths; there were ornate iron crosses as well as simple marble ones and everywhere—flowers. She saw a few women carrying watering cans and one with a dustpan and brush, doing the housework, lovingly sweeping particles of gravel from her ancestors' threshold. It was one of the most touching things she had ever seen.

She retraced her steps and eventually found Miguel not far from where she had left him, sitting on a stone bench.

"Sorry I've been so long," she apologized.

"Don't worry. Time stands still here."

"That's true." Sonia smiled.

She sat down on the bench beside him. It was late morning now. The sun was strong, and they were grateful for a shade-giving tree. Opposite them was a huge wall. From top to bottom, there were six tiers of memorial stones. In front of each one was a ledge where people had placed small vases of flowers.

"Do you recognize those names?" asked Miguel.

Directly in front of them, second row from the bottom, she read aloud three names:

Ignacio López Ramírez

28–1–37

Pablo García Ramírez

20–12–45

Concha López Dominguez

14–8–56

She noted the plant that Miguel had bought earlier, its pink blooms just brushing the letters of the last name, and next to it a bouquet of glorious red roses now slightly wilting.

"It looks as though someone else has been to visit them too," said Sonia.

There was no response from Miguel, and she turned to look at him. He was shaking his head.

"Just me," he said, his old eyes glistening. "Just me."

Sonia now had to ask the question that had been on the tip of her tongue since the previous night, when she had recognized the depth of his emotion on telling her the Ramírez family's story.

"Why?" she quizzed him. "Why were you so attached to this family?"

For a moment it seemed hard for him to speak. He swallowed, and it was as though he had to gulp for air before he could say the words.

"I'm Javier. Javier Miguel Montero."

Sonia gasped in disbelief.

"Javier! But . . ."

There was only one gesture that seemed a natural response to this revelation. She gently took his old hands, and for a while they looked into the watery depths of each other's eyes. Sonia recognized what Mercedes had seen all those years earlier, and Javier gazed at the reflection of Mercedes that he saw in the face of her daughter.

Eventually Sonia spoke.

"Javier," she said. It seemed strange to use this name now, and the old man interrupted her.

"Please, call me Miguel," he said. "I've used the name for so long now. Ever since I first arrived back at El Barril."

"Of course, if that's what you prefer," said Sonia. She waited a few minutes in silence. There were so many burning questions, but she did not wish to cause him any more pain.

"Can you tell me what happened?" she asked eventually. "When did you come back to Granada?"

"I was released from my duties at El Valle de los Caídos—the Valley of the Fallen—in 1955," he said. "I had 'redeemed myself through labor,' that's what they said. The fact that I hadn't committed a crime in the first place was neither here nor there. I turned up at El Barril one day, completely unannounced. I had no family left in Málaga or in Bilbao, and I was physically destroyed by my time at Cuelgamuros. Two of the fingers on my left hand had been broken and were badly deformed, so I knew I couldn't make my living out of being a *guitarra* anymore. I didn't really know what to do with myself."

Miguel paused for a moment.

"Quite simply, I couldn't think of anywhere else to go. Concha made me feel welcomed and invited me to make my home with her. She treated me like her son."

"But Concha died not long after you came back," commented Sonia.

"Yes, she did. She became sick quite quickly, but I nursed her as well as I could."

"Did she ever write to Mercedes to tell her that you were here?"

"No," Miguel answered bluntly.

"I suppose it would have come out that she had known for years that you might still be alive . . ."

" . . . but she had told me that Mercedes was living in England and that she was settled."

"But she loved you so much." Sonia choked as she spoke. "And you loved her?"

"I did," he said, "but I knew she was happy, and I was glad for her. It would have been cruel to take that away. She had experienced enough unhappiness . . ."

For an hour or more, the pair of them sat in the sunshine. Sonia felt in no position to judge her grandmother's decision to withhold information from her daughter. If she had not done so, then Sonia would not be here now.

She sat there admiring this nobility, this fathomless love.

# CHAPTER 39

Unlike Spain, which was moving into summer and not looking back, April in England still seemed caught in the depths of winter. It was icy cold when Sonia's plane landed that night, and there was a thin layer of snow on the ground in the car park. Sonia's hands were blue by the time she had scraped her windscreen.

She arrived home to an empty house and felt like a stranger breaking and entering. It was as though she was examining the clues to someone else's life. She peered into the drawing room. A vase of dead roses sat in the middle of the coffee table, and petals were scattered over copies of *Country Life* and *Tatler*. On the mantelpiece, there was a row of invitations to drinks parties and a couple of invites to formal corporate events, which required the use of card several millimeters thick. One of them was to a buck shoot in Scotland. The invitation was for that day. Perhaps that was where James was now.

On the floor by the kitchen door were a dozen empty bottles of red wine and in the sink, uncharacteristically for James, who loathed anything not to be washed up and put away, was a glass with sediment encrusted in the bottom.

Sonia took her bag upstairs and went to bed, automatically going into the spare room. It had almost slipped her mind, until of course she turned the key in the lock, that her growing estrangement from James had been one of her reasons for going to Granada. London had seemed so remote while Miguel was telling his story.

The week passed frostily. Sonia would not have expected anything different. Her highlight was a salsa class that Friday from which she came home invigorated.

After the deadening few days of being back in the office and the strange domestic atmosphere, the life-enhancing, heart-lightening enchantment of dancing lifted her once again.

That weekend there was a long-standing invitation to visit James's parents. She dreaded it even more than usual, but James clearly expected them to go. Appearances needed to be kept up, and canceling would raise all sorts of questions. For James and Sonia it was much easier to continue in silence, and they managed to maintain it for the entire journey. It would have been the perfect opportunity to tell James about her extraordinary discoveries, but she had no desire even to mention them. These were precious things, and she could not bear the thought of either his mockery or his lack of interest.

Some old family friends, including James's godfather, were invited for dinner, and Sonia observed that she was the only one of the five women not wearing pearls. For her this defined absolutely her sense of not quite fitting. She looked across the tarnished silver and best Wedgwood at James and realized that there was not the slightest possibility that anyone would give the lack of warmth between them a second thought. None of the married couples around the table seemed to address any remarks to each other. Perhaps this *froideur* within marriage was completely normal in the shires.

The big, drafty rectory had last been redecorated in the 1970s, and in the twin room she and James always shared when they were staying, there was an apricot-colored sink in the corner and shreds of wallpaper hanging from the walls like peeling skin. The curtains must have been grand once, with their swags and drapes and silk trimmings, but now they looked depressing. Diana, James's mother, barely noticed the gradual stages of dilapidation and left her husband to fix the odd broken door handle or dripping tap. This, Sonia told herself, was how the English upper-middle classes liked to live, in a sort of genteel decay, and perhaps it explained why James was so fastidious about the décor of his own home.

After she had renovated the house all those decades ago, Sonia's mother-in-law had turned her attention to the garden and was now a slave to its carefully laid out borders and tyrannical vegetable garden, which supplied them with astonishing gluts of courgettes or lettuces at certain times of year, obliging them to live at times on a very limited diet, and then for months providing nothing at all. As an essentially urban creature, Sonia found this lifestyle baffling.

The single beds had allowed Sonia and James to keep their distance, but that night, when James came upstairs after a late session of port and cigars with his father, he sat clumsily on the edge of her bed and poked her in the back.

"Sonia, Sonia . . ." he drawled, the last word right in her ear.

Already rigid with cold, in spite of the hot-water bottle she clasped to herself for comfort as much as warmth, Sonia stiffened.

"Please—leave—me—alone," she willed him.

He reached under the blanket and shook her shoulder.

"Sonia . . . come on, wake up, Sonia. Just for me."

Though she was good at playing dead, he knew full well she was awake. Only the truly dead would have slept through the level of noise he had made and the roughness of that shaking.

"Bugger it, Sonia . . . for Christ's sake."

She listened as he stamped across the room and to the sound effects of his clumsy preparations for bed. Without looking, she could picture the corduroy trousers, shirt, and pullover lying in a twisted heap on the floor by the bed and the highly polished brown brogues randomly left, ready to trip them should they have to get up in the night. Then she heard the noisy spitting as he cleaned his teeth and dropped his brush back into the tooth mug, yanking the cord to turn off the light above the sink, and her ears, acutely tuned in to these sounds, picked up the sound of the little plastic knob gently banging against the mirror.

He threw back his quilted counterpane and the bedsprings creaked as he finally lay down. Only then did he realize that he had left the ceiling light on.

"Bugger, bugger, bugger . . ." It was his mantra. He stomped across to the switch by the door and then stumbled in the darkness back to bed, tripping predictably over his own shoe. There was one further expletive and then silence.

Sonia exhaled with some relief and then rolled over. James's consumption of port would keep him soundly asleep all night.

Early the following morning, Sonia went downstairs to make herself some tea, her breath emerging in clouds of vapor. Her mother-in-law was already sitting at the kitchen table, her gnarled, gardener's hands wrapped around a steaming mug.

"Help yourself," she said to Sonia, pushing the teapot across the table toward her, scarcely looking up from the newspaper.

Perhaps it was their drafty houses that made these people so cold inside, reflected Sonia, watching the stewed brown liquid splash into the chipped mug that sat on the table.

"Thanks . . . so how's the garden?" she asked, knowing this was one thing that her mother-in-law had feelings for.

"Oh, you know. So-so," she said, still not lifting her eyes from the newspaper.

To an outsider, this understatement would have been hard to interpret, but Sonia knew her dismissive attitude conveyed a level of indifference to her daughter-in-law.

As was routine, they all went for a walk with the Labradors that morning. Diana looked imperious in her full-length Barbour and mocked Sonia for her urban faux fur jacket. She strode ahead with James, determined to keep the pace of the outing going while her husband Richard brought up the rear, a slim figure limping slightly, still dependent on the stick he had used since a hip replacement a year ago.

For some inexplicable reason, Sonia felt slightly sorry for her father-in-law today. He looked worn-out, faded, like a very old shirt. When she tried to make conversation, he was monosyllabic, with the coolness of someone who preferred the company of his own sex. On the whole, he was a man who was quite happy with silence as long as it was occasionally punctuated with the sound of a barking dog.

By the time they arrived back at the house, they were all numb with cold.

For the first time in the past couple of days, the house actually felt warm. James stirred the embers of the fire in the drawing room, and soon the fire came to life.

It was a solid enough scene, observed Sonia, as she set the big kitchen table for lunch. For a moment she questioned her own restlessness. Then James walked into the kitchen, and she remembered at least one reason for her dissatisfaction.

"Where will I find the corkscrew?" he demanded, swinging a bottle of claret in each hand.

"In the top drawer, darling," replied his mother indulgently. "Lunch is nearly ready."

"We're just having a pre-prandial," he told her. "It can wait half an hour, can't it?"

It was a statement rather than a question, as he proved by leaving the room before his mother had time to protest.

After lunch, James and his father drained a second bottle of wine and the remains of a bottle of port, retiring eventually for a game of snooker in the old derelict stable. By the time they returned, Sonia was ready to go, and her bag was packed in the hall.

"What's the hurry?" asked James groggily. "I need some caffeine!"

"Okay. But then I would quite like to get back to London."

"We'll go when I've finished my coffee."

Sonia let him have the last word. She was already bored with the exchange and would conserve her energy for when it mattered.

Diana appeared in the hall now. "So are you leaving soon?" she said, addressing the question to James.

"Sonia seems to think so," said James facetiously, hamming up the part of the hen-pecked husband.

During the four-hour journey to London, while James listened to an entire Dan Brown novel, Sonia mulled over the proposition Miguel had made before she had left Granada: that she should now inherit the family business.

At five o'clock the following morning, James threw open her bedroom door.

"I'm still waiting," he said.

"What for?" asked Sonia sleepily.

"An answer."

Her genuinely quizzical expression irritated him.

"Dancing or our marriage. You *remember*?"

Sonia looked at him blankly now.

"I'm flying to Germany until Friday, and it would be nice to have the answer when I get back."

Sonia picked up the hint of sarcasm in his voice, and she could see he had not quite finished.

"I assume you won't be out as usual," he added.

Sonia literally had nothing to say. Or nothing that she wanted to say now. James picked up his bag, and a moment later he was down the stairs and gone.

# CHAPTER 40

Sonia went to the office and worked furiously that day. At lunchtime she rang her father and asked if she could come and see him in the evening.

"I promise I won't get there too late," she said. "And there's no need to worry about supper or anything."

Jack Haynes liked to have eaten by six and was normally in bed by nine thirty.

"All right, darling, I'll make you a sandwich. I think I've got some ham. Will that do?"

"That will be lovely, Dad. Thank you."

She had a lot of ends to tie up in the office that afternoon, and by the time she left it was already six thirty. The rush-hour traffic out of London was heavy, and it was past eight by the time she rang her father's bell.

"Hello, my sweet. This is a lovely surprise. A Monday evening! How lovely. Come in. Come in."

Jack's delight in seeing Sonia never diminished. He bustled about as usual, putting on the kettle, finding a napkin for her, getting out the biscuit tin. Her sandwich, on white bread, cut into triangles with a few slices of cucumber arranged on the side, was already on his small dining table set against the wall.

"Thanks, Dad. This is lovely. I hope you didn't mind me coming in the week."

"Why would I mind? The day of the week doesn't make too much difference to me, does it?"

He went off to make the tea. When he returned, she had not touched her food. She could not eat.

"Sonia! Come on. Eat up. I bet you haven't had anything all day. Do you want me to get you something else?"

"No, Dad, really I'm fine. I'll eat it in a minute."

"Are you feeling all right, darling?"

Sonia smiled at her father. Nothing seemed to have changed in thirty-five years. He had always fussed over her eating and worried about her looking "peaky."

"I'm fine, Dad," she said gently. Sonia was so nervous she could see her hands shaking, but she had come here to tell him something and she could not leave without doing so.

"I've been in Granada again," she said quietly. "I met someone who knew Mum. I never knew her name was really Mercedes."

"I always called her Mary. No one here could pronounce her Spanish name."

Jack carefully pulled out the chair opposite Sonia and sat down.

"How wonderful to come across someone from her past! You lucky girl! And did they remember much about her?"

Her father was smiling, eager, curious to know everything Sonia had been told.

His daughter told a carefully edited version of the story. She mentioned Javier once in passing but decided that her father should not be made to feel second-best to anyone. He had given Mercedes Ramírez the happiest years of her life, and that bright gem should never be tarnished. She would work out how to introduce Miguel when the time came.

Jack Haynes had known none of this. He had respected his wife's desire to leave her past behind.

"She always told me that she could dance away sadness and bad memories," he said reflectively. "And I believe she did. While we were spinning around the dance floor, she became as light as a feather. She couldn't have danced like that with the weight of the world on her shoulders!"

"It must have been such a huge help to her," said Sonia. "Perhaps it

really was all that dancing, all that exhilaration, that helped her to survive. I know exactly what she meant by dancing away sadness."

They sat for a while. Jack looked at his watch. It was hours past his
bedtime.

Sonia sipped a glass of water.

"And the man who took El Barril has offered the café back to me."

"What? He's giving you the café?"

"Not exactly, but technically it still belongs to the Ramírez family,
and I am the only surviving member of it."

Jack was more astonished by this than anything.

"What would you say if I went to live in Spain? Would you come and
see me?" said Sonia, her voice now full of unconcealed excitement. "Because I wouldn't go unless you did."

"But what about James? Does he want to go?"

"James isn't coming with me."

Her father needed no further explanation. He would not have
dreamed of prying into her relationship with James.

"Oh, I see," was all he said.

It all seemed rather sudden to Jack, whose life had only changed in
small increments from one decade to another, but this younger generation saw things differently.

"Yes, of course I would come and see you. As long as you cooked me
something nice and plain! And would you still come and see me?"

"Yes, Dad, of course I would," she said, touching her father's hand. "We
will probably even see more of each other than we have done in the past.
The flights are really cheap too. And there was something I wanted to ask
you. Do you mind looking after a few boxes of mine? Just for a while?"

"Of course not—they can go under my bed. I've got a bit of room
there."

"I'll pop back with them tomorrow, if that's OK?"

"It will be lovely to see you twice in one week! Just ring and say when."

Jack Haynes had not seen his daughter looking so happy for years.
They held each other in a long embrace.

"You do understand why I'm going, don't you?" Sonia asked him.

"Yes," he said. "I think I do."

After a small whiskey, Jack Haynes slept soundly and had sweet dreams of doing the *paso doble* with a dark-eyed Spanish girl.

The journey back to Wandsworth took less than twenty minutes at this time of night. When she got in, Sonia collapsed onto her bed. At seven the following morning, she woke up, still fully clothed. There was a busy day ahead of her, and she needed to get going.

She began with her clothes. Most of them would be completely inappropriate in her new life. Suits and long dresses she packed into carrier bags, along with winter coats she had hoarded for a decade, and scores of high heels that she would never wear on the Granadino cobbles. There were hats that she had worn to weddings, and handbags in every shade of most colors. She had dozens of scarves, most of which she did not even recognize. By the time she had finished, there were twenty-three bags bursting with contents. She drove them immediately to the Oxfam shop, in case she had a change of heart. There was one garment over which she had demurred. It was the dress she had been wearing at her engagement party in a champagne bar in Mayfair. It was a flimsy piece of lilac chiffon that James had bought and she had been obliged to wear. It had not been quite "her," but its association with a time of happiness lingered on.

There were other things that went straight into the dustbin: a filthy old Barbour and some wellies that would definitely not be needed in Spain. She had files full of old paperwork, job application letters, CVs, and bank statements dating back to university days. All of these could be thrown away.

She made up a box with her favorite CDs. Most of it was music that James did not listen to anyway, so he would not miss them, and on the top of the box she threw in the few stuffed toys from childhood that she would never part with.

Sonia kept herself busy all day, deliberately burying herself in trivia in order to detach herself from the enormity of her actions. Only when she stopped for ten minutes to make a cup of tea did the reality of what she was doing hit her. She was removing herself from James's life. There was terrible sadness but as yet no guilt. As she stirred milk into her tea, she looked around the kitchen and realized that she had left no impression on this room. It had always been James's place and it still was.

There were a few more things to sort out in the bedroom, so she climbed the stairs with her tea. One thing she was absolutely resolute about was that she should take nothing that was not hers. The house would remain absolutely intact; she had no desire even to take anything that was jointly theirs. Men are rarely on their own for long, she mused to herself, and she was fairly certain that someone else would soon slot in to take her place. It was as this thought came into her mind that the jewelry box on her dressing table caught her eye. She opened the lid and took out some of the junk jewelry on the top layer. Underneath, there were some small drawers and inside these some family heirloom jewelry that James's mother had given her to wear for formal occasions: emerald earrings, a ruby pendant, and some rather hideous if very valuable brooches. Sonia removed them and put them in the safe, which was where James had always told her to keep them. In a little drawer all on its own, she remembered there was a gold chain. Her father had given it to her when her mother had died. She found it now and put it around her neck. Her hands trembled as she did up the clasp.

Then she went back to see her father. He was his usual sweet self, if a little subdued.

"Are you sure you are doing the right thing?" he asked as they stowed two boxes under his bed. "I'm a little worried about you."

"I know what I'm doing looks rash, but I have never felt so sure of anything, Dad," Sonia answered. "I promise you I've thought about it."

"Very well, darling. But if you change your mind, you can always come back here, you know that, don't you?"

He said nothing else.

"I've got something here," said Jack, shuffling across to the other side of the room. "I thought it would be nice for you to have these now."

On top of the dresser was a brown paper bag. He handed it to her.

Sonia knew immediately from the shape and weight what was inside.

"Your mother never even considered throwing these away," he said. "She would love to think of them being taken back to Granada."

The paper rustled as Sonia reached into the bag. There they were. The dancing shoes, their soft leather and the steel toe- and heelcaps worn right down, just as Miguel had described them.

"They even look my size," said Sonia. "Perhaps I shall wear them one day . . ."

They were both silent for a moment.

"Why don't you come out soon, Dad?" she said to break the tension, caressing the shoes absentmindedly as she spoke. "Come in a few weeks. I'll have sorted out where I'm living by then."

They embraced warmly, and Jack watched as she disappeared down the stairs.

It was her last day in London; tomorrow she would be flying back to Granada. She rang Miguel and told him she was returning.

"I'm so glad," he said. "I hoped you would be back soon."

Now all that remained was to write a letter to James. She had been dreading this, but she did owe him a response to his ultimatum and perhaps an explanation too.

*Dear James,*

*I think you probably know my answer now. It's as simple as this: for me, dance is an expression of being alive. I can't give it up, any more than I can give up breathing.*

*I don't expect you to forgive or understand my decision.*

*I do not want to take anything from you. I have no interest in a share in the house or a proportion of your income. I think what we owe each other now is simply our freedom.*

*The solicitor has my address, so he will forward correspondence to me there.*

*I wish you well, James, and I hope in time you will wish me the same.*

Sonia

She wrote several drafts of the letter, many of them much longer, but this simple, uncomplicated note seemed to express all that she wanted to say. It was left on the kitchen table. That was the first place James would go to on Friday, when he arrived from the airport and needed a drink.

She had already packed a suitcase, essentially containing favorite clothes that had not gone to the charity shop, and ordered a cab for the following morning.

At five o'clock, the alarm went off. After she had showered and made the bed impeccably, Sonia went downstairs. Taking a final, sad glance around, she dragged her case over the threshold, double-locked the door, and posted the key back through the letterbox. She walked toward the waiting car.

Flying north to south later that morning, she watched the changing landscape of Spain through the plane window. She observed the jagged peaks of the Pyrenees melting into gentle foothills and then giving way to the vast open expanses of land now cultivated on an almost industrial scale. Images of Jarama, Guadalajara, and Brunete flashed through her mind, but the scars of warfare had long since been erased.

When the plane began its descent from a cloudless sky, she thought of how many weeks it had taken her mother to travel the same distance. For Mercedes it had been months, for her less than an hour. There was a glimpse of Granada in the distance as they came in to land and her heart raced with anticipation.

The plane was half full, so it was only moments before Sonia was at the top of the steps and feeling the sweet warmth of the Andalusian breeze on her face. Soon she was crossing the tarmac. It was only a short distance to the terminal building, and she knew that Miguel was waiting for her.

Her footsteps were light. Her heart was dancing.

The military coup led by General Francisco Franco in July 1936 was meant to be swift and decisive, but instead it led to a three-year civil war that devastated the country. Half-a-million people died and an equal number went into exile.

After 1939, hundreds of thousands of Republicans still languished in prison, and many faced the firing squad and burial in unmarked graves. Those who had fought against Franco experienced years of repression, and even when the Fascist dictator died in 1975, many people in Spain still remained silent about their experiences. There was, in effect, a *pacto de olvido*, a pact of forgetting.

Thirty years after Franco's death came a significant step forward with the passing of the Law of Historical Memory in October 2007 under the Socialist Prime Minister José Luis Rodríguez Zapatero, whose own grandfather was executed by Francoists. The law formally condemned Franco's uprising and dictatorship, banned symbols and references to the regime on public buildings, and ordered the removal of monuments honouring Franco—the last of these was finally taken down in Santander in December 2008.

The law also declared the political trial of Franco's opponents during the dictatorship to be illegitimate and obliged town halls to facilitate the exhumation of those buried in unmarked graves.

In January 2009, the 500,000 people whose families had to flee Spain under the Franco era were given the right to apply for Spanish citizenship. These are the children or grandchildren of those who fled for fear of persecution or hardship between 1936 and 1955.

Almost seventy years since the civil war ended, the *pacto de olvido* has finally been broken. In my view, this is a cause for celebration.

*Victoria Hislop*
*April 2009*

The Return *brought back many memories of things past. Chapter 28 was particularly poignant for me, as I remember vividly* The Habana *and our departure from Bilbao.*

*I am seventy-eight-years-old, and one of those who never returned to Spain. I served in the British Army for seven years in the infantry and have had a wonderful life in the UK.*

*Your chronology of events in Spain at that awful time will be read by thousands of people as a consequence of the popularity of the book. I have read commendable histories, but your narrative of events in the story brings to many the evils of living under a dictatorship.*

*Marcel R. Everton*

*I have enjoyed every minute reading your book. You have done the story so well, and it is so true what happened in Spain.*

*It brought so many of my* querida papa. *He was in Bilbao prison and was sent to be shot but then was given thirty years in prison and sent to Burgos. Like so many, he suffered.*

*Josefina Antolin Stubbs*

# ALSO BY
# VICTORIA HISLOP

## THE ISLAND
### A Novel

ISBN 978-0-06-134032-1 (paperback)

The Petrakis family lives in the small Greek seaside village of Plaka. Just off the coast is the tiny island of Spinalonga, where the nation's leper colony once was located—a place that has haunted four generations of Petrakis women. A richly enchanting novel of their lives and loves unfolding against the backdrop of the Mediterranean during World War II, *The Island* is an enthralling story of dreams and desires, of secrets desperately hidden, and of leprosy's touch on an unforgettable family.

"A page-turning tale that reminds us that love and life continue in even the most extraordinary of circumstances."
—*Sunday Express* (London)